Witchfire

Book Two of The Dark Inbetween

Sam Thorne and Lauren Ivey

PUBLISHED BY THORNE & IVEY BOOKS

CONTENT WARNING

This work of fiction contains scenes of sexual abuse, graphic violence, and mutilation.

This edition first published in 2025
by Thorne & Ivey Books
Athens, Georgia
www.thorneandivey.com

Cover Design by Benjamin P. Roque
Author Photo by Jacqueline Aleace Photography
Chapter Emblems by Arthur Balitskiy

ISBN 978-1-955221-05-4 (paperback)
ISBN 978-1-955221-06-1 (hardcover)
ISBN 978-1-955221-07-8 (ebook)

Chapter One

"It's too bad about the rain," Barrett murmured, turning his head so he caught his lover's kiss on his cheek.

With an indignant huff, they grabbed his chin and turned his head, planting an inelegant kiss right on his lips as he laughed. "There will be other nights," they insisted, stretching on their tiptoes as he lifted his head.

"Eventually," he conceded, grinning like an idiot at his lover's annoyance.

"You…" They let go of his chin, grabbed his tunic with both hands, and pushed him back against the wall. They held him there, glaring up at him. "If you don't want to kiss me—"

Barrett wrapped his arms around their shoulders, and drew them into an embrace, pressing a kiss to their forehead the way he knew they hated. "Who said anything about—"

There was a pull. The unmistakable sensation of magic from beyond the house. Barrett stiffened, his head swinging automatically in the direction he felt the power from like a lodestone.

"Barrett? Is it…?"

"Yes."

They swallowed, their grip on his tunic tightening. "Graces cursed bastards. Of course, a demon would show up here. Tonight."

Barrett reached for their hands, letting a bit of his magic seep out, warming their damp fingers. "Griswold's here, and it feels pretty weak. I'll go. You stay here."

They let out a tight sigh, not quite meeting his eyes. "No, I'll fight."

"We don't all have to go out in the rain. There will be plenty of nights chasing demons once we get to Oareford."

They chewed their lip as water beaded along their forehead, dampening their hair. "Are you certain?"

"I'll be fine. I'll go and take care of this and be back before you can even miss me." He touched their cheek, waiting until they finally picked their head up. "I promise."

They held his gaze, eyes crinkled with worry, before they rocked up on their toes and kissed him—properly this time—and Barrett wished to all the Graces he didn't have to leave.

"Come back to me," they whispered, stepping out of the embrace, cheeks faintly pink.

"I will," he said, taking a breath to regain his composure. "Keep Kat safe."

They crossed their arms with a huff. "Of course."

Patting his hip to ensure his dagger was where it should be, Barrett let himself from the room, only to meet another hunter's impatient stare. The man was shorter than Barrett by a head, only coming to his chin, and built almost sickly thin, but the way he looked at Barrett always made him feel small and stupid, and he hated it. But the man was his sister's guest, and this was her house.

"Let's go," Griswold said, leading the way out the front door.

It was still raining outside. Barrett's breath clouded in front of him as he broke into a quick trot down the lane behind the shorter man, following the pull of magic. There was no glow of any fires nor the sounds of anyone screaming. Maybe they would get there before the beast had time to climb out of whatever cellar it had crawled into.

But as they got closer, the sense of the demon began to fade, until there was barely enough of it to follow.

"It must have retreated," Griswold reasoned.

"Course it did," Barrett groaned. Right after it had pulled him out of his lover's arms and out into the rain.

"We should keep searching to be certain. You take—"

There was another surge of magic, stronger than before. Overwhelmingly. And in the complete opposite direction.

Barrett glanced at Griswold. "Another one?"

The air began to stir around the older hunter as he broke into a run. "So it would seem."

"But why…?" Barrett's question faltered as he pinpointed the direction he sensed the demon from. That was where Kat's house was. "Oh, Graces, no."

"I'll meet you there," Griswold said before the wind around him roared into a gale, and he took off down the lane, kicking up a choking spray of mud and rain.

"Bastard!" Barrett shouted, wiping his face on his sleeve as he raced after him. "Please let me be wrong," he pleaded between breaths. "Please let it be anywhere else."

Orange light bloomed in the distance, and he pushed his legs to move faster.

He had to grab the low stone wall on the side of the lane as he skidded around a turn, his boots losing traction in the mud, but he could see it now, clear as day.

Kat's house was burning.

"No. Please, Graces. No."

Fire licked the eaves from where it had chewed through the walls, steadily spreading and engulfing the house. The house he had grown up in, where all his childhood memories were. Where his sister was. Where Raleigh was.

A shadow moved in the open doorway, and he called his fire to hand, ready to strike, only for Griswold to appear with Kat on his arm. They were hard to make out in the harsh light and shadow from the fire, but something was wrong with his sister. Her head was down, and she was cradling one of her arms close.

"Is she—Where's Raleigh?"

"Engaging the demon," Griswold said. "I had to get Katherine—"

Barrett didn't stay to hear whatever else Griswold had to say. Without hesitation, he turned and plunged into the burning house.

Instantly, it felt as if his lungs had caught fire as he gulped down a lungful of noxious smoke. He covered his face with his sleeve, blinking furiously as his eyes began to sting and water. He nearly ran into the bedroom door and hardly felt the bite of the hot metal as he turned the latch and threw the door open.

Black smoke rolled over him, swamping his vision and sending him staggering, sputtering as he sucked down air hotter than any oven. He felt his way forward, crouching to stay beneath the noxious cloud, when his eyes locked on something in the dissonant half-light of the fire.

Time stopped, the roar of fire fading to a ringing silence as he struggled to take in what he was seeing.

It was crouched, its body jerking as it tore off pieces from something lying beneath it. It reminded him of the stray dogs he'd once watched eating a fawn they had caught. Only, this wasn't a deer. It had a face that was looking at him, its mouth moving as it said the same word over and over and over.

Run.

He knew that face, even drenched in offal and blood. Even laid open to the bone, glistening white in the inferno's light. Had dreamed of seeing that face at his side every day the rest of his life.

But it couldn't be.

"Raleigh?"

"Barrett?"

Barrett flinched at the sound of his name, lifting his head to find Captain Griswold looking back at him with what might have passed for concern writ into his passive features. The creature was gone, vanished along with the house and that awful face he could still see in his nightmares.

"Barrett?" Griswold repeated slowly.

"What?" Barrett asked, trying to sound nonchalant as he focused on the captain again, but it was strained, even to him.

"You dozed off. Are you all right?"

"Never better," Barrett said as he glanced round him, slowly recollecting that he was at an inn in Avonmouth and not a burning house. Behind the captain were tables filled with other patrons drinking and talking amongst themselves. The place was packed to the rafters with merchants and sailors trying to keep dry from the storm howling outside that had dogged their entire journey back from the Isles. It was a small favor. It wasn't still a blizzard out there.

"It's just…been a long journey. That's all," Barrett assured him.

Whether the captain believed the lie or not, Barrett marked the faintest softening of Griswold's frown before the captain's attention returned to his supper. "You should eat. It's getting cold."

Looking down, Barrett was surprised to find a second plate set in front of him with stewed greens, a hearty slice of bread, and a pile of chicken with one, greasy leg on top, the bone showing white against the grey pink flesh. "I think my stomach is still sour from the boat," he excused, pushing the plate away.

"Has Kyran eaten?"

Barrett shook his head. "I doubt he'll take this, either. I'll ask for something else for him and Effie."

"Don't hesitate to come and fetch me if anything is amiss," the captain said as Barrett got up from the table.

"*Aye,*" Barrett dismissed him. As if he would want to spend any more time with the captain after being stuck with him for nearly two months now.

Rising from the table, he went to the bar and flagged down a barmaid to give his order, who poured him a fresh drink and hurried off to fetch what he'd asked for. He gulped down nearly half his ale in a single pull before he lowered the tankard, observing the other patrons watching him and the captain. Their glances were wary and stern. No one had approached either of them since they had arrived, sodden and steaming from the storm bringing its wrath down outside.

To his surprise, he found it made him miss Oareford. He was never short a table of folks at the Drunken Wind to talk with, sharing stories and asking him questions about what was going on in a hunter's life. They'd all known his name, and he knew them. He wouldn't be alone at the guild, but he didn't remember having the sense of camaraderie there like he did in Oareford.

Except for Raleigh.

At just his name, the pain, and the guilt and grief Barrett had buried for months under worry and drink welled up in a geyser, and he quickly lifted his drink again. Graces, it had been… He had to think, before he realized it must nearly be the day. He had lost track of the days while in the Isles, but it couldn't be far now. It would be two years then since that demon had killed Raleigh and maimed Kat. Two whole years. It felt like an eternity, and yet, somehow, it still felt like yesterday. By all the Graces above, did Barrett miss him.

The barmaid returned a moment later with what he asked for. "You certain I can't get you something more?" she asked, topping off his drink.

"Thanks, but my, ah, friend isn't feelin' well. Wanted to bring him his food."

She hesitated, her eyes flicking down to his chest where his amulet rested beneath his threadbare tunic before she smiled. "Of course. I can carry it if you'll show me your room."

"That's all right. I can manage," Barrett assured her, gently taking the tray from her hands. "May your lanterns stay lit."

"Yours as well," she said with a curtsy, hurrying away.

Chapter Two

BARRETT PICKED HIS way across the inn, nodding and smiling at the various looks he got from the other guests. It was a small wonder Kyran had retreated to their room as soon as they'd received their key. They were meant to all have separate rooms, but the letter the guild captain had written ahead to secure their lodging had never made it across the sea, likely swallowed by the storm. The innkeeper had managed to free one room for their use, but there simply weren't enough beds for them all.

Griswold had volunteered to stay in the outpost, citing letters and work to be done. Barrett figured he'd find a table someplace to lay his head whenever he got tired to give Kyran and Effie their privacy.

Ducking under the stairs, he knocked on the door with his boot. "I brought supper," he announced, leaning in to catch any response over the noise of the tavern.

There was a stilted tapping, then a pause, before he made out Kyran's voice. "Come in."

Juggling the drink in his free hand, Barrett managed the latch and pushed the door in. Inside there were at least two small beds on either side of a window, and the burning stumps of two candles hung on the wall. It was uncommonly dark for an inn room in Tennebrum, but perhaps he'd grown too accustomed to the Drunken Wind's treatment of its local hunter.

Kyran was seated in the farthest bed, the quilt pulled up to his waist and dressed in a dry shirt, his wet hair swept back from his face, the burnished copper waves curling at the nape of his neck. The mage had fared about as well as Barrett with the rough sea. Kyran had only emptied his stomach once at the beginning of the storm, but he had weathered on by hardly eating and only sipping at any drink offered to him. What little weight he had regained during their too brief stay with his family had quickly melted off, leaving hollows around his eyes and cheeks, and clothing that hung off a frame shrunk to frailty.

Despite his health, the mage had been in better spirits than Barrett had ever seen him. There were still moments when Kyran seemed to forget where he was, and he hadn't slept more than a few hours at a time since waking at the guildhall, but he smiled more, and his devious sense of humor he definitely shared with his brothers had shown its head more and more.

Barrett had barely gotten the door shut behind him when Effie bounded over to him, reaching for the wooden server with one hand, the other clutching her wet doll to her clean, dry dress.

"Back up," Barrett chided her.

Sticking out her lip, Effie let out a huff, and backed away, bouncing impatiently on the balls of her bare feet as she watched Barrett, her damp black hair sticking to her cheeks

"She's a mite hungry," Kyran remarked, managing to pull a weak chuckle from Barrett.

"So, I see." He carried the tray to the meager table that had been forced into a corner of the room, and set an onion pie down in front of the only chair. "There you are, lass."

Effie didn't move, looking from the meal to Barrett to Kyran, and back.

"Go on," Barrett urged, stepping out of her way.

After a moment, she raced to the chair, climbing up into the seat and snatching the pie up.

"Hey! Don't—"

The girl quickly dropped the pie, snatching her hands back with a sulky pout.

"You know better," Barrett said, picking up the fork and handing it to her. "Kyran's mother would be ashamed."

Effie stuck her lip out as far as Barrett thought it could go, then sullenly sat up in her chair and stabbed the top of the pie with the fork. She was the only one of the four of them that had been unbothered by the storm, sleeping her way across the sea. She'd really come a long way from the filthy, frightened little girl he'd rescued from the demon realm alongside Kyran.

Graces that felt ages ago. He supposed it was, when he thought about it. Almost half a year now.

Barrett watched until the girl managed to get the first bite to her mouth with the utensil, before carrying the other bowl to Kyran. "I got you some porridge," he said, setting the bowl next to the candles on the bedside table. "'Bout the only thing they had that didn't have any meat in it."

"Thank you."

Leaning over, Kyran plucked the kerchief he had been borrowing from Barrett off the side table where he'd laid it out to dry, and used it to pick up his bowl. "I dinnae ken another time I've been more pleased ta see Tennebrum," he said conversationally as he carefully wiped his spoon down.

Considering the last time Kyran had landed in Avonmouth, he had been fleeing Connal's persecution after what the man had done to him, Barrett couldn't imagine a truer statement. "I wish we might've stayed a while longer in the Isles," Barrett remarked. And not only because he could appreciate a country of men that wore kilts, though it was a considerable factor. "I liked meetin' your family. They're good folks. Though, honestly, I'll be surprised if Tavish doesn't appear from one of the barrels on deck."

Kyran snorted. "Na if he kent what ma would do ta his hide when she found out."

"Are you certain that would stop him?"

The mage opened his mouth, then sighed, shaking his head. "I'm na."

Kyran's brothers had snuck into Castle Erchleis to break Barrett and Kyran out of imprisonment, and then single-handedly held off the laird's men while Barrett, Griswold, and Kyran fought a demon in the castle's dungeon. They had then, Barrett found out afterwards, conspired to be present at Kyran's trial in case it had gone south, despite being explicitly forbidden. Kyran had expressed his fear that Connal would retaliate against the mage's family for escaping his accusations, but Barrett was starting to wonder if perhaps it wasn't Connal that should be worried.

Picking up one of the wet garments hanging from the end of the second bed, Barrett made himself comfortable on the mattress opposite Kyran. "I'll get these dried for you. I'm much faster than any fireplace."

Kyran chuffed drily, and Barrett smiled to himself as he spread Effie's sodden dress out on his lap. "It took me a while to figure out how to do it without burning anything," Barrett admitted. "I went through quite a few shirts before I could dry them without scorching the fabric." Kyran only shook his head. "Won't be long before you get to see the capital and the guildhall," he remarked to fill the quiet room as he ran his gloved hand over the first piece of clothing, the water beginning to steam out of it. "They're really somethin', especially compared to Oareford."

"Oh, aye?" Kyran responded absently.

"*Aye*," Barrett teased, grinning at the mage's flat look. "It's bigger, of course, and they have street lamps they light at night so you can still go out safely."

The mage looked up at that, eyes wide in open curiosity. "Is that so?"

Barrett's grin broadened. "Aye. Every street and window and even the city's wall is lit up like the Day of Lumen Festival. Oh, and the festivals. Just wait until you see one of those. There's not much that can top The Drunken Wind for drink, but Graces, the food."

He prattled on, describing the city and its wonders as best he could, trying not to linger on the fact that the last time he had been there and done any of the things he was describing had been with Raleigh. Instead, he focused on the idea that in just a week, he would be back at the guildhall, and all of the terror and anguish of these last few months would finally be behind him and Kyran both.

Chapter Three

KYRAN HELD UP the bit of wood he'd been scratching at to the candlelight, examining it for imperfections or details he'd missed, but it was complete at last. It had taken almost a week of work to finish, though the storm they'd weathered while crossing the Isleish Sea was mostly to blame.

He already missed the Isles. Not the lonely years spent on Cairngorm or the terrifying night beneath Erchleis, but the rare nights with his brothers and Barrett, of hours spent talking about nothing and telling stories before falling asleep wherever they lay. He wished he could have stayed, but the price of his freedom hadn't come cheaply.

He was a bondsman now, a servant in all but name. But while he was still furious at the captain for tricking him, he had slowly come to accept that if it weren't for Griswold's, and by proxy the guild's intervention, he would have died in Erchleis for nothing.

And now, he was to become a hunter, the very thing he had hoped for almost in vain just this past summer. He wasn't hiding or running. He would be somewhere people accepted mages, somewhere he wouldn't have to hide what he was. Somewhere he could use his power to fight and kill the beasts that had hunted him. He would finally be doing something to make his da proud. It almost felt like a dream after all the terror and horror of the last two years.

He slipped the trinket into his purse and pulled out his charm, bending his head to his morning prayers. The sun's carved rays dug into his fingers as he prayed his thanks for the gift of the risen sun, and asked the stars to keep their vigil by night.

There was a soft shush of fabric, and a gentle sigh from the bed opposite him, and he quickly said the last of his prayers. Pressing the wooden sun briefly to his lips, Kyran opened his eyes and met Barrett's bleary gaze beneath a tangle of yellow hair.

"Mornin'," the hunter mumbled thickly. He'd fallen asleep while drying their clothes and apparently worked his way beneath the quilt at some point.

"*Madainn mhath*," Kyran returned, leaning to slip his charm back into his purse on the bedside table and take up the comb his ma had given him before he left.

"Too early for that kind of talk," Barrett groaned and pulled the quilt stubbornly over his face so that only his blond hair stuck out.

Kyran smiled, working his comb through his snarled hair. "Careful, Effie, it seems a bear must have gotten in last night."

Effie lifted her head from where she had curled up next to Kyran as Barrett made a noise from beneath the quilt that might have been a curse or poor imitation of a bear.

"A verrah peevish one."

Barrett punctuated his point with another sleepy grumble. "All right, you had your fun. I'm up. I'm…" He trailed off into a yawn, finally sitting up.

"Aye. I can see that."

Barrett shot him a look, but Kyran could see the smile the hunter was trying to hide.

"You get any sleep?" the hunter asked, gathering his hair at the back of his head with a few perfunctory combs with his fingers. He looked as battered as Kyran felt, his long, yellow hair tangled and knotted in its tail at the base of his neck, and his beard had grown in unevenly. His clothes had seen better days, though many of the holes in his tunic had been patched by Kyran's ma, despite Barrett's red faced protests.

"Some."

Barrett glanced up at him. "Nightmares?"

Kyran bent his head. It didn't matter how many days passed, or if he had felt the demon die in his grasp, he couldn't shake the lingering fear he might open his eyes to those same ashen grey walls looming in around him again. It was better some days, nothing more than a faint doubt he could easily brush away. But other days, he swore he could see flickers of that dark place beneath this one. The impression of bricks. The sound of nails scratching against stone.

"Aye," he answered after a moment, reaching to settle a hand on Effie's shoulder and gently shaking her awake.

"I'm sorry."

Effie whined, turning her face into the mattress stubbornly, and Kyran felt a smile tug at his mouth. "For what?"

"That you're havin' them, I guess. The nightmares. I…get them sometimes too. I—"

There was a sharp knock on the door. "It's your captain," Griswold said through the door. "Are you decent?"

"Aye," the mage said, pulling his quilt closer.

The door swung in, admitting Captain Griswold, looking much more himself than the night before. His shirt and vest were dry without a wrinkle to be found, his dark hair neatly combed above his pale face. "I've made our arrangements to leave. As soon as you have eaten and collected your things, there will be a wagon and horses waiting."

"You in a hurry, Captain?" Barrett asked, plucking his leather thong from the side table and tying his hair off.

"As a matter of fact, I am, so if you wouldn't mind—"

"All right," Barrett cut him off. "Don't worry. We'll be ready."

Griswold held the hunter with a long stare until Barrett ducked his head, scratching the tip of his nose. "Very well." With a brief nod to Kyran, the captain exited again, closing the door behind him.

Barrett shook his head, yanking his first boot on. "Always somethin' with him," he grumbled. He got up, stamping his feet down into his boots. "I'll get us some breakfast before Griswold comes bangin' down the door again. Let you get ready."

"Ye hear that lass?" Kyran said, giving Effie another gentle shake. "It's breakfast time."

She sat up at those words, dragging her doll to her chest and peering blearily around.

"Go on." Kyran gave her a gentle nudge, and she stumbled onto her feet over to Barrett, who took her hand. "I willna be long."

"I'll get us a table," Barrett assured him, grabbing his pack at the foot of the bed and leading the lass out into the muted noise of the tavern.

The door latched behind the hunter, but Kyran didn't move, taking a moment to soak in the calm silence of the empty room before he reached for his walking stick. The silverbark was rough in places with scorch marks and deep scars from nails and teeth, but it had survived the ordeal beneath Erchleis, just as he had.

Rummaging through his sack he'd taken to replace his lost pack, he retrieved the last few rolls of clean bandages, and set them where he could reach by the bowl of water that passed for a wash basin.

He carefully removed his shirt, trying not to use his left shoulder. While greatly improved, it was still quite tender. He picked the loose knot of his bandages on his chest free and held his breath as the smell of old blood and his own body odor wafted up from the soiled cloth. Beneath were scattered at least two dozen dark, pocked scabs where the demon's too many teeth had buried into his shoulder, surrounded by faintly glowing bruises where his blood pooled beneath his skin.

The first time he had gotten a good look at it, his shoulder had been nothing more than a ragged mess of thread holding what was left of his flesh together. But every day it had improved, faster than he'd seen any wound heal. He did his best not to contemplate why, tending to it while he trained his thoughts to anything else—the weather, breakfast, where he might wash his clothes—anything but the nagging sense that he knew why the demon had called him half-breed.

Letting his shoulder dry, he pulled his kilt up to his waist, and removed the bandages from his left leg and hips. He felt along the thick, scarred edge, mouth set in a grim line. No matter how many days passed, it was still jarring for his leg to end so abruptly in the middle of what was once his thigh.

It too had healed, though it was difficult to say if it had healed well. It ached fiercely whenever he did not apply the cold of his magic to it, enough to wake him during his scant hours of sleep, and the thick scar was still so sensitive that even the brush of air was almost too much at times.

Satisfied it hadn't suddenly gone off, he gently cleaned the limb, then began to rebandage it, careful to maintain pressure on his leg.

Unpleasantness done, Kyran redressed, and carefully put away his soiled bandages. He packed his scant belongings, then allowed himself a long moment to breathe in the quiet and ready himself before he left the room.

It wasn't as crowded as it had been the night before, but Kyran could feel the other patron's eyes tracking him as he made his way across the tavern. He gave his sleeves a quick tug, mouth tightening at the sight of his blood showing faintly through his skin.

While he no longer woke to walls glittering in frost, he still hadn't managed to bring his power entirely to heel since his time in the demon realm. Yet, even as it unnerved him to have to struggle for control he couldn't help a sense of excitement. He was stronger, and any demon that tried to take him now would regret its choice.

He found Barrett at a table set off to one side, away from the crowd at the bar. Effie waved between bites of thick pottage, her face scrunched in excitement.

"She really seems to like this stuff." Barrett chuckled, kicking the chair out across from him for Kyran. "You just missed Griswold. He just stepped out to sort more guild business. Said to come out when you're done."

Lowering into the seat, Kyran tucked his walking stick into the crook of his good knee, and fished in his purse for his borrowed kerchief. It was still damp, the fabric dingy and cold. He ran his thumb over the embroidered K.B. the same way he had done a hundred times now. "I need ta get a new bit of cloth so I can give this back ta ye."

"There's no hurry," Barrett assured him, pushing a bowl of the pottage and slice of bread across the table. "I know you'll take care of it."

"But it's yours." Kyran laid the cloth over his palm, using it to pick up his spoon and wipe the handle clean.

"And I gave it to you to use, which you're doing. Just keep it until you find another one."

Kyran frowned down at his bowl. It wouldn't be difficult to find a new kerchief, if he had any coin to spend. Every cent he'd earned had disappeared when he'd been taken by that needle-toothed demon into its realm, and he had yet to find more. But the kerchief was precious to Barrett—a memento from his mother. Far too precious to simply *lend*.

"I know you'll take care of it," Barrett added and leaned to wipe some of the mess from Effie's face. "Eat your breakfast before Griswold shows up to interrupt again."

Kyran cut him a look, and the hunter laughed. "Verrah well."

Chapter Four

IT WAS WITH a sinking disappointment that Barrett realized there weren't going to be any more inn rooms on the way back to the guildhall. The last inn lay at least an hour behind them, and the next city was some ways down the river road, while the sun was steadily moving lower, and lower.

He supposed he should have seen it coming. They had camped every night on the way to Avonmouth in order to avoid attracting any demons into the populated areas. They numbered far less this time, but the risk was still higher with hunters and a mage around.

At least the weather was better this time. For now.

It was near sunset when Captain Griswold finally called a halt for the night, directing the driver he had hired for their wagon to a flat spot off the road.

"Barrett, if you will fetch the wood from the cart and start the fire. A small one," the captain added with some emphasis.

The hunter narrowed his eyes at his captain. "What's that supposed to mean?"

"This is farmland. We only have what wood is in the wagon unless we find a copse. A small fire will need less wood."

Barrett grunted in reply and dismounted, his legs wobbling. He ached from riding all day, but it was better than having to walk.

"Bet you can't wait to be out of that," he said to Sweetheart, patting her shoulder fondly.

The mare huffed without lifting her head intent on nibbling at a patch of not quite brown grass. She had been odd all day, refusing to go anywhere near the wagon, no matter how he tried to guide her to it. She would either veer away or prance backwards or sideways until she deemed herself far enough from it to be satisfied. The horse pulling the wagon had been nervous as well, requiring constant soothing from the driver until Barrett and Griswold had dropped back behind it a ways and followed them down the road.

Tucking the reins under one of the stirrups to keep it from falling and tangling in the horse's hooves, he made his way to the wagon. Kyran was seated in the back on a bundle of firewood, Effie across from him. The mage had something in his lap he was focused on, his expression intent but calm. It was a marked difference from the way he had looked at Barrett when they had followed this same road to Avonmouth. Barrett hoped he'd never have to see that look again—the suspicion and anger and naked fear.

"Working on an amulet?" Barrett guessed when Kyran didn't pick his head upup, keeping his voice soft so as to not startle him.

"Just a trinket," Kyran said, holding up a piece of wood. It had been whittled down, but it was hard to say what it was going to be.

"What is it?"

"It's a bit of wood."

"Oh, is it?" Barrett said with feigned surprise, but his composure crumbled when he noticed Kyran's smirk. "Thanks for clearin' that up. No, really, what's it gonna be?"

"A horse, eventually," Kyran said, setting the piece aside and brushing the curls of wood off of his lap.

"Somethin' for Effie?"

"Aye. She's been watching, too. Seems ta like it." Kyran leaned across the cart and ruffled the girl's hair, earning an aggrieved whine before she swatted his hands away. "I ken I'll have ta watch my knife around her when she's older."

"You'll have to teach her how to throw it. After me, of course."

The mage picked up his walking stick, easing towards the back of the cart. "Oh, certainly, though I dinnae promise you'll be able ta hit a thing afterwards. I canna work a miracle."

"Just full of vinegar today," Barrett feigned a scowl, leaning over the side of the cart to grab one of the bundles of wood and hefting it out. "Your brothers were a bad influence on you."

"Is that so?"

"Aye, it is. Bring some of those shavings, will you?" Barrett called, lugging the bundle over to what he judged a suitable spot for the night and set about getting their fire going.

His own fire had been easier to wield and call forth since wresting control of it from his demon. He hadn't heard a whisper from the beast since leaving the Inbetween in the Isles, and he couldn't determine if that was a good or bad thing.

"Does the guild always camp like this?" Kyran asked, leaning into his walking stick as he watched Barrett tend the fire.

"I can't say. I haven't done much traveling before now."

"Isna it more dangerous out here?"

Barrett didn't like how nervous the mage sounded. He wasn't too thrilled about the idea of sleeping in the dark outside, either. It held more weight than it used to. "We'll be taking shifts tonight so nothing can sneak up on us and to keep the fire going."

Kyran's mouth thinned, his eyes flickering across the darkening landscape. "Does the fire even matter?"

"Course it does," Barrett answered before his head caught up with his mouth. In all honesty, most demons could only come through at night in the deepest shadows. But there were a rare few strong enough to do as they pleased. The needle-toothed demon that had taken Raleigh and Kyran had done so in lantern light and even during the day. "If they come, we'll be ready for them," he mollified. "They'll regret they ever tried us."

The mage managed a wan smile, but it was far from the comfort Barrett wished he could give Kyran. He wanted to assure the mage that he was safe, that he wouldn't let anything happen to him. But it was an empty promise. It didn't matter how hard he tried to keep it. The last two years of his life had proved through and through that demons didn't care for promises.

Once he was certain the fire had caught, he doubled back to the cart to retrieve the bedrolls to lay out around the fire. He sat next to Kyran, and Griswold joined them, producing a bundle of fresh vegetables and meat he began to prepare for their supper. Effie sat by him, helping in her own way by feeding little sticks and bits of grass into the fire.

Barrett looked around, searching for some way to distract Kyran from the falling gloom around them, when his eyes landed on the horses being tended by their driver.

"Y'know, the guild horses were bred around hunters and mages. They're a mite less skittish than you'd expect if you spend enough time around 'em."

Kyran frowned, looking up from the fire. "Aye?" he said slowly.

"I just thought maybe you'd like to try and start gettin' friendly with Sweetheart."

A flicker of something bright appeared in Kyran's eyes. "Do you think I can?"

Barrett grinned at the mage's evident excitement. "Course I do."

"Do any of the mages at the guild ride?"

The image of Raleigh astride the old red mare, laughing and hooting as they splashed along a stream outside of the city struck Barrett like a slap. Graces, he hadn't even thought of that day in nearly a year, how it ended with them behind a clump of bushes, giggling as they kissed under the warm sun and made promises neither of them ever had the chance to keep.

"The mage I knew—" he tried to say, but his voice broke with a quiver. He reached for his hip, and the flask waiting in his coat pocket, swallowing a pull almost without tasting it, letting the burn of the Isleish whiskey fill the hole threatening to open up in his chest and swallow him.

"He, uhm. He had an old mare he liked to take on short walks," he said, forging ahead through the pain. "She was a slow, lazy bastard who only ever liked to bite me, so I don't know how he managed to get on with her other than persistence." Barrett cleared his throat and gestured to his grazing mare. "But, ah, if you wanna try, I can hold her still. She's a little fussy at first but she's sweet."

"Is that so?" Kyran asked, and Barrett chuffed at the familiar phrase.

"Aye, it is," he countered, taking another swallow of whiskey before he pocketed the drink and levered to his feet. "But, let's see if we can't introduce you to Sweetheart, then. Just gimme a second to get her ready."

"Ready?"

"Her bridle."

"Ye are na going ta put the poor beast back in her bridle, are ye?"

Barrett scratched at his beard. "Shouldn't I?"

"Just put the reins around her neck under her chin. Like this." Kyran held his fist under his chin. "She's had that bit in all day and Sean already hobbled the lass when he took their saddles off. She willna go anywhere unless she has a mind ta, and none of us are going ta stop her then."

The hunter managed a small, embarrassed laugh. "I guess you would know. Just give me a moment then."

Sweetheart picked her head up at Barrett's approach, nickering loudly.

"I wasn't gone that long, silly girl, and you could still see me," Barrett teased, stroking her neck before reaching for the bridle hanging on a nearby bush.

She nibbled playfully at his tunic sleeve while he lay the reins over her neck.

He shooed her, gathering the reins under her chin as Kyran had described before he turned to the mage. "We're ready when you are."

Kyran murmured something to the captain and Effie before he carefully got up from his bedroll. It was an ungainly process, but one Kyran was getting better at. He rolled off his hip to his knee and set the end of his walking stick firmly in the earth next to him. Then, leaning heavily into the stick, and using his other hand for balance, he stood straight up, hopping to keep his balance as it threatened to pitch forwards until he could get his stick under his arm.

Barrett clenched his fists, fighting the urge to rush over and do something stupid. Kyran didn't need his help, and offering would only insult the mage.

Sweetheart's ears flicked straight forwards, her posture going rigid, and nostrils flaring wide as she took in the mage slowly approaching. She stamped unhappily, dancing in place until Barrett shushed her with a hand at her neck.

"It's just Kyran," Barrett murmured. "You know him, you silly lass. We followed him around the whole length of the Isles."

A muscle twitched along the mare's flank, one of her ears briefly flicking to Barrett, but not an inch of her posture changed. She let out a grumble of complaints, to which Kyran replied in a tumble of soft, lilting Isleish.

"Pretty, innit?" Barrett whispered to his horse, smiling when she paid him no mind. "I bet you'll like him more than me by the end of the day."

It was a slow process. Murmuring almost nonstop, Kyran approached the horse, pausing whenever she laid her ears back. He kept at it, creeping closer and closer until he was well within reach of the mare, who pressed her shoulder into Barrett's side, as if he were going to protect her from the mage.

Then, moving very slowly, Kyran extended his hand, fingers curled limply, and simply held it there between them.

Sweetheart snorted, stretching her neck up away from the mage's hand as if it were something poisonous. But Kyran waited until, at last, Sweetheart stretched out her neck and snuffled curiously at the mage's hand. Barrett grinned in triumph before, without any warning, the mare's ears pinned back against her head, and he knew in an instant what was coming. He'd seen that look aimed at him before.

"Kyr—"

The mage jerked his hand back as Sweetheart snapped at his fingers, tossing her head furiously.

"Sweetheart!" Barrett scolded, fighting to keep hold of the reins beneath her chin. "That was rude."

"I ken she's had enough for the evening," Kyran said, backing away as hope dimmed from his eyes. "Best ta let her go before she hurts herself."

Barrett started to disagree when Sweetheart yanked her head free of the reins and with a surge of her entire body, hopped in her hobbles away from them. Barrett sighed, frustrated his plan had panned out so poorly. "I'm sorry," he said, turning back to Kyran to find the mage still watching the horse, his smile turned wistful.

"Dinnae be," the mage said. "She's her own mind, and enough fire ta light the dawn."

"That's for sure," Barret agreed and folded his arms. "I'll bet we'll have better luck if you had some treats."

"What does she favor?"

"Just about any fruit, I'd wager. Mihai's lads always had apples for her, but she near took my fingers off once when I offered her some berries."

"A sweet tooth, aye?"

"Oh, aye, much like yourself," Barrett teased.

Kyran rolled his eyes, leaning into his walking stick. "You are na ever going ta let me forget that, are ye?"

"Not likely," Barrett grinned, then added, "unless it really bothers you, then I'll stop."

The mage waved a hand at him. "You'll ken when you're a real bother."

"I'm certain I will," Barrett acknowledged, then looked to where Sweetheart had wandered over to. "And I'm certain Sweetheart will warm up to you. We can try again another day."

"With a pocket full of berries and turnip greens."

Barrett laughed. "We'll spoil her rotten at this rate."

"Oh, too late for that."

Barrett started to agree, when Captain Griswold called out to them for supper. "I suppose we'd better hurry before Effie finishes the lot for us," he sighed, casting a last look at his mare. His plan hadn't quite worked out, but it hadn't fallen apart either. Kyran was joking and smiling again, the hollow fear gone for the moment. Barrett would take that small victory.

Chapter Five

K YRAN STARED INTO the fire watching as embers rose from the logs in fading arcs like falling stars, unable to sleep. It felt strange, lying in the grass under the stars along nearly the same path he had taken himself when he first arrived in Tennebrum. It had all the trappings of familiarity, and yet, it felt anything but like that first time. The novelty of seeing a new landscape and feeling grass beneath his head had been almost wondrous.

Now…

Now, every animal and insect scratching in the night was suddenly the step of that needle-toothed beast crawling out of the Inbetween to take him back to its dark prison.

At least there was the small comfort that Griswold and Barrett were nearby. Whenever Kyran gave up on his fitful attempts at sleep, Barrett was almost always awake. Just like he was now, prodding at the fire between wide yawns, utterly disheveled with bits of grass poking from his tangled hair.

"*Madainn mhath*," Kyran murmured, disentangling himself from Effie, who had wrapped herself around one of his arms during the night, her bedroll kicked in every direction but over her.

Barrett picked his head up with a tired smile. "Mornin'. See you got yourself a barnacle."

Effie let out a soft whine as Kyran finally slipped free and tossed the bedroll back over her. "A *wean*." He reached for his walking stick, and painstakingly pulled himself upright. It wasn't normally so difficult to stand, even after his injury, but over the last few weeks, his back had begun to ache and stiffen. He blamed the long cart rides, and miserable boat crossing for his troubles.

"You headed to the cart?" Barrett asked, preemptively rising from where he was seated.

"Aye."

"All right." He shuffled to the opposite side of the fire, putting his back directly to Kyran and the cart. "Just shout if you need anything."

Kyran let out a drily amused chuff, and made his way to the cart, cautious to keep a wide berth of the horses dozing and grazing nearby. Their ears pricked his direction, but they merely watched as he clambered gracelessly into the back of the cart. He propped the canvas up with his walking stick, then dug out a bowl and skein of water, pouring out a measure to wash with.

He worked as quickly as he could, then redressed and carefully put away his soiled bandages, flicking the bowl of dirty water out the back of the cart before he climbed out again.

Barrett was standing with his back still to him, conversing with the guild captain and the driver while Griswold prepared breakfast over the fire. At Kyran's approach, they broke from their conversation about which cut of back bacon was the best and, while Griswold cooked, Kyran and Barrett packed away camp into the back of the cart.

They were nearly finished when Barrett and Captain Griswold both stiffened and whirled to face the road. Kyran's blood flared, the grass frosting in the early morning, and the horses whinnied anxiously in their hobbles, leaping away from him and the driver.

He flexed his control, ready to fight tooth and claw if it was that needle-toothed bastard come back for him, when he made out a rider on the road headed their way.

"It's a courier," Griswold said, his posture easing, and he moved to greet the rider.

"Doesn't look like Alex," Barrett said, dropping his hand from his hip.

The rider slowed as they drew near and swung down off their chestnut mare. "Glad I left when I did," they said, pulling a scarf down from around her face. She looked to be about as old as Kyran's ma, with soft lines writ into her features.

"Finley," Captain Griswold greeted her. "I presume you bring word from the guild."

"I do." She reached into her saddle bags and produced a sealed letter. "Orders from Selah herself. You and your hunter are to head to Culfield to escort a supply train to Belldale."

"Really? Why?" Barrett asked, and Finley shrugged.

"Orders. I'm supposed to take that wagon over and finish escorting your other member back to the guildhall."

Kyran stiffened, his fingers drumming against his walking stick.

"What does that mean?" Barrett demanded. "He's not coming with us?"

"He is not a guild member yet," Griswold said, looking up from the letter. "Finish packing. We will eat on the road. Finley, if you wouldn't mind, I want to speak with you."

"Of course." She followed the captain back to the cooking fire, trailing the mare behind her.

Kyran watched them go, a dawning dread spreading through him.

Barrett let out a single short curse. "Of course they would ask me to go right after I've only just gotten back."

"How far is it?" Kyran asked, ignoring the growing pit in his belly.

"I don't really know. I guess I'll find that out on the way. Hopefully not far. Hopefully I can go and be back in no time. Graces give me strength, I'm sorry to just—"

"It's fine." Kyran picked at the end of his sleeve. "I can take care of myself and Effie."

Barrett sighed, clenching his fist uselessly. "You're right, but it doesn't make me feel any better about leavin'."

"Ye'll be back, aye?"

"*Aye*," Barrett said, smiling at Kyran's dry look, and bending to lift the last of their bedrolls into the back of the wagon. "I just hope it won't be too long."

"Aye, me as well," Kyran said, surprised to find he meant it.

"Well, I didn't think I'd have to keep my promise so soon," Barrett said, scratching at his beard. Kyran frowned, and the hunter let out a soft chuckle. "To write you."

A flush crept up Kyran's cheeks. "I canna read it."

"I'll write all the same. You can read it later once you learn how."

A flutter of light shone from beneath Kyran's shirt before he quickly tamped his magic down. "You're daft," he muttered, fumbling in his purse as he suddenly remembered himself. "Here."

Barrett's brows shot up at the sight of a small, carved whistle resting on Kyran's palm. It was about as big as his finger, and every inch of it had been carved in minute detail to resemble a flowering vine with tiny clusters of berries.

"I finished it after you fell asleep. Now you willna lose your mare while you're traveling."

Barrett's cheeks flushed pink, but he smiled as he picked up the whistle, careful not to touch Kyran's palm beneath. "Oh, havin' a gaff, eh?"

"Well, you seemed ta need it."

Barrett snorted, shooting a sarcastic glare in the mage's direction. "Well, thank you anyway," he said, turning the whistle over in his hand. "I promise to report if Sweetheart cares to listen to it."

"If she doesna, you had best take her ta your horse master for a shaming."

"Me or Sweetheart?"

Kyran smirked. "Both."

Barrett shook his head, muttering about ungrateful mages, but he was smiling as he tucked the whistle away in his coat pocket.

Griswold and Finley returned a moment later. "Are you both ready?"

"I guess," Barrett said.

Kyran opened his mouth to give Barrett his final goodbye, only to find he wasn't entirely certain what to say. It felt strangely final to say goodbye like this. It was ridiculous, of course. The hunter was coming back. He might not even be gone more than a few days. But Kyran still couldn't quell the baseless anxiety stirring in his belly.

"Well, I suppose this is goodbye for now," Barrett said, and looked down at Effie clinging to Kyran's kilt, his expression softening. "You watch his back, eh?"

The lass nodded gravely, pressing closer to Kyran's leg.

"May your lanterns stay lit," Barrett offered.

"And the stars guide and keep you," Kyran said in turn. There was a beat between them where Kyran felt like he ought to say or do something more, when Griswold spoke up.

"If you are done, Barrett, I need you to see to your horse."

"*Aye*," Barrett mumbled, grinning at Kyran before he walked off.

"I suppose we'll be on our way, then," Finley remarked, patting her coat breast. "I'll deliver these soon as we arrive, Captain."

"See that you do. And Kyran." Griswold inclined his head to the mage. "My condolences that you must make this journey without us. May your lanterns stay lit."

"And yours as well," Kyran offered in turn, watching as the captain followed Barrett.

"Well, well," Finley said, her gaze lighting on Kyran with a look of speculative interest. Her mousey brown curls had been cut short as a lad's and she smiled with an utter insouciance that could only be rivaled by his brother Duncan. And Barrett, of course. "I must say, it's good to finally meet the man that has the guild all a twitter at the moment. Kyran?"

"Aye," the mage confirmed. There was a tug at his hand, and he glanced down as Effie sidled behind him.

"You know, it's been a long while since I've met another mage that isn't ten years old."

Another.

Kyran's attention snapped back to the woman. "You're a mage?"

She smiled, showing her teeth, and extended one of her hands. Lines of ruddy light blossomed beneath her skin, and a crimson and black flame flickered to life in her palm.

"Stars above," he whispered. She had runelines, just like him. It had been one of the first things he'd noticed about Barrett—the hunter had no lines when he cast his magic. But the demons did, a fact that had preyed on Kyran since his time in their realm. But she…

"Am I the first mage you've met?" Finley asked, quenching her fire, the lines of her magic fading.

"Aye."

"That's hardly surprising. There aren't many of us, and the guild keeps us spread fairly thin trying to keep the demons at bay. I can only imagine how many questions you must have if you've never had anyone else to talk to," Finley said, shushing the cart horse as it snorted nervously. "Pardon me. I'm letting my enthusiasm get ahead of me. If you're ready, let's get going and talk on the road. I'd like to take advantage of the sun before it remembers to hide its head behind its winter blanket again."

"A—aye," Kyran stammered, bending to help Effie into the back of the cart while Finley mounted her mare.

Another mage. Stars above, but he never thought he'd see the day. Perhaps there was more to the guild than a means to make something of his life after all.

The driver clicked his tongue, coaxing their horse until it finally started off down the road. Kyran looked back just long enough to catch a glimpse of Barrett watching him before a turn of the road took him out of sight, and despite his anticipation of what lay ahead, he couldn't help a pang of anxiety over leaving the hunter behind.

"It won't be long," he assured himself, turning back around to face the road ahead. If Barrett could find him in the demon realm, he could certainly find his way back to the guildhall.

Chapter Six

"WE BETTER STOP here," Finley announced, stirring Kyran from his drowse in the back of the wagon.

He'd only meant to rest his eyes a moment, but that moment had apparently eaten up most of the day. Pushing up on his elbow, he peered over the side of the wagon at the vacant fields on either side of the road, faintly recalling his journey to Avonmouth in the back of another wagon. His memory of that time was all a nightmare smeared blur, but there were points he remembered clearly. Bowls of hot soup. Barrett's face. Effie. The sound of rain.

"I'll get the fire started if you'll unload the bedrolls," Finley said, coming around the back of the wagon to grab a bundle of firewood.

Kyran nodded and, using his walking stick as a brace, eased himself over the side of the cart, gripping the rail to keep his balance as his muscles spasmed painfully in his back and hips. He set his teeth against the simmering frustration that had been slowly building each day with every staircase or chair he struggled with. He was ill, he reminded himself. He still needed time to heal, to regain the strength the demon had starved from him.

"Come on, lass," he finally said, taking Effie's hand as she climbed down after him.

Grabbing the bedrolls, he dragged them one by one out of the back of the cart, tossing them onto the grass like hay bales. He started to move them into place, when he noticed Finley bent over the sticks she had arranged, her skin glimmering with lines of red light. Nails clicked roughly on stone above him and a lipless grin of needle teeth leered down at him as he was torn apart inside his head and out.

The scent of smoke wafted past him, and Kyran was once again looking down at Finley, settling back on her heels as she observed her fire.

He shook his head, dragging the bedrolls into place on opposite sides of the fire she was building, and rolled them out.

"Supper will be a bit," she said, retrieving a cooking pot from the cart. "But in the meantime, I thought we might have a little demonstration. I'm really curious to see your magic after I've heard so much about it, and I presume you would appreciate the same of me."

"Aye," Kyran blurted. After a lifetime wishing and dreaming of this moment, how could he say anything but yes?

Finley beamed, tossing another log onto the fire. "Wonderful. I'll tend to Mistral after I get this on the fire, then we can find a spot."

Kyran frowned, settling down on the bedroll next to Effie, who watched the fire enraptured. "The mare? It will let ye tend it?"

"The guild horses are a sturdy lot next to the common plough horse."

Except when it came to him, apparently. "Are ye certain?"

"I've been riding all day, haven't I? I'm certain there will be time for you to go and meet the horse master eventually. Mihai will find one that will take you. It might be some time though. First, you'll have to make it through the guild's mountain of records the scholars will want from you."

Kyran huffed. "You sound like Barrett."

"Oh, he hasn't the faintest idea yet. Just you wait until *he* makes it back to the guildhall. The scholars are all in a frenzy to speak with him."

And Barrett would hate every minute of it. The thought made Kyran chuckle. Barrett was skilled at facing down demons with his fire and dagger, but when it actually came to fulfilling the scholarly side of his position, Griswold had made a point to tell the hunter he was woefully underwhelming. "Do ye ken when that might be?"

Finley shrugged. "Whenever he finishes whatever task the guild asked of him." She settled the pot into the logs and poured out a flask of water into it, along with several handfuls of oats, bits of vegetables, and some sort of seasoning, giving it all a stir. "There." She stood, dusting her hands off. "We'll just let that boil a bit. Let me get the horse while you pick out a spot. Maybe over by that stump?"

Kyran craned his head, picking out the rotting stump some ways away from their camp before he carefully got up from his bedroll. "I'll be right back, lass," he told Effie, smiling when she cocked her head up at him. "You stay here and keep watch."

She seemed to take his meaning, pulling her knees up against her chest before she fixed her gaze back on the fire. When he was certain she wouldn't do something foolish, he picked his way across the field to the stump. The ground was deceptively uneven, and he had to move slowly to keep from tripping over the hidden ruts and holes beneath the grass.

Finley joined him not long after. "What should we start with, hm? We can use the stump as a target. Then we can really see what the magic is doing." She considered the stump, the lines of her blood beginning to glow beneath her skin. "I suppose I can go first. You've been around the hunters, so I assume you've seen them working fire. Mine is much the same except for my means of accessing my power." Her runelines flared bright under her skin, and the grass beneath her feet flashed to embers.

Fire shot out from her body, curling around the stump in a crimson and black burst before it disappeared, leaving only orange embers behind. She hadn't lifted her hand.

"How did you do that?"

"Do what?" Finley asked, smiling like the cat that got the cream. Before Kyran could elaborate, another blast of fire licked the stump, the scent of smoke filling the air.

"That."

"Do you usually use your hand to direct your magic?"

Or his teeth.

He shuddered at the too-fresh memory. "Aye."

"Well, our magic comes from our blood, and our blood runs through our entire body. There's no reason you cannot simply use it from any part of you." She stepped back, nodding to the stump. "You should try."

Kyran started to object, inexplicably apprehensive, then tamped it down. He was a guild member now. There was no one to tell him he could not use his magic.

He clenched his hands around his walking stick to keep from lifting them as he loosened his hold on his magic. The air crackled, filling with a fine white mist that glowed with the light of his lines. His hand twitched as he focused on the stump and let his control slip for just a moment.

The grass flashed silver as a wake of cold scythed through the air, colliding with the wood with a sharp hiss, quenching the lingering embers all at once. He started to smile in triumph when he realized the ground was frosted in every direction around him. The stump had merely been incidental.

"Brr." Finley laughed, clothes steaming as she approached the stump. "Don't worry. You'll get the hang of it with some practice." She knelt by the stump, pressing her fingers to the crags of ice clinging to the char. "Your magic isn't quite what I expected after reading the reports. I wish I had more time to see what else you can do, but I suppose there will be time for that when you are recovered." She turned his way, eyes bright with runelight and excitement. "I'll admit I'm curious how you've managed to do so well for yourself without any guidance. You have remarkable control."

Her praise caught him utterly by surprise. His control over his magic had always been necessary. If he didn't have it, he had nothing. Nothing but a lonely cabin at the top of a ben. "Thank you," he said, his chest strangely tight. "Did you...have a teacher?"

"Of a manner." She started back towards the fire, and Kyran had to stretch his walking stick to keep up. "I was living in the ward at the guild when my power awoke. One of the older mages was summoned to teach me how to control it once I survived the fever, but he was a terrible teacher. We muddled through it eventually, but I think I would have been better off without him. Old bastard. How do you think of it?"

"Think of what?"

"Your magic. What do you use to keep it in check? That old bastard had me imagining a fist that I had to keep clenched around it like a particularly hard to hold snake." She shot Kyran a wry look. "I detest snakes."

He chuckled at that. "Oh, aye?"

"Immensely. But what about you?"

"I dinnae have ta deal with them on the *ben*."

"Not snakes. Your magic."

"Oh." Kyran considered his answer. At one time he would have had a ready answer, but his magic had changed while he'd been in the demon realm, as had his understanding of it. "It is like...fencing a herd of unruly stallions. They kick and jump and try ta get free, but if they canna be tamed, they can at least be trained."

Finley smiled warmly. "That's surprisingly poetic. You would have been a much better teacher than the one I had."

"I dinnae ken about that," Kyran demurred modestly. "I—"

"Managed to figure all of this out on your own as a child while I was being led by the nose. I'm certain you'll fare well enough. Take the compliment."

Kyran shut his mouth, embarrassed yet indescribably pleased. After a lifetime wishing and dreaming of this moment, he couldn't believe it was another mage complimenting his skill. Perhaps it hadn't all been for naught.

"You and I will have to talk more once you're approved to begin training."

"Aye, I would like that," Kyran agreed earnestly. Finley's excitement was contagious, and he found himself eager to see what a guild trained mage might teach him.

"Good. You do your best to recover in the next week, then, and we'll see if I can't loosen some of those restrictions they've placed on your martial training. The chirurgeon's mean well, but they don't always know best. I can't wait to see what you can do."

Kyran smiled in real excitement. "I look forward ta it."

Chapter Seven

Barrett rolled the whistle Kyran had given him between his fingers as he scratched his quill across another sentence. Belldale had turned out to be a great deal farther from Avonmouth and the guildhall than Barrett had hoped. Six days they were bound to travel across the whole of Tennebrum, and to top it off, the rain had returned the moment he and Griswold had set foot in Culfield.

Leaving Griswold to hash out the details of their journey, Barrett had followed the wagon drivers to a nearby tavern where he was promised one last night of drink and a bed before they were off in the morning.

The tavern was warm and dry, and with a pint of ale at hand, he had pulled out his writing kit at the first table that opened up, intent on keeping the promise he'd made. He smiled absently, holding onto the image of Kyran's baffled expression at receiving a letter as he tried to think of what to actually put down on parchment.

Two more pints in, he had scrapped three letters, and was little closer to figuring out what to write. He would have expected a friendly letter to be far easier to write than official guild documentation, but every sentence he wrote addressed to Kyran felt awkward and clumsy.

"What's this, then?"

Barrett startled upright, dropping the quill on the parchment. Ink splattered across the lines he'd written, ruining another draft. He whipped around to find Alex, of all people, standing behind him, grinning.

"Alex! What are you doing here?"

She shrugged. "Same as you, I guess. On my way to the guild to deliver more mail. I got pulled from Oareford to help. What's all this chicken scrawl you're working on, though? I didn't take you for a writer."

"Oh, Graces, no." Barrett chuckled, dropping the whistle back in his pocket and crumpling the parchment, smearing the ink. "I'm absolutely no good with words for that."

"Practicing your calligraphy, then?"

"No, I—"

"Is it a love letter?"

"No!" Barrett's entire face burned like fire, and he quickly gathered his discarded drafts in case she tried to look at them too. "It's just a letter."

Smiling cattily, she glanced pointedly the empty seat at his table. "Is Kyran here?"

"No, he's on his way to the guild."

Her smile widened to show her teeth. "Ah, I see."

"It's just a letter."

"And I'm just a courier. You need help with that?"

"No. Graces, I've got this."

"All right. Have you written up a motion of transfer?"

Barrett blinked, the sudden shift in topic catching him by surprise. "No. I haven't. I just got back to Tennebrum. How did you…"

She gave him an arch look. "Didn't you tell Kat you didn't want to stay in Oareford any longer?"

He had, though he had utterly forgotten in the midst of everything else that had been happening at the time.

"You'd better get it done before they ship you back," she chastised, and nodded down to his letter. "I'm going to get my supper. You let me know when you finished your poem and I'll take it for you."

"It's not—" Barrett argued, but she had already slipped away through the crowd. He glared after her, then down at his crumpled paper, a trickle of doubt starting at the back of his head before he quashed it. He'd made a promise. Silly or no, he intended to keep it.

Chapter Eight

Aside from turning the roads to slick muck that claimed more than one wheel off the supply wagons, the cold, miserable rain had dampened any conversation, turning the days into boring, lonely slogs. There wasn't even a chance of finding a stranger to talk to in the evenings. Captain Griswold ensured they camped outside of any towns, much as they had last time, and everyone was content to care for their animals and retire to their tents to get out of their wet clothes.

Which left Barrett to mumble to Sweetheart and stare at the inside of his greased tarp. He often fiddled with his whistle, twisting it in his fingers idly, envious of the mage's hobby of whittling bits of wood. At least that would have whiled the hours.

He caught himself more than once wishing he had been able to go with Kyran, but at least he had been able to send a letter. Hopefully they would only need to deliver the supply wagon to Belldale, and then they could head back to the guild.

"Halt!"

Barrett snapped out of his reverie and squinted into the rain, but it was difficult to make out anything further than a few yards.

"We've reached it," Griswold said, nudging his horse forward, and Barrett followed him up the line of wagons to where a single figure stood at the center of the road, the pull of their magic undeniable. A hunter then. They really had finally made it.

"Hunters," they were greeted by a firm, feminine voice from beneath the other's hood. "Just the two of you?"

"It is," Griswold replied. "Hunter Barrett and Captain Griswold."

"Captain Fairclough. It's good to see you both. I'll give you your inbriefing as soon as the Lightbringer's done with his sermon." Fairclough looked up at Barrett, teeth flashing white against her dark skin as she grinned up at him. "Another Barrett, huh?"

Barrett was more than a little chagrined at the number of guild members who knew his family name. "That I am."

"Well, if you're anything like your sister, I'm glad you're here." She nodded towards the gate. "Come on, then. The guardsmen will sort the wagons. I'd be much obliged if you told me those were supplies for us."

"They are," Griswold answered. "There will be a second train coming in another week."

"Thank the Graces."

Their company rode down the path into the village proper, which was strangely devoid of people. The windows of every home and shop glowed with light, assuring Barrett the town was not as abandoned as it felt. He could smell the wood fires from chimneys filling the air, no doubt getting an early start to ward off the early winter dark quickly descending in the foothills.

They reached the edge of what looked like the village square, and it was only then Barrett noticed the incredible pull of power from ahead of them where the fog glowed like fire. He started to reach for his dagger when a familiar voice spoke above the nervous jangle of the horses' tresses.

"If you will wait here, there will be an evening brief just before sundown," Fairclough said quietly. "Afterwards, we can talk and I'll bring you up to speed on events and what your expected duties will be."

"Of course," Griswold answered, but Barrett wasn't paying attention any more, fixed on the voice in the fog. It couldn't be…

"Myles?" He eased Sweetheart around Fairclough, nudging her forward until he could make out the congregation gathered in the street. People of every age and creed, a few Crown Guardsmen with their close cropped hair and red surcoats, all stood clutching candles with faces upturned to the sky as the Lightbringer standing on the House's steps in his orange robes prayed for them, calling on the Graces and the Light to protect them from harm and guide their paths.

It was difficult to make out any fine details through the fog and drizzling rain, but Barrett was certain it was Myles. But what in the world was the old Lightbringer doing all the way out here?

The congregation murmured their reply to the prayers, and the Lightbringer raised his voice again, when a bell began to toll, and the overwhelming press of magic suddenly thickened in the air. Sweetheart whinnied sharply, prancing anxiously in place, her ears pressed back, and the hair shot up along Barrett's arms and neck.

A demon.

"Lumen's Graces protect us," Myles prayed before a deep, rasping howl sounded over the village, drowning out the Lightbringer's voice.

"Hunters!" Fairclough bellowed over the square, striding with purpose past Barrett towards the House. "Form up. Get these people in the House and hold the door!"

Barrett swung down out of his saddle, glancing about for a safe direction to send the horse when the reins were wrenched from his hand as Sweetheart wheeled and plunged into the fog.

"Graces cursed…" There was nothing for it. She was trained not to go far, and she had always managed to stay safe before. He would have to trust she would be all right this time as well as he joined the other hunters appearing from the fog in the circle of the House's light.

"But it's not even night," someone wailed, and he dared a glance upwards, but he couldn't tell anything beyond the low hanging fog.

Another howl shivered through the air, joined by a second throat, and then a third. Panic rippled through the crowd, and all of a sudden, people were running in every direction. There was a crush for the House, but some, seeing the press at the door, took off down the road away from the howls instead.

"Wait!" Barrett called. "Come back. Go into the House."

"Hunters, on my mark!" Fairclough's voice rose above the clamor. "Aim outwards and unleash your fire. Ready."

"But the people—"

"Fire!"

A torrent of red and black fire roared into the fog, and Barrett had to raise his free hand to shield his face as the heat threatened to scald him, the rain hissing and spitting around them.

"And cease fire!" came Fairclough's command, and the blaze stuttered to a halt.

Around them, the fog had cleared for nearly twenty feet in all directions, burned away, but already it was slowly rolling back in. There was a scream from somewhere in the village, and Barrett jerked into motion, when Griswold grabbed his arm, dragging him back.

"Hold here. We have to protect as many as we can."

"But the people that ran—"

"Are scattered throughout the village by now. We will save more by staying together."

"Again on my mark," Fairclough's voice carried over them.

Barrett glared at Captain Griswold's calm expression, tugging his arm, but the captain held firm. "I can help them."

"You will be killed and cause more of these people to die. Stay where you are."

"Fire!"

Another blistering wave of fire churned through the fog with an almost bestial howl.

"Cease fire!"

The unnatural half-light of their fire dropped away, leaving them in the glow from the House's windows again surrounded by a tightening ring of fog. Another scream punctuated the quiet left in the wake of their fire, and Barrett considered punching the captain right in the nose to get him to let go when a twisted silhouette slunk out of the fog.

"There!" he shouted, wrenching at his arm. "I see—"

Several of the hunters unleashed blasts of fire, but the silhouette flickered back into the fog, untouched. No unearthly howl. No lunging attack. It simply withdrew.

"What... Why isn't it attacking?"

"I am not certain," Griswold said, finally relinquishing his grip on Barrett. "That is why we cannot go running into the dark alone. Stay in the circle."

Barrett shivered. This felt far too familiar for his comfort.

The hunters around him shifted nervously, and a few more bursts of fire went up from the opposite side of the circle. Most of the villagers had finally made it into the House, but some were still scrambling to squeeze through the doors, and he could hear people sobbing from inside.

Reaching for his hip, Barrett withdrew his dagger, running his gloved thumb along the jewel set in the pommel, but he couldn't quite quell the fear rising through him with every second that passed with no enemy in sight. What if it had gone and done what the needle-toothed demon had done before, and simply taken someone? What if it was that same demon?

There was another flicker of movement before Barrett felt his attention pulled in a hundred different directions. He had the space of a breath to feel the cold dawning terror at what he was sensing before the growing night around them exploded into pandemonium as beasts of every description lunged out of the fog.

It wasn't one demon. It was many.

Chapter Nine

"WON'T BE LONG now. We should make it before the rain," Finley said confidently as the last miles before the city gates rolled past. A week had come and gone in a flash between Avonmouth and the capital. Kyran wished he could have spent more of it learning about the guildhall and about Finley, but he had spent the majority of the trip dozing in the wagon under the high sun, and awake much of the night on watch.

Ahead of them, grey beneath the heavy clouds, were the city's walls. Clusters of ramshackle houses flanked either side of the road, growing denser the closer they got to the gates. Faces peeked out from doorways and windows, watching the wagon roll by, and Kyran quickly clamped his control down tightly over his power and tugged his sleeves down.

As they neared the gate, a distant bell began to ring, and Kyran felt the first trickle of familiarity from the night he met Barrett.

"That can't be," Finley muttered, glancing up at the sky. "It's too early."

Kyran started to ask her what she meant, when a second bell above them began to ring loudly.

Finley dug her heels into her mare, leaping into a canter, lines blazing beneath her skin. "Come on!"

The driver snapped the reins, and the wagon leapt forward, nearly unseating Kyran. He grabbed Effie, holding her tightly, and clung to the wagon's railing as it jolted over the gate's threshold onto the uneven cobblestones of the city lane.

"What's going on?" he shouted over the din.

"That's the guild's bell!" she shouted back. "Demons!"

A stone dropped into the pit of Kyran's stomach. Demons. During the day again.

The fear that had kept him awake night after night in the Isles and followed him all the way back to Tennebrum gnawed at his insides—had *that* demon survived? Had it come back to try to take him again?

"It is dead," he whispered, nails biting into the rail. He had won. He was alive because it was dead.

There was nothing visibly burning, but the familiar smell of smoke steadily thickened as the cart rattled past rows of shops and pubs lit by the rows of lamps glowing on the sides of the road.

Then, he heard it. As the gate's bell began to grow distant, he finally made out the sounds of distant shouting melded with inhuman shrieks. A shiver rolled down his spine. Stars, it reminded him of the first night he met Barrett. He'd had no idea what he was facing then, and he'd still thrown himself headlong into the fight. It was a grace Barrett had come in time.

Kyran knew better now, though, and, he reminded himself, knew how to properly kill them.

They followed the dreadful sounds until they came to a crossroad where the lamps were dark.

"Hold on!" the driver shouted, yanking the reins back and slamming the brake on the wagon. The horse let out an irritable bray, tossing her head against the bit, the wagon bouncing and juddering behind her. Kyran nearly crushed Effie against him as the wagon threatened to turnover before it crashed back down on both wheels and skid to a stop.

"What are you doing?" Finley demanded, bringing her horse around.

"You said there are demons?" the driver asked, leaping down from the front of the wagon. "I can't—I'm not a hunter."

Finley tutted impatiently. "You're right. Go. Find someplace to hide and make your way to the guild when it is safe. You will be compensated."

"But—"

"Go. Now," Finley barked, sending the man scrambling back the way they had come and out of sight. She sighed, swinging down out of her saddle. "Leave the girl and follow me," she ordered, marching towards the darkened lamppost. "I'll scout first."

"Wait. I canna—" But she didn't slow, disappearing between the buildings.

Cursing to himself, Kyran twisted in place, but he had no idea which way the guild might lay, or where anyone else was. The street was quiet and empty, as if he had been plucked up and dropped into someplace Inbetween.

A gout of fire went up from the direction Finley had gone, curling up the wall of a building. The wagon jerked beneath Kyran, throwing him and Effie into the bottom as their horse lunged forward away from the flames, knickering anxiously.

"Effie, lass. Hold tight." Kyran scrambled for his walking stick as the wagon lurched forward again. He tossed his walking stick out and pulled the lass under one arm, when the horse's nerve finally broke and it bolted, throwing Kyran and Effie over the rail.

Kyran just barely managed to get between Effie and the ground before they landed, tumbling across the cobbles. He lay there a moment, letting the control of his magic slip just a measure, the cold of his blood easing away the aches and pains.

"Ye all right, wean?" he wheezed, checking Effie, but the lass was unharmed, if frightened.

Cursing after the flakey mare, he stretched as far as he could and managed to snag his walking stick, and it was only then when he noticed *it.*

It was almost vaguely humanoid in the harsh shadows cast by the flames, crouched on all fours. It bristled with a feline yowl, row after row of spines standing up along its back and flanks before charging straight for them.

Spitting an Isleish curse, Kyran flung his arm out, letting his magic howl out of him. The street bloomed with blue-white light and the demon squealed as its skin ruptured, dark crystals bursting through its hide. It skidded on the frosted cobbles, spinning, and slammed into a lamppost, the wooden post snapping in half with a deafening crack. But it didn't slow.

Legs kicking, the demon scrabbled onto all fours and bolted down a narrow alley between two buildings, kicking flames up behind it that licked up the stone to the wooden shingled roofs. At this rate, the whole block would be up in flames.

"Come here, lass," he ordered, pulling Effie up onto his back as he got up. He waited until he felt her grip around his neck and waist tighten before he started after the beast.

It was difficult, his walking stick catching in the gaps between the cobblestones and the uneven ground casting his balance in every direction.

Kyran swore and cursed, but no amount of vitriol could make his body move any faster. He just couldn't move his walking stick fast enough to keep up without pitching himself over in the street, and he hated it. Hated how difficult even simple things were now because of his leg.

He turned a corner, only to nearly collide with a second demon running straight at him. He thrust his walking stick forward blindly, frost and fog boiling off of his skin, and the creature let out a deafening howl as it leapt over him. He pivoted, following its arc, and the demon collapsed to the cobbles with a solid, frozen thunk.

There was a quiet whimper at his ear, and he quickly helped Effie down off his back. Frost clung to her lashes and hair and she shook from head to toe, teeth chattering loudly.

"Stars, I'm sorry lass. I canna—"

The lass's eyes flicked behind him, stretching wide as wagon wheels, and Kyran spun to find himself eye to eye with another demon. Time seemed to slow, every detail of the creature's body—from its rippling, greasy fur, to the fleshy tongue lolling between its triangular teeth—coming into sharp relief in the blue white light of Kyran's lines. He fought to move, to throw himself out of the way, but he couldn't make himself move fast enough.

Then, in a flash, white hoarfrost began to scrawl over the demon's tongue, the inside of its mouth, its nose, freezing its hair into solid peaks.

With a strangled cry, the beast twisted in pain, missing Kyran by a fraction of an inch as it collapsed to the ground in a convulsing, squealing heap.

The mage staggered to catch his balance, walking stick sliding on the cobbles, and barely missed a swipe at his ankle from the writhing beast. Planting his stick, he rounded on the creature when a blast of fire connected with the demon, knocking it away. Finley followed it down, flames roaring from her palms as she pinned the beast writhing to the stones, the heat rolling off in choking waves.

Grabbing Effie, Kyran pulled her behind him, shielding her from the worst of the heat, when another bell began to ring. It was tinnier, higher than the others.

"We've got to get to the guildhall," Finley shouted, kicking what was left of the demon beneath her viciously. "The gate bell is ringing! The guild is under attack! We have to go!"

"Wait!" Kyran called, cursing the other mage as he bent to help Effie onto his back again before he hurried after Finley, towards the guild and the only future he had now.

Chapter Ten

BARRETT CAUGHT A glimpse of twisted, animalistic forms before they were swallowed in a bank of crimson and black flames as he and the hunters around him all unleashed their fire at once.

There were so many. He'd faced more than one demon before, not to include the one he, Kyran, and Griswold had fought in the Isles that had been able to divide itself. It had been a pair of demons that had attacked when he was just an apprentice, but he had been assured it usually only occurred when two or three demons happened to come through at the same time. This felt like an entire legion hiding out in the fog beyond their fire.

"Keep it up! Don't let them through!" Fairclough bellowed.

But demons didn't work together. Graces, they could barely keep from eating one another even when faced by hunters. And why here? A village in the middle of nowhere? What in the world would they—

CRASH.

Glass shattered somewhere behind him, and people began to scream.

"They're coming around the back!" someone yelled.

Fairclough swore fluently. "Griswold, take ten down your side! You—"

Barrett didn't wait for her to finish. Dropping his fire, he twisted out of Griswold's reach before the captain could stop him, and raced down the side of the House in the direction of the screams.

The fog closed in around him, a glowing wall of mist that cut him off from the world as solidly as the darkness of the Inbetween.

There was another crash, and Barrett skid to a stop as shadowed outlines loomed out of the mist, resolving into not one or two, but a full half score of demons. They crowded around the side of the House, climbing over one another as they attempted to scale the stone wall. No two looked alike, the smallest no bigger than a dog and the largest the size of Sweetheart with enormous reptilian claws where there should have been hooves. It had punched through a window on the side of the House and was clawing at a hanging shutter, pulling itself inside, where the villagers had taken shelter.

"No you don't!" Barrett shouted, launching a stream of fire into their midst, focusing on the tail of the beast in the window.

The creatures let out a cacophony of shrieks and howls as they tumbled from the wall, scattering into the fog. The largest demon whipped its head out of the window, fixing him with one hollow socket as its head split near in half to reveal rows of small, razor-like teeth as it shrieked its fury.

Barrett returned with a furious snarl of his own, raising his hand to throw another gout of fire when a burst of air collided with him, knocking him sideways. He hit the ground with a hard roll and a demon landed where he'd been a moment before, teeth like shards of rock bared at him. He scrambled to his feet as another blast of air knocked the demon off balance, and he lunged for it, burying his dagger in one of its many empty sockets.

"Thanks Gris—" Barrett looked up only to find it wasn't Captain Griswold, but another hunter standing over him, trembling hand raised as wind stirred his clothes and hair. Graces, he couldn't be more than an apprentice, he looked so young. "Who—"

"Behind you!"

Barrett whipped around as another demon tumbled away beneath a blast of wind and fire, only for it to instantly be replaced by three more. And then another.

Swearing darkly, Barrett ripped his dagger free of the dissolving corpse beneath him and grabbed the younger hunter's arm, yanking him back towards the wall of the House as more demons appeared from the fog. Graces, how were there so many? Even the needle-toothed bastard hadn't managed to make so many parts of itself at once.

He locked gazes with the nearest demon, lips lifting in a sneer as he raised his dagger, daring it and its friends to come any closer, when a wall of fire rolled over the beasts, scattering them again.

"Hold fire!" came Captain Griswold's voice from the fog as a group of hunters appeared from the way Barrett had come. "You both all right?"

"We're good," Barrett answered, glancing back at the other hunter with him, who nodded.

"You two cover this part back to the front, then. The rest of you, keep moving. Pair off when I tell you."

"Aye," Barrett called after the captain as Griswold took off in a flurry of wind after the others. He glanced back at the hunter at his side. He was small compared to Barrett, barely up to his ribs, with shaggy black hair and an oversized tunic that only made him look younger than his soft, round features already leant. "You watch back towards the front, and I'll keep watch this way," he said, turning his dagger over in his hand as the fog slowly closed in around them again. "Name's Barrett, by the way."

"I'm—"

"Elijah?" somebody shouted from the fog.

The hunter with Barrett went rigid, eyes wide in naked terror. "That's Marcus!"

"Elij—AH!" The voice broke in a ragged scream, and the younger hunter bolted into the fog.

"Marcus!"

"No, wait!" Barrett shouted, but the mist had already swallowed the other hunter. Spitting a curse, Barrett raced after him, barely catching sight of him and another pair of figures grappling on the ground as a flash of fire lit the fog up ahead.

"Get away from him!" the younger hunter screamed.

There was a boom of thunder before a blast of wind hit Barrett's chest like a mule kick. He staggered back, wheezing as he struggled to draw breath. Tendrils of fog spun past him just before another gale of wind roared past, and Barrett had to brace to keep from being torn off his feet. Graces above, the hunter had wind magic just like Griswold, and none of the captain's precise control.

Squinting into the wind, Barrett could see the young hunter standing over someone else on the ground, dagger pointed at a demon bristling with spines like a hedgehog, its claws sunk into the earth to brace against his wind. They didn't see the second demon sprinting full tilt out of the fog behind them.

Barrett tried to shout a warning, fire roaring out of his hand at the demon. But the moment he opened his mouth, the words were sucked right out of his throat into the wind, his fire bending back on him and blowing searing heat right into his face. There was another scream, and he swore up and down, straining against the wind until, without warning, the gale vanished.

Dropping his fire, Barrett staggered into a run only to see the demon galloping away, dragging the younger hunter by his arm, leaving the other bleeding on the ground.

"Get back here!" Barrett snarled, pumping his arms as he broke into a dead sprint, racing after the pair, when the spined demon slammed into his side, knocking him to the ground in a flurry of limbs and teeth. They rolled to a stop with the demon on top, its bulk crushing Barrett into the earth beneath it. Teeth snapped in his face, and terror lit through him as its throat began to glow with molten light.

Slinging an arm over his face to protect his eyes, Barrett wrenched his other hand free and plunged the end of his dagger through the demon's throat. With a gurgling scream, the beast bucked in pain, tearing the blade from his hand. It made a few loping strides into the fog, before its limbs fell into ash beneath it and it collapsed to the earth.

Barrett shakily got to his feet and staggered to the demon's remains to collect his dagger from the quickly disappearing ash. Pressing a hand to his side, he took a long, ragged breath, wincing at the sharp ache that lanced through his ribs. "Cursed demons," he muttered, forcing his hand away before taking off in the direction the other demon had gone.

He made it no more than a few steps when another horrid shriek filled the air and a gust of wind rolled over him.

"Hold on!" Barrett called, rushing after the scream.

On the ground ahead of him he spotted the hunter's boots, the rest of him hidden beneath the bulk of the demon. Planting one boot, Barrett kicked the beast as hard as he could in its soft flank where the spines didn't reach, rolling it off the hunter. He had fire in his hands ready to burn it to nothing before he caught the pommel of a dagger buried in its shoulder, and a glimpse of what looked like black, bloody crystals protruding from its feet before the beast began to fall apart.

"I got him?" the hunter asked, his voice unexpectedly soft.

Barrett couldn't help a relieved smile. "You did." But his smile faded at the sight of the hunter's mangled arm. "Graces, can you—"

"Is Marcus all right?" the younger hunter asked, rolling upright and cradling his arm against his chest.

"Last I saw. We've got to get back to the House. You—"

"But Marcus—"

"We're goin' to get him. Come on." He bent, grabbing the hunter's dagger for him while he painstakingly got to his feet. "What's your name?"

"E… Elijah."

"Elijah, I'm Barrett. Your arm all right?"

Elijah clutched his arm more tightly against his chest, blood squeezing out between his fingers. "Ye… Yes."

Barrett grimaced. If he'd been a little faster… He shook his head. There was no time for that. Keeping Elijah on his left, Barrett started back in the direction he was certain the House was, but he had gotten further out into the fog than he thought, and he could barely tell which way was forward.

"Your wind," he said softly to Elijah. "Do you think you can—"

An outline formed in the fog and Barrett's hand lurched up of its own accord, fire conjuring at the ready before the shape coalesced into another hunter.

"Marcus!" Elijah cried, rushing past Barrett and throwing himself around the other man with a sob.

"I'm all right," the other hunter grunted, slipping an arm around Elijah.

Barrett felt his cheeks flush unexpectedly when he realized the two were embracing. He cleared his throat and held out Elijah's dagger. "We need to get back."

Marcus nodded, pressing a kiss to the top of Elijah's head before he took the dagger. "Come on. We've got to protect those people inside."

"All right," Elijah sniffled, and looked up at Barrett with a nervous, guilty smile. "We'll be right behind you."

Taking the lead again, Barrett kept his senses peeled for any other demons, but strangely enough, they didn't cross any by the time they reached the House, and he didn't feel the wild, random swells of power any longer. He itched to follow the direction Griswold and the others had gone, but that would leave the open window unprotected. He glanced up at the broken window, its shutter hanging by a single nail, and let out a frustrated sigh, running a hand over his chin, surprised when it felt slick under his palm. Pulling his hand away, he was even more surprised to find it was blood.

He prodded at his face, wincing when he found a tender cut that ran across his cheekbone and over his nose. He reached into his coat for his kerchief, a note of panic racing through him when he couldn't find it before he belatedly remembered he had left it with Kyran.

"Keep your eyes out for anything creepin' out of that fog," he warned the other two, wincing again at the sight of them propped against the wall together, faces pale and bloodied. They needed a healer, but Barrett couldn't leave and he hadn't the faintest notion of where to send them, or if it would be any safer wherever they went.

Grinding his teeth, he tightened his grip on his dagger, and prayed silently that this wouldn't last much longer.

Chapter Eleven

FIRES LICKED UP the walls of the shops on either side of Kyran and Finley as they hurried towards the clanging guild bell. The air thickened with heat and smoke, blotting out what little light there was from their magic, the crackle and roar of fires surrounding them drowning out all other sound. Stars, but it felt too much like that first night outside of Oareford. Except Barrett wouldn't be coming this time.

Effie squirmed on his back, her cries and weak coughs barely audible over the sound of the fires. He reached back, touching her arm, and swore when he felt how hot her skin was. "Stars, no." Searching the street, he found a spot to stop where the fire hadn't spread yet, and leaned against the warped panels of a shop to keep his balance as he flipped the extra fabric of his kilt up around her, tying it across his chest.

"Just hold on," he said, making certain the cloth covered her head securely before he took off after Finley again. "I willna let any of them hurt you."

Another woman emerged from an alley ahead of him, headed in the same direction. Crimson flames wreathed her hands and arms with no trace of red light beneath her skin. A hunter then.

At last, what could only be the gate to the guildhall came into view at the end of the road. Demons darted to and fro, shadows against the fire lighting up the night air, and Kyran kept his power ready, lines glowing bright.

But as they drew closer, Kyran could make out something in the shifting firelight that wasn't quite a demon. At least, not as he had come to know them. It looked human. Not in the way the toothy demon had been—a parody of the human shape—but as if a man had somehow grown demonic features, its face all too human in the orange light but for its night black eyes as it gazed across the field of chaos straight into Kyran's eyes. Its lips turned in an ugly sneer.

Dropping into a crouch, it craned its head up towards the walls and, in one ungainly leap, latched onto the stone edifice with long, hooked claws.

"Blessed Lumen!" Finley gasped as Kyran finally caught up to her at the end of the road. "Is that—"

"Hunters!" bellowed a man's voice from the gate, and Kyran made out an older man with close cropped white hair and another hunter defending the gatehouse with fire and sword. "The abomination! Don't let it get over the wall! Bring it down!"

"Let's go! Stay behind me and watch my back!" Finley shouted, plunging ahead with the other hunter

Mouth set grimly, Kyran snugged the knot on his chest more securely and followed the other mage. They'd only made it halfway across the street, though, when the pack of demons turned to meet them.

"Here they come!" Finley bellowed, unleashing a scorching burst of fire that split the charging pack of beasts like water across the keel of a ship. But the demons didn't retreat, circling left and right. Kyran pivoted on his walking stick, magic lashing into the wet, drooling snout of a wolf-like demon as it snapped at his ankle. It retreated with a yelp, only to be replaced by two more as the pack surrounded them.

"Blessed beasts, get out of my way!" Finley snarled, her back bumping into his as their circle tightened. "How are there so many?"

"I don't know," the other hunter shouted back. "But the abomination—"

"I know! But I can't—"

Kyran missed whatever she said as another demon braved his magic, darting in low. With a snarl of his own, he smashed the side of its head with his walking stick, forcing his magic down into the beast. Black and silver crystals of ice burst from the sockets of its eyes and from between its teeth, and it turned aside, colliding with another demon before it collapsed, clawing at its face.

He glanced behind him over Finley's head at the monster on the wall. It was nearly to the top. If it climbed over, there was no telling what damage it could do. It wasn't only hunters that lived at the guild.

Letting his control slip, he thrust his hand forward, his power rolling over the demon lunging for him and the two behind it, sending them scattering. He glanced backwards again, judging the distance between himself and the abomination. It was far, but if he didn't do something, it would reach the top. He steeled his will.

"Hunter, I need your dagger!"

"What?" the woman shouted without even casting a glance in Kyran's direction.

"Your dagger!"

"Here." Finley spun, tearing the dagger from the hunter's hip, and thrust it into Kyran's hand, the grip hot against his palm.

A faint shiver ran up Kyran's arm with a memory of the touch of leather, warm fingers, and quiet snow. He quashed it, whirling to face the wall. Raising his arm, he took careful aim, reared back and threw the dagger.

The blade turned one full revolution and sank into the abomination's back nearly up to the hilt. The beast screamed, the sound far too human, as it clung to the wall, thrashing and wailing as the unnatural features of its body began to dissolve.

There was a flash of blistering heat against Kyran's cheek, and he flinched as a demon shrieked a mere foot from him, and was sent skittering away. Finley, arm outstretched towards it, hardly glanced his way before she whirled to meet the next charging beast.

Another demon came at Kyran, and the mage braced against his walking stick, sweeping his hand at the beast. His magic raked across it, its legs buckling with a shrill squeal of pain as its face ploughed into the earth. With a contemptuous flex of his control, he focused his power, driving every trace of warmth from the creature until its cries of pain choked off and its body stiffened, black crystals bursting in clusters through its white frosted skin.

There was a sickening wet thud against the cobbles behind him, and the last remaining demons scattered, tails tucked. Kyran, Finley, and the hunter started after them, when another group of hunters emerged from one of the lanes, blocking the demons' escape.

"Kyran!"

Kyran pivoted to find the white haired man standing over the body of the abomination. Only it wasn't an abomination anymore. All of the demonic features had vanished, leaving only a twisted, broken man that couldn't be much older than him.

He turned away with a whispered prayer, gorge rising at the back of his throat, and he had to swallow to keep from retching. He reached behind him, pulling his tartan down over Effie's head completely, shielding her face. "Dinnae look lass."

"That was a mighty good throw." There was the sound of squelching flesh and Kyran's guts churned. "This your first time facing an abomination?"

"Aye," Kyran said thickly.

The man chuckled darkly behind him. "You'll have to get used to it if you really want to be a hunter. Turn around, mage."

Digging his nails into his walking stick, Kyran forced himself to turn and look at the broken body. What was left of the man's face was contorted in a scream of terror, his fingers twisted at wrong angles, and there was a smell Kyran was familiar with from hunting—the unique stench of offal and still warm blood. His stomach jerked, and he swallowed hard to keep from retching.

"Take a good look, mage," the man said, nudging the body with the tip of his boot. "This is what really happens when you let a demon—Is that a child?"

Keeping his teeth shut tightly around the bile in his throat, Kyran peeled his eyes away from the body, but it lingered with him behind his eyelids, waiting for the next time Kyran was alone in the dark fending off nightmares.

He dropped his hand to one of Effie's hands around his throat, his chest tightening at her frightened whimper as she burrowed her face into his shoulder. "A-Aye. Is there—"

"Graces above, you should have said something. Come on. This way." He led Kyran into the gatehouse, gesturing to a small door inset in one of the walls. "In there."

Leaning against the wall, Kyran eased the lass down off his back, his eyes widening fearfully at her blue lips and fingers, her little body trembling from head to toe with wracking shivers. "Stars, lass. I'm—" He started to reach for her, then saw the lines glowing under his skin, and the cascade of frost it sent across her hair, and he withdrew. He could have killed her, the way he almost had Tavish once. "I'm sorry. I dinnae mean ta…"

She sniffled, shuffling forward to lean against his leg where he could feel her violent trembling.

With every ounce of fortitude, he cinched his magic under his control and bent to brush the frost from her hair. "I'm sorry I cannae keep ye warm."

"Mage…" the other man said impatiently, and Kyran flicked him a cold glance.

"I have ta go, lass," he told her, gently touching her back to guide her towards the door. "Warm yerself, and I'll be back soon as I can. I just need ye ta be safe."

She let out a soft whine, digging her heels in as he tried to urge her forward.

"Lass…"

Another bell began to ring, brassier than the one over their heads and nowhere near as deep as the central bell still tolling over the guildhall.

"That's the northern gate," the man said and pointed over Kyran's shoulder, and he glanced back to see Finley approaching. "You! Take these two and go to the other gate!"

"We're on it," Finley confirmed. She turned away, and Kyran's lips slid back in a sneer of frustration at being left behind again.

The man at the door grabbed Effie's arm and the lass let out a deafening shriek, kicking and scratching as he pulled her to him.

"Effie!" Kyran lurched after her, stumbling over the uneven cobbles.

"She'll be fine," the man said over the lass's cries. "Go with the others before there's no guildhall for you to stay at."

The mage looked from the lass to the man and back, the sound of her cries eating away at his insides. "If you hurt her—"

"She'll be safer here than with you."

Kyran's head snapped back, his anger draining into the pit of his stomach, and his heart seemed to shrink.

"Now go. You're wasting time."

Taking in Effie's tear streaked face, still pale and blue from his magic, he nodded and stumbled after Finley, desperate not to hear the lass's cries as she called his name. Stars above, what he would do to never hear that again.

The other mage had waited just out of earshot with the other hunter, and she started down the road as he joined them. They met no demons as they circled the hall, but as they drew nearer the gate, Kyran heard a deep, rattling boom, as if an avalanche had started.

"Oh, Graces," Finley swore. Another boom followed and a loud, splintering crack. "That sounds like—"

They rounded the side of the gatehouse containing the northern gate to find another pack of smaller demons, these no larger than a *wean* of Effie's age with knobby, lumpy bodies, crowded around the bodies of two guards, or what was left of them. And behind the beasts, its shoulders and lower body grotesquely swollen with ashen flesh, was another abomination.

The demons shrieked in alarm, scattering like locusts with a clatter of too many legs as first Finley, then the other hunter unleashed a blast of fire into their midst. But the demons quickly regrouped, moving as one over the ground like a living wave of teeth and limbs.

Focusing his magic, Kyran banged the end of his walking stick on the street, sending his power down through the damp and the mud still left from the rain. The demons squealed as the muck flashed to ice, trapping more than half of them as their limbs froze to the road.

"Stay on them!" Finley shouted as one of the demons lunged for her face. With a swift kick, she knocked the beast to the ground, setting its flesh to burning before she rounded on the next one caught fast in the icy mud. It snapped and snarled, tearing at its own flesh trying to get to her even as she immolated it.

One by one, Finley waded through them while Kyran held them fast and the other hunter fended off any that tried to approach, but it was slow going, and Kyran could only watch as the abomination, unhindered, reared back and slammed its armored shoulder into the gates. The wood and iron bowed with a crash like thunder and breaking boughs. He could reach it from where he was if he concentrated, but that would mean allowing the demons free of his icy grip. It was taking most of his focus as it was to keep from freezing Finley or the hunter while keeping the ground frozen against the heat of their fire.

The abomination backed several steps, lowering to all fours as it waddled into a better position. It ducked its head like a goat squaring up against a rival, and charged the gate, both feet and hands leaving the ground as it rammed the gate.

With a shriek of tearing metal, the gates buckled, their hinges tearing from the stone archway as they fell inward.

The guild was breached.

"Stop it, now! Don't let it get in!" Finley shouted and staggered forward, but there were too many demons in her path. She would never make it before the abomination made it through the broken gate.

Kyran looked at the mass of demons left, grit his teeth, then raised his hand at the abomination, and focused his will around his power, shaping it as he had done before. "Back ta the pit with ye," he sneered, and drove his magic through the beast, cleaving deeper than its flesh and into its very essence.

It was easy. So much easier than before.

The sensation of falling filled his senses as the dim street gave way to torchlight. He dropped through night air, the claws of his hind feet spearing through a lass's belly, knocking her down on the cobble path. He clamped his mouth down over her screaming face, his teeth tearing into her soft cheeks, swallowing her cries. Then her face became another demon, smaller, faster, grappling for control as he tore its fingers off in his teeth.

The scene changed again to the familiar ashen roads of the demon realm.

"Help us, and there will be no more hunters, and you will be able to feast to your hearts' content."

Refocusing his intent past the horrors of the beast's mind, Kyran drove his magic deeper into it, past the thing's tangle of memories. Its entire being screamed with pain as his magic tore a path through it. But he wanted to do more than just hurt it. He wanted it gone, wanted to carve the infection out to leave behind the man just as the hunter's dagger had done to the other, like he wished he could do for himself.

There was another sound, beyond the screams and the chaotic swirl of memories that weren't his, distant and distorted, as if he were deep underwater. It came again, louder and clearer, and he swore it sounded like his name. But before he could focus on it to listen, the abomination cried out as a new pain lanced through its thoughts like lightning, all the way to Kyran, setting his nerves, his thoughts, every inch of him aflame.

His eyes snapped open with a ragged scream, the pain vanishing in an instant. He had enough time to blink, to see he was back in his own skin before something collided with him, knocking him to the ground.

"Let go!" Finley snarled above him, fire pouring from her palm into a demon latched onto her arm by its teeth. Dropping from her, it let out a horrible shriek and fled out of reach.

Finley spat an ugly curse, chasing the demon with a curtain of fire that made Kyran's eyes water before he let his magic slip free enough to shield him from the heat. But the beast was fast, circling Finley to lunge for her wounded flank only to meet a pointed spear of Kyran's power. Icy magic plunged down the beast's maw, its entire body convulsing midair before it connected bonelessly with Finley's hip and spiraled to the ground where the other hunter plunged her dagger deep into its frozen hide. It died with hardly another sound.

"Are you all right?" Finley asked, holding her hand out for Kyran.

Help us.

"It's fine," Kyran assured her, waving off her hand. "I'm na—" He sniffed, a tickle starting in his nose. "—hurt."

Finley's gaze drifted down his face, her eyes tightening. "Your nose is bleeding."

Kyran swiped the back of his hand over his lip, a smear of dark blood coming away. It brought back unpleasant memories, memories of things scratching about inside of his skull, pulling images and faces out of it. "It isna anything," he said quickly, sniffing again as the tickle grew stronger. "It will stop. Are there any more demons?"

"I don't sense any others. At the moment," the other hunter answered nearby.

Kyran nodded, hauling himself upright onto his walking stick. Blood began to trickle in earnest from his nose, and he pinched his nostrils shut as he turned away from Finley, taking in the destruction.

Around them, the ground was littered with broken stone, charred wood, and flecks of ice. Behind them, the abomination lay sprawled on the ground in the wreckage of the guildhall's gate, rendered no more than a broken man once again that Kyran couldn't bear to see.

Such destruction, and by so many demons. After his first encounter with a single demon, he had never imagined having to face more than one at a time, but this had been a horde. At the guildhall itself on the day of his arrival.

Thunder rumbled in the distance, and all at once, the bells fell silent, leaving only the distant roar and crash of burning buildings taking their dying gasps. Smoke was settling into the streets, the noxious tang of it biting at Kyran's eyes and lungs. He looked back at the guildhall again, at the wreckage. He wanted to believe it was a coincidence, that he would be safe here, but couldn't quite shut out the nagging knowledge that it hadn't been a coincidence last time.

Blood ran down over his fingers, so dark it appeared black in the firelight.

You're nothing more than a demon blooded monster.

Chapter Twelve

BARRETT WAITED IN the growing quiet, every nerve on edge as he and Marcus used their fire to maintain a small, tight ring of clear air around them. But as minutes dragged by, nothing appeared to attack them or the House. He tried to sense if there was anything hiding in the fog, but try as he might, it was impossible to tell hunter from demon by sense alone.

It felt wrong, just standing there and waiting when he could be helping somewhere else he was needed. He almost considered doing it anyway, but another glance at the two hunters with him quickly changed his mind.

Neither looked older than sixteen, maybe even younger. It was difficult to make out more than their rough features beneath the harsh shadows cast by the light from within the House. Marcus was the taller of the two, with a broader build and short hair, while Elijah was much shorter and stouter beneath an ill-fitted tunic, his shaggy hair clinging to his face.

Had he ever looked that young? Sixteen wasn't so long ago for Barrett, but it already felt lifetimes away. So much had happened since then.

Whatever injuries Marcus had obtained, he was weathering them better than Elijah. Elijah's face had become pale and clammy, his sleeve torn and soaked with blood from where the demon had bitten him, and his hand was twisted oddly. Barrett was no chirurgeon, but he knew a broken arm when he saw one.

"Is there a healer here?"

"In the House, but it's not that bad," Elijah said firmly, meeting Barrett's gaze with a wan smile.

It looked bad, and Barrett hated to see the young hunter in so much pain. "I can hold this position while you two head to the front of the House to find the healer."

"The doors will be barred," Marcus said, lifting his hand. "We have to hold until a captain tells us we are clear."

Barrett set his jaw, raising his hand alongside Marcus's as he prepared to repel the fog again, when something caught his eye. A jolt of raw anxiety flashed through to the tips of his fingers before Captain Griswold stepped into view. "Graces above," he sighed in irritated relief, quenching his fire. "What's going on?"

"I am not certain. I am accounting for everyone while there seems to be a break in the attacks." The captain looked past Barrett to the other two, then back to Barrett. "I will find another hunter to cover your place here. I want you to take those two, and go to the front of the House. They've set up an infirmary inside."

"But—"

"Barrett, I understand this is a very different experience for you, but you aren't working alone here. Someone else will be standing here when the next demon comes if you are not. Now I need you to take care of them so I can focus on ensuring we all go home at the end of this."

It was everything Barrett could do to keep his teeth grit around the retort he had for the captain, and simply nod stiffly.

"Good. Now go."

Turning on his heel, Barrett waved for Elijah and Marcus to follow him, his ire softening at the sight of Elijah's arm. Whatever he felt personally about being sent away, Elijah didn't need to be out here with an injury like that.

He led them past several other hunters holding places along the side of the House until he got to the front steps where Fairclough was standing.

She spared them a glance, quickly counting their number before she fixed her attention back on the other hunters spread out before her. "Injured inside," she said brusquely.

Nodding, Barrett stepped out of Marcus and Elijah's way. "I should be headin' back. I'll come check on you all later."

"What are you talking about?" Marcus asked. "You should come with us. You're hurt, too."

Barrett touched his face before he could stop himself, wincing. "It's just a scratch," he dismissed, but now that he was focusing on it, he couldn't ignore how badly the scratch was throbbing, or the way his side and head hurt, or how heavy and tired he was.

"You don't want it to go off. There's been a few hunters that have gotten real sick from their wounds since I've been here," Marcus admonished.

Barrett immediately thought of Kyran's leg. How awful the wound had looked and how sick the mage had gotten before they had reached the guildhall. The chirurgeons had to remove more of the leg to save him.

"All right," Barrett relented, following them past the hunter guarding the door into the House.

Inside was barely contained chaos. The area immediately around the doors had been walled off by benches to create a small corridor. Cots lined the center of the House, stretching all the way to the raised altar. The walls echoed with the sounds of frightened conversation and sniffling children, the distinct smell of blood and bodies filled the air, and everywhere Barrett looked there were more people taking shelter.

Graces above, he had never seen anything like this, even in the guild hospital. Just what—

"Oye, you there. Are ye needing healing?"

The hairs stood up all along Barrett's arms at the gruff Isleish burr, and he couldn't help but stare as an older woman came stomping up. She wore much the same as the other Tennebrumians around her. Her hair was caught up in a kerchief, her plain skirts muddy about the hem, and her sleeves were rolled above the elbows.

She glared at them from behind sun baked wrinkles, then jabbed a finger at Elijah. "Find a cot that's empty. I'll tend ta ye first." She turned a hard eye on Barrett, flicking a critical glance over him. "Ye'll hafta wait."

Barrett didn't know quite what to say. Of everything he might have expected to encounter in Tennebrum's far west, he never would have guessed an Isleish woman. He'd only met a few Isleish before Kyran, and they'd all been in the capital or further north. He wondered if she might have known any Roches or if she belonged to a different clan. She wasn't wearing any tartan. Perhaps he could ask her?

"Kristopher?"

Barrett jolted out of his thoughts at the sound of his name, and turned, recognizing the man approaching him immediately. "Myles? Graces, I thought that was you I saw."

"Graces be praised, indeed, young man." Myles offered Barrett a hand and, with surprising strength, pulled Barrett into an embrace. "I prayed every day for you and Kyran." He clapped Barrett on the back and stepped back, smiling up at him. "Is he well?"

"Yes. Yes, he's recovering back at the guild."

"Blessed is Lumen. Come. I can help you with that nasty cut there."

"I meant to write," Barrett said apologetically, his attention wandering to the wounded as Myles led him down the rows of cots. "I never could seem to find the time with all the traveling."

"That's quite all right. I confess, I am not certain your letter would have found me all the way out here—"

"No!"

Barret jumped at the shrill cry, turning on the spot to see Marcus pushing himself between Elijah and the Isleish woman.

"Hunter," the woman sneered, voice heavy with exhaustion and disdain. "I need ta see your arm."

"You can see it just fine," Marcus argued as Elijah drew further behind him.

Myles let out a tired sigh. "I am sorry, but please excuse me a moment." He stepped past the hunter, approaching the other three with a stilted gait Barrett hadn't noticed before. "Is there something I may assist with?" the Lightbringer asked, looking from Marcus to the woman.

The woman folded her arms, mouth pressing in a tight line. "This lad has a verrah clearly broken arm, but he willna remove his tunic so I can examine his injuries. There are plenty of people that need treating, and if he willna—"

"Georgie," Myles cut her off delicately, his voice mild and patient. "Have we asked him why he does not want to remove his tunic?"

Barrett's hand drifted to his own sleeve and the witch marks beneath. He'd been careful to bathe and change only when he was certain he was alone since getting them, even going so far as to wear gloves near constantly to prevent even a glimpse of the marks from showing.

"It doesna matter one way or the other. I canna treat a broken arm I canna see, and I dinnae have the time ta—"

"We can take him to my quarters in the back," Myles interjected again. "Let his friend come along if it will make him more comfortable. We are not so dire that we cannot take the time to help."

Closing her eyes, Georgie took a long breath, then reached to sweep a loose piece of grey hair from her face. "If ye insist."

"I do." The Lightbringer gestured to Marcus. "If you will please help your friend, I will be right along."

"Thank you, Lightbringer."

"Think nothing of it."

Scowling, Georgie marched away without even looking back to see if anyone was following.

Myles turned to Barrett again, his smile turning sheepish. "I am sorry to be such a boor, Kristopher. I will, of course, see to—"

"Don't worry about me. I can take care of this little thing," Barrett assured him. "I think they need you more right now."

"Well, I don't quite agree with that, but I had better go and see to it that I haven't put Georgie entirely out for the evening. You and I will have to make time now that you are here so we can talk, if you don't mind humoring an old man."

"Of course, I don't mind. I'm looking forward to it," Barrett assured him.

"Oh, bless you. Lanterns guide and keep you, Kristopher."

"And yours as well."

The Lightbringer hurried after the others, leaving Barrett amongst the rows of cots with a fading smile. He looked the rows up and down, and, with a heavy sigh, found one to sit on and wait his turn to be tended. Perhaps it was a good thing after all that Kyran hadn't come.

CHAPTER THIRTEEN

KYRAN KEPT HIS eyes trained out on the streets, searching the faces of the people as they wandered out of the smoke towards the guildhall, dazed and frightened. It gave him something to do, somewhere to look other than the broken body lying behind him.

He'd known what the final fate of a witch was, but to see it, to see how twisted and monstrous it was… How could anyone ever take a demon's bargain knowing that was their fate?

There came a soft, familiar cry, and Kyran whirled to see Effie racing towards him, trailed by the older hunter from the other gate and another wee lad. He knelt in the muck and opened his arms to catch the lass in an embrace, holding her tight as she burrowed into his shoulder.

"I'm all right, lass," he soothed. She was warm again, her cheeks rosy, and her hair dry.

"Well," the older hunter drawled as he neared. "I suppose I should have guessed you had returned. Welcome back, mage."

Kyran cut his eyes up at the man. Mage. Like a smear of something unmentionable he couldn't wash off. "It's Kyran," he said, tugging at his sleeves.

"I remember," the man said loftily. "Though, I suppose it stands to reason you don't." He straightened, touching his chest as he bowed shallowly to Kyran. "Guard Captain Nowell. Are you injured?"

"No."

"Good. Alf here will show you where the ward is. I want you to take the girl there, then return here to receive orders from me. Understood?"

The ward. Kyran had nearly forgotten about that part of their arrival at the guild. Finley had explained on their way to the capital the ward was dedicated to raising any weans of hunters or whose parents were the victims of demons and had no other place to go when the Houses of Light were unable to accept any more.

He agreed with the other mage that it was the best place for Effie. She would still be near enough they could see one another, but she would be with folk that knew how to properly raise a wean, and, hopefully, be with other weans her age. But the lass wasn't likely to see it that way, and, if he was honest with himself, the thought of having to finally say his goodbye with her was surprisingly hard to comprehend.

"Aye."

"Good. You." The guard captain stepped past him, addressing the other hunter that had fought with Kyran. "Are you injured?"

"No, Captain."

"Good. Start looking for any injured and bring them to the hospital. We're opening doors to anyone that needs aid, guild members or no. If you find another hunter out there, stick together."

"Yes, Captain."

"Associate Kyran?"

Kyran peered down at the sound of his name to find the young lad that had come with the guard captain gazing expectantly up at him. He looked to be about Tavish's age with a small, round belly under his tunic and a mess of brown hair sticking in every direction.

"Aye?"

"Are you ready to go?"

Effie clung to his hip, already half asleep, and a pang of something keen and sharp struck him right between the ribs. "Aye," he murmured, smoothing away the wisps that had escaped the braids he'd twisted in the lass's hair to help tame it.

Alf led them under the gate's stone archway, and Kyran slowed, craning his head back to stare in awe above him. Ornate carvings of plants, animals, and people who stared down their noses from above a shield depicting a pair of crossed arrows above a field of stars, held by the forelimbs of a stag and a hound, an eagle perched above.

The inside of the guildhall proved to be as strange and wondrous as the city surrounding it. Everywhere Kyran looked, there were lamp posts lighting paths between buildings that soared over his head like small castles with moats of grass. People moved across the lawns, going about their business within the guild's walls the same as the people without, apparently unmoved by the darkness.

Effie kept close to Kyran's side, staring in every direction at once, trying to take everything in between sleepy yawns.

The ward was an older building shaped like a long, tall rectangle of stone with a well-cared-for pitched wooden roof. As they neared the closest door, Kyran could make out a murmur of voices inside, weans and a woman's voice speaking over them.

Alf stepped up to the door, and tapped his knuckles against the wood. A moment later the door opened, revealing a blonde lass no more than seven or eight years. Behind her, a group of weans gathered in a semi-circle around an older woman seated in a hardback chair with a roaring fire at her back.

The blonde lass beamed when she spotted Effie before she turned to look back in the room. "It's Effie, mum!"

The woman leaned in her seat, peering out the door before she set aside the book she was reading, and got up to come to the door. She was quite short, barely coming to Kyran's middle, with warm, brown skin and a frame built of curves beneath her plain dress. Her silver hair was twisted into several neat braids and pinned at the crown of her head, and she squinted up at him through glass lenses.

"You must be him," she said, a note of satisfaction in her voice that put off Kyran's initial balk at her recognition. "I'd say you looked better than I'd last heard, but you look like you could use some of my cooking. You come by anytime and help us wash dishes, and I'll see you're fed properly for a growing young man."

Kyran flushed, picking at the wood of his walking stick. "Aye."

"It's Sophie," she said gently, squinting down at the lad that had come with them. "Hello, Alf."

"Hello, mum."

"They've got you working when the bell's out ringing."

The lad squared his shoulders, raising his chin. "Of course, mum."

"I hope they aren't working you too hard, now."

"No, mum."

"That's good to hear. You keep up that hard work, but don't forget to get some shut eye, too. And don't let that man work you into the ground."

"Yes, mum."

She finally looked down at Effie, setting a hand on her knee as she leaned forward to be closer to her level. "You went on quite the adventure, little one. You'll have a lot of new things to draw and show everyone." She held out her hand, palm up. "Come on. Everyone's waiting to see you again."

Effie peered up at Kyran, fingers clutching at his kilt and her eyes wide and nervous. "It's all right, lass," he assured her, but her lip began to tremble. "No, no, there now." He lowered himself to his knee, and had no more than set his walking stick aside than Effie flung herself around his neck, squeezing tightly. He wrapped his arms around her, holding her as tightly as he dared as she began to sniffle. "I'm na leaving. I'll still be here, and I'll come ta visit ye. Ye'll get ta be with other weans and learn things."

"That's right, little one," Sophie said, smiling kindly. "You've got so much to learn, and Moira missed you when you ran out on us. Cried for three whole days, poor thing."

"Ye hear that? Ye were missed, wean."

Slowly, Effie's grip began to loosen, and Kyran pulled back, his chest unexpectedly heavy at the sight of her wee teary face. She had been the reason he survived the demon realm as long as he had and helped make his every day a bit brighter. But she deserved something better than he could ever give her, something close to normal. This wasn't goodbye, no matter what it felt like.

"Go on." He nodded to Sophie, who leaned forward and took the lass's hand.

"There's a good girl," the woman murmured, gently towing Effie towards her. The lass came, if reluctantly, looking back over her shoulder at Kyran. "Have a good evening, both of you. May your lanterns stay lit."

"And yours as well," Alf replied before the door shut.

It was intensely quiet with Effie and the matron gone, the sound of the weans inside muffled to a vague nighttime sound. Pushing the hair from his face, Kyran used both hands on his walking stick to get up from the ground, suddenly eager for bed. But there was more work to be done.

Nowell was waiting at the gate, along with a group of other hunters he was giving orders. Kyran lingered back from the group, uncertain what he was supposed to do, when the guard captain finally turned to him.

"You. Come here." Nowell ordered as the other hunters dissipated into the city. "I want you and Finley up on the walls tonight keeping watch. It's going to be a long night, and I expect you to rotate shifts between you so you can get some sleep. I've already sent a runner to the mess hall to have something brought out to you all for supper. If a demon does appear at your post, one of you rings the gate bell while the other engages. I will send others up once the city is clear of injured. Finley will be in charge of giving orders. Any questions?"

"No."

"Good. The stairs are in the gatehouse. Right side. Finley's already up top."

The guard captain turned away to address someone that was approaching him, and, so dismissed, Kyran went to find the stairs, carefully navigating the broken remains of the gate scattered across the lawn. To his relief, the body from earlier had disappeared.

He found the door leading up to the walls and took in the stairs. They were steep and cramped. He'd have to stoop the entire way up to keep from banging his head. Lifting his stick to the first stair and setting his hand, shielded by his kerchief, against the wall, he managed to hop up the first stair without trouble. But by the time he reached the top, his leg and arm were shaking. Not even a season ago, he wouldn't have even thought about stairs or hills, but now, even sitting in a chair was an exercise in control and balance he found uniquely mortifying, and he was grateful there was no one to see him catch his breath.

With a small effort, Kyran straightened and looked about until he saw Finley's outline at the edge of the wall, backlit by orange light.

Fires.

Eerily bright patches of orange glowed beyond the wall of the guildhall. The fires must have spread. He wished he could be out there, helping, but here he was, stuck on a wall, keeping a lookout for demons while the city burned down. "Does this happen with every demon?"

"No. Not like this," Finley said without turning away from the scene. "They've never come in such numbers before."

Until he came. Everywhere he went, there followed demons.

"Port's out that way," she noted, pointing off to their right. "Normally a bit more to look at."

The mage's walking stick clicked against the stone as he joined Finley gazing out over the wall. Buildings obscured most of the view, and a thick haze of smoke hid the rest, but he swore he could make out more of the orange glow that way.

"I can take first watch," Finley offered, tapping a nearby stool with her boot.

"I can take it," Kyran insisted.

He could feel the other mage eyeing him before she shrugged. "Fine. I can't sleep right now either. We'll both keep watch until one of us gets tired."

Kyran drummed his nail against his walking stick. "Because I'm na a hunter."

Finley leaned against the wall next to him. "Because I just faced more demons at once than I have seen in the last ten years at the guildhall, and I don't know if I can sleep after that tonight."

Kyran made a soft noise of acknowledgement, but her words did little to assuage the dread sitting heavy in his middle. That this was his fault. That by being here, by being what he was, he had brought this to the guildhall, to this city. That it would happen again. And again.

The guild wasn't safe. Nowhere was safe. It was only a matter of time before he was taken again, and Barrett wasn't there to save him this time, couldn't be there every time. The only way Kyran could see forward was to become stronger—strong enough no demon could ever take him—and go someplace no one else could be hurt when the demons followed him.

A place like *Cairngorm.*

CHAPTER FOURTEEN

"ARE YOU FINISHED?"

Barrett flicked his eyes over the head of the man smearing salve across his face to find Griswold looking down at him.

"He's just got the scratch, he says," the healer assured the captain, sitting back to observe his work. "Not much else I can do for it."

"You need something, Captain?" Barrett asked, unable to keep the exhaustion out of his voice. Despite the throbbing ache from the cut, he'd nearly nodded off at least a dozen times before the healer had gotten to him.

"Fairclough has asked to speak with us."

Barrett let out a heavy sigh, and nodded. They'd just been attacked by a score or more of demons. They would need everyone. Sleep would just have to wait. "Has there been any more trouble?"

The healer looked up at the captain as well, expression full of naked hopefulness.

"We should speak with Fairclough before we try to guess at the situation here," Griswold said firmly.

Resisting the urge to roll his eyes, Barrett levered up off the cot and followed the captain out. He felt like he'd been beaten black and blue from head to toe, and he was more than a little bow legged after so many long days in the saddle.

Fairclough was still on the steps, her head bent as she consulted with a crown guardsman and another hunter, and her body steaming gently in the drizzle of rain. Griswold stopped a few feet away, waiting until Fairclough finished with the other two and turned to address them. A bit of blood had dried black above her eyebrow, but she had otherwise made it through the fracas unharmed. "Glad to see you two came through all right," she remarked. "I will try to keep this brief. I understand it has already been a long day for you both, but I am going to need you to join in on our patrols while you are here."

Barrett groaned in agreement, and Griswold gave him a cool look.

Fairclough smiled, flashing her teeth. "I know I promised you a briefing, and I will gladly field any questions you have, but if it isn't important, I'd rather wait until the morning when the sun is high. We have a stable prepared across the square and a few hands that can tend to your horses once you bring them there."

The bottom dropped out of Barrett's belly. Sweetheart. Graces above, he had completely forgotten about the mare in all of the chaos that had happened since they arrived. If she was hurt…

"If you don't have any questions, I want you to get some supper in you, then stay together and begin patrolling the east side of the village. We're looking for dead, injured, and demons. The first two come here. The last, I trust you to handle."

"We'll see to it," Griswold said, and gestured for Barrett to follow him out into the square.

"Where do we look?" Barrett asked as the fog closed in around them again. In Oareford, Sweetheart always stayed nearby while he took care of whatever demon had appeared. But there had been so many demons, he almost hoped she had run off somewhere safe.

"I'm not certain. I don't know this area well. Hopefully they are close enough to hear us." Pursing his lips, the captain whistled into the fog, then cocked his head to listen.

Of course. Barrett had completely forgotten Sweetheart had been trained to come to a whistle. That had been why—

"Oh!" Shoving his hand into his pocket, Barrett grabbed the whistle Kyran had given him, eager to finally give it a test. Raising it to his lips, he blew a single, long, sweet note.

There was a nickering cry from nearby, and Sweetheart came trotting out of the fog, followed closely by Griswold's red mare, Nettle.

"Sweetheart!" Barrett flung his arms around the mare's neck, winding his fingers through her mane. "I'm so glad you're all right."

The mare snorted impatiently, bending her neck to nose at his back and pockets, searching for treats.

"I don't have anything." Barrett chuckled, blinking rapidly as his eyes began to water in sheer relief. "Come on. Let's get you out of the rain and that saddle, hm?"

Sweetheart huffed loudly in what he decided was agreement, and he couldn't help a soft laugh.

"We'll have to let Kyran know his whistle works."

Of course it does, Barrett could almost hear the mage telling him with that flat look he gave Barrett whenever he thought the hunter was saying something incredibly daft.

Taking the mare's reins in hand, he led her back to the front of the House and across the square in the direction Fairclough had pointed, still smiling to himself as he remembered the look Kyran had given him that first night they'd met after Barrett confessed he couldn't whistle.

Regardless of everything that had happened since that night, some things still hadn't changed.

CHAPTER FIFTEEN

DESPITE THE TERROR and rush of their arrival to Belldale, the rest of the night passed with an almost excruciating lethargy. Back and forth, Barrett and Griswold paced the muddy streets between empty, silent houses whose windows slowly dimmed as fires began to burn low. The village was quiet, unnervingly so. Every strange sound and dark shape turned into a demon in Barrett's mind before it inevitably resolved into another pair of hunters pacing the same street, or a rat scurrying between hiding places. By the time the mist began to lighten, Barrett felt like a bit of rope stretched to the point of fraying.

A bell broke the pall of silence, and Barrett jerked into motion before Griswold held out a hand to stop him.

"It's the morning call to worship," he said calmly.

Barrett trailed to a stop, opening his mouth to ask Griswold if he was certain before he realized he didn't feel the surge of power that normally accompanied a demon coming through. "Graces. I thought…" He rubbed at his face, taking a moment to collect himself. "Is it really morning?"

"Just barely," Griswold assured him. "We can make our way back to the House, though, and get our next orders from Fairclough."

Barrett nodded numbly, falling in next to Griswold as Myles' voice began to call out over the streets, a soft and distant murmur at first, growing into words of affirmation and hope as they reached the edge of the worshippers gathered in the square. Other hunters emerged from the mists all around the square, faces haggard with exhaustion as they staggered into the light of the House.

There was a gentle touch at his elbow, and Barrett turned to find Griswold gesturing mutely towards the House's steps. He followed the captain, legs leaden as he trudged up the stairs.

"Morning, Captain," Fairclough greeted them just inside the doors. "There's breakfast in the kitchen at the back. When you are done eating, come and find me. There's something we need to discuss."

"Of course," Griswold said, and Barrett nodded in affirmation before they joined the line at the back of the House.

The same gruff woman that had treated Elijah was doling out bowls of soup, bread, and beer as other people rushed about busily behind her in the kitchen proper.

Her glower deepened as Barrett stepped up to receive his portion. "You have a lot of nerve going through the trouble of embarrassing me last night."

"Pardon?"

"That lying wee tart ye brought in that made a scene in front of everyone." She tossed her ladle into the cauldron with a clang, setting her fists to her hips. "I dinnae ken what kind of prank ye lot were trying ta pull, letting that lass call herself a man in front of Lumen and everyone."

Barrett blinked thickly, utterly failing to understand what in the world she was talking about. "Elijah?"

"Aye, that's what she was callin' herself."

"Elijah's a—?"

"What he says he is," Griswold cut in, a breeze ruffling the kerchief over Georgie's hair. "And I will not hear any more of this."

Barrett had never witnessed the captain angry, but there was no mistaking the cold, sharp edge to his words as he stared the woman down.

The hard dourness faded from Georgie's face as the shifting breeze began to stir more strongly, an edge of fear creeping into her expression. "Light protect us," she whispered, snatching her ladle up and slopping soup into a bowl, shoving it into Barrett's hands.

The wind ceased in an instant, and Georgie muttered another quick prayer as she shoved a second bowl into Griswold's hands and jabbed her finger at the trays of bread and beer.

Barrett shuffled forward, grabbing the rest of his meal and moving out of the way as Griswold followed, mouth set in a hard line.

"I would take it as a kindness if you forgot what that woman said," the captain said once they were out of earshot of the serving table. "And please do not mention it to him."

"Of course," Barrett said without hesitation, and Griswold's shoulders eased a fraction.

"Thank you."

Barrett marveled at the captain's genuine concern over the younger hunter. He'd never seen Griswold worked up enough over anything to break his composure, not even in the Isles.

They found a bench that was unoccupied and sat, tucking into their meal. It was bland compared to the food the Drunken Wind had served, but Barrett wolfed it down all the same, slumping against the wall once he was finished. Graces, he was tired.

"I want you to come with me when I speak to Fairclough," Griswold said as he got to his feet, gathering their dishes.

Barrett sighed, but pulled himself up from the bench as well, grumbling at the ache that consumed every inch of him. They carried their dishes back to the kitchen, leaving them with a pile of others on an empty table. Georgie never even looked their way.

Fairclough was waiting near the front of the House, leaning against the wall. She lifted a hand as they got close, gesturing for them to follow her out.

Myles was leading his flock in another prayer as they slipped out of the House and down one side of the stairs. Barrett had hoped to find a little time that morning to speak with the Lightbringer, but he doubted he could keep his eyes open much longer.

"Later," he promised himself. There would be time later.

Fairclough led them down the road a ways until they were quite alone, away from the House and the idle mill of the hunters, Myles' prayers distant enough to easily speak over. "I'll be brief," Fairclough said, facing them, her eyes darting up and down the road. "Griswold has vouched for you as a senior, Barrett, but to make certain we are clear as the Avon, what we discuss does not leave this spot in the road unless Griswold or I instructs otherwise. Clear?"

Barrett looked between the two captains, utterly bewildered. What in all the Graces... "Ay—Yes. Clear."

"Right then." She rolled her shoulders, checking the road again, and Barrett had the distinct, creeping impression he didn't want to hear what she was about to tell them. "Griswold?"

The wind stirred around them, and Barrett felt a pressure against his ears, the sound of the Lightbringer's prayer vanishing.

Fairclough let out a tight sigh. "Thank you. In short, demons have been attacking in large, apparently organized groups for months. As you know, it's not uncommon to see demons here, given the tower's proximity, but recently, they destroyed the guild's post here and have been attacking in larger numbers more frequently."

"Tower?" Barrett asked.

Fairclough's brows went up. "The wizard's tower. Certainly you've heard of it."

Barrett's hand drifted to his chest, touching the amulet hidden beneath his tunic. "The wizard?" The one that had created the artifacts that all hunters used to house the demons that gave them power and consumed the demons they hunted.

"The very same."

"Do the demons…know?"

"We have yet to have a conversation with one that could tell us, but we suspect they must sense something about the place. What's more disturbing is they have started showing signs of using tactics. Retreating after short, fast, concentrated attacks, like you saw last night."

"The guild has recorded instances of small numbers of demons actively working together," Griswold noted. "But it never lasts long before they turn on one another, and it is usually limited to the older demons that show human-like intelligence.

"But they attacked before sundown," Barrett pointed out. "I've only seen one demon that could do that, and it wasn't able to stay very long."

"It wasn't the demons, but the abominations that attacked first last night to take advantage of the protection from the sun they are afforded and surprise us. That is a new tactic we will have to account for," Fairclough said, voice tight.

"Were you able to confirm if the abominations came from the Inbetween like the rest of the demons?" Griswold asked, a line appearing between his brows.

"You know as well as I there is no way to determine that, but we were able to determine a linking factor between all of the remains." She looked to Barrett. "How familiar are you with the Cult of the Guiding Light?"

Barrett straightened. "Some. Myles told me about them."

Fairclough arched a brow at him. "The Lightbringer?" At his nod, she shook her head. "To make it brief, they are the ones that started the riots in the capital under the last king. The unrest they caused attracted a swarm of demons into the capital at the same time as the protests. You can imagine what that would have been like."

"Graces," Barrett whispered.

"You've found something," Griswold said, brows lowering.

"Something like that. I had the Lightbringer examine what was left of the abominations with me. He was able to confirm by looking at the remains from the abominations we killed last night that the scars on both of their hands were likely related to the cult."

Griswold frowned, his usual calm composure turning contemplative. "And you have…examined everyone in the House for similar signs?"

"Yes, and we have asked the Lightbringer to keep his own vigilance among the villagers in case there are those we have missed among the injured."

"Good. I will bring this to Selah's attention and urge her to ask the Crown for more support. With this they should be more amenable to offering assistance," Griswold said, and the pressure around them began to lighten. "It will take a few days before we can be ready to leave," he said, the wind dissipating around them and the sound of prayers fading back into the air. "We'll take the wagons with us to send more supplies."

"Better send back salt. That's all this earth will be good for if this carries on much longer," Fairclough sighed.

"Are we dismissed?" Griswold asked, and Fairclough waved a hand.

"Ask someone to show you where to sleep and turn in for the day. Be back at the steps by the evening worship."

"Good day, then, Captain. Barrett." Griswold gestured for him to follow, and Barrett fell in at the captain's shoulder as they walked back towards the House.

"Griswold," Barrett murmured, keeping his voice low. "*What* is going on—"

The air shifted in an instant, and Barrett slapped his hands over his ears with a pained cry. "Fuck—"

"Do not mention anything you have heard," Griswold's voice said almost inside his head. "We will discuss it when we have returned—"

"No!" Barrett snapped, cutting the captain off. "If we have to work together, I want to know what's goin' on. Why hasn't the guild evacuated these people or gotten more help?"

"We did," Griswold said, glancing up and down the street before he pulled Barrett into the space between two houses. "The people you've seen left in this town volunteered to stay to help support the guild members here to defend them. Everyone else was relocated when the attacks increased in frequency."

"But…why? Why are there so many demons attacking here? And… and abominations? I've never seen so many."

"We are investigating the cause."

"And?"

Griswold glanced past Barrett at the street then back, the purpled hollows of his eyes beneath the layer of ash and sweat betraying his exhaustion. "And we are investigating the cause."

Barrett glowered at the captain, but relented with his own exhausted sigh. "Fine." The pressure vanished again, and Barrett nearly stumbled into the mud. "Bastard," he sneered.

"We should see to the horses before we retire," Griswold said, following the outside edge of the main square as the House came into view again. It was easier to see the marks of night after night of battle in the daylight. Gouges in the wood and stone from claws, boards blackened by char, windows broken and boarded. And still the people of Belldale bent their heads on the stairs of that place in prayer and hope against the beasts preying on them. It was like something out of a nightmare.

A tired boy raised a hand in their direction as Barrett and Griswold stepped into the stable. The spicy scent of hay and the sounds of restless horses filled the air, and Barrett couldn't help a smile. He always felt like a guest in stables, someone that knew his way vaguely around, but was otherwise a stranger to the inner workings of the place. He knew just enough to make his mare ready and keep his seat in the saddle, and he had thought that was enough, until he'd listened to Kyran talking to his father and youngest brother about their stable. It was like listening to a foreign language, even when they didn't slip into Isleish.

He found Sweetheart in a small stall near the back chewing placidly on a mouthful of hay. One ear swiveled forward as he reached over her door, and she plodded up to him, nudging his palm.

"Morning," he mumbled, rubbing her soft nose. "Still no treats yet, but I'm sure I'll find something for you."

She snorted in reply, as if to say she would believe him when he produced his promised berries, and he chuckled.

There was a loud sigh in the stall next to him, and he leaned back to see Griswold gently patting Nettle's neck.

"They don't seem to be shivering or favoring any legs," the captain noted.

"And Sweetheart seems content with what she's got to eat," Barrett agreed, snickering when the mare blew out another dramatic sigh. "Do you know where we need to go?"

"I'll ask." The captain gave Nettle a last pat on the neck, then walked back down the row of stalls to where another hunter had come in behind them.

Barrett ran his hand along Sweetheart's neck, scratching at one of the mare's favorite places, grinning as she leaned into it. "Bet it feels good to be out of all that weather," he told her.

"Barrett," Griswold called, and he gave her a last pat.

"Enjoy your breakfast," he told her and joined the captain as he and the other hunter stepped outside.

"We're being quartered in the village," Griswold explained, beckoning Barrett to follow. "He's going to show us where there are a few places left with beds."

Barrett didn't quite understand what the captain meant, but the promise of a real bed with a roof over it was all he needed to hear.

That was, until they stopped outside of what was very clearly someone's home.

"In here?" he asked, even as Griswold was pushing the door to the house open.

"Yes, the villagers that aren't in the fields are staying within the House so we can have places to sleep."

"But shouldn't it be the other way around?" Barrett asked as he ducked under the lintel into the tiny common area of someone else's house, with chairs around a dining table, and a hearth burning low. The rafters were all hung with drying things—herbs, flowers, and vegetables alike, and there was a spinning wheel on the other side of the room, with half a spool of thread pulled and a basket of raw wool still waiting to be finished by the foot of the stool.

"It makes the most sense to keep the villagers together where they are safest. They are, of course, allowed to come and get anything they need from their homes."

Allowed. Barrett didn't like that word much. "How much longer will they have to stay in the House?"

"Until the attacks stop, I imagine."

"And how long—"

"I don't know, Barrett." Griswold stopped next to one of the beds crammed into the backroom. There were just two. "For their as well as our own sake, I hope it is soon."

Barrett let out a tight, irritated sigh, and dropped onto the side of the bed. "Me too," he grumbled, peeling out of his coat and boots. The bed was far too short, but he made do with hanging his feet over the bottom edge, and despite his protest, he barely had his eyes shut before he was fast asleep.

Chapter Sixteen

THE NIGHT ON the guild walls passed with a deceptively quiet calm. Smoke hung thick in the air, indiscernible from the heavy fog that rolled up from the ocean and blanketed the city in smothering, somber grey. But it wasn't to last. As the sun rose, the city woke screaming from its nightmare.

"Guard Captain Nowell requests you both at the gate," Alf said, pitching his voice over the ruckus rising from the streets below the walls.

"What's going on?" Kyran asked, trying to peer over the wall through the foggy murk.

"A mess," Finley groaned, stretching stiffly. "Hopefully one we don't need to be involved in."

The guard captain was waiting at the bottom of the stairs, barking orders to other lads like Alf who scurried off across the guild lawns to deliver their messages. Beyond him, a makeshift barrier had been erected using wagons filled with debris from the broken gate. The smoke and fog swallowed the street beyond, but the noise of overlapping voices and shouting from beyond them was even louder down on ground level.

"You two!" Nowell said above the noise, pointing to Kyran and Finley. "I am relieving you from watch. I want you to—" He was interrupted by the abrupt bellowing of a deep, masculine voice, followed by a general building uproar from the fog.

"What now? You two, with me," Nowell growled, striding through the gate's heavy arch.

Kyran and Finley followed, stopping just outside next to Nowell. Across the road, standing at the narrow corner of two streets in front of the charred remains of a pub, was a group of six or seven people, mostly men, in the midst of a shouting match with a man wielding a club like the watchman in Oareford.

"Should we—?" Finley asked, gesturing to the lot.

"No," Nowell interrupted. "You don't want to antagonize them anymore than they already—"

"Demon dogs!" one of the men howled as he noticed Nowell, Kyran, and Finley. "They're in league with the guild!"

Kyran's belly twisted, and he tugged his sleeves down as far as they would go, checking his hands, but his lines weren't showing.

"Don't pay them any mind," Finley said. "They hate everyone involved with the guild."

"Why?" Kyran couldn't fathom resenting the only thing that stood between this world and the demon's.

"Why does the sun rise every morning?"

The other members of the group had noticed them by now and were chanting and shouting vulgarities at them.

"Witches!"

"You're the ones selling us to them!"

"Whores of the Pit!"

"...dead because of you!"

Kyran swallowed, the twisting feeling in his middle growing until he could feel it at the back of his throat. Stars, it was like being back in the Isles again.

"What's this then?" Nowell murmured, his hand drifting down to the pommel of his sword. "See his hands?"

"Bandages," Finley whispered from Kyran's other side.

He squinted through the murky haze, and could just barely make out the filthy cloth wrapped around both of the man's hands.

"I'd wager what's underneath," Finley added.

Nowell pinched the bridge of his nose. "And I'd wager Hammond is going to be in a twist when I tell him."

One of the rabble bent and picked up a rock, hurling it at the watchman trying to talk them down. It bounced off the man's shoulder, the impact loud even from across the street. The watchman staggered, and another member of the group lunged for him, taking him to the ground as other members of the group started picking up rocks.

"Ah, curse the Graces. With me," Nowell said, sprinting across the street as the corner erupted into chaos.

Kyran followed, ducking as a rock came hurtling his direction.

"They're coming!" a woman shrieked before pelting out of the fray, down the road.

"Watch our backs, Kyran," Nowell shouted, grabbing the first body he could get hold of—one of two men grappling with the watchman—and hauled, flinging the man into the street.

Kyran hovered nearby, uncertain how to help, when one of the other men turned and swung at him. The mage barely got his arm up in time to deflect the blow before the man careened into him, knocking them both to the street. Panic gripped Kyran's chest, his blood flaring bright as the man straddled him, fist raised, before he was yanked sideways.

"Hold still," Finley snarled, twisting the man's arm up between his shoulder blades until he cried out in pain.

Gulping for air, Kyran fought his magic back down, the power bucking his control as he tried not to feel the places on his skin where the man had touched or the way it made him think of Connal and dried hay.

"You, watchman," Nowell barked, setting his knee into the back of the man he'd thrown into the dirt. "Do you have shackles?"

The watchman slowly pulled himself up, face spattered with blood from a broken nose and busted lip. He leaned forward, letting the blood dribble onto the stones as he fished in his pouch and produced a pair of shackles.

"Take hers," the captain ordered.

"I've got him," Finley growled and looked over her shoulder. Other than the man she had and another Nowell was restraining, the rest of the group had scattered.

Kyran eased upright, anxiety easing at the solid click of the shackles fastening around the man's wrists.

"I'll handle the rest of this mess," Nowell said, glaring at the watchman when he tried to step in and help with the man he was restraining. "You take that one, Finley. Kyran, back to the guild. Get some sleep. I'll send a runner by if you're needed for watch tonight."

"With all due respect," the watchman said thickly, earning a withering look from Nowell. "There's no need for the guild—"

"The bloody Pit there isn't. This isn't a request," Nowell snapped. "You can send your complaints care of the guildmaster. Now let's go."

Scowling, the watchman bent to take the man on the ground by one arm, while Finley took the other, and they hoisted him upright. She left the man in the watchman's care before joining Kyran's side.

"Well, then," Finley sighed, brushing off her coat. "Are you all right?"

Kyran nodded stiffly, pulling his hand from his walking stick where his nails had carved a line into the wood.

"I'll show you to the dormitories, then, before I go and see the scholars."

She led him to a long rectangular building at the far side of the grounds. It was tall, its flat stone edifice marked by rows of windows. Inside, the narrow hall was lit by lanterns mounted to the walls at intervals between the rows of doors on either side.

"This one is yours," Finley said, pulling the key from the lock and swinging the door open. The room was small, about the size of the inn room Kyran and Barrett had shared in Avonmouth. The bed was situated to the left of the window, a table and chair right of it along with a washstand. A small chest at the foot of the bed served as the only storage.

Kyran instantly disliked it.

"At least you're not in one of the bunked rooms," Finley remarked, peering into the sparse room. "When I first joined, I had three roommates."

Kyran shuddered. Sharing a room with three brothers was one thing. Sharing it with three strangers was quite another. "I dinnae envy that."

"It's what they usually do with initiates." She stepped back, looking up and down the halls. "I'll have your things brought round when they find the wagon."

"Aye," Kyran murmured, his gaze straying to the dim window, its shutters left open.

"Get some sleep," she said, smiling perfunctorily when he looked back at her, and handed him the key, waiting for him to use his kerchief to take it. "May your lanterns stay lit."

"And yours as well."

The door clicked shut behind her, and Kyran was, for the first night since waking to find himself free of the Erchlais's dungeon, alone. It wasn't so long ago that he would welcome the quiet—the chance to gather himself and relax. But the empty room felt anything but relaxing.

Dropping the key into his purse, he considered the place he was to live for the foreseeable future. He should be happy. He'd finally gotten what he wanted. And yet, before he had even set foot upon guild soil, he had been hounded by demons and now the people of the city. Was that to be it? For the rest of his life?

Demon dogs!

Demon-blooded bastard!

Mageling…

Chapter Seventeen

Something was in his room.

Kyran bolted upright in his bed, his runelines quickening beneath his skin, setting the room aglow with blue-white light. Nothing moved. Nothing but the flickering wick of the lantern and the steady patter of rain at the window.

Slowly, he leaned for his walking stick, his eyes raking over the dim corners of his room, when there was a shush of fabric from the foot of the bed and a tiny arm stretched up over the frame.

"By all the stars above," he muttered, throwing the quilt back and straining to peer over the end of the bed where he spied a wet head of black hair. "Effie?"

The lass's head snapped up, and she smiled, her bare feet pattering on the stone floor as she came around the side of the bed. She was drenched from head to toe, her entire body quaking with shivers.

"Stars above, you're blue as the ice. Get up here." He held the corner of the quilt up, and she gleefully clambered up and burrowed under the bed cover until just the top of her head and eyes showed.

He shook his head, patting at her hair with the quilt. He doubted she had gotten here any way other than sneaking out, somehow. "You spent too much time with Tavish," he scolded her gently. "How did you even get in?"

The lass only made a small noise in answer, and he puffed out a sigh.

"Someone is going ta come looking for you. Soon as you're warmed up, we're going back ta the ward."

She didn't respond this time, and when he peeked at her face, he could see her eyes closed. Asleep already.

Drawing himself up to lean against the headboard, Kyran pressed his power down until his runelines faded, leaving him with only the light of the lantern and what scant grey light the window allowed.

"Stars," he sighed, fingers drumming against his thigh. Sleep had been slow to come, and reluctant to stay, peppered with fragments of nightmares and memories that weren't his, of places and faces he had never seen before—except within that abomination.

Kyran paled, the vivid image of that man's broken body filling the space behind his eyes.

"No…" he whispered, pressing his fingers into his eyes. "Stop."

There was a knock. "Kyran?" Finley called through the door. "Are you all right?"

"Aye," Kyran called back, drawing his hand from his face. He blinked several times, squinting. The room was brighter than it had been a moment ago, though still grey. Grabbing his walking stick, he made his way to the door, using his kerchief to turn the latch.

Finley stood just outside, snugged in a coat with a scarf and hat pulled down over her ears. She smiled apologetically. "Sorry to bother you, but I thought you might want some dinner before you go to see the scholars."

Kyran glanced back at the window, uncertain when so many hours had passed. "What time is it?"

"Nearly three." Her smile faded. "Are you certain you're— Oh my. It seems you already have a visitor."

"Aye." Kyan moved to one side so Finley could see the lass sitting up on the bed, quilt pulled up to her eyebrows. "She showed up drenched as a wet rat. I dinnae ken how she found the room, but she's mostly dry and warm now."

"We should get her back to the ward. I'll come with you. There's something I want to show you while we have the time."

Effie peeked over the top of the covers at them, then pulled the quilt up over her head, burrowing underneath and out of sight.

"Oye, lassie. I can still see you," Kyran snickered, returning to the bedside and poking at the lump beneath the covers. "You have ta go back, you wee scamp, and apologize for frightening Sophie. You could have frozen out there."

The lass let out a sound of protest and swatted at his hand, burrowing more deeply beneath the quilt.

"Oh no, lass. It's time." He grabbed the quilt and with a sharp yank, pulled the whole thing down to the foot of the bed.

Effie squealed, scrambling for the quilt, and Kyran simply dropped it to the floor. She glared up at him, lower lip sticking tremulously out, and he nearly laughed. "You learned that from Tavish," he accused, holding out his hand, which she glared at even more fiercely. "Come on. You want dinner, dinnae you?"

Her expression softened at that, her eyes sliding over to Finley watching from the doorway.

"The lass isna going ta kidnap you. We're going together." He shook his hand.

She resisted for a long moment, pretending not to see his hand until he shook it again. Shoulders sagging, she finally took his fingers and allowed him to pull her from the bed.

"This way then," Finley said, leading the way out into the hall.

The grounds were sodden with rain, still falling in a cold, steady drizzle. Puddles pooled on the grass, oozing over the stone walkways. Effie was delighted, skipping along at Kyran's side and jumping with both feet into each and every puddle, splashing water everywhere, her sullen mood forgotten.

It wasn't until they were nearly halfway across the lawn that Kyran realized they had bypassed the ward entirely. "Where are we going?"

"Somewhere no one else will think to show you. But I want you to see it, especially after what you saw and heard since you've arrived. I don't want you joining this guild without some idea of what you are stepping foot in, curse the laws to the Pit." She looked back at him, scarlet lines tracing beneath her skin as the rain began to sizzle and hiss where it touched her. "It's what I wish someone did for me."

Her words sent a trickle of unease through Kyran. No matter where he turned since coming to Tennebrum, he found secrets. Everything he had ever known turned on its head again and again until he was dizzy with it.

"This is it," Finley announced at last, stopping at a fork in the path that led behind the college to a piece of lawn tucked discreetly between the furthest outbuildings and the northern wall, lined with neat rows of headstones.

"Why have you brought me here?" Kyran demanded, unable to look away from the headstones as he thought of the man lying twisted and broken at the gates after Kyran had buried a dagger in his back.

"I wanted you to see them. I do not know the customs in the Isles, but in Tennebrum, mages are not allowed to be buried in the blessed ground at their Houses of Light. They are instead brought here."

The shock of surprise at her words quickly turned to bitter pain. Of course, they would not be afforded rest in Lumen's embrace even after death. Cursed in death the same as in life.

Kyran eased forward, his stick sinking in the soft, wet earth, until he could see the nearest name carved into the small, grey stone. Except he could not read it.

"Iona Swyft," Finley murmured from behind him. "She died aged twenty-four years." He moved to the next, and she read it too. "Thurstan Dunn. Nineteen years." Kyran's age.

"They're so young," he murmured, reaching for Effie's hand as the lass eased up to his side.

"Mages do not often live long lives. Our nature draws demons, and most of us eventually draw one we cannot overcome."

As nearly happened to Kyran, and would have without Barrett's interference, and would continue to happen for as long as he fought to live.

He kept looking at them, kept walking the rows with Effie trailing at his side until he stopped in front of one he recognized when Finley read it.

"Raleigh Fields. Seventeen."

Kyran knelt in the wet grass, his fingers closing on the carved sun he kept in his purse as he whispered a prayer. This had to be him—Barrett's partner, in perhaps more than one sense of the word. The lad had been taken by the very same demon that had taken Kyran. Yet, somehow, Kyran had managed to survive while Raleigh lay beneath him without any token of affection, or even of Lumen. They all did, and he was heartsick for them. For all their neat rows and carved headstones, the mages' graves lay barren, surrounded and tended by strangers. And he would lie here with them when he died if his feet still touched Tennebrumian soil.

"Does anyone visit them?" he asked, his thumb worrying the dull points of the sun's rays.

"A few." Finley stopped in front of another grave, gazing down at the headstone. "I do. For my sister."

"I'm sorry for your loss. I dinnae ken—"

"Don't be," Finley cut him off. "My mam prayed harder than she ever has for anything in her life that she wouldn't get pregnant after what happened. And then she prayed even harder she would lose the baby. And then again that at least the child would be normal." She let out a bitter sounding chuckle. "My sister died from fever when her talent woke, though not before she set the house on fire. Wouldn't you know the only prayer Lumen answered, he did it with the back of his hand."

Grief and horror rose in equal measure through Kyran. Had he been born to any other family in the Isles, it very well could have been his story. "I'm sorry."

"So was I," Finley said, her expression filled with old, worn in sorrow that hollowed her eyes and picked the grey out of her hair. "What do you know about the guild, Kyran?"

He looked askance at her. "It's a guild that uses mages and hunters ta kill demons."

A look of annoyance flickered over her face before she recovered with a tight smile. "True, in a sense, in the same way those men at the gates were right. Do you know how hunters gain the same powers as the ones mages are born with?"

A hole opened in the pit of Kyran's stomach, his nails digging into his walking stick as he tried and failed not to think of what he'd seen beneath Erchleis, the way Barrett's eyes had turned to scarlet and coal.

"Only a demon can kill a demon."

Demon-blooded.

Half-blooded.

Kyran clutched his walking stick, the world swaying around him as he finally faced the truths he had closed his eyes to. Barrett and every other hunter was a witch, carrying a demon within them. And Kyran was a half-blooded monster.

"Why?" he gasped, clutching at straws as the lies he told himself crumbled around him.

"Demons aren't flesh and blood like humans or animals. They are, in the purest sense, magic. Destroying their bodies, the things we touch and see, merely disperses them for a time, like splashing a puddle out of its hole. The guild has recorded many occasions where a demon has returned after its body was destroyed by sword or fire.

"They can only be destroyed by magic, in essence, by themselves. They do it amongst themselves by hunting and eating their own kind—not because they need nourishment like we do to survive, but it is how they gain power. They are a being of raw force devouring more raw magic."

As the beast had done to him while imprisoned by it. Fed nothing but the flesh and blood of demons, he had felt his magic swell until he could barely control it. It had lessened after the demon took his leg, but his magic remained stronger than it had been before.

And now he understood why.

"It is a dangerous game hunters play," Finley continued, "allowing a demon to feed for as long and deeply as they do, passing them down through generations. They are creating their own folly, both in the sense that the stronger it is, the more it attracts its kind, and the very fact that one day, it will be strong enough to decide it does not need its host any longer. And then we face abominations."

Kyran repressed a shudder, vividly remembering the twisted, part human, part demon forms sieging the walls. The way ashen flesh had sprouted from human. He'd seen something very similar in the Isles, when Barrett had removed his gloves—spots of dark flesh against the pale of his arm. And the way his eyes had turned in the Inbetween. What if it happened again? What if he didn't turn back?

There was pity in Finley's eyes as he looked up at her again. "I know it comes too little too late, but I am sorry you had to learn the truth this way."

She moved as if to come to his side, and Kyran flinched away. He wanted to be somewhere, anywhere else. Not in the Isles where he would have to look his family in the face, knowing what he was, knowing his da wasn't...

"Kyran? Are you..."

"Aye." He staggered upright, twitching when he felt a faint tug at his kilt, only to find Effie looking up at him again, eyes wide with concern. "I...need ta think."

"All right. Do you...?"

"I'll take the lass."

Finley said something in parting, but his head was still swirling with the terrible realization.

Connal was right.

Chapter Eighteen

Barrett groaned as he woke, blinking in the afternoon sun streaming through the window near his head. He ached from head to toe, his face the worst. Dragging his arm up, he gingerly poked the cut, wincing at the tenderness. He hoped it hadn't gone off.

Resting his arm over his eyes, he started to drift off again, when his stomach let out a plaintive growl. He nearly laughed, immediately thinking of Kyran and his ever growling stomach. Graces, he hoped the mage was eating.

He tried again to let himself fall back asleep, only for his stomach to let out another deafening roar. Grumbling, Barrett swung his legs down and bent to rifle through his pack for a comb to tame his hair back into an oily tail. What he wouldn't give for a hot bath after days of traveling and a foggy night of fighting.

Leaving his things, he left the bedroom and was surprised to find Elijah curled up in a rocker and wrapped in a pile of blankets with his bandaged arm laid atop it. Marcus was sitting at a nearby table with a book open in front of him.

"Mornin'," Barrett greeted quietly once Marcus looked up at him.

"Afternoon," Marcus corrected with a tired smile. "You about to go on duty?"

Barrett shook his head. "Not yet. Couldn't sleep." He gestured to Elijah. "How's he?"

"All right, I suppose. They gave him something to help him sleep. Griswold came to check on him a while ago."

Barrett blinked. "The captain?"

"Only Griswold I'm aware of," Marcus said, grinning.

"Weren't we all supposed to get some sleep?"

Marcus shrugged. "Must be something important. What about you?"

Barrett's stomach let out a low, rumbling growl, and he felt his face flush. "Hungry."

"They were handing out meals at the House when I passed it," Marcus suggested, laughing.

"I'll head that way first, then."

The rain had passed during the night, thankfully, but the sky was still a heavy grey and a low mist hung just along the ground in the village, giving the clusters of small houses an eerie look. The streets were quiet and vacant as Barrett wound his way to the House, the hunters all resting while there was sun left. Above him loomed the tower. It was shrouded by the mist, but even then, he could still make out its outline. It stood straight as a pin with no windows or doors, no wider than the House of Light. He had heard of it, the place where all the hunter's amulets and daggers had been created, but had never come to see it himself.

"Ah, good morning, Kristopher," a familiar voice called from the House's door.

Barrett met Myles' playful smile with one of his own as he glanced up at the sky to assure himself it was indeed afternoon. "Morning?" he teased.

"Well, you don't look like you've been awake more than a few minutes at most," the Lightbringer said, shuffling aside to let Barrett in.

Barrett touched his knotted hair, and winced self-consciously. "I heard there was food this way."

"Right this way. Those supplies you brought were a tremendous help."

"I wish we could have brought more." He followed Myles to the far end of the interior where tables had been dragged together. There were a couple of hunters waiting to be served bowls of porridge. "Did you sleep all right?" he asked while Myles ushered him over to a bench. "All things considered, I mean."

"I don't do much sleeping at my age," Myles said lightly, taking a steaming bowl from the table and carrying it to Barrett.

"Thank you." The hunter stirred the bowl, blowing gently across the surface before taking a bite. It was a bit bland, even with greens and meat in it, but his stomach didn't care. He had half of it down before he came up for air, much to the Lightbringer's amusement.

"I'm glad to see your appetite has returned," Myles remarked. "The bakery has been stoked, and they are working on getting more bread made, so your next meal should be a bit heartier now that we have more flour."

Barrett's brows furrowed at the Lightbringer's words. "Was there a shortage of food before we arrived with the supply caravan? Even with all the farms?"

"The farmers here only put away enough for themselves before they had to leave. Those stores wouldn't have been enough for an entire platoon of hunters and soldiers, and there's no one to tend what crops haven't burned or gone off without a guiding hand to care for them."

"Ah." Barrett's cheeks flushed, looking down at the bowl of food as unease wriggled in his gut. "I hadn't thought of this many hunters as bein' that sort of inconvenience."

"It wouldn't be for the capital or perhaps even Oareford for a short term, but the guild has been sending people here for months."

"So I finally heard," Barrett grumbled.

"Oh?"

Barrett stirred the bowl of food, fishing out a piece of carrot. "Well, we only just got back from the Isles, and that was…" Graces, a whole ordeal.

"The Isles? Did you wind up going there with Kyran?"

Barrett looked up, surprised. Somehow, it had completely slipped his mind that Myles had no idea what had happened after he left the House. "Yes. The guild had to take him back to the laird up there to be tried for that warrant Griswold came to Oareford about. But Kyran was innocent. The laird's son lied, and said Kyran attacked him, when he…" Barrett stopped himself from saying it, his chest aching as he remembered what Kyran had told him.

He shook his head. "He was the one that attacked Kyran, and he threatened Kyran's family to keep him from defending himself."

"Oh, please do tell me Kyran is safe."

"Yes. He is. Captain Griswold was able to pay the laird. Kyran's name was cleared but no one would say anything against the bastard that hurt him."

"He will face his own judgment one day," Myles said solemnly.

Barrett's judgment, if he had any say in it. He scowled down into his porridge.

"Did Kyran return with you after all this?"

"He did, but he went on to the guildhall with another guildmate." He sighed, guilt or something like it sitting heavy on his chest.

"Oh my, that was quite the sigh."

Barrett flushed. "It's just… I know Kyran is all right, safe with the guild and all, but I… I feel bad, being away. After everything that's happened, I don't want him to have to be alone."

"Is he alone at the guildhall with the rest of your guild?"

Barrett twisted the spoon between his thumb and forefinger. "I mean, he doesn't know anyone. And I… I wanted to be there. To help him adjust."

Myles leaned forward, his eyes bright as he looked up at Barrett. "You miss him?"

"Nh—" Barrett started to deny the suggestion as his face grew hot and he nearly choked on the thick porridge. He covered his mouth around a cough, swallowing roughly. Myles chuckled, and Barrett's face only got that much hotter. "I mean, I… Yes," he finally admitted and looked down at his food, too embarrassed to look at the old man still laughing. "I… I guess I do."

"That's quite understandable. There's a stream of couriers that have been taking correspondence from your captains to the guild. I am certain one more letter wouldn't be amiss to them," the Lightbringer suggested gently.

"He's um… He can't read," Barrett said softly, but the excuse was weak and he already felt his lips twitching into an amused smile. "But I did write a letter to him when I realized I'd be gone longer than expected. I don't know if he'll be able to read it, but I think he'd recognize my initials, and he'd know it was from me, and that might cheer him up."

"And he'll have it to read when he does learn," Myles encouraged.

"I do have time before I'm due for my next patrol," Barrett reasoned. "Although I'd like to hope I'm back before he's learnt— I mean, I imagine it'll take awhile, unless he's a fast learner, which…" What *if* the mage was a fast learner and could read the letters? It wasn't as if they were full of embarrassing details, but the thought flustered Barrett all the same. This was silly. He was being silly. *Daft.* "I'll write something once I finish eating," he resolved at last.

"Is there anything you need? I found a very well stocked desk in the back of the House."

"I have a few things in my pack, but I wouldn't mind taking a look. My quill isn't the best…"

"I'll show you the desk as soon as you finish eating," Myles said, face creased with amusement that Barrett couldn't help but share.

Chapter Nineteen

THE RAIN HAD strengthened from a drizzle to a steady downpour by the time Kyran made it to the ward with Effie, and they were both drenched from head to toe. Before he could even knock, the door opened, and the same wee blonde lass that had answered before peered up at him through wide eyes and tangled hair.

"You're glowing!" she gasped, bouncing up and down in place.

Kyran looked down, and, to his mortification, his runelines were faintly visible in the dim morning. He hadn't even realized. With an effort of will, he tightened his control, and the pale light vanished.

The lass jumped back, eyes searching up and down him before she stuck her lower lip out nearly identical to how Effie had earlier. "Awh, they're gone," she whined, clearly put out.

"Moira, invite the guests in out of the rain," came Sophie's voice from somewhere out of sight.

The lass clapped a hand to her mouth, then looked up at Kyran again. "Come in. Come in," she said, waving her hand frantically.

Ducking under the lintel, Kyran moved to one side as the lass shut the door behind him and Effie.

In one motion, Moira swooped down on Effie and pulled her into a hug. "You're back!"

Effie made an uncomfortable whine, and Moira quickly let go, though she didn't move away.

"She sneaky-ed out," she told Kyran, pursing her lips in her best imitation of seriousness.

"Moira," came Sophie's voice again before the matron appeared from an attached hallway. "If you've got time to gossip, you've got time to help the little ones wash up for dinner. Go on."

The lass peered up at Kyran, then the matron, then back to Effie before she gave a small huff and hung her head before marching past Sophie into the hall, disappearing from sight.

"And you," the matron continued, her gaze now turning to Effie. "What are we going to do with you, little one?"

Effie found someplace on the wall to stare, her mouth set in a firm line, but Kyran felt her lean against his leg.

"I doubt there's a lock in existence that would keep you inside," Sophie continued, shaking her head. "I don't know how they do it, but when little ones like her get it into their head to go visiting, there's nothing I've found that can stop them."

She stepped out of the doorway into the front room and made a small shooing motion. Effie twitched, then looked up at Kyran, worry showing in the crease between her brows.

"He'll still be here when you get done cleaning up," Sophie said, now looking at Kyran with a knowing smirk. "We'll feed him some dinner for his trouble."

Kyran squeezed Effie's hand, and smiled in encouragement. "Go on. Listen ta your mam and dry off."

She still looked uncertain, but at last, the lass let go and slowly, head ducked, passed the matron into the hall, disappearing in the same direction Moira had gone, leaving a trail of water.

"There's a basin in the kitchen you can wash with," Sophie said, gesturing for Kyran to follow her into the hall as well. "We'll put a chair by the fire for you."

"You dinnae need ta trouble yourself," Kyran insisted, ducking under the low door to follow the matron. "I can manage—"

"Nonsense." Sophie turned and entered the next doorway that led to the room directly behind the entrance hall, which turned out to be the kitchen. The other side of the hearth from the entrance hall blazed with light and warmth, a cauldron and a smaller kettle burbling over the flames. Several baskets with cloth draped over their contents sat on a long counter, waiting to be served. "There isn't room on the benches, so, of course, you'll need a chair," Sophie continued, pouring fresh water into a bucket and setting a chunk of soap next to it. "Here," she said before bustling off to another part of the kitchen. "Do you eat pork pie?"

"No," Kyran answered sheepishly, dunking his hands in the cold water.

"Neither do I. I've got porridge for us and a few of the other children." She reappeared next to him, and set a rag on the edge of the bucket. "When you've finished, come back to the front. Brady and the rest will be in soon to get the tables set up and serve the meal."

She left him, continuing down the hall in the direction the weans had all gone. Kyran finished washing up and patted his hands dry before timidly returning to the entrance hall. He felt out of place, like a cow in a castle. But he didn't want to disappoint Effie. So, he tugged the single hardback chair over to the fire and sat, stretching out.

"'Scuse me."

Kyran picked his head up to find the blond lass at his hip again. Glancing around, he realized there were a few other weans that had suddenly appeared in the room with him. Stars, he must have dropped off. "Aye?"

"Why did you glow?"

"Magic," Kyran said, even as he felt his guts begin to squirm.

"But hunters don't glow!"

Kyran's mouth went dry. "Aye. I'm a…" He hesitated, struggling to say the word. What if the lass knew? What if she knew just what he was, and it frightened her?

"You're a what?" Moira prompted.

Kyran swallowed, his tongue sticking to the roof of his mouth.

"He's a mage," Sophie explained gently, crossing the room. "Let the poor boy rest now, Moira."

"Oh!" the lass gasped, bouncing on the tips of her toes. "I knew that. I learned all about mages in class. They're people born with magic. Can I see your magic?"

"Moira," Sophie chided gently, offering Kyran an apologetic smile.

"But I wanna see!" she protested, stamping her foot.

Kyran smiled nervously, despite himself. "I need a cup of water first."

"Why?"

"Ta show ye."

"Oh! I can get that. Wait here." The lass scurried off around the corner into the kitchen.

Sophie shot him an amused glance. "You'll never be finished showing her tricks now."

"I dinnae mind," Kyran assured her, focusing on staying upright in his seat. Stars above, he needed to finish his amulets. "Reminds me of Tavish."

"Oh? And who might that be?"

There was a tug at Kyran's kilt, and he glanced down to find Effie peering up at him. "My wee brother," he said, reaching to ruffle her hair fondly.

"Oh, it's no wonder you get on with the little ones so well."

Moira came barreling around the corner of the door, nearly upending on the wood as she slid.

"We do not run, Moira," Sophie chastised the lass.

"Yes, Warden Sophie," the lass chimed back without slowing even an inch, and thrust a small cup of water almost into Kyran's nose, a bit slopping over and dribbling onto his lap. "Here you go."

Plucking his kerchief from his purse, Kyran took the cup and gave the lass a pointed look until she backed away a few steps. Then, he let his control slacken just enough to focus his blood down his arm and fingertips into the water. Moira darted behind Effie, eyes wide as she watched. Behind her, other weans were staring, jaws slack with awe or fear.

There was a sharp crackle, and he switched his attention back down to the cup. "There you are," he announced, pressing his magic back beneath his control before he held the cup out for Moira.

The lass approached timidly, taking the cup and peering inside with an excited gasp. "It's frozen!" She looked up at Kyran with something almost like awe. "I've never met anyone with ice magic!"

"Is that so?" Kyran said, voice cracking.

"I just said so."

"Aye," Kyran agreed, his shoulders easing a fraction. "You did."

She poked at the ice, excitedly holding the cup out to Effie. "It's frozen!"

The other weans began to flock to the lass, gasping and cooing in awe, all reaching to press their fingers against the ice. They all began to talk excitedly, voices rising rapidly.

Kyran swallowed against the knot that had lodged in his throat. This, the *weans* and their reaction, was so…*vastly* different from anything he'd ever known. From even the conversation he'd had just minutes ago standing on the graves of people like him buried outside of the Light because of their blood. His blood.

"Children, leave Kyran be and go and wash your hands," Sophie said over the din of their excitement, shepherding them back towards the kitchen.

"Awh," Moira whined, but at a look from Sophie, she shuffled over to Kyran and set the cup down in front of him before taking Effie's hand and tugging her along. Effie let out a soft, distressed cry, and Kyran tried to smile, even as he felt his eyes prickling sharply.

"I'll be here, lass," he said, voice thick. "Dinnae worry yerself."

Chapter Twenty

THE SAME TIRED boy raised a hand in Barrett's direction as the hunter stepped into the stable. Sweetheart nickered softly as he followed the aisle back to her stall. She swung her head over the door, ears pricked at his approach.

"Feeling better?" he mumbled, scratching the white star on her forehead. "Enjoy the rest while you get it. Won't be too long 'til—"

He was cut off by the gentle clang of the village bell announcing the House's evening service, and the hunters' call to rally for the night.

"I'll find you something to nibble," he told the mare, giving her a last pat.

He paused just outside the door, blinking at the dregs of sunlight still lingering beneath the storm clouds on the horizon.

Myles' voice carried across the streets as he ministered to his crowd on the steps of the House. The old Lightbringer caught his eye as he came into the square, flashing him a quick smile without missing a word of his prayer.

Barrett returned it, suppressing a threatening yawn. He hadn't managed more than a few hours of rest after he'd finished his letter, and he was already starting to feel it.

At the prayer's conclusion, Myles ushered the villagers inside the House while Fairclough took to the steps.

"A supply wagon has arrived, and I will need a number of hunters to help unload. Those of you patrolling north, you will help unload. Captain Griswold will coordinate the rest to cover for them until they are able to return to their duties. I want everyone to eat and then those that are going to help with the wagon will meet behind the House of Light. The rest of you will meet back here within the hour to be briefed by Captain Griswold and given assignments. Any questions?" Fairclough waited a moment, scanning the silent crowd. "Good. May your lanterns stay lit."

"And yours as well," Barrett murmured with the crowd, automatically following the flow of people into the House for his supper. Breakfast. Meal. He gulped it down almost without tasting it, then joined the others on the steps, waiting to be sent off to roam the streets.

"Good morning, Barrett," Elijah said with a wide yawn, appearing at Barrett's side along with Marcus.

"Evenin'," Barrett corrected with a strained chuckle.

"Oh, you're right," Elijah mumbled, his eyes slipping closed, and Marcus looped an arm around him.

"Don't make me carry you," Marcus threatened playfully, to which Elijah mumbled something in reply. Barrett looked away, conscious of how his chest ached. "How is your…" Barrett looked up to see Marcus gesturing vaguely to his face.

Barrett affected a reassuring smile, and winced when it tugged on the tender scab across his face. "Stopped bleeding at least." And hadn't turned into a black witch mark, for which he was grateful.

"It still looks—"

"It seems we are all present," Griswold's even voice echoed over the crowd effortlessly. More of the same magic he used in Erchleis's dungeon, Barrett was certain. "If you will pay attention, I will divide you into your new groups for tonight's patrol."

In just a few minutes, the captain broke the crowd into small groups, and Barrett was briefly surprised to find himself pulled aside.

"We are leaving with the wagon once it is unloaded," Griswold explained once he had dismissed the rest with their orders. "Go and help the others behind the House."

"And what about you?"

"I have arrangements to complete."

Barrett rolled his eyes, stepping off onto the muddy cobbles. "Course you do."

He found his way to the back around the side of the House he had defended just the other night. The broken window had been patched with salvage from the homes that had been destroyed, parts of it black with char.

Graces, but he couldn't imagine living here, day after day, watching his and his neighbors' homes be destroyed as demons came night after night after night. For what reason?

He stared up at the tower as he rounded the back corner of the House. Its outline was hazy even in the lamp light illuminating the wagon and hunters ahead of him.

That had to be what had called them. It was the only thing that made sense. It was where the guild's amulets were made. Or had been. As far as he knew, no new amulets had been produced since before his father had been a hunter. Maybe longer.

Why it was not where the guild had been built, he couldn't understand. Then none of this would be happening.

"Oh, Kristopher." Myles waved him over as he got close, smiling brightly. "Are you joining us back here?"

"For now," Barrett said as he approached the Lightbringer and reached to take his outstretched hand, warming the knobby knuckles between his palms. "It sounds like I'm headed back to the guild after all."

"So soon?"

The hunter chuckled. "Apparently. I wish I had a bit more time to catch up with you. But I'll be glad to see Kyran." Barrett turned to accept a heavy crate from one of the other hunters, balancing it on his hip. "But now that I know where you are, I'll be certain to send you an annoying amount of letters."

"Oh, you will have to try very, very hard to annoy me," the Lightbringer said with a broad smile. "Don't let me keep you though, or I am certain that grouchy captain of yours will be along to glare sternly. Here, carry that inside with the others."

Barrett did as he was told, setting his crate down wherever the next person told him to. It looked like a bedroom that had been converted into a storeroom, crates and barrels stacked next to a shabby dresser and rickety beds. It reminded him keenly of the rooms back at the House of Light in Oareford.

Graces, that was almost half a year ago now. It still took him by surprise every time he reckoned with how long he had been fighting to keep Kyran out of the hands of the needle-toothed demon, then the guild, then the laird and that…that *monster*, Connal. The Pit be cursed, if he *ever* had the chance…

Fire flickered along his fist, and Barrett shook it away as he doubled back along the hall to the wagon, falling into the rhythm of the work. No one was talking much, despite the close quarters, and Barrett could read the exhaustion in all of their faces. All but one.

None of the other hunters looked thrilled about their task, but there was one man in particular that caught Barrett's attention. The man was scowling at something, but when Barrett looked over his shoulder, all he saw was Myles directing someone to follow a different direction inside.

Shuffling forward in line, Barrett reached up to take whatever was next, only to receive a laugh from the man up top. The wagon was empty.

"That's the last of it," the man on the wagon said.

"Thank the Graces," Barrett said and watched the last box get hauled away by two hunters sharing the weight. "Do you know when the wagon is leaving?"

"Shouldn't be long. We're letting the horses get watered up before we hitch them again."

Which meant Barrett had at least a little while before he had to begin the miserable trek back to the guildhall.

Looking around, he spotted Myles leading the last two hunters with their heavy box inside, and Barrett followed after them, trailing the others headed inside to receive their assignments for the rest of the night.

Squeezing past the others, Barrett followed the sound of the Lightbringer's voice to the room they had been unloading into, pressing to one side as the hunters exited. "Do you need anything else before the captain hauls me away, Myles?"

"Well, I would normally say I don't need much, but I'm rather glad to have this." The Lightbringer gestured to the supplies surrounding him. "Are you leaving right now?"

"As soon as Griswold tracks me down," Barrett said with a wink.

"We'd better hide, then," the Lightbringer said, grinning broadly at Barrett's laugh. The Lightbringer shuffled towards the door. "I know a place."

"Lightbringer Horn?" A man appeared in the doorway. Barrett recognized him from the wagon. The scowling man.

"You've found me," Myles said, folding his hands. "How may I help you?"

"One of the injured. He's asking for a Lightbringer."

Myles' face sobered at that. "Very well. Where is he?"

"I'll take you. We should be quick."

The Lightbringer nodded gravely. "I understand. Sorry to leave you again so soon, Kristopher."

"It's no trouble," he assured the Lightbringer, moving to one side to let him by, when he caught a glimpse of the man's hands.

They were both covered by bandages.

He started to dismiss it for any number of injuries people had after the attack his first night, but Fairclough's suspicions about the abominations lingered with him.

He set his hands to his hips, watching the two walk past the turn to the front of the House before he started after them. He'd rather be wrong, than sorry.

He kept his distance, meandering after the two far enough he could only hear the barest murmur of their conversation over the noise of the other townsfolk working in the House. They passed the kitchen, stepping through a door at the far end of the hall. Barrett hurried a little then, making the corner just as they went through another door. He could see stairs down beyond it. There was no reason they should need to go down stairs to what he could only assume was a basement or crypt beneath the House. Something was wrong.

"Myles?"

The man with the Lightbringer glanced back at Barrett, his lips drawn back in a snarl before he shoved the Lightbringer down the rest of the stairs.

"No!" Barrett screamed, racing after them as the bandaged man chased the Lightbringer down the stairs.

"Traitors will burn in the Light!" There was a surge of power, and the man lunged for Myles, mouth open wide to show a set of wolf-like canines.

Snatching the dagger from his hip, Barrett launched himself from the stairs, but he wasn't fast enough. He could only watch in horrid slow motion as the abomination's teeth snapped shut around the Lightbringer's arm, yanking him off the floor.

Barrett landed hard, staggering to keep his feet as he threw his hand forward, sending a stream of fire licking over the abomination's hide.

It shook like a dog shedding water, flinging the Lightbringer left and right before it finally released him, sending him tumbling across the floor into the wall with a solid thud of impact.

The Lightbringer wasn't moving.

"You!" The air around Barrett burst into scarlet flame and he lunged for the abomination, grabbing what was left of the rags clinging to it and shoving it to the floor. Screaming in fury, Barrett slammed his hand down on the abomination's face with a burst of fire so hot its skin caught like tinder. The violent stench of burnt meat and hair filled the air.

The beast let out a terribly human shriek, thrashing blindly beneath the hunter until, with a last shudder, it fell still.

But Barrett didn't relent, pouring fire into the beast, the roar of the fire punctuated by the pop and crackle of bones cracking and flesh melting away.

"Why?" he shouted. "Why!?"

And then, the fire under his hand snuffed out.

He tried to pull more magic, cursing his demon, but there was nothing. With a furious snarl, he pulled his fist back, when he caught a glimpse of his hand. His entire hand was ashen, the same as the abomination. Tendrils of the color were going up his wrist. The tips of his fingers were darker, almost bony, and a shock lit through him from where he had seen it before. In the Demon Realm, when he had lost control, when he had contorted to the demon's will.

"No." He tried to catch his breath through the pounding in his head, but he couldn't even manage a thready gasp in. He pulled harder, his chest heaving, but it felt as if he were trying to breathe in stone.

"What..." The words were nothing more than a whisper, and he felt the first threads of panic begin to worm their way into him. Something was wrong.

He stood up and stumbled towards the stairs, only to find someone standing there.

Griswold.

The captain's hand was outstretched towards him, and his face was set in a cold, impenetrable expression. Barrett looked down at his blackened arms, with thick veins pulsing against his taut skin, and long, pointed claws where his nails should have been. He tried not to look beyond his arms, at the thing at his feet. The abomination was turning back into man, naked and bloodied, except for his face, which was in complete, unrecognizable ruin. He couldn't even gasp at the sight.

With a shock of panic, Barrett suddenly recognized the sensation of air being ripped from his mouth. "Cap—" He looked towards the captain, pleading with what little air he had remaining. "Stop—Gris—"

Black edged his vision, his limbs growing heavy as the pounding in his skull became a slow drumbeat. He fell to the floor, unable to even scream as his body burned, starving for air, chest convulsing as he horribly recollected the familiar sensation of suffocation.

But there was no Kyran begging for him this time. He might never see him again, or anyone else. Black filled his vision just as the voices around him escalated to a crescendo, then faded to nothing.

Chapter Twenty-One

KYRAN STARED UP at his ceiling, his eyes burning for lack of sleep, but he couldn't stop his thoughts from chasing each other into the silent corners of his room, where every shadow and shift of lantern light became a demon waiting to form. Stars above, he was near as bad as the nights after Connal.

And he hated it.

He hated that he felt so fragile, as if one wee thing could shatter what was left of him. He had faced down a demon, and now he could hardly face an empty room.

Giving up on the idea of sleep entirely, he got up and moved to the chair he'd set by his window, cracking the shutters open. It wasn't quite night yet, but the sky above was black with clouds and he half-expected to see a ring of stone outlining it above his head. Only the stinging scent of smoke still thick in the air, and the rough texture of cloth against his fingers reassured him that he was awake.

A clink against the stone brought his attention round where little chips of ice bounced off the sill, gathering in drifts that reflected back the blue of his blood. He hadn't even realized it had slipped free again, and he felt a coil of shame.

For the longest time, he'd tried not to use his magic. Growing up, he had struggled hard for his control while living alone on *Cairngorm*, and every slip of power was a failure. When he came down from the *ben*, he had to hide his lines lest he be found out for a mage. His magic was a thing of shame and fear, his control that of pride and necessity. That was, until he faced that needle-toothed demon in the Inbetween in the Isles.

It had felt good to finally have the power to face that monster as its equal, to be strong enough to stand his ground and fight back. To hurt it for hurting him. Even if it was only possible because it had fed the monster inside of him. And what did it matter? He couldn't go home.

Even if his bond was paid, he couldn't look his da in the eye knowing he wasn't his son, but some demon's bastard git. And his ma… He couldn't even think on it.

Lifting his hand, he focused on his magic, tightening his concentration down upon it until all of his attention was absorbed in the task. He started to shape it, as he had done in the Inbetween, picturing a rope stretching between him and the strange, floating paths of ashen stone he had tried to escape down after climbing free of the pit he'd been kept in.

The image came easily enough, and gritting his teeth, Kyran pulled. His lines flared bright, but there was no sinking sensation, no slogging against a tide. He pulled harder, leaning into it with every bit of power he could force to the action. Nothing.

He let go of the image, tamping his magic down with a short curse, when the flickering light of the lantern caught his eye. Demons always crossed in the dark. Barrett had told him that. What if he needed to do the same?

With a quick flash of power, the lantern guttered out, leaving him in a deep murk of shadow. His skin prickled, the gnawing at his middle quickening into mute terror, but he pressed on. He needed to know he could do this.

He closed his eyes, picturing the rope again, but instead of walkways, his mind went unbidden to that horrid pit. He tried to shift his thoughts away, absolutely not desiring to see that place again, but the rope was already anchored, and somehow stronger. The connection was almost tangible this time, pulling on him as he pulled on it. Perhaps it was because the place was so personal to him. Perhaps it was because he had never quite left. Maybe he would cross into the other realm and find another him still shuddering in the bottom of that pit, waiting to be saved.

Drawing a deep breath, he pulled.

The world flexed around him, the firm reliability of earth and stone turning to thick porridge and cloth. He tugged, hard, and felt the fabric of things give just an inch, resisting, a steady pounding starting in his head.

"Come on," he whispered through his teeth, sweat beading along his brow and flashing to tiny crystals of ice. The pain in his skull built and built, and he fought to keep the image of the rope suspended in his mind, but it was getting difficult to even remember to breathe. "Let me in."

All at once, the resistance against him gave, tearing like wet fabric. He didn't have time to even gasp in relief as he was swallowed down the throat of the world.

Dark, smothering heat pressed against him, and when he opened his eyes, he found himself in the same familiar nothing. The Inbetween. He'd done it. He was there.

But whatever elation he felt was tempered by the sheer exhaustion the effort had cost him. It hadn't been nearly so hard last time, though it hadn't been easy. It could have been the place, or the fact that he'd already been in the Inbetween and had been merely navigating it. He didn't know enough about it to do more than speculate.

He considered if he should go further, or simply turn back. As much as it had taken for him to get this far, he doubted he could go much deeper, but the thought of going back had little appeal. What was he going to do there? Sit in his room and frantically carve bits of wood by the light of his fire to keep the walls from closing in around him?

Steadying his thoughts, he began to gather his will around his magic again, when there was a sudden weight against him, not nearly so overbearing as the demon's had once been, but undeniably familiar. He wasn't alone. He spun to face whatever it was, hand extended, when something's grip closed on his arm. Before he could react, he was yanked from his feet.

The world spun, lights blinking into existence around him before he hit the ground and pain lanced through his leg up into his hips. He quelled it with magic, quickly rolling onto his back to find himself on the lawn surrounded by faces lit by lantern light and black fire.

"You stupid mage!" barked a man's voice before its owner stepped out from the darkness. Nowell. "You all can go," the guard captain scowled at the others. "False alarm."

A few of the faces began to dissipate, but others lingered, looking between Kyran and the guard captain.

"I said false alarm!" Nowell snapped again, and the rest scattered hastily. He bent as if to grab Kyran by his arm again, and the mage snatched the knife from his boot in an instant, pointing it at the man. The guard captain looked at the knife, then straightened, settling his hand on the pommel of the sword at his hip. "You don't want to go crossing blades with me, mage. Now get up."

"Lay hands on me again, and we will see what ye think of my blade," Kyran snarled, his lines beginning to glow again as he focused his magic to the tip of his knife, the metal beginning to frost.

Nowell held his gaze steadily, unphased by his threat. "Do you hear that bell ringing?"

Kyran did. It had been a background noise until the man pointed it out, but now that he noticed it, it was impossible to miss, thundering over the guildhall.

"That bell rings when something—usually a demon—tries to make its way into the guild from the other side. It's ringing right now because of you. Hunters are out of their beds looking for you because you didn't think. Now get up, or I will drag you to the stocks myself."

A nearly hysterical laugh caught at the back of Kyran's throat as any last doubt he might have clung to melted away like snow in the sun. He had done that? He'd rung a bell used to warn of demons. Him. It really was true, then.

Nowell gave him an odd look. "Are you all right, mage?"

Gathering his walking stick where it lay nearby, Kyran hauled himself upright, keeping his blade tucked close. "Aye," he said at last. "Bonny and bright as—" Something drifted past the lantern's light, then another. He held out his hand, releasing just enough of his control on his magic to set his lines glowing and make out the tiny drifting flakes. It was snowing.

The other man took notice and muttered darkly at the sky. "Going to be an awful winter. Come along, mage. We'll talk in the guardroom."

"Why na here?"

"Because it's not for everyone's ears," the man argued, tone exasperated. "Start moving. I'll tell you where to go."

"Th—"

"Or we can negotiate this conversation from the stockade."

Kyran glared at the guard captain, but there was truly little he could do. He was to be a guild member. He was a tool of the guild. Bought and paid. A monster in a menagerie of monsters whose usefulness was defined by how well they could destroy other monsters. The sheer absurdity was enough to make him laugh. Or scream.

Something else caught his eye as he turned to leave, and he bent awkwardly to pick up the kerchief from where he'd dropped it, brushing off the grass and mud before he tucked it safely back in his purse.

"Nowell!" Finley came running up, slowing to a brisk walk as she neared, but her eyes were wide, face flushed. "What's happened?"

"It was a false alarm. You can stand down."

"I asked what happened," Finley snapped, her breath fogging thickly in front of her.

"And I said—"

"It was me," Kyran cut the guard captain off. "There wasna a demon."

Finley's brows nearly met, they furrowed so deeply in confusion beneath her knitted cap. "Are you all right? What were you doing to set the bell off?"

Kyran dug his nails into his walking stick. "I was practicing."

"Practicing what?"

"Magic," Kyran snapped.

"And just happened to accidentally slide out of our realm?" Nowell accused, scoffing. "I don't think so."

Finley's expression softened in undisguised surprise. "He... Did you really?"

Kyran shifted under the intensity of her stare. "Aye."

The other mage smiled, and Kyran had the distinct impression of watching a wolf spy a lamb. "Let me speak with him, Nowell. I will sort this out."

The guard captain dragged a hand over his face, but after a moment, he nodded. "I honestly do not have the time now. Just see to it he understands he cannot do it again."

"Certainly," Finley said, not without a little dryness to her tone. "Come on, Kyran. I'll walk you back to your room."

"I can find my way," Kyran said, voice tight.

"I'm certain you can, but I want to talk to you. You entered the Inbetween tonight all on your own, did you not?"

Kyran glanced at the guard captain's retreating back, and started down the pathway back towards the dorms. "Aye."

"Do you think you could get all the way to the demon realm?"

Kyran's brow furrowed as he considered the question. It had taken an enormous amount of his power to simply enter the Inbetween, and it would take more to even reach the depths the other realm must lay. But if he were to take enough amulets... "Aye."

"And would you be able to teach someone—someone like me—how to do it? Because if we and others like us could travel to the other realm at will, we could finally take this endless war to their door. We wouldn't have to wait for demons to come here and murder innocent people. We could finally wipe them out for good. And if there are no demons..."

Then there would be no more mages. No more cursed bairns born. No more weans like Effie taken to that dreadful place. "You believe we could? Be rid of all demons?"

Finley's eyes crinkled with a smile beneath her scarf. "Where else would they go if not to fall on our swords?"

A flicker of hope, like a dying star, lit in Kyran's chest, and for the first time in longer than he cared, he felt like there was something in his life he was meant to do. "It is a strange thing ta grasp, but...aye. I ken I could teach you how ta reach their realm."

"Thank you," Finley said with genuine relief in her voice. "You don't know how much this means to me, Kyran."

Kyran thought of Raleigh's headstone she had shown him, of the rows of silent headstones of mages cursed for their existence they did not choose. "I ken I might."

Chapter Twenty-Two

"I'll handle him."

"Is he…"

"…can't be…"

"…abomination."

Barrett jerked awake with a sharp gasp, lurching into motion. "Myles?" he slurred, his knees buckling at the throb that went through his head, catching himself against a set of bars. He squinted at his surroundings, trying to make out where he was when he noticed his hands. His gloves were missing, showing two pale, completely normal hands.

"Thank the Graces," he sighed, reaching to touch his amulet. Only it wasn't there. "No." He slapped his hands against his clothing and hip, but the amulet wasn't there, and neither was his dagger. "Oh—"

You fool, a voice hissed in the back of his mind.

Barrett scowled, trying to keep his breathing even as he looked around. "What did you do to me?" he muttered. "What in Lumen's name did you—"

Me? You are the one that drew on my power. You were simply too weak to hone it, so I assisted.

"You—"

You would have hurt yourself without me. And now you've lost my amulet.

"I haven't lost—" Barrett paused when a door latch turned, pressing against the bars of his prison cell to see Captain Griswold step into the room.

The captain's expression was empty as he faced Barrett, as cool and unreadable as it had been the entire time Barrett had been stuck with him in the Isles.

"How are you feeling?" Griswold asked, voice devoid of any discernible care. It never failed to infuriate Barrett, and this time was no different.

"Like I've been beaten and choked to death. Where is my amulet?"

Griswold stared down at him for a long moment before he spoke again. "It will be returned. Tell me what happened."

Barrett scoffed, trying not to think about how terrifying the captain was with that heartless stare. It was the same look he had given him when he had choked him, both times. "There was an abomination. One of the men from the wagon. He attacked Myles. Is he all right?"

"How often have you been manifesting your demon since becoming a hunter?"

"Tell me Myles is all right."

"Have you—"

"Tell me!" Barrett demanded, his voice cracking.

"He is alive. Now—"

"What does that mean?"

"The sooner you answer my questions, the sooner I can release you."

Liar.

"I don't believe you. Why am I locked in here? Where are we?"

The captain was silent, watching Barrett with those same cold, calculating eyes. "How often have you manifested your demon?"

"What?"

Griswold raised his hand, and Barrett looked down at his own pale hand again.

"I haven't— That's never happened before."

"I would not advise lying again," the captain warned, a hint of ice creeping into his voice.

Barrett swallowed tightly. "You're asking about…in the Isles."

"I am asking about any other time you have let your demon through like that."

Griswold knew about the Isles. Barrett swallowed against the sudden gag of nausea. If the captain had any reason to believe Barrett was a threat, he doubted Griswold would hesitate to kill him. The thought was terrifying and he found himself searching the captain's face for any sort of sympathy or concern. There was none.

"I—I… When I… When I was in the demon realm, when I went to get Kyran, I needed its help. But before, earlier. I don't know how or why."

"So three times now?"

"Yes," he confirmed quietly. "Griswold, what— What's going to happen?"

The captain's hair stirred as the air in the room shifted again, pressing in on Barrett's ears. "You will be monitored for influence, and if it is determined your demon has gained sway over you, you will be retired."

Barrett let out a shaky sigh of relief. He didn't want to lose his power, but retired was better than dead. Unless his demon overtook him, then he would be better off dead, like any other poor soul that became an abomination. "I understand," he said quietly.

"Good. In the meantime, we have a new mission." The pressure against Barrett's ears increased, the noise of feet and muffled voices from above vanishing. "We are going to escort Myles back to the guildhall to be seen by our chirurgeons."

"How bad is he?"

Griswold's mouth thinned in what Barrett might almost call concern. "I'm not a healer, but Georgie did not have encouraging words."

It didn't feel real. "When are we leaving?"

"There is a wagon ready and I've had our horse's saddled." He stepped forward, reaching into the pocket of his coat. Dangling from his fingers was Barrett's amulet.

"Now? Right now?" Barrett quickly rose to his feet, immediately regretting it as a nauseating lightheadedness washed over him, a litany of aches greeting him. Graces, what he wouldn't give for a strong drink to dull the aches and settle his nerves. He gestured to the amulet dangling from Griswold's hand. "Am I gettin' that back, then?"

"For now."

With a grunt, Barrett pushed off the wall and reached through the bars, but Griswold made no move to bring it within reach. He gave the captain a tired look, and turned his hand over, until, leaning just far enough to reach, Griswold laid the amulet in his hand.

Ignoring the protest in his shoulders, Barrett looped it over his neck and tucked the amulet back under his clothes, sighing as some of the nameless anxiety coiled in his chest eased. He waited for the captain to move or say something, but he simply stood there, watching Barrett, a line of tension showing in his neck. Then, without warning or even a change in stance, the pressure on Barrett's ears vanished, the noise of the House rushing back in to fill the silence.

"Can you walk?" Griswold asked, hands slowly opening and closing at his sides.

"Well enough," he answered, eyeing the stairs leading out.

Following his gaze, Griswold let out what might have possibly been a sigh before he stepped over to Barrett's side, offering his arm. "Come on."

"I said well enough," Barrett muttered, but accepted the captain's help when he did not step away. It was quite awkward, considering Barrett was taller than Griswold, but they staggered up the stairs together.

They came out in the back hall Barrett had followed Myles and the other man down. Griswold led him down the hall away from the constant low drone of voices, and Barrett noticed ahead of them a place in the wall that was a different color and even texture of stone from the rest. The patch went all the way from floor to ceiling and was wider than his outstretched arms.

"What is that?"

"The tower," Griswold said simply, continuing past it.

"The wizard's tower?" He reached out to brush his fingertips over the stone, half expecting some foreign shock in return. It was just cold, grainy brick.

"The same," Griswold confirmed, pulling the next door open and dragging Barrett through it out into the light rain.

Barrett had once been fond of the rain. But over the last couple of years, it only made him miserable. Normally, he would call on his magic to warm him and evaporate the moisture from his clothes, but after his interaction with Griswold, he didn't dare draw on his power. "Is anyone else coming with us?"

"We bribed the driver to man the cart. It will just be us so we can focus on making good time."

If Barrett didn't feel so poorly, he might have laughed at the thought of Griswold bribing the driver. It was dark between the sparse lanterns lighting the area, and they walked all the way to the edge of town without meeting a single person. "Do the others know what's going on?" he asked abruptly.

"No. I told them I would handle you. That's why we have to leave before anyone sees you."

Griswold was essentially sneaking him out. Barrett looked down at the muddy ground, confused at the guilt that hit him from the realization. "What'll you tell 'em?"

"Only as much as they need to know and will keep the peace."

Barrett eyed the man. That didn't sound like Griswold, the man that had demanded to know everything from Kyran before he would help him. Then again, the captain hadn't exactly been forthcoming with his own plans.

"There they are."

Barrett nearly jumped out of his skin as the cart and two figures appeared from the weather. Elijah, waving his good arm, and Marcus, holding Sweetheart and Griswold's horse's reins, stood huddled near the back of the cart.

"Evening," Elijah greeted them, smiling brightly.

"Hello," Barrett greeted cautiously, taking his weight from the captain. "Did you bribe them, too?" he teased Griswold weakly.

"I didn't have to," Griswold said stiffly, looking over the cart. "Elijah is my apprentice, and Marcus is his devoted companion."

"Devoted com—?" Barrett looked at the two hunters, who were pointedly not looking at each other, their faces matching shades of scarlet. "I see."

"Regardless," Griswold continued. "We should be off."

"Right." Barrett moved over to Sweetheart, smiling when she reached to sniff his hand. "No treats today, sweetie. I'll get you some berries when we get home, I promise."

She let out a snort, shoving her nose against his hand. He rubbed her damp neck and nodded to Marcus before he awkwardly climbed up into the saddle. Graces, his whole body hurt, but at least he wouldn't be walking on his own two feet.

"May your lanterns stay lit, hunter," Marcus said, stepping back as he handed off the other reins to Griswold.

"Yours as well," Barrett said as he turned Sweetheart to face the road. "Light keep you all safe." He looked at Elijah, who was holding his arm close to his chest. "Be careful."

"Don't worry," Marcus said, his arm slipping protectively around Elijah's waist, who turned a faint shade of pink in the low lantern light from the wagon. "I won't let him out of my sight again."

Barrett grinned at the two of them, nudging Sweetheart closer to the wagon while Griswold mounted.

The man leading the cart let out a sharp whistle and the horse began to pull. Barrett clenched his hands around the reins and took one last look at the young hunters. "I suppose I'll see you all back at the guild."

He followed behind the cart, staring at the back where Myles must have been lying beneath the tarp to stay dry. It felt eerily similar to when he brought Kyran to the guild for help. He only hoped he reached the guild quick enough that Myles could get the care he needed. If they didn't make it in time, he wasn't certain how he would handle the Lightbringer's death. There was no shortage of nightmares lately.

You just need more power to protect them, his demon whispered. *More control to use it.*

Barrett flexed his jaw, hating the truth in its words. He did need to be stronger to protect those he cared about. He just wasn't certain he could afford the cost of that power.

Chapter Twenty-Three

"Associate Kyran?"

Kyran's eyes flashed open, flicking around his room until he heard the sound of a small fist pounding on his door. He squinted at the window, a faint glow of grey light showing beneath the shutters. Was it day already? He swore he had only just finally fallen asleep.

There was more knocking at the door, and he surrendered to the day, pushing his hair out of his face as he made his way to the door.

Alf stood just outside, hand raised, as if he'd been about to knock again. "Morning, Associate Kyran. Here with a message for you."

Kyran waited for more, until he realized the lad expected a reply. "Aye, go on."

The lad cracked a smile, but dutifully continued. "You are to report to the hospital as soon as possible."

Kyran's nail found a sliver of his walking stick, worrying at it at the thought of someone touching and looking at his healing wounds. "I'm well enough. I dinnae need ta—"

"I have been instructed to show you to the hospital before I can be dismissed," Alf interrupted.

Kyran narrowed his eyes, and the lad stood up straight and stiff, but didn't back his statement down. He would wait. "Aye, just a moment," Kyran muttered, retreating into his room to wash his face and give his hair a quick comb.

The scent of smoke still lingered in the air outside beneath the heavy, threatening cloud cover. Kyran followed just behind Alf as they passed the ward and turned down a short path that led up to a heavy set of doors.

He craned his head back, his mouth going dry as he took in the imposing stone edifice, unable to compare it to anything he'd ever seen but the foreboding entrance of Erchleis.

Inside was a large open area where people sat on benches, most of whom looked positively miserable or bored. A wide set of stone stairs led up to another floor.

"Wait here," Alf told him, pulling the door shut behind them, but he'd hardly made it more than a few steps into the waiting area before someone wearing a canvas coat came hurrying up from the direction of the stairs.

"You're Kyran?" they asked, squinting at Kyran through a pair of crooked spectacles.

Kyran shifted uncomfortably, pinching the bottom of his sleeve. "Aye."

"Good. If you'll follow me." They waited just long enough for him to nod in agreement before they led him down a hall at the far end of the waiting area and through an open door.

The room beyond was lined with a row of wooden framed cots on either side, a few of which were already occupied by other people. The person in the canvas coat stopped by an empty cot, gesturing to it.

"If you'll wait here, she'll be by when she's finished with her patient." Kyran barely got in a nod before they hurried off.

The mage had hardly sat down before a woman entered. She was older, her short dark hair spotted with silver, and clothed in an identical canvas coat. She smiled as she approached, teeth white against her earth brown skin.

"Welcome back," she greeted, rubbing her palms idly together. "My name is Tacita. I oversaw your care while you were here before. If it is all right with you, I would like my apprentice to be the one to look you over."

"Look me over?" Kyran questioned, suddenly uneasy with where this was headed.

"Yes, to see how you are healing."

Kyran's nails clicked against his walking stick. "I ken verrah well."

"That's good to hear. This shouldn't take too long then." She turned towards the door, where a younger woman was entering pushing a tiered cart ahead of her. "Here she is. This is Lilyanna."

She was stockier and younger than Tacita, her expression set and calm as she approached them. She stopped next to the foot of the bed, and stepped from behind the cart, hands clasped in front of her and Kyran couldn't help but notice the dark speckles spattered across her identical canvas coat that looked suspiciously like blood.

"Good afternoon," she greeted Kyran without moving any closer or extending him a hand, her voice soft and even. "If you are amenable, I would like to examine your leg. Given the length of time that has passed since you were brought here, I believe it should be well enough to progress to the next phase of healing, but I will have to examine it to be certain."

"Aye," Kyran said, his voice tight.

"You would not have to remove your clothes, just expose your leg," Lilyanna continued. "You will be behind screens, and it will only be the two of us, if that would make you more comfortable."

Kyran clenched his fingers around his walking stick as he felt a splinter of wood come away under his nail. She was a healer, he told himself, but it did nothing to ease the rapidly rising dread at just the idea of having someone look at or touch him without even the scant protection of his clothes.

"Tacita, if you will help me set them up before you go."

"Of course," the chirurgeon said, immediately moving to grab the screens Lilyanna pointed out behind the cot. They were sturdy things, the canvas thick enough over their wooden frames that Kyran couldn't see a thing through them.

They set them up one each side of the cot and then across the foot, effectively shielding it from sight.

"How's that?"

"That will do," Lilyanna said from outside the screens. "Kyran, if you will remove your bandages."

Kyran swallowed, his knuckles aching from his grip around his walking stick. She was only looking at his leg. Unknotting his hand from his walking stick, he laid it aside on the cot and, lifting his shirt and kilt, began to slowly remove the bandages from his hips and leg until the tender scar was laid bare. He felt so exposed even with all of his clothes on, fingers knotted in the wool of his kilt as he pressed it down between his legs, his stomach writhing anxiously. She was a healer, he reminded himself again.

"All right," he finally said, trying to take a deep breath to steady himself, but his lungs simply refused.

"May I enter?" Lilyanna asked.

"Aye."

The screens' frames creaked, and the apprentice let herself in, carefully closing the gap behind her. "I am going to examine your leg now," she said, her voice still low and even. "Is that all right?"

Kyran grit his teeth, looking anywhere but at the apprentice. "Aye."

She moved closer, bending to examine his leg, and Kyran had to fight the urge to lean away and cover himself. Stars, he hated this.

"I am going to touch your leg and examine your scar now."

Kyran braced in anticipation, but at the first featherlight touch against his leg, he flinched, jerking out of her reach. She didn't say anything, though, simply waited patiently as he settled back against the cot, trying desperately to calm the frantic thunder of his pulse in his ears. He squeezed his eyes shut, clenching his hands in his kilt until his fingers went numb, but a second touch never came.

Peeling his eyes open again, he found Lilyanna watching him, absolutely unphased by his reaction. He tried to swallow, but his throat wasn't working, his breaths coming in fast pants through his nose. "I'm sorry. I…"

"You are all right," the apprentice said in that same, calm tone. "Tell me when you are ready to try again."

He nodded, unable to get another word out. Slowly, painfully slowly, he was able to take deeper breaths, but his pulse wouldn't steady. "Just do it," he finally told her, bracing again.

"All right. I am going to touch your scar this time. It may hurt, but I will try to be quick."

The touch came again, pressing more firmly this time against the ropey scars on the end of his leg. He sucked a breath through his teeth, hissing at the sharp pain that shot through his leg.

"The scar is tender," Lilyanna noted. "But that is normal for this stage." She stood up, backing up as much as the small space would allow. "Have you been washing it and changing your bandages every day?"

"Aye."

"Good. Make certain to continue and to keep it dry. You are also going to need to start desensitizing it if you intend to wear a false limb."

Kyran's attention piqued at that. He hadn't even thought so far as to what might come next with his leg.

"If you will watch," she continued, holding out her first. "You will want to massage the end of your leg like this, starting out as gentle as you need." She pressed against her knuckles, moving her fingers in gentle circles. "You will also need to rub and tap it, like this." She switched to tapping the pads of her fingers against her knuckles. "It will likely be very uncomfortable, and even painful at first, but as it becomes less uncomfortable, you will need to increase pressure. You need to do these every day. When you are ready to have a false limb fitted, the guild will assist in furnishing you with one."

She clasped her hands again. "Senior Robin thought to inform me that it is common for you to have hip and back pain after losing a lower limb, and asked me to tell you the kitchen can provide warm water for compresses to ease the pain. He would be someone you could speak with if you have any other questions."

Kyran nodded, more than ready to be done with the examination and leave, when Lilyanna's eyes moved up to his shoulder.

"Captain Griswold noted in his letter that you had a shoulder injury."

Silently cursing the guild captain, Kyran nodded, and reached up to pull his shirt down over his shoulder, exposing the unbandaged scars stippling over the front and back. "The demon bit me," he explained as she leaned close to look over the marks.

"It seems to have healed well. Was it tended?"

"Aye. At Castle Erchleis and by my ma."

"They did well." She stepped back again, looking him over. "Do you have any other complaints?" He shook his head. "Then I will give you clean bandages to reapply and allow you privacy to tend to it. Please do not hesitate to call upon me if you have any further complications or questions."

She let herself through the screens, and Kyran pulled his kilt back down over his leg, wincing at the texture of the wool against his scars. It was done then. She reentered a moment later with several rolls of linen, setting them on the cot next to Kyran before taking her leave.

He didn't immediately move, clasping his hands as his pulse finally began to slow until, at long last, he could take in a deep breath. Then, picking up the first roll, he began to wrap his leg again.

"Kyran? Are you in there?"

Finley.

Kyran hurried to finish his task. "Aye."

"My apologies for bothering you, but the runner said you would be here."

"Aye, just a moment." Tying off his bandage, he got up from the cot and wound his way from behind the screens. Finley was waiting nearby, a cap pulled down so far it nearly covered her eyes.

"First things first, you've a letter, and a note from the chirurgeon."

Kyran fumbled out his kerchief, taking the folded piece of parchment she held out for him. A daub of green wax sealed the letter shut, and Kyran recognized the shape pressed into it from the initials he'd traced a hundred times embroidered into the corner of his borrowed kerchief.

K.B.

Kristopher Barrett.

A smile pulled at the corner of his mouth. The daft fool had actually written him. "Thank you."

"You're welcome. And here." She handed him another piece of folded parchment. "Lilyanna says to post it to the guild's artisan in the city if you decide to get a false limb. As to the other business, Nowell asked me to tell you to come to the arena tonight for training."

Kyran's back snapped straight. "He did?"

"Ah, so you do know what I'm talking about. Good. He wants us to show up an hour after sundown."

"Us?"

"Oh, yes. Nowell will be there too. The three of us, if you are still willing."

"Aye. I'll be there," he said, feeling the weight on his heart and shoulders lift for the first time in days, and was surprised to find he looked forward to the evening.

"Good. Make certain you rest plenty. I'm certain you know how much hard work you're in for.

That he did after his first few attempts. It took a lot of magic to move into and through the Inbetween. He wasn't certain how long he would last at a concentrated effort. Unless… It was early still. He could work on remaking at least one of his amulets and still have time to rest before he was expected.

"Aye, I ken it verrah well."

"I'll see you then."

Chapter Twenty-Four

IT WAS RAINING again when Kyran ducked out of the dormitory, nothing more than a drizzle, but more than enough to turn the grounds to slick mud. He stuck to the brick paths, moving as quickly as he dared following the directions Finley had given him, but by the time he reached the arena at the far end of the grounds, the drizzle had become a downpour.

"Stars above." Kyran muttered, flicking water from the ends of his fingers. "At least on the *ben* I only had snow ta deal with."

His kilt wasn't quite soaked, the wool doing a fair job of shedding the rain, but his shirt was drenched.

Wringing out his hair, he took in his shelter. Rather than a building, the arena simply had a low wall delineating its perimeter. Within the wall, the ground had been sunk several feet and covered in sand, with wide shallow stone steps to access it. It had its own lanterns hung on the walls and set on posts in the middle of the arena floor to keep it lit.

On one end were training dummies, all badly charred wooden mockups of demons. At the other were several targets that could be used for arrows, also badly charred. The center of the arena was mostly bare but for a lamppost and four shorter wooden posts lined up next to it, likely for securing dummies or other targets.

There was a press against Kyran's senses, a ghost of the sensation he remembered so keenly from the Inbetween and that monstrous prison deep in the demon realm. Like a finger trailing across his thoughts.

His runelines flared bright and cold, his head snapping towards the source of the sensation as a figure limned with glaring, red lines appeared at the entrance to the arena.

"Ah. You beat me here."

Kyran pressed his magic back under his control, shoulders easing as Finley resolved from the haze of rain and white fog.

She pulled her scarf down, steam drifting up in lazy curls from her clothes, and smiled at him. "How are you?"

"Well enough," Kyran said, taking in her lines bright and bold as glowing coals along her cheeks.

She looked him up and down, and giggled. "Your magic isn't quite suited for our weather here, is it?"

Kyran ducked his head, uncertain how to take her remark, and the rime of ice clinging to his hair and shoulders crackled at the movement, falling in bits to the ground, his shirt creaking threateningly. It had all frozen.

"Glad to see you could both make it," Nowell interjected as he came in behind Finley, steam trailing behind him. "Shall we get started before we waste any more time?"

Finley waved a hand dismissively at the captain. "Of course."

"Good. I'll get the lanterns when we're ready to begin."

"Insufferable man," Finely muttered, descending the stairs to the center of the arena.

"Did Finley tell you any of what we are trying to do here tonight?" Nowell called as he strode across the sand to the first lantern and quenched it.

"Some," Kyran said, carefully navigating the stairs behind him.

"Our goal is to enter the demon realm and return safely, like Hunter Barrett reported doing. Originally, it was only going to be me and Finley, a mage and a hunter, to test some scholar's theory about why no one has ever made it to the demon realm or returned from it until now. It's clear the bastard has never made the attempt himself, because if he had, he'd realize how bloody difficult it is simply entering the Inbetween, let alone traveling it."

Kyran let out a dry chuckle. "Aye, that's the truth of it."

Finley gave him a tight smile, glancing past him at Nowell. "Since you've made the attempt before, I take it you understand the principle of how it is done."

"I do," the guild captain said, quenching another lantern, blanketing one corner of the arena in darkness

"Good. Kyran, you said you could teach me?"

"A—aye." He stepped off the bottom of the stairs onto the wet sand, his walking stick sinking slightly. "It sounds a bit mad, though."

"We are trying to go to the demon realm voluntarily," Finley laughed dryly. "I'd say we're already a bit mad."

Kyran let out a soft snort. He described the process of what he had figured out to Finley, keenly watching her expression. But she seemed to only be listening intently, even when he fumbled for words.

She looked thoughtful when he finished, brow furrowed. "I was already planning to have us take turns entering and exiting the Inbetween to test the preparations Nowell has made, so why don't you go first so we can observe your technique."

Kyran nodded, taking a steadying breath as he moved to the center of the sand away from the two of them. He lifted his hand, concentrating on a point before him.

Without warning, the last lantern within the arena winked out, leaving them in a stark darkness lit only by the golden-red glow of Finley's lines. Kyran's skin prickled, his breathing coming faster, and he closed his eyes, focusing all of his intent on shaping his magic, and not how much Finley's lines reminded him of the toothy demon.

There was a sharp crackle as the sand beneath him froze, and he could taste the change in the air as his magic seeped out of his blood. The image of the rope came easily enough and, reluctantly, the vivid charnel house of his imprisonment. Then, gritting his teeth, he pulled.

It was no easier than last time, the darkness flexing and folding, but refusing to tear easily, the pain in his head building and building until it seemed as if a hammer were slamming against the inside of his skull with every heartbeat.

He pulled and pulled until he thought his brains might come splattering out of his head onto the sand, before it finally gave, and he fell into the crushing, hot embrace of the Inbetween.

A whimper of relief slipped past his lips, and he clutched his head, allowing himself a moment to exist as the pain faded.

When he could think again, he gathered his nerves, and pictured his rope, only this time, he needed to pull himself in the opposite direction. He had never quite gotten this far before. Captain Griswold, Nowell, and even Barrett had all taken him from the Inbetween whenever he had entered it before. He'd never needed to move in any direction but deeper, but it should work by the same process, he reasoned. But when he tried to think of the arena or Finley to pull himself back to, the image wouldn't come easily. It had been the same when he'd tried to imagine the endless, floating walkways. He needed something more familiar.

Closing his eyes, he pictured Barrett. Tangled, golden hair, broad shoulders under tatty clothes, and a warm, crooked smile. A stone as unmoving as the bones of a ben.

When he pulled this time, it was easier, the pain less. There was no sensation of tearing, but of the dark simply bending out of his way until the thick heat of the Inbetween vanished. He took a deep breath of the clean night air and opened his eyes to a shroud of white fog lit by blue and yellow light.

"Welcome back," Finley said, materializing at his elbow from the fog. "I suppose it is my turn now. You can take a seat with Nowell and rest."

She pointed behind him, and Kyran joined the captain at the base of the stairs as power began to swell in the arena. The fog rolled and swirled, dissipating as the air turned warm, and then hot. Finley stood where Kyran had been, hands clasped before her, every inch of exposed skin glowing like yellow moonlight. The air grew warmer and warmer, building into a furnace until Finley vanished.

It was…unnerving to witness, despite anticipating it.

"You might as well relax while she's in there," Nowell noted, reclining on the stairs. "It will be a little while before she returns."

A little while became nearly an hour before Finley returned and joined Kyran on the stair while Nowell stepped up for his turn.

"Hopefully, next time, Nowell will agree it is a better use of our time to attempt to bring all three of us at once and work on discovering how to reach the demon realm instead of practicing like this," Finley remarked as they waited for the guild captain's return. "That is the goal, after all."

Kyran mumbled an affirmative, fumbling in his purse for the bit of wood he had been saving.

"What's that?"

He held out the shapeless bit, drawing his knife from his boot. "Ta pass the time."

"How charming. What are you going to make?"

He considered the wood, imagining what it might be, and felt the first inkling of a calling. "A charm," he said, scoring a rough shape into the surface of the wood.

Finley laughed. "I suppose I should have seen that coming. Do you mind if I watch?"

"I dinnae."

The night continued much the same, the three of them trading out practicing going into the Inbetween. It was easier the second and third time than the first, like climbing through a hole already made. Even so, by the time Nowell finally called their practice done, Kyran was exhausted, teetering on his walking stick.

They parted on the promise Finley would write up a report tomorrow, each going their separate ways.

Collapsing into his bed, Kyran made a solemn oath to work on his amulets as soon as he was awake again, before dropping into a fitful sleep.

CHAPTER TWENTY-FIVE

BARRETT STRAIGHTENED IN his saddle, all the misery of riding an entire week through the rain vanishing at the sight of the capital's walls twinkling ahead.

"Finally. We've made it, Myles."

There was no answer from the wagon. Barrett hoped it was because the Lightbringer was asleep. Myles had improved somewhat on their way back to the guild, but he was far from well.

The guards at the gate waved them through, but they had no sooner set foot within the city that Barrett knew something was wrong.

The streets of the capital were always a marvel. Not just the architecture and towering lanterns that lined the streets, but the sense of safety the citizens felt to still be out walking after nightfall. At this time of day back in Oareford and elsewhere, most folk would be in their homes, nursing their hearths and lighting candles in every room. But here, many people would still strolling about together, laughing as they went to find a pint while the lamplighters went about their business with long poles sporting lit wicks on the end to light the streets and ward off any demons.

At least, they should be.

A pall rested over the city. Barely half the lamps were lit, and what people were in the streets sat huddled beneath the strangely scant pools of light from the streetlamps and what made it through the cracks of shutters on houses. People that appeared to have nowhere else to go and who glowered at him as he passed, a few spitting curses his way, though none were so bold as to approach him.

Then, they reached the fires—blackened skeletons of buildings left to crumble and fall and the lingering scent of wet heat and char. Barrett's hands went slick and cold, his pulse thudding against his ribs. A demon. It had to be. And Kyran… It was a coincidence. There was no way it was the same demon. Unless…

He glanced aside at Griswold, who had for his part been silent for much of the journey, his attention divided by the missives he received and sent with the couriers that always found them along the roads. He wanted to believe the captain would have told him if anything like that had happened here, and yet… "Griswold—"

"Here, Captain." From out of the foggy dark, Nowell appeared, accompanied by several other guardsmen.

"I take it things have not settled, then," Griswold remarked from beneath his hood.

"Quite the contrary," Nowell said, directing his men to form up around the wagon. "Keep close and don't stop."

"Wait. What's—"

"I'll explain once we're inside," Nowell said, moving to take a position by Griswold's mount.

Barrett started to insist he tell him now, when he heard them. People, chanting and shouting.

They'd all gathered around the outside of the guildhall, fists raised as he and the others entered the street just before the guildhall.

Demons and witches! Lords of lies! Get out of our city! Get out of our lives!

Barrett touched his hands to reassure himself his gloves were still on, looking between his other guild members to make certain he wasn't the only one hearing what they were chanting. Graces, what in the world was going on? It felt like all of Tennebrum had gone mad in the last few months.

"Quickly, quickly!" Nowell barked as they thundered in through the archway, and waiting guardsmen shut the gates behind them.

The relief from the noise was immediate, the heavy gates sealing the outside world away.

"We'll handle getting the Lightbringer to the hospital," Nowell said, taking the reins of the wagon horse to keep it steady. "Griswold, Selah wants to speak with you right away. Barrett, report to the hospital if you have injuries, otherwise, you are dismissed for food and rest. Report to the library in the morning with a report."

Barrett groaned. Of course, there would be a report. He swung down out of his saddle and handed his reins off to Nowell. The guards quickly and efficiently worked to lift Myles from the wagon on the same stretcher they had carried Kyran in on.

Guilt settled heavy on Barrett's shoulders. Both of them could have been spared if he had just been faster, or stronger. Instead, Kyran had suffered all that time in the demon realm, and Myles… Graces, the man might not recover.

"Your mage is probably in the ward," the guard captain said after a moment, nodding in the direction of the children's ward with a smirk. "He's been spending his free time there visiting his kid."

"Effie?"

"That's the one. Go on. We can handle this one. I'm certain you're both looking forward to seeing each other again."

Barrett smiled before he could stop himself. Despite the circumstances that had brought him, he was glad to be back. "You behave," he told Sweetheart, patting her neck fondly. "Maybe there will be some berries for you soon."

The mare snorted, nudging his hand, and he gently tickled her nose.

"Not yet. But maybe tomorrow. If you're nice to my friend when I bring him to visit, I'll give you something special."

Sweetheart let out a warm puff of air against his glove, and looked away, ears pricking as she watched more volunteers unload the remaining supplies from the back of the wagon.

With a last pat on her shoulder, Barrett finally turned away and started across the lawn towards the ward.

Chapter Twenty-Six

"YOU SHOULD TALK to the chirurgeons about their sleep remedy," Sophie said as she lowered into the seat opposite Kyran.

"Oh, aye?" Kyran replied, looking up from the fire he had been watching flicker over the logs in the fireplace. He'd given up on sleep that evening, and been caught out wandering by Alf carrying supper to the ward with several of the other older weans, and invited him back. Kyran had resisted, feeling he might not be welcome to intrude more than he already did, and Alf had simply assured him Effie would like to see him more. Kyran's resistance crumbled.

It was an honest relief to see Effie every day, well and happy amidst the orderly chaos of the other weans. Whatever else had gone right or wrong in his life, this at least was something good.

"I had to take it when I hurt my back a few years ago," Sophie continued. "Couldn't sleep for anything with it like that, and nothing was helping it. One cup of that tea, and I was in the Graces' hands. I know it's easy to dismiss potions and powders, but sometimes we need a little help."

Kyran stared down into his lap, blood creeping up into his cheeks. "It isna so bad."

She squinted one eye, giving him a critical look. "If you say so. I might still have a little on hand if you'd like to try it. Or some of my own special blends. I think you might like some honey bush or perhaps some mint. They're both very lovely to have by a fire."

"What are they?"

"Oh, they're teas, dear."

"Teas?" They didn't sound anything like the tea his ma made whenever he was at home—barley sweetened with honey and sometimes a few berries.

"Yes. As a matter of fact, I keep a pot going in the kitchen when the weather starts to turn. I'll just go and fetch us some."

"Oh, ye dinnae have ta—"

"Nonsense." She waved him off and she got up from her seat. "I think a spot of tea sounds lovely. You just wait right there—"

She was interrupted by a knock at the door, and Moira sprang up from her seat at the table, racing to answer it. A blast of chill, moist air rolled across the ward, the sound of rain turning to a roar. Moira chimed an excited, "Hello!" that pierced through the rain before turning to smile at Kyran. "Someone's looking for you."

Kyran's grip tightened on his walking stick, nails digging into the wood as a figure stepped into the ward, closing the door behind them. His spine stiffened as they looked at him through wet strings of yellow hair, smiling broadly.

"Good evenin'," Barrett greeted in a tired, but pleasant tone. He swiped a hand over his face to get the rain water off, sweeping his hair away from a very bruised face. "Nowell said I might find you here."

Kyran sat, frozen and staring, unable to discern what exactly he was feeling from the tumult of emotion seeing the hunter was stirring in him, only that it ached fiercely.

"I'm sorry for the mess," Barrett said, looking down at the puddle forming under his dripping clothes.

"That's all right. We're used to it in here," Sophie assured him, rising stiffly from her seat. "Let me get a few rags."

The hunter lingered by the door, grinning sheepishly. There was a deep cut that ran from his cheek and over the bridge of his nose, the skin around it and in random spots across his forehead and cheeks mottled by greenish bruises. It was almost unreal that the hunter could be standing right in front of him.

"Sorry I didn't, ah, write ahead that I was on my way," Barrett said after a long beat of silence. "Well, I did write, but we left before I could post it."

"A—aye," Kyran managed to force past the knot in his throat. He felt ill. Too hot and too cold all at once, his face and eyes burning, fingers working themselves numb over his walking stick. He needed a moment, air, something to clear his head before he unraveled.

"Kyran?" The hunter's smile faltered and his brows creased. "Are you all right?"

"Aye." Kyran lurched up out of his seat, clutching his stick hard as the room faded in and out of focus.

"I guess it is late." Barrett chuckled.

"Aye, I…need ta sleep."

"Oh, I can walk you back to the dorms," Barrett offered.

"No, I…" Kyran scrambled to come up with a reason, even as he lifted the latch of the door. "It's fine."

"It's no trouble," Barrett insisted. He might have said something else, but Kyran opened the door to the deafening sound of torrential rain.

Fog swirled up around him as he fled, rain turning to ice, piling up in his hair, along his sleeves, and the tops of his boot, mud crackling with every step. It wasn't until his door clicked shut behind him that he realized Barrett hadn't followed him. He was alone, and it wasn't the comfort he hoped it would be.

"Curse it all," he whispered, rubbing at his eyes when he felt the first grain of ice build at the corners. "Curse this whole place ta the Pit."

CHAPTER TWENTY-SEVEN

BARRETT'S CHEST ACHED as the ward door swung shut. He had imagined seeing Kyran again would have been a relief. Not just for him, but the mage too. He had expected a smile, or at least a sarcastic barb. Not this.

"Where's he going?" he heard a child whine at his side and looked down to see Moira. And next to her was Effie, eyes watering as she lowered her head.

"Oh, sweetheart," Barrett sighed and knelt before reaching to touch the girl's shoulder. "He's not mad at you. You didn't do anything wrong." Effie picked up her head to look at him, but didn't smile. She just wiped at her cheeks and eyes.

"That's right," the warden spoke up behind him. "He just needed a little fresh air."

"But it's raining!" Moira pointed out loudly. "He'll get wet!"

"I'll make certain he's all right," Barrett assured her, levering himself up with a groan. Everything ached.

"I think—" The older woman set her hand against his arm. "I think we should give Kyran some room. Things have not been easy since he arrived."

"What happened?"

The warden shook her head. "I don't rightly know, and it wouldn't be my place to say anyway, but he's been troubled. Perhaps he wasn't ready to be surprised?"

Barrett let out a resigned sigh. He had been looking forward to seeing Kyran since they had separated. He couldn't imagine what could have happened to make the mage make that face at him. He'd looked faintly terrified, like he had on the ship when he'd woken with no idea of where he was. Could the nightmares have gotten worse?

"You're right," he conceded. "I should— I should go. We just got back and I haven't really had a hot meal, or a bed…"

"Or soap," the warden added with a dramatic wave of her hand in front of her nose. Moira giggled at the gesture. "You go on. I'm certain everyone will be in better spirits tomorrow."

Barrett smiled thinly, clinging to the hope in her words. Tomorrow. He'd try again tomorrow, when the sun was high.

He reached to ruffle Effie's hair. "I'll see you soon, all right? Be good and listen to your warden." The girl gave the barest nod that she understood him. Barrett adjusted his coat before he opened the door and ducked out against the sluicing rain, finally breaking into a run for the dormitories. What had started as a drizzle late last night had finally turned into a fully-fledged storm.

"Cursed rain." He scowled, yanking the door open and nearly catching his head on the lintel before he remembered to bend lower.

Water pooled in an instant at his feet, and his boots sloshed as he moved to one side to wipe the rain from his eyes. He felt a wistful pang for the Drunken Wind. What he wouldn't give for a hot fire and as much warm drink as he could put down, especially the drink. Maybe he should go to the mess first before he tried to get some sleep.

He'd barely finished thinking the idea before he turned to grab the door again, only to miss the latch as someone else pulled it open.

"Kristopher?"

Barrett blinked, almost not believing what was clearly standing right before his eyes. "Kat?"

He hadn't seen his sister since leaving for the Isles with Kyran, and he wasn't certain how he felt about seeing her now, the heat of their argument in Oareford still warm in his memory, even as she smiled at him.

"Where—What are you doing here?" he asked as she pushed inside. She was dressed well for travel—sturdy leather boots covered in mud, thick trousers, even a jerkin that hid her blouse, and a heavy cloak over her shoulders to keep the rain off.

"I live here, in case you forgot. Shouldn't I be asking you that?" she said rather pointedly, reaching up to wring water from her braid. He hadn't seen her with her hair fully up in years. She'd taken to wearing it down to hide the scarred half of her face.

"I just got back."

She frowned suspiciously, tossing her braid back over her shoulder. "Did something happen? I've heard some of the rumors of what happened in the Isles, and some of the trouble your mage has been causing, but I haven't met him yet. It isn't related to that, is it?"

Barrett's stomach knotted. "Kyran? What happened with him?"

Her brows went up. "Oh, you must have *just* gotten back."

"That's what I said," Barett insisted.

Kat gave him a flat look and blinked. "Tell you what, you let me put this pack down, and we can talk."

The knot in his belly twisted. He really didn't want to go and chat with his sister, who would inevitably find some excuse to chastise him, probably for drinking. She'd only tried to *talk* to him about it nearly a dozen times in Oareford before she finally stopped coming around the Drunken Wind. "I…"

"Come on, this thing is heavy," she said, starting down the hall without looking back to see if he was following.

He looked at the door, already imagining the warm taste of mead and the soft numbness it always brought him, before he sighed, and turned to follow Kat.

"So, did you and Hammond return to help with the protests?"

Barrett sputtered a moment before he could respond. "The what?"

"I take it not, then."

"What protests?"

She shot him a disbelieving look over her shoulder. "You mean to say you walked in those gates and didn't notice the people gathered out there shouting at us or that half the lamps in the entire city aren't lit?"

"I saw them," he scowled. "But why are they out there?"

"It's not good." She stopped outside of a door, producing a key from someplace under her cloak. "There was a demon attack that burnt half the quarter down and sank a ship in the harbor that was carrying a shipment of oil." She pushed the door in, ducking inside, and Barrett followed.

"Before that, the Crown's ration has been getting tighter and tighter as the oil prices have been getting higher. There's a rumor the Crown is nearly bankrupt at this point." Dropping her pack from her back, she all but fell into a chair. "No one's saying it outright, but if the Crown doesn't find the money soon, Tennebrum will have to give in to whatever demands the Ijeichon Empire might require to continue to supply us with oil, and given how direly we need it, they could ask quite a lot."

The idea of Tennebrum running out of oil was terrifying. "That's ridiculous. We need it for the demons."

"It's politics, I'm afraid."

"Well, why would the people protest against us for that if it's the Empire causing the shortage?"

Kat shrugged. "We have lights and money, and they don't."

"But that doesn't make any sense."

"They're scared, Barrett, and not everyone has forgotten the riots."

Barrett thought of the man in Belldale with the burn scars, the one who had attacked Myles after shouting about the Light. Clearly, not everyone had, but the idea that the two things were connected was fairly farfetched. Right?

"Well, if it wasn't for that, why did you two get sent back?" Kat continued, propping her foot on her knee and prying at the sole of her boot. "I was under the impression things were rather dire in Belldale."

"I—Wait, how did you know I was in Belldale?"

Kat arched her brows at him, smugly amused. "Hammond told me."

"Hamm—He told you?"

"Yes, so I would know where to direct any letters."

"Bastard," Barrett sneered, folding his arms over his chest. Of course, the guild captain had simply *told* Katherine where they were going when *no one* would tell him, even though Barrett was the one going. Next thing he was going to find out Kat and Griswold were secret lovers. He nearly gagged at the thought. It was more reasonable that the two of them were communicating to *keep an eye on him*.

"What is that look for?" She looked amused.

"You…mentioned Kyran has been involved in some sort of trouble?" he said, shifting the conversation.

Kat snorted, leaning to settle her elbows on her knees. "He set the bells off, for one, practicing some sort of magic. Then, there was that attack on the guild, and he apparently impressed Nowell during it." She paused, frowning as she scrutinized Barrett. "Have you…been to the hospital yet? You look like something dragged you out of the Pit this morning."

"I'm fine," Barrett grumbled. "Just need a drink and some sleep."

"You're not *fine*. You look like shit."

"A demon—"

"I don't mean that cut on your face," Kat interrupted. "Have you slept or even eaten recently?"

"What do you care?"

"I care because I don't want you winding up like our father."

"And what is *that* supposed to mean?"

"Bitter, drunk, and with nothing to show for your life outside of how well you served the guild."

"I'm not bitter or a drunk," Barrett snapped. "If all you want to do is criticize me, you can—"

"I didn't say you were," Kat interrupted, raising her voice over his. "But you're well on your way. You think our father was the way he was all his life? He started the same as both of us. He just wanted to help people the same way his father, and his father's father did." She took a deep breath, her face aging in front of him until he hardly recognized her. "The guild is good at doing what it was made to do. It saves lives and protects people, but it does it at the cost of our lives, its hunters."

Barrett's gloves creaked, his nails biting into his palms through the leather. "I'm not quitting."

"I'm not telling you to. Just not to let the guild be your whole life."

"I'm not quitting!"

She sat up, facing him, her face wrought with something like pity, and Barrett had enough.

"If you're just going to lecture me and try to bully me into leaving the guild, then we're done. I've had enough of people telling me what to do just being around Griswold. I don't need more of it."

"Fine!" The pity was gone, replaced in full by the contempt he had always known from her. "Do whatever you want, like you've always done."

"I will!" He turned away, storming out of her room and slamming the door shut behind him. Of course, it had ended in a fight. Kat never could resist the urge to criticize and mock him.

He stalked back down the hall to the door to the outside, and stopped, listening to the rain sluicing down. He didn't want to go to his room, where Kat might come and find him, but his appetite had vanished. He considered just getting a drink to help him sleep after nearly two weeks of barely catching more than a few exhausted hours a night, but even that small pleasure soured with Kat's words.

The drink helped him sleep. Helped him not think. But he always felt worse afterwards, and between Kyran's abrupt standoffish behavior and Kat's chastising, he wasn't in the mood to feel any more miserable. Spitting a curse, he shoved the doors open and stormed back out into the rain. He pushed out the barest amount of magic around him, so that as soon as each drop of rain hit him, it steamed off.

If he couldn't sleep, then at least he could get his Graces' cursed report over with and whatever other paperwork he needed to submit. At the very least, it wouldn't be raining there, and he could take his Graces' cursed boots off.

Chapter Twenty-Eight

BARRETT DIDN'T RECOGNIZE the young woman behind the desk at the library, and she spared him hardly more than a glance as he passed her to enter the winding stacks. It took him a bit to remember how to get to the scholars' study, but at last, he found the corner of the library where several desks had been arranged with readily available materials for writing.

He gathered a few sheafs of parchment from a drawer, and settled at one of the desks with a sigh. As much as he wanted this over with quickly, his head was already pounding trying to think of how to word his report. Maybe he should start with something else. There was still the matter of his transfer request to have his station moved to the guildhall, as Alex had reminded him. He'd meant to submit it the moment he and Kyran got back from Avonmouth before everything had gone entirely wrong.

Staring at the parchment, he tried to quote what he thought the captains might want to hear—about the rising frequency of demon appearances and missing persons, and his own experiences in dealing with demons over the last six months, how he would be a boon to the capital. But the more he tried to extrapolate on his reasoning, the more it felt like he was making up excuses, when what he really wanted to write was, "I don't want to. There's nothing worth going back for."

Alex would have laughed at him. He missed having her help with phrasing his official documentation for the guild, but he strongly suspected he wasn't likely to see her again anytime soon, as busy as Belldale must be keeping her.

"Good evening, Barrett."

Barrett started nearly out of his seat, almost upending the bottle of ink. He glared at Ilham, who giggled as she approached his desk, peering at his draft over the heavy stack of tomes she carried.

"What a surprise to see you here," she said, shifting the tomes in her arms to push her spectacles back up her nose.

"Afternoon," Barrett mumbled awkwardly. "I was just…working."

"Something official, then?"

"Yes. I'm afraid I'm not very good at it, though. Back in Oareford, there was a courier who always helped me with my reports."

"Oh, you mean Alex?"

Barrett's eyes darted up at the woman. "You know Alex?"

"Of course I know her." Ilham chuckled, setting her books down and pulling a chair around to sit across from Barrett. "She writes very prettily."

He smiled, feeling a little charmed at having found a mutual acquaintance and more than a little curious how the two knew each other. "I suppose I am a little helpless with getting these words on paper."

"I'm rather adept at teaching literacy. What are you working on?"

"I'm writing a motion for transfer."

"Ah, I see." Her dark brows rose and she pressed her lips together as she reached for the parchment. She set her fingertips to it and looked at him in question until he nodded. She skimmed over it, humming occasionally in a neutral tone he could not decipher. "This isn't bad," she said at last. "It's a little unorganized but that's easy to fix. May I see your quill?"

Barrett was surprised. Perhaps he had picked up a thing or two from Alex after all. He passed the quill to Ilham and moved the inkwell to her side of the desk. "Do you think they'll accept it?"

"It's very likely," she said without explanation and dipped the quill in before setting it to the parchment. She circled a phrase he had written and drew an arrow up over a few lines. "I'll see what we can salvage from this and we'll start on fresh parchment."

"I would appreciate that," he admitted around his fluster.

Even with Alex's help, a letter to the guild could have taken a few hours. But Barrett had the request finished, signed, sealed, and ready to deliver to the chancery so it could be taken up the proper channels for approval in less than an hour with Ilham's revision.

"Thank you," he said sincerely.

"Of course. Before you go, though, I wanted to talk to you about some things, if you're not busy. It's about the Old One," she said quietly. "I wanted to speak to you about it after you returned, but I read the reports. Your friend… Is he all right?"

Barrett picked his words carefully. "He's…been through a lot. Too much. But he's recovering. I know he'll be okay, but he needs time."

"Time helps," Ilham agreed. "So do friends. I know we'll need to conduct an interview with him eventually, but the things the report was describing… It can't be easy to speak about. Perhaps, when the time comes, we can have you sit in with us."

Barrett inclined his head, though he wasn't certain how much his presence would help Kyran. Maybe it was a question better asked of the mage. "You were sayin' about the Old One, though?" the hunter prompted, changing the subject.

"Oh! Yes, right!" Ilham got up from her chair and picked up her stack of books again. "Just let me put these away. I'll be back in just a moment."

"I'll be here," he said as she ducked out of sight. He thought she'd return right away, but when she didn't, he settled back into his chair and resisted the urge to pick the quill up and scribble on the parchment to pass the time.

At last, she scurried back into sight, a stack of papers in her hand, spectacles balanced on the end of her nose. "I'm sorry that took so long," she said, taking her seat across from him again.

"It's all right," Barrett assured her as he reached for the first paper on the pile, eager and curious to see what she had found. "I 'ppreciate your help. I know you've got other things you could be doin' instead of helpin' me do research."

"Of course. But—" She pulled the stack out of his reach, her smile sobering. "This is… Well, I have been instructed only to give this to you under a few conditions."

That sounded serious, but very like the guild. "What is it?"

"This," she tapped the stack of papers, "is a copy of all of the guild's knowledge about the Old One. The guild believes it would be beneficial for you, due to your…proximity to Kyran."

The hunter raised his brows at her choice in words. "And what *are* these conditions?"

"They want information. About Kyran."

"What…" He leaned back in his chair, the wood groaning with his weight. "What do you mean? Can't they just talk to him? That's what interviews are for, right?"

"And you saw how well it went in the Isles,"

"In the Isles—" She couldn't mean… "Just how much do you know about what went on up there?"

"I have reviewed everything that was recorded for the guild's records. For privacy, much of it has been removed from the transcriptions available for anyone to access in the library."

Barrett felt the blood drain from his face. "You can't mean… What Kyran told us about… About what happened to him?"

Ilham swallowed, looking down at the desk, her own face paling. "That was removed."

But not from the records. "Kyran told us that in confidence."

"It needed to be recorded to justify the guild's payment to the laird—"

"He trusted us," Barrett growled, his voice raising. "Trusted me that what he told us wouldn't leave that room."

"It is only for the records. It won't be—"

"Read by every scholar and guild captain around?" Barrett all but shouted. "I don't know who—" Barrett stopped himself, his fists clenching until he felt his nails bite skin. "Griswold wrote it, didn't he?" He didn't have to hear her answer. It couldn't have been anyone else. That bastard. There wasn't a low he was above stooping to. "Why should I help you?"

Ilham fingered the corner of the pages, folding them back and forth. "They don't believe it would be helpful or useful to try to ask Kyran directly again. But, since you're his friend, they assumed you would be able to answer their questions."

"I'm not saying a Graces' cursed thing without him standin' next to me. What more could they possibly want to know?"

She tapped the papers against the desk, her eyes moving over the writing. "How much does Kyran know about his parentage?"

"I don't know. I mean, I've met his parents. His entire family. Back in the Isles." Barrett watched the librarian fidget with the papers, straightening them against the edge of the desk. "You're— You're not askin' about them, are you?"

A strange expression creased her mouth and brows for a moment, almost a grimace. "No." Her fingers tightened until the edges of the papers crinkled before she let out a tight sigh. "How much do *you* know about mages?"

"About the same as anyone else in the guild, I imagine. I mean…it's passed down through bloodlines."

"Well, you're not quite right." She turned over the first sheet, revealing a sketch of the Old One staring off the page. "The Old One isn't Kyran's ancestor. It's his sire."

Chapter Twenty-Nine

A KEEN, FAMILIAR throbbing dragged Kyran from the pleasant nothing of his sleep. Peeling his cheek off the rough surface of the table, he slowly eased himself upright, loosening his hold on his magic until pain in his back and hips dulled to something bearable.

"Oh stars," he slurred, his tongue still thick in his head with sleep. He arched his back, trying to stretch his stiff muscles. Glancing down, he found his knife and the tiny sun he had been carving resting on the table before him. He hadn't meant to fall asleep at the table, only get in a bit more work to stave off the nightmares, but apparently he had misjudged how worn out he was.

His walking stick was propped up against another chair within easy reach. He dragged it to him, digging his nail into the scorched wood as he tried to decide what to do. He knew he was hiding by staying in there, but he just couldn't bring himself to face Barrett, couldn't bear to face the anger and the hurt and other things it stirred in him. After everything Barrett had done to save him, the hunter had still lied, just like every other person Kyran had known. Even his family.

But this was his home now. He had nowhere else to go. He was a bondsman and a mage. He had the guild and nothing else. A guild Barrett also belonged to. A guild full of other hunters. Other witches.

There would be no escaping that truth.

Kyran hung his head in his hands, trying to scrape together the will to rise and leave his room when his belly let out a long, plaintive growl of protest. He pressed a hand to his middle, scowling with embarrassment, and pulled himself up out of the chair. He had to catch himself against the table as his back and hip let out twin complaints, and he took a steadying breath, only for his stomach to interrupt again.

"Aye, I hear ye," he grumbled, fishing out his borrowed kerchief, when something shifted on top of his bed.

He choked on a gasp, and for a split second, Kyran felt his heart stop.

It couldn't be— Not again.

The blankets stirred again before a small, dark head poked out from beneath the bedcovers, and Kyran sagged in relief.

"Stars above, lass. Ye near did me in."

She blinked owlishly up at him before sitting up with an enormous yawn.

He leaned into his walking stick, trying to figure out just how she had gotten in. "I dinnae suppose this is a planned venture by your warden?"

Effie beamed up at him, and he couldn't help but chuckle. He supposed she must have missed him.

He reached to ruffle her hair, and fair laughed at the tousled mess. "Let's see if we can do something about that mane of yours before I take you back or Sophie will be even more cross"

She scooted closer as he sank onto the side of the bed, turning so her back was to him. Taking up his comb from the side table, he started picking at the snarls as gingerly as he could.

"Stars above, did you let a cow go at it?" he chuckled in disbelief. "It's as bad as Barrett's most days."

Effie peeked over her shoulder at the familiar name.

"Aye, you ken him. Great big daft idiot with straw hair."

"*Ee-dot,*" Effie mimed back.

Kyran almost choked. "Aye," he laughed. "Aye, that's the word."

"*Ee-dot,*" she repeated with glee. "*Kee-rin?*"

"No, na Kyran. Barrett."

"*Ber-ret.*"

"Aye. Barrett. I dinnae ken if I've met a man with less sense. Except Murray." Kyran took a moment to free the comb from a particularly bad snarl, then continued, prattling to the lass about whatever came to mind. But somehow, his topic of conversation kept circling back to Barrett.

"I swear he'd jump off the highest *ben* if he thought it would help someone," he said, running the comb from top to bottom through the lass's hair, pleased when it only caught in one place. "There you go, lass. Fine as any sunrise."

She patted her hair, beaming up at him. "Tank oo."

Kyran's smile widened, an unfamiliar warmth trickling through his chest. "You are verrah welcome. When it gets longer, we'll have ta braid it ta keep it from turning inta a snowberry bush."

The lass's giggle was interrupted by a firm knock at the door.

"Your warden, I ken." Or Barrett.

But when he opened the door, it was Nowell and Captain Griswold. The captain must have returned with Barrett.

"Afternoon," Nowell greeted him. "May we come in?"

"Aye," Kyran said, looking between the two as he stepped out of the way.

"We just have some questions," Griswold said once Kyran had closed the door. The guild captain looked nearly as haggard as he had in the Isles after they had escaped the Inbetween. His clothing was neat, but he stood with more of a slouch than before, the lines at the corners of his eyes and mouth more pronounced, and there was a shadow of a beard along his jaw. It made him look much older.

"To start with, what is this little one doing here?" Nowell asked, gesturing to Effie, who watched them from across the room

"I ken she snuck out of the ward."

"Not the first time either," Nowell noted with a chuckle.

"Is this what you came ta talk ta me about?" Kyran asked curtly, drumming his fingers against his walking stick.

Griswold shot Nowell a quelling look. "No. It concerns the report drafted based on the interview you gave for the demon attack that originated in the city."

"Oh, aye?" Kyran prompted, watching as Nowell dragged the chairs at the table around and sat in one.

"Take a seat," the guard captain said, gesturing to the bed. "No point in standing around. Plenty of that to do these days. And nights."

Hesitantly, Kyran lowered himself onto his bedside and tucked his walking stick in the crook of his arm. Effie edged behind Kyran, clinging to his arm as she peeked around him.

Griswold took the last seat at the table next to Nowell.

Kyran watched the men's faces, but it was impossible to read the air. He shifted uncomfortably on the bed, unable to shake the sense they were there to reprimand him for something, though he couldn't think of anything he might have done.

Griswold plucked a heavy envelope from the inside of his coat, and Kyran's skin pimpled with gooseflesh. The guild captain removed several folded papers from within, flattening them over his knee. "In your report, there was a reference included to an unusual use of magic against one of the abominations you faced. Could you describe it for us?"

Kyran tugged the end of his sleeves down his wrists out of old habit, looking from one man's face to the other. "What's this about?"

"We're not asking because you did anything wrong," Nowell said, shooting Griswold a wry look. "We're hoping you might be able to do it again."

"Aye. I can. I've done it before."

Both men's brows shot up.

"In the Inbetween in the Isles," Kyran elaborated. "That's where I first learned it."

"And just what is *it?*" Nowell asked.

Kyran tried to explain in a way they might understand without making him sound absolutely out of his head mad. He didn't know how hunters experienced magic or their own demons, or what it was like for them to face down an enemy demon, so he started in the same place he had when forming the idea.

"You ken how demons can…get in a man's head, aye?" The men nodded. "I do that ta the demon."

"With your cold magic?" Nowell asked, skeptical.

"No, it is…" Stars, how could Kyran describe it? "—a different sort of magic. Like the kind I use ta enter the Inbetween."

Griswold tapped the papers. "Are you able to discern the demon from the man when you attempt this magic?"

Kyran shook his head. "I dinnae ken if I can or na. I dinnae have a lot of time."

"Could you with more time?" Griswold pressed.

Kyran lifted his palms, and shrugged. "I dinnae ken," he repeated. "I havena tried."

The two men exchanged another look. Griswold looked unconvinced about something.

Nowell shrugged, then leaned back in his seat. "We have a proposition we would like you to consider," he said. "It may be our only way of preventing what is coming."

"And what is that?" Kyran asked.

"A lot," Nowell said through a yawn, gesturing to Griswold.

The guild captain tilted his head, holding Kyran's gaze. "You must first swear not to tell anyone what we discuss. It is vitally important that this conversation not leave this room."

More secrets. Kyran wrinkled his nose in distaste. "Is that so?" he challenged.

Griswold's eyes narrowed. "It is. If you will not agree, then our conversation is—"

"Just tell the boy," Nowell interrupted, earning a dry glance from the guild captain.

"Do you swear?" Griswold asked again, and Nowell rolled his eyes.

Kyran narrowed his eyes, reaching to take Effie's hand with a gentle squeeze. He didn't like this one bit, but he'd rather hear the lies then continue to have his eyes closed to them. "Aye."

"Good." Taking another breath, Griswold described their plan.

Chapter Thirty

BARRETT SAGGED IN his chair, knees bumping the hospital cot next to him. He felt ragged and exhausted, his head pounding with every little movement, but he couldn't stop his thoughts from circling after that conversation with Ilham. He'd told her no, of course, but by every Grace, he hoped Kyran never found out.

You dinnae ken the first thing about me.

Barrett rubbed his face. Blessed Lumen, everyday proved that truer and truer. He was such an idiot.

He heard a sigh and lowered his hand to see Myles awake, turning to look at him.

"Mornin'," Barrett said, moving his seat closer.

"Is it morning again?" Myles mumbled, smiling weakly up at Barrett. "It seems it's always morning."

Barrett managed to return the jest with a weak smile of his own. "How're you feelin' today?" he asked, turning away to pour a cup of water from the jug at the bedside.

"Grateful, as Grace would demand, but I believe I might summarize my other feelings as *oof.*" He shifted tenderly on the cushions he'd been propped up on and took the cup, his gnarled hands shaking.

The hunter winced at the sight, the guilt that haunted him every minute since he had failed to protect the Lightbringer sticking thickly in his throat. Graces, it was a miracle Myles had survived at all.

You might have managed if you had more training, a hideous whisper slid through his thoughts, and Barrett's hand twitched almost of its own accord to swat the voice away. *I could teach you.*

"Now, don't go making those faces on my account," Myles said, patting Barrett's hand in reassurance, the hand marred by the hunter's black witchmarks. "These things happen, especially in a life like mine. I had honestly expected it to come when I was younger, but I suppose it is difficult to plan for misfortune. These things take time to gain momentum."

"I didn't realize Lightbringer's lived such daring lives," Barrett joked weakly.

Myles raised both shaggy brows, pursing his lips in wry amusement. "Oh, you know very well I meant my life before the cloth. I upset a great many people in my youth. And a few more as I've gotten older." His face creased with a broad, chagrined smile. "Wiser doesn't mean faultless. Don't you forget that."

It was hard to imagine the Lightbringer as anything other than wise and faultless. Barrett clasped the Lightbringer's hand, trying not to notice how frail and papery it felt. "I'll do my best."

"Good. That's all we really can do, anyway." Myles sank into his cushions with a raspy sigh, patting his chest beneath the quilt pulled up almost to his chin. "It's here a wiser and better Lightbringer would tell you to be content with your circumstances, but I haven't met a day that wasn't improved in some way by a nip of old medicine or hot tea, preferably both."

Barrett chuckled. "I can ask one of the orderlies to bring you some hot tea, but I can't promise I can sneak a nip of *medicine* in for you."

"I suppose I will have to settle for just the tea, then. When do you think we will reach the guild?"

Barrett's smile faltered at the question. "What do you mean?"

"Oh, I just thought we might be there soon."

"Myles… We *are* at the guild. We arrived last night. You're in the hospital."

"Am I?" The Lightbringer looked around, as if just noticing his surroundings for the first time. "Well, bless my bones. Would you believe I've never been inside the guild's walls before?"

"Now why do I find that surprising, of everything you've told me?"

Myles' nose wrinkled with mirth. "Next thing you know, I'll be telling tales of how I've never been sailing, or that I like to stand on my head every sunrise."

"Graces, how will I ever know?" Barrett laughed. "I'm sorry I don't have any exciting tales to spin for you."

"Oh, that's not true," Myles insisted. "You've had a number of adventures, and you're still young."

Barrett tried to laugh and smile at the Lightbringer, but something about the statement stung. He wasn't certain everything he had gone through—everything Kyran had gone through—could be called *adventures*.

"That is quite the frown, young man."

"Hm? Oh, it's nothing. Just tired," Barrett excused.

"That much is obvious, but what else is troubling you? Is your friend all right? Have you gone and seen him?"

"Who? Kyran? I haven't… He seemed well." The Lightbringer tilted his head, and Barrett winced at being caught in a half-truth. "I think he's upset with me."

"And why would he feel that way after you haven't been here?"

Barrett picked at a hole he hadn't noticed in his trousers, unraveling the thread. "I don't know." There was a pregnant pause, and Barrett's belly coiled in nameless anxiety.

"If you are certain there isn't anything you can think of, perhaps you could ask him," the Lightbringer prodded gently.

"I'm not good at talkin'," Barrett said, rolling the thread between his gloved fingers. "I always say the wrong thing or not enough or too much. Especially to Kyran."

"Perhaps, but you cannot expect to know your friend's mind without asking, and you cannot expect him to know yours if you do not speak."

"It's not that easy. I always seem to set him off, and I never know why or what might do it."

There was another pause, and the cot creaked before Myles' hand settled on Barrett's shoulder. "These things take time and care. You haven't known Kyran very long. I imagine there is much for you both to learn about one another. Even if you do not get it right at first, if you wish to continue being friends, you will both have to open yourselves to each other. Secrets make for poor friends."

"I don't mean to keep secrets," Barrett said, his voice small as he pressed the heel of his hand to his forehead where an ache had begun in earnest. "I just…don't know what needs to be said."

"It doesn't have to come all at once. I imagine it will take a lot of practice. You seem like someone that hasn't had many people he can share his burdens with."

A bitter chuckle gathered at the back of Barrett's tongue, and he swallowed it down. Apart from Myles, he hadn't confided in anyone since Raleigh died. There had been no one else but ale and mead to comfort him.

But maybe that had, in a way, been his fault. He had decided he would rather feel nothing all those months than the bleeding hurt where Raleigh had once been. And he was still living that way. Living demon to demon, drink to drink. It kept the hurt buried, but he didn't know how much longer he could keep going, or if he could stop. He couldn't go back to the way he was that night, cradling Raleigh's bloody body against him, but he didn't know how to move on. If he could. If he wanted to.

"I don't know where to even start," he said, his voice cracking.

"Well, first, you might ask what is troubling your friend. That ought to give you some sense of direction."

Barrett did laugh then, a soft, watery cough. "All right."

"Good. I wish you the best, Kristopher. I know things have been troubling—"

The Lightbringer was interrupted by a light knock, and Barrett twisted in his seat, quickly swiping at his eyes, to see Tacita stepping in. She looked much the same as Barrett recalled, dressed in her canvas coat with a scarf covering her calico patched hair.

"Afternoon, hunter," she greeted him, coming up to the opposite side of Myles' bed. "And hello, Lightbringer. How are we doing today?"

"I would be quite happy to vanish an entire loaf of bread with a pot of tea," Myles said cheerily. "Ah, but, and this might be my old mind failing me, but what is your name, dear?"

"Tacita," the chirurgeon answered without missing a beat, peering into Myles' face. "How is your head?"

"Oh, it still feels very much like I fell down and hit it, but not quite as thunderous as it has been."

"That's good to hear. Hunter, if you don't mind, I need to examine the Lightbringer, and he needs to rest."

"Of course," Barrett said, standing quickly. "I'll be back soon as I can," he told Myles

"Oh, take your time, Kristopher. I promise not to go off cavorting while you do what you need to do," Myles assured him, smiling warmly.

Barrett tried to smile back, but it was hard to manage around the tight knot in his throat. If he'd only been faster… "All right."

Ducking out of the room, he hurried towards the stairs before the knot could choke him, when he saw a flash of copper ahead of him.

Kyran.

He swallowed, coming to a stop on the stairs, a thousand doubts swarming him. What if? What if? What if?

What if this was his only chance to make whatever had happened right?

"Oh, curse the Graces," Barrett muttered, and hurried down the stairs.

Chapter Thirty-One

Nowell and Griswold's words sat heavy with Kyran as he left the hospital, his leg tended. He wished he could feel proud or even important to be involved, but he kent very well why they had asked him, and not a hunter.

Only a demon can kill a demon.

"Kyran?"

The skin at the back of Kyran's neck and up and down both arms prickled as he turned at the voice he knew well. "Barrett."

The hunter smiled, the expression strained. "I need to talk to you."

Kyran dug his nails into his walking stick, a stone dropping from between his ribs into his belly. Not now. There was too much. He wasn't… Not now. "I dinnae—"

"Please. I don't know what's going on, or what has happened since I've been gone. I need to talk to you."

"Oh, aye. Now you do," Kyran snapped, shrinking at the inquisitive looks from the other people waiting in the hospital's entrance.

Barrett's smile vanished. "What do you mean now I do? You left when I came to see you last night, and I haven't seen you all day."

"Aye, and I dinnae have time now."

"You don't have time? Not to catch up? Not a hello? What is—" Kyran turned away, and Barrett stepped in front of him, blocking the door. "Kyran, what's goin' on? Talk to me."

The frustration, the betrayal, and the raw horror Kyran had felt as the lies he had been fed—that he had sustained himself with for years—had crumbled came roiling up out of him in a vicious fury that set his lines glowing. "Why? I dinnae ken what ta ask first. Ye and this whole star blighted place and your secrets."

The hunter's expression tightened, but he didn't budge. "Kyran," he said the mage's name quietly, gently even. "What happened?"

"I found out. About mages. About demons. About hunters. This guild… It's a lie. Everything ye have told everyone is a lie."

"It's not like that," Barrett said quickly, his voice dropping very low as he looked down the hall. "Listen, I didn't—There's a reason. I wanted to tell you, but I—I didn't want to alarm you—"

"So, it's true?" Kyran cut him off. "About my da? And the amulet you wear—Is there a demon in there?"

The hunter paled, his hand drifting to his chest, where the shape of his amulet lay beneath his tattered tunic. "Kyran, it's not what you think. There are laws. Guild laws. It would've been considered treason if I—"

"So, it's true, then?"

"Kyran, please, we can go back to my room or yours, and we'll talk. I'll tell you everything. I promise. Please."

The soft plea in the hunter's voice cut at Kyran. He wanted to believe Barrett, wanted to believe in something, but how many times had he caught the hunter lying to him now, or simply withholding information? What was to say anything else Barrett told him would be the whole truth? "I…"

"Ah, Hunter Barrett? Associate Kyran?" The lad that had taken Kyran to the ward and brought him messages appeared beside them, his brown hair sticking in every direction.

"That's us," Barrett answered before Kyran could muster a response.

"Captain Griswold has requested you both meet him at the college. Says it's urgent."

Barrett groaned. "This better not be about that bloody report. We'll head that way, Alf."

Alf bobbed in a quick bow, and Kyran watched as he trotted away to deliver another message.

"I…suppose we'd better go," Barrett said after a moment. "I meant what I said, though. After we see what Griswold wants, we can get a drink and just…talk."

Kyran wrapped his hand around his walking stick, his nails cutting into the wood as he started down the path. "As you say."

Chapter Thirty-Two

THE SILENCE SAT tangible and heavy between Barrett and Kyran as they crossed the guildhall. Despite knowing he should say something, Barrett simply couldn't find the words. He knew what he wanted to say—that he was sorry, that the guild had forbidden him, that he had planned to tell Kyran everything once he was a hunter. But it was all too late, just like last time, only last time had nearly cost Kyran his life. This time, it might cost Barrett a friendship.

"Morning, Hunter. Kyran," Nowell greeted them at the door. The man was hunched over a stool and blinking up at Barrett in the weak afternoon light. "You look like something a rather determined cat dragged in"

Barrett rolled his eyes. "Well, thanks. You know where Griswold is?"

"First door on the left just behind me," the guard captain said behind a smothered yawn.

"Right…"

"Left," Nowell called as Barrett stooped under the lintel, Kyran close behind.

Turning left down the first hall, Barrett found an open door, and was surprised to find the room full of people arrayed around a large, central table. He noted the faces he recognized: Lane, one of the hunters that had helped escort Kyran to the Isles with him, Finley, the guild member that had picked up Kyran and given Barrett and Griswold their reassignment orders, and Captain Griswold, pacing at the far end of the room beside Selah, the Guild Leader. He frowned. What was so important that Selah would be there?

Griswold looked up from his conversation with Selah, taking in Barrett and Kyran in the doorway, and made his way over to them. "Thank you both for coming promptly. Barrett, if you will find a seat. Kyran, I need to speak with you."

"What's this about?" Barrett asked, growing suspicious as Kyran moved to one side.

"You will see soon enough," the captain assured him, gesturing for the mage to move ahead of him. "Kyran, if you will over there—"

"Griswold—"

"If you will be seated, we can start soon," the captain cut Barrett off curtly

Barrett's jaw creaked, and he opened his mouth to tell the captain what use he could find for a chair right then, when he met Kyran's cool gaze watching him. "Fine," he ground out.

Inclining his head, the captain ushered Kyran away, leaving Barrett to find his seat in the gathering. He slunk to one near the back with several empty on either side, keeping an eye on Kyran and Griswold as the captain began to speak to the mage at the far side of the room, but Barrett couldn't make out even a note of the captain's voice. More of Griswold's wind magic, he presumed.

"Bastard," he muttered, folding his arms. He scanned the rest of the room, the faces he didn't recognize. There were maybe fifteen people present, most of them hunters by the pull of their magic against Barrett's senses. Their ages ranged widely. Some looked younger than him, while another couple looked old enough to have retired ages ago. He wondered idly if he was looking at a gathering of every hunter stationed in the city. Were they really stretched so thin with the attacks in Belldale, or had their numbers dwindled even further in the few years since he'd left the guildhall?

"I think that's just about everyone," Captain Griswold said over the murmur of voices, approaching the gathering. Kyran lingered behind him, fingers worrying a staccato into his walking stick. "If everyone will take their seats, we will commence."

Someone shut the door and the last few voices went silent as Selah stood from her chair. To anyone from outside the guild, she appeared unassuming. She wore a plain, if finely made gown, and stood no higher than Barrett's chest, the sharp, severe lines of her face unadorned by any makeup. Yet she spoke with the air of someone that expected to be heard and their words obeyed.

"Good afternoon," she said, her voice carrying over the length of the hall. "I have called this meeting to discuss the very real threat facing us not only in our city, but within our very own walls."

A murmur of unease went through the crowd, and Barrett sat up a little straighter.

"It is through your tireless efforts, and many reports—" There was a wry chuckle at that. "—that we have been able to grasp the nature of that threat.

"As you all are aware, Belldale has been under tireless assault by demons that appear to be working together with abominations. An unprecedented event, and yet less than a fortnight ago, our guildhall faced this same threat. It is our belief these two events are not unrelated." She looked around the room, at the uneasy shifting in seats.

"But that is not all. The common people of this city are frightened and blaming us for what has happened, despite our efforts at reparations. You have heard them at the gates, and what they have been shouting. Some of you may even be old enough to remember the last time such a thing happened. As such, given the evidence our captains have gathered, and the similarity of these events to those that occurred in the last days of King Edrick's rule, we fear that what we are experiencing could be a return of the Cult of Light. But, given the unusual involvement of demons and abominations, they have found either a witch or a misguided hunter as their accomplice."

Barrett's belly coiled and he looked around the room. The punishment for sharing guild secrets outside the guild was to be tried for treason against the Crown, the very reason he had let Kyran assume he was a mage when they met. The same guild law that had been put in place after the riots Myles had been a part of.

Barrett glanced towards the mage before he could stop himself, and noticed Kyran wasn't looking at Selah either. The mage was staring silently off to one side, his expression fixed somewhere between concentration and exhaustion, eyes lidded, and runelines faintly glowing.

It wasn't quite the same look he'd seen on Kyran's face when he went somewhere else, but there was clearly something wrong. Whispering a curse, he started to rise when there was a knock at the door, and every head turned as one to see Nowell enter pushing a wheeled chair. Seated within was Myles.

"This is Lightbringer Horn," Selah introduced as Nowell wheeled the man over next to her. "I have asked him here at the recommendation of Captain Griswold as a witness to the Crown and to inform our decisions regarding the likely goal of this cult's return."

The Lightbringer bowed his head, clasping his hands, drawing Barrett's eye to the scarred skin. "It is unfortunate," Myles said, addressing the room, "that once again my presence in this city brings ill tidings, but Lumen lights for each of us a winding path. I am glad to offer my assistance to you all in preventing any more tragedy, and I will call upon all the Graces to guide us with mercy."

There were no whispers among the hunters seated at the table. A few moved in their seats, no doubt digesting the information, but Barrett's eyes gravitated towards a still point at the table.

Finley. She looked… He could hardly place her expression above the scarf hiding most of her face, but she looked angry. And she wasn't the only one. Nowell looked far less than pleased to see the Lightbringer.

"Thank you, Lightbringer Horn," Selah said when no questions or remarks came forth, dismissing Myles. "In the interest of not keeping our watch from their duties, I call this meeting adjourned. Your questions are welcome, but I ask that everything that has been said—"

Magic swelled and surged from somewhere on the guild grounds a moment before a bell began to clamor above them. The hair on the back of Barrett's neck rose and he whirled in his seat towards the doors when the guard captain gasped.

"Bar the door!" Nowell bellowed, racing for the door. "Everyone ready—"

The latch exploded and the door slammed open, just barely missing Nowell as a gale came howling through the door, quenching every wick in an instant.

Barrett threw his arms over his face to shield it from the buffeting wind, lurching up out of his seat. "What in Lumen's name?"

With an abrupt pop of his ears, the wind in the hall ceased, leaving only the panicked cries and scrape of chairs as hunters raced for the door.

Barrett lowered his arms, surprised to find Griswold at Kyran's side, his hand lifted and face creased in concentration.

"Nowell, remember the plan," Captain Griswold said over the unnatural quiet.

"Everyone—" Nowell began when something burst through the doorway like a tempest, bowling through anyone in the way. Wind whipped across Barrett's skin like a lash, tearing at his clothes, his hair, his eyes. He twisted, trying to get away, to protect himself, but it didn't matter where he faced, the wind found him, pulling the breath out of him.

For a long, horrible moment, he thought of Belldale, and of lying on the ground, gasping vainly and clutching his throat as he fought to suck down even a dreg of air. Of suffocating on dry land.

Fire rippled up his back and down his arms, and he spun to face whatever beast was responsible, a scream kindling at the back of his throat as he fought to keep his streaming eyes open to see through the gale when the air went dead.

With an ugly wheeze, Barrett sucked down an icy breath, peeling his eyes open to the bright, blue-white light of Kyran's runelines setting the room aglow, and illuminating the figure encrusted in frost and writhing atop the table. It was long, as if someone had taken a man and stretched his body out like pulled sugar. Its chest was deep and broad, heaving like bellows as it moaned and shuddered, sending out fitful gusts of wind.

An abomination.

"Don't attack it," Griswold said, leaping up onto the table with barely any visible effort and placing himself between the abomination and the room. "We will handle it. Everyone outside. Assess and subdue any others that came through."

"But—"

"We will handle it," Nowell snapped, climbing up onto the table with Griswold. "You take the Lightbringer back to the hospital. Make certain a hunter stays with him." Dropping to his knees, the guard captain seized the abomination by its arm and twisted it up behind its back while Griswold knelt to take its other arm.

Barrett stared, utterly bewildered. They had daggers. Both of them. "What are you—"

There was a tug at his sleeve, and Barrett looked down to where Myles' gripped his arm, the swollen, knobby knuckles hard against his forearm, eyes wide and his breaths coming in loud, whispering pants.

"Myles?"

With a ragged gasp, the Lightbringer sagged in his chair, eyes fluttering, his breathing growing more labored. Something was wrong. He needed help, but something here wasn't right. A year ago, he would have trusted that his captains had a good reason for whatever they were doing, but now? He would leap into the Pit itself before he left Kyran at their mercy. But neither could he abandon Myles.

Gritting his teeth, he grabbed the back of the Lightbringer's chair and wheeled him out of the room.

Outside on the lawn, chaos reigned as crimson and black fire swirled through the air, caught on errant gusts of wind as hunters pursued a second abomination fleeing across the lawn. He quickly searched the faces he could see until he recognized one.

"Lane," he shouted over the din until the man finally looked his way. "Take him, please," Barrett urged, relieved when the hunter hurried over. "Griswold wanted me to take him to Selah but he needs a hospital."

"I'll see to it."

"Thank you." Barrett hesitated, taking in the Lightbringer's unfocused eyes and the ugly, thin whistle of breath. It reminded him disconcertingly of Kyran lying in that sunken hole and Raleigh as he choked out his last words.

Tearing his eyes away, he raced back up the stairs, praying silently that this time he wouldn't be too late.

Chapter Thirty-Three

CARVING INTO THE abomination's mind had been easy. Not effortless, but compared to how hard Kyran had to struggle to claw his way into the needle-toothed demon that had tortured him, this beast was as easy to enter as diving into a lake. He wasn't certain how he should feel about that, but there was hardly room for him to feel at all.

Memories that weren't his washed over the mage one after the other, scenes of hunting and scrabbling amongst the floating ruins of the demon realm, of the feel of rope in his hands, of kissing someone passionately, of burying his teeth up to the gums in tough flesh, and the bite of a lash along his back. A nauseating smell of blood and salt and fish mixed with ash pervaded everything. Hideously monstrous faces of ashen flesh and the carefree laughter of friends.

Man and beast, tangled together, screaming from the same throat as he struggled to separate them, to consciously look, but he was groping blindly.

You have made a grave mistake, mageling.

Kyran flinched, nearly breaking his concentration at that word—mageling.

You may have caught me off guard, little one, but it will not happen again.

A low, guttural growl reverberated through Kyran like a thing alive, growing louder and sharper, scraping along the inside of his skull, until the sound itself nearly burned him.

Let me see you.

"No!" Kyran lashed at the itch in his thoughts, frantic to get it out, to not let it inside of him again. "Get out!"

Come now, just a peek.

Out. He had to get it out, now, before it could—

The demon probed deep, tracing old scars to soft places that hadn't quite healed. Kyran's thoughts raced back to home, to bens and barns, then to Tennebrum, inns and fires, then to darkness, and the Pit filled his vision, illuminated by the glow of a demon grasping his leg, dragging it towards an open maw, its nails cutting into his thigh.

It was digging now. Not content simply to look. He could feel it digging, its nails sinking into the soft meat behind his eyes. He wanted to scream, but he couldn't choke down the breath to make even a whimper.

More power. If he had more power, he could force it out, like before. He just needed the power to do it.

He groped at his side, fumbling blindly for his purse's ties when the bald memory of being held down and teeth sinking into his shoulder, and a fiery pain seized his arm.

"Kyran!" A dozen familiar voices called his name in unison. "Kyran!" There was his pa, Connal, his brothers, Ben, Laird Dunbar, Barrett... "Kyran!"

So you're the one, the demon growled, the sound of its voice ploughing through the flickering voices and faces. *You're the one he hunted. He nurtured you. Tasted you.*

Kyran forced his fingers to open, dragging his useless hand along the pleats of his kilt until he finally brushed soft leather, but he couldn't figure out how to work the knot.

So much pain you've suffered, it simpered, and he felt it cleave deeper, vividly remembering the sensation of teeth sliding into his thigh.

"No," Kyran whispered, frantically tugging at the ties, but the knot wouldn't loosen. "No no no no..."

The growl evolved into a purr that vibrated through his leg, down into the very bone, the pain so intense, he couldn't even draw breath. *Oh, what anticipation.* The razor teeth connected through his flesh and he could scarcely shut his eyes to the memory replaying before him. *What a treat you must have been. Let me see it again.* And then, suddenly, there was his leg, whole again, teeth closing around the flesh.

A strangled, desperate sound, almost a scream, tore out of Kyran's throat, and with a panicked determination, he shoved his fingers through the tight aperture of his purse. The ties snapped, and, following the pull of his own blood, his hand closed around the sharp rays of his newly carved amulet, its edges blunted by the kerchief tangled with it.

"Get out!" he snarled, focusing just enough to give the flood of magic direction.

He felt it dislodge, the sheer relief in his head invigorating him. While the visage faded, that same growl seeped in, and the pressure began to redouble. *Clever mageling,* it sneered.

He held his ground, his magic keeping the thing from him, but for how long? His magic had an end, one that couldn't be too far off after the long night practicing in the arena, and his amulet was far from abundantly laid in. He knew too well what would happen if he fell, and let the thing in with no defenses to protect him, but he couldn't hold out forever. If he was to come out of this, he would have to kill the demon first.

But how? If it were simply a matter of destroying it, he could freeze its flesh until it simply fell apart. But that wasn't what Nowell had asked of him. He was supposed to be looking for something, or, at the very least, saving the poor soul caught in the ugly tangle of the demon inside of them.

Because this wasn't like all the beasts he'd faced before. There was a man—a human—caught in the middle. A man that might be able to tell them who was behind these attacks.

Kyran needed to remove the demon without hurting the man, but how? He could hurt the thing, claw and thrash gracelessly through it to make it feel pain, but how could he destroy it?

The answer came more easily than he was comfortable admitting. How else did a demon destroy another demon?

His mouth watered, and a thick nausea began to rise at the back of his throat as his mouth flooded with the taste of blood, but he forced himself to concentrate, to remember he was a mage. A half-blooded *demon*.

The wall he had built of his magic crumbled, and the demon howled in victorious laughter as Kyran quickly reshaped his magic

Weak, it mocked, slithering back under his skull. *I don't know why he—*

Its voice broke in a ragged, keening wail as Kyran's new teeth found its soft belly. He envisioned his power tearing, swallowing, pulling bits of the creature back to him. Images flickered through his mind, disjointed scenes of him standing amongst other demons while someone spoke. Power washed into him, the same way as if he had touched an amulet. It was working.

He went for another bite when the demon's will slammed into him like a physical blow, threatening to cleave him in two.

You teething, impudent mageling!

"*Deamhan gòrach!*" Kyran snarled back, tearing another bite out of the beast.

It howled against his mind, but its presence didn't retreat, instead digging deeper and deeper, tearing a fiery hole through his head that tasted like blood. But Kyran knew this pain, knew how to push through it, goring the beast even as he screamed his throat raw.

More images of the demon realm flit through his mind. Of other demons. Of people. That had to be what the captain was looking for.

Kyran sank his power into the memory, worrying at it like a dog with a rag, tearing it free.

The demon squealed, its thrashing becoming more frantic. *No! I won't die to some mageling!*

Kyran tore out another bite.

You will not consume me so easily!

The sensation of wood under his palms, and heavy weight on his back flashed through Kyran's senses, laced by the smell of salt, fish, and hay. He flinched from the memory, and the overwhelming scent of hay abruptly filled his senses.

Soft.

A hot, whiskey laden breath rolled across the back of his neck.

Kyran froze, the sensation of wooden boards materializing beneath his knees along with the scratch of dry hay on his cheek. "No…" He tried to push himself upright, tried to crawl away, but he was too heavy, his limbs uncooperative, and his head throbbed as if someone had beat it in with a rock.

"It isna real," he whispered, trying to focus on his magic, to shape it again. "It isna real."

Something scuffed in the hay behind him, and panic seized him as out of the corner of his eye he caught a glimpse of a yawning, needle-toothed maw before it clamped down on his shoulder.

Pain, bright and hot and jarringly real, tore a scream from his throat as he felt every one of the beast's teeth tear through skin and muscle to grind against the bones of his shoulder.

So soft.

A hand ghosted over Kyran's hip, and he screamed, kicking and thrashing against the thing at his back, his magic lashing blindly into ashen flesh, but the teeth only sank deeper. "Let go! This isna—No! No!"

Such a treat.

Chapter Thirty-Four

BARRETT HAD HARDLY reached the top stair, when a ragged scream echoed down the hall. His heart nearly twisted in two. "Kyran!" he shouted, sprinting for the room. He made to throw open the door and snatched his hand back with a hiss. Turning his palm over, the skin was pink, as if it had been burned. He looked at the doorknob, frost scrawling over the dark metal. Summoning his fire, he grabbed the knob again, the frost spitting at the contact, and shoved the door in.

Cold, bright and sharp, slapped across his face, stinging his nose and lungs. The mage stood at the center of the room, clutching his walking stick as if he were holding on for dear life, his breaths coming in deep, heaving gasps laced with pained whimpers.

"Oh Graces, Kyran? Kyran, can you…"

"Stay back," Griswold ordered, leaning into his knee on the creature's shoulder, pressing it into the table more firmly. "Do not interfere."

"With what? What are you doing?"

Kyran gasped, the sound like a knife through Barrett's belly, his body arching as if a blade had been buried in his back. The abomination on the table let out a low chuckle. It was doing this. And the captains were letting it happen.

Snatching his dagger from his belt, Barrett lunged for the table, only to meet a solid wall of air. For a moment, his boots left the ground, his body perfectly weightless, before he was sent tumbling across the floor, coming to a stop against the wall.

"I said not to interfere!" Griswold bellowed, his eyes cold as he watched Barrett get to his feet again.

"It's killing him!"

"He knew the risk."

Something deep in Barrett cracked, and a cold, bottomless fury rolled through him with a roar of flame. He grabbed the chair next to him, the wood igniting under his fingers, and flung it, narrowly missing the captain. He felt the wind stir around him, and grabbed the next chair, throwing it and the next, one after the other, pushing forwards as the air resistance began to fade.

"Captain—" Releasing the abomination, Nowell shoved Griswold away as one of the chairs whizzed through the place the guild captain had been just a moment before, shattering against the back wall.

The pressure against Barrett vanished, and he lunged, burying his dagger in the beast's back.

The abomination shrieked, arching up off the table, knocking Nowell, Griswold, and Barrett back as it began to thrash violently, curling in on itself until, with a last convulsing shudder, it collapsed to the table. Its demonic features melted away in a crumble of black ash, leaving behind a man. Barrett's stomach lurched as he took in the vacant eyes, the broken, twisted body, but most of all, how young the man was. He hardly looked older than Barrett did, but his hands were the same as the man that had attacked Myles. Scarred.

"Griswold, don't," Nowell said before wind tugged at Barrett's clothing and hair.

In an instant, Barrett was on his feet, hands wreathed in crimson and black fire, ready to tear Griswold apart with his bare hands. "You bastard," Barrett snarled, shaking with wrath. "What in the bloody Pit were you doing?"

"It was a trap, Barrett," Griswold said, his voice eerily cool and calm. "And your interference may have cost us our only chance to figure out who is behind it."

"By letting it kill Kyran?"

"I wouldn't have let it go that far."

"You already were!"

There was a choked whimper from behind Barrett, and Kyran crumpled to the floor, his walking stick clattering loudly as it tumbled away.

Cursing every Grace, Barrett ran to the mage's side and dropped to his knees. The mage twitched, rolling onto his side, and the bottom of Barrett's stomach fell out. Blood, a whole dark smear of it was frozen to Kyran's face.

"Kyran," Captain Griswold called sharply. "What did you see?"

"Graces, give him a minute," Barrett snapped back at him. "He's not even—"

Whispering something in Isleish, Kyran curled on his side, his hand clamping over his eyes. This close, Barrett could see every muscle clenched tight under Kyran's skin, the cords of his neck and down his arm standing out.

"Hammond," Nowell said, stepping forward. "Barrett can handle this. We should see to the rest of the guild."

"Then go," Captain Griswold replied almost tersely. "I will salvage what I can of this."

"What was that?" Barrett sneered, getting to his feet to face the captain.

"Captain," Nowell said, his tone crisp. "I believe Hunter Barrett is capable of taking this associate to the hospital to be examined while you fulfill your duties as captain elsewhere."

"I have an obligation—"

"To the guild," Nowell reminded the guild captain.

"Yes, and that is why I must know what the mage saw."

CRACK.

Griswold stumbled back, clutching his face where Barrett's fist had connected.

"His name is Kyran." Barrett snarled, planting himself between Kyran and the captains. "Not mage or associate or the Old One's… It's Kyran."

"Noted," Griswold said coolly, pulling his hand from his cheek as wind began to stir his hair.

"Well, you heard him," Nowell said, not bothering to hide his snickering as he stepped up between the two of them, his hand resting lightly on the pommel of his sword. "I'll let you handle what's left here, captain. Barrett, take Kyran to the hospital. If the captain here follows, take down a statement of whatever Kyran says for him, then make certain you all eat and get some rest. I'm certain there will be another meeting about this tomorrow."

Barrett scoffed at the guard captain, "Another meeting?"

Nowell swept his arms out grandly, his mouth twisted in a sardonic smile. "Welcome back to the capital." Offering Griswold a very slight nod, the guard captain spun and strode from the hall, barking orders for a status report before he'd even fully crossed the threshold.

Griswold lingered where he was, the line of his jaw set as he contemplated something. "I will send round for the report later," he finally said. "Please see to Kyran, and…" The guild captain hesitated before adding, "Please give him my condolences for what has happened. It was not my intention."

"But you let it happen anyway," Barrett sneered.

The guild captain looked at him, then Kyran, his shoulders inching higher. "I did."

Barrett fumed with another ready insult, his fist clenching at his side, when he caught another glimpse of the dead man on the table, and felt his guts lurch. He turned away, ignoring the captain instead. He would have it out with him later.

"Kyran?" he called softly, lowering to his knees again, but the mage didn't respond.

A tight knot seized in Barrett's gut. It couldn't be—

"Kyran? Kyran, can you hear me?"

Nothing.

"No. Graces, no." He reached for the mage's shoulder and Kyran flinched at the contact, a sob wrenching out of him. Barrett winced and retracted his hand. He wanted to scream, wanted to throttle Griswold. "It's Barrett. I don't know what you're seeing, but you're here at the guild with me."

He wished he could comfort Kyran in some way. Hold him or even throw an arm around his shoulders, but Kyran had made it clear that kind of contact was not welcome—what it reminded him of. There was that one night, though, standing in the snow, vulnerable and raw, when Kyran had shown just how much he had come to trust him. Perhaps it was enough.

Cautious and slow, Barrett settled his hand over Kyran's. The mage twitched, but didn't pull away.

"I'm here," Barrett soothed, moving his thumb over the back of Kyran's hand. "And you're here with me. This is real," he added, keenly recalling the mage's painful confession that he often could not tell if the world around him was real or not after what the demon did to him.

Kyran's hand moved beneath his again, and Barrett lightened his touch, ready to pull away, but instead of withdrawing, the mage turned his hand and clasped Barrett's, squeezing tightly.

Barrett's heart hit his ribs and his fingers tightened around Kyran's. "I'm here," he whispered again around the lump that had lodged in his throat, clasping his second hand around Kyran's. "I'm right here. I'm not going anywhere."

Chapter Thirty-Five

DEMON BLOODED MONGREL.

Meet me at the pub, eh?

I will not make that mistake again, mageling.

I think I love her, Jacob. I really do.

What about us?

We must work together, or the guild—

"Did the abomination strike him?"

Kyran twitched in surprise as Lilyanna's face came into sudden sharp focus above him, glowing orange in lantern light.

"I don't know," Barrett said from somewhere above and behind the mage. "I don't think so."

"I see." She leaned closer, and Kyran shrank away, a sudden prickle of gooseflesh running down his neck and arms as he finally realized he was lying completely prone on the floor of the room he had faced the abomination in.

"What—"

"It's all right, Kyran," Barrett said, and there was a ghost of a touch at Kyran's shoulder, and he flinched away.

"Please hold still so I may examine you," the chirurgeon said softly. But instead of reaching to touch his face or even leaning closer to get a look at him, the chirurgeon lowered her head and closed her eyes.

The prickle of unease only got stronger, but before Kyran could settle on what exactly was unnerving him, Lilyanna opened her eyes. Only, they weren't *her* eyes looking back at him. The whites had turned a coal black that swallowed the light so completely that they looked more like holes the fiery ring at their center floated upon.

They looked just like Barrett's had in the Inbetween in the Isles.

Kyran didn't have a chance to react, to flinch or even draw breath to shout, before her power struck him. Not the customary hammerblow, but the precise thrust of a fine edged knife.

"No!" Kyran's magic came roaring out of his blood, and he shoved her away.

In an instant, Barrett was between them, his dagger out. "What did you do?" he demanded, steam rising from his coat, curling around Kyran in a frozen fog.

"She was in my head," Kyran croaked, dragging himself up onto his elbows just before he began to retch, his stomach emptying itself in a wet, nearly black spatter.

"Graces—"

"I was ensuring no part of the demon had been left behind," Lilyanna replied.

"You could have warned him," Barrett insisted, at Kyran's side again, his face a mask of concern.

"It would have warned anything within him into hiding."

"Within him—?" The hunter's voice faltered into a discomforted sigh. His brows knit together and he looked to Kyran with a worrisome expression. "Are you all right?"

Spitting a mouthful of bile and blood, Kyran looked blearily around, taking in the frost scarred room of the college, and the glimpse of a man he could see lying on the table above him.

"Kyran?"

The mage gingerly shook his head, sniffling before wiping his face. He could feel the maelstrom the abomination had kindled in him spinning still. A tangle of thoughts and feelings and memories so loud, they drowned out everything else. Even now, as he tried to focus on Barrett, on what to say to reassure him, he could feel himself sinking beneath the deafening fog inside his thoughts.

"There was no demon, but I would advise a draught of sleeping tea and rest for at least a day for your injuries," Lilyanna said, watching him with cool brown eyes once more.

"Tell that to Griswold," Barrett growled, turning to Kyran again, his expression softening. "Do you—"

"I can walk," Kyran insisted, dragging his walking stick to him from where it fell.

"All right," Barrett relented quietly, easing back.

The mage struggled to get up, limbs shaking, and he leaned heavily on his walking stick once he was upright, his exhaustion finally beginning to sink in. Stars, he was tired, and yet even the thought of lying down to sleep made his belly curdle with anxious anticipation, knowing those big, white hands would be there, waiting for him.

He glanced towards the table, and Barrett stepped between him and the grisly sight.

"Griswold said he will deal with it."

"Aye," Kyran croaked, ignoring the way his gut twisted at those words, or the way he could still see the broken body under his lids when he closed his eyes. He'd failed the task Nowell and Griswold had asked of him, and more people might be hurt or worse because of him.

"I'll walk you to your room," Barrett offered quietly, holding the door as they stepped out into the night. Thunder rumbled in the distance. Another storm was coming.

Kyran's gaze fell to the bit of cloth twisted up between his fingers stained almost entirely black. Barrett's kerchief. Ruined, like so much else.

Chapter Thirty-Six

BARRETT KEPT HIS eyes trained on the path in front of his feet, watching his boots slosh through the quickly gathering puddles. He felt like he was in a dream, weightless and tired. Except the knot in his chest was very real, and he did everything he could not to think about what had caused it. Tried not to think of the memories, the feelings that had surfaced again after so long of not having to face them. The sound of Kyran screaming. The sight of the man on the table. Or how it could have been him.

The thought haunted the hunter, his throat tightening as he remembered the frightening powerlessness of being trapped within his own skin, his body twisted and changed by his demon to suit its needs. His demon had eventually given him his body back, but what if it hadn't? What if he had stayed like that? An abomination. Would he have been the one that attacked Kyran? Myles? Kat?

His knuckles ached from clenching his fists so tightly, trying to calm his pounding heart, but he couldn't stop thinking about what had happened inside that building. How Kyran had simply stood there, screaming as if something were turning him inside out, while Griswold and Nowell had simply…watched.

He wished Kyran would say something, anything that would distract him, but the mage was silent but for the tap of his stick. Barrett's belly coiled at the fresh memory of their most recent conversation. Though *conversation* was putting it a bit too strongly. They'd barely gotten more than a few words out before the bell had interrupted them.

It probably wasn't the time to try to apologize and explain himself. But then again, there never seemed to be a *good* time, and if he kept waiting, kept putting it off, Kyran might not keep waiting around either.

He stepped ahead of the mage, and grabbed the door to the dormitories, holding it open. "We should talk."

"About what?" Kyran replied after a moment.

"I hardly know where to start," Barrett confessed, letting the door swing to behind them. "Are you…certain you're all right?"

Kyran's gaze faded out of focus, drifting down to his hands wrapped around his walking stick, still clutching the kerchief Barrett had given him. "I'm na hurt," he said after a moment.

"Kyran," Barrett insisted. "You're bleeding. You fainted. You were… were screaming."

The mage's face wilted and grew pale. "Aye, but this isna something a bit of linen can fix."

"What do you mean?" Barrett begged, moving so he could look the mage in the face, but Kyran would not look at him. "Kyran, what's wrong?"

"I… I wasna strong enough."

Barrett's chest ached at the words. "I know the feeling. But I… Look, I don't understand exactly what happened back there, but…" He watched Kyran wipe his nose again, the blood not quite frozen this time and smearing across his lip and hand. He had seen it like this once before. "Your nose bled in the Isles too, after we fought that other bastard. I thought you'd taken a hit, but you didn't, did you?"

"No. I dinnae."

"Then what… What did you do to it?"

"The same thing that demon did ta me in its pit." He touched the side of his head.

"You were…in its head?" Barrett guessed, the concept utterly foreign to him. Except… "Like the Old One?"

Kyran cut him a look. "What do you mean about the Auld One?"

Barrett opened, then closed his mouth, groping for words. Any words. Anything to clarify and understand what had happened and how the mage had done it. "When we were in the Isles, when the Old One was there, he looked at me… I mean, looked at me, and he saw… everything." He shuddered, doing his best not to reflect on that raw, helpless feeling of being flayed by the demon's will alone. "But you're saying, you can do the same thing?"

Kyran squeezed his eyes shut and shrank into himself as he nodded stiffly. "And they can do it ta me. It isna just looking, though. It's tearing, and digging. It's teeth without a mouth."

The words clicked into place, and a terrible realization dawned on Barrett as he finally understood what Kyran had endured locked in the demon realm, what had put the mage in a coma, trapped in nightmares he couldn't wake from until the Old One had…done something.

It…hurt him, but the hurt was…better than what had been. Like…breaking a bone to reset it, or.... Or removing a limb to save the life.

Or taking away a memory.

"But…why?" he finally asked. "Why were you…?"

A piece of the walking stick splintered under Kyran's nail, his scratching turning to digging. "I was…trying ta take the demon out of that lad. But I wasna strong enough ta…ta do that and protect myself."

And Barrett had killed him. Kyran had been trying to save him and Barrett had—

"I—I didn't know," he whispered, the nausea returning so quickly he had to shut his eyes.

When he opened them back up to look at Kyran, the mage had shrunk even further, his head ducked and his hair flaked with ice from the rain. He couldn't imagine what the mage had seen or felt.

"Do you want to talk 'bout it? What happened or what you saw?"

Kyran shook his head, and Barrett swore he heard the mage's breath hitch. "Ye ken what it saw. It saw everything. The other demon. My leg. Connal… Everything."

"Graces. I… I can't imagine. I'm sorry. I wish Griswold hadn't… Why did he ask you to do it?"

"Ta find out what I could about the demons' plans."

"But there had to be another way. He and Nowell could have done something."

"And why na me?" Kyran bristled, and Barrett quickly backpedaled.

"You're strong, Kyran, but you're still…" His eyes moved over the hollows of Kyran's face, the sunken spaces of his collarbones and shrunken frame. "…ill."

The mage scoffed, pulling a key from his purse as he stopped in front of a door. "Demons dinnae care."

"Well, I care."

Kyran's glare softened, his cheeks coloring faintly. "Aye." He shoved the key into the lock, the metal chattering. "But ye willna always be there."

A stone dropped into Barrett's chest as he watched Kyran walk into his room. The truth stung, but it wasn't the whole truth. Maybe Barrett couldn't be there every time a demon attacked, but he was here now, and Kyran was at the guildhall. He should have been safe. Instead, there were secret files and secret missions and secret truths.

Secrets make for poor friends.

Grabbing the door, he stepped in after the mage.

CHAPTER THIRTY-SEVEN

THE BACK OF Kyran's neck prickled with gooseflesh as the door's latch clicked shut behind him, closing him in with Barrett. He could feel the air crackling like thin ice between them. "The captain will be looking for ye," Kyran reminded the hunter, his fingers drumming against his thigh as he stood, frozen, at the center of his room.

"Griswold can hang," Barrett said, his voice heavy with exhaustion. "I… We still need to talk."

"We did."

"You did." There was a scuff of a boot, and Kyran twitched, resisting the urge to retreat across the room when Barrett stepped past him, tending to the lantern that had burned low in his neglect. "I want you to know I never meant to keep things from you."

Kyran felt his lips curl. "Oh, aye? Is that so?"

"Yes, it is," Barrett insisted, pinching the end of his glove and tugging it off, laying it on the table. "There are laws. We're not supposed to talk about the guild or demons. But you're a member now…"

"Na yet," The mage looked down, his gaze sliding down to his wrist and the lines glowing faintly beneath his skin even now. "I'm only a bondsman."

"That's as good as a member—"

Kyran's eyes burned, and his lines flickered beneath his skin as he wrestled to keep himself under control. "No. It isna. You can walk away from this one day. Do something else with your life if you want."

"You…don't want to be here?" The hunter looked almost ill with anticipation, his starkly bare hand clenching the bottom of his sleeve, but Kyran couldn't tell if it was fear of Kyran knowing the truth or leaving.

Kyran spread his hands, inviting the hunter to look at him, all of him, glowing with fey light the way no human would. "I couldna leave if I wanted. The guild *owns* me. And where else would I go? I'm na good for anything else. Only demons can kill demons, aye? I…" His voice cracked as a sob fought its way between his teeth. "Connal was right about me."

"Connal's a bastard and doesn't know the first thing about you."

"He kent what I was." Kyran pulled his sleeve up, letting his lines brighten, his breath fogging white. "Demon blooded."

"No, you're—" Barrett started towards him, then stopped when Kyran shied back. "You're wrong. Connal was wrong. You're not a demon. You're a *person*, and you have every right to be here and do whatever it is you want, no matter what anyone else says about you."

"And every right ta be buried in a grave a country away from my kin, in unblessed soil and no Lightbringer ta speak over it because Lumen doesna take demon kin inta his House. Even in the Isles they'd have at least buried me on the *ben*."

"You're not demon kin, Kyran. You can't think that way."

"I couldna have done what I did ta that…that abomination if I werena…werena…" The bastard get of a demon and a human woman. Of the Auld One.

His da had to know. He had to know Kyran wasn't his son. That had to be the real reason he'd sent Kyran to *Cairngorm*. But why didn't he just leave Kyran in the woods? Why go through with the farce? Why risk so much for something that wasn't even supposed to be? For his ma? What had she suffered to conceive Kyran and then see his blood waken? Why had they let it go so far? Why was he here?

"Kyran, you're not—Look at me. Please."

Blinking against the gathering crystal of ice at the corner of his eye, Kyran finally looked up at the hunter. Barrett's face was earnest, his pale-blue eyes soft with worry.

"You're not your blood, all right? Your blood doesn't make you a bad person."

"But—"

"You're still Kyran, the same person I met in Oareford tryin' to protect a village of people you didn't even know against something you'd never seen before then. You saved that boy from the Inbetween and Effie, too, and you were willin' to let that laird kill you to protect your family. Your magic might come from demon blood, but all of that, all the rest of you, is human."

The word struck through Kyran's chest like an arrow. *Human*. He searched the hunter's face for any indication that he was lying, that he was simply trying to say whatever would calm him, and found only a warm sincerity.

The sob that had been building in his chest broke, and Kyran folded beneath it.

It hurt. He hurt, in every way imaginable. But there was relief in it as well, like poison let from a wound with every ugly wail.

When at last, the tears began to slow, he found himself inexplicably calm for the first time in longer than he could clearly remember.

There was a clomp of boots against the wooden floor moving away from him, and Kyran flushed in embarrassment as he remembered Barrett was still there, and had seen him utterly collapse. He tried to lift his head and compose himself, only to find his hands had frozen to his face.

His embarrassment deepened to mortification. He gently worked one hand free, but the other was fastened quite firmly to his eyelid, and he found he could not open either eye through the crust of ice built up over them. He couldn't imagine what he must look like to the hunter, but the man did not say a word.

There was a splash of water behind him, followed by Barrett's footsteps returning. "I, uhm, here." He felt something warm brush the very edge of his hand and flinched. "It's—It's just a rag. Warmed it up."

Kyran hesitated, anxious to let the hunter see what he'd done to his face. He angled his head away from Barrett's voice and timidly held out his hand to take the rag.

After a moment, something hot and damp was laid gently into his palm, the heat soaking into his fingertips in an instant.

Kyran pressed it to his eye, blinking and gently rubbing as the cloth quickly cooled, until the ice came free and the room swam back into view. Cool, blue light danced over the walls in time with every lub of his pulse, and he turned his hand over to take in his runelines. He hadn't even noticed the slip in his control.

His breath shook as he focused, reining in his power until the soft light vanished back to where it belonged.

He started to lift the cloth again, only to find it had frozen in his hand already, the fabric stuck lightly to his fingers and palm.

"I can fix that," Barrett offered, offering his hand.

Kyran turned the cloth over, dangling it over Barrett's palm, and using just the tips of his fingers, the hunter tugged the rag free.

Almost immediately, the cloth began to steam as Barrett closed his hands around it, thumbs smoothing over a thick patch of ice until it dissolved. "There you are," he said, handing the rag back.

"Thank you," Kyran mumbled, pressing the rag between the fingers of his other hands to melt the ice underneath.

"I'm…sorry all this happened." Barrett said after a moment. "I know I'm not so great with words, and I don't think about sayin' things when I should. I know there's things I haven't said that I probably should have, but I want you to know that you can talk to me, whenever you want, about anything."

An ache rose through Kyran at Barrett's words, his throat tightening until all he could manage was a nod, clenching his teeth to hold back the sound that threatened to escape him again.

"Or… or if—It feels like you've been avoidin' me since I got back, and if—if I'm just botherin' you with all this, you can tell me not to bother you again, and I'll—I'll leave," Barrett offered.

Kyran thought about it. Honestly considered telling the hunter to leave, to just let him be, but the warmth he'd felt at the notion of simply disappearing had faded. It left only the hollowness behind and a bitter acknowledgement that the certainty he had those long years on the side of Cairngorm was gone. It felt like falling, like there was nothing to stop him from crashing into the rocks below, except…

He brushed his thumb over his finger tips, remembering keenly the warm grip wrapped around his fingers and palm. "I dinnae… I dinnae ken why you'd want ta stay."

"Because that's what friends do. Because I… I care about you, and I want you to be all right. As all right as you can be, y'know? You've been through things no one should ever have to experience. And I… I have bad memories, too, but I don't think about 'em as much when I'm around you. And I—I want that for you, too."

Kyran didn't know what to say, or even feel, his chest squeezing down around his pulse until he could feel it in his throat. He…

A light knock on the door interrupted whatever the mage was about to say, and Barrett swore softly. Stomping over, he eased the door open a sliver. "Kat," he said drily, and Kyran stood up a bit straighter. That was Barrett's sister. "What do you want?"

"Hammond sent me."

"Come back later," Barrett growled.

"If I go back empty handed, he'll be down here next."

"I'll tell him the same—"

"Let her in."

Barrett looked over his shoulder at Kyran. "You don't have to—"

"Aye, I do," Kyran said, peeling the rag from his face. "Either now or later, and I'd rather na have ta think about it tomorrow."

The hunter's face softened. "If you're certain… Just a moment, Kat." Pushing the door shut again, he came to stand in front of Kyran, shoulders hunched nervously. "Is it all right if I… I know you don't like folks touching you. I just…thought I might help." He looked meaningfully at Kyran's fingers still frozen in place. "May I?"

Kyran nearly refused out of hand, shrinking at even the imagined sensation. But his hand was stuck fast, and Barrett had never grabbed him or touched him without asking first or letting Kyran initiate the contact. They'd shared rooms and other stranger places, and despite Kyran's apprehension, the hunter had never acted less than courteously.

"Aye," he managed to croak, even as every line in his body went taut with anticipation.

Moving slowly, the hunter laid his hand atop Kyran's fingers. The touch was featherlight, hardly more than a warmth Kyran could feel through the hunter's gloves. Even then, he couldn't help but fixate on the point of contact, keenly and intimately aware of being touched.

"Tell me if it's too much," Barrett said, the warmth growing, and water began to trickle from between Kyran's fingers down his cheeks until he finally felt his lashes part.

"That's—"

Barrett pulled his hand back, stepping away from Kyran. "Is it—"

Kyran blinked, rubbing the last few wet crystals from his lashes. "Aye. Thank you."

The hunter smiled, turning to pick up his glove from the table. "You are very welcome," he said earnestly. "Are you certain you want to talk to Kat right now?"

Kyran sighed, wrapping his hands around his walking stick. He wasn't certain of anything more than that he would rather be anywhere or do anything else just then. But it would be waiting for him, and putting it off might risk wasting the time Griswold and Nowell had hoped to buy with this plan. "Aye."

Chapter Thirty-Eight

Hand on the latch, Barrett took a moment to gather himself before he opened the door again. He really wasn't certain if he had been more relieved or aggrieved to find his sister outside rather than Griswold. Taking a deep breath through his nose, he opened the door.

Kat was still where he had left her, two steaming mugs in either hand, her hair pulled tightly back in a single braid. She cocked her head, a smile tugging at the unscarred side of her mouth, and Barrett was sorely tempted to shut the door again. But she would only come back later. Or Griswold would.

"Kyran, this is Katherine, my sister," Barrett introduced, shuffling to one side to admit her. "Kat, Kyran."

"Pleasure to finally meet you," she said as Barrett closed the door behind her. "And welcome to the guild, by the way. It isn't normally this chaotic, or…" She tilted her head, considering. "I suppose it wasn't when I was younger."

"When Tennebrum still had lords," Barrett said, earning a sharp look from Kat.

"Well, one of us had to accrue some wisdom, and I'm afraid the rocks in your head crowd it out."

"Wha—You!" Barrett protested, his scowl deepening when a ghost of a smile flickered across Kyran's face. "Just hurry up, already."

"I'm tryin' to," Kat said, the same accent Barrett had unlearned in the capital colored her words. "Kyran, if you don't mind taking a seat, we can get started. Griswold has only asked for whatever you deem the most important of what you saw or heard, and said the rest could be taken down later by a scholar. Barrett, you will still have to give a full report."

"Of course, I will," Barrett groaned, following Kat to the table where she finally set the steaming mugs down. "What's that?"

"Tea? I took it off a runner I caught at the door. Said Lilyanna had it sent over for you both."

"Oh." He vaguely recalled mention of a sleeping draught, but no instruction on where or how or when to get it. "I'll…send her my thanks."

"Right." Sighing, Kat dropped into one of the chairs at the table, and propped her foot on one knee. "When you are ready, Kyran," she prompted, producing a piece of parchment and a pen.

Kyran slowly sank onto the very edge of his bed, tucking his walking stick into the crook of his arm. "I can tell you what I took from the beast, but I dinnae ken how much will be useful. I couldna get much."

"Anything at all will be more than we had," she said, scratching in something at the top of the parchment. "So, were you able to find anything when you…" She waved one hand vaguely. "…*attacked* the demon?"

"Aye. The lad was a sailor. I dinnae see how he was taken or turned, but I was trying na ta hurt him." He looked down at his lap, nail clicking against his walking stick in a sharp, quick staccato. "I dinnae think the demon has ever left its realm before. I only saw it there. There wasna a lot useful, but I saw it with other demons and someone was speaking ta them. I couldna make it out, but it was…familiar…"

Barrett shook his head, struggling to wrap his mind around what Kyran was describing even after the mage's explanation of what he had been doing. If the Old One hadn't done the same thing to him, he wasn't certain he could even imagine such a thing. Kat did not even act phased, head bent to her parchment, and Barrett wondered how much of it was her professionalism and how much Griswold had told her, like with Belldale.

"Would you be able to identify it if you heard it speaking again?" Kat pressed.

"It was the same one I heard in the abomination that attacked the gates."

Barrett looked up sharply. "The same as *what?*"

"Shush," Kat hushed him. "What did the voice sound like? Can you describe it?"

Kyran faltered. "It's…hard ta say. It sounded familiar, but I only heard it for a moment."

"Was it a demon speaking?"

"Aye," Kyran answered almost immediately, then frowned. "That was how the abomination saw it."

"And can you tell me what it said?"

Kyran lowered his head, his eyes moving over something Barrett couldn't see. "It was calling them ta fight," he said slowly. "Against the hunters."

Kat's pen froze, the sudden silence underlining Barrett's shock. Did this mean…

"Fairclough was right," Kat murmured, almost to herself, her pen flying over the parchment. "This…changes everything."

"How's that?" Barrett asked.

"It means the attacks in Belldale and here in the capital aren't a coincidence," she said, rising from her seat. "We need to speak with the Lightbringer."

Barrett cut his eyes at her remark. "What do you mean by that? What does Myles have to do with what's going on now?"

"It means the Lightbringer may know more than he's let on."

"You're wrong," Barrett said, rounding the table to catch his sister's eye. "Myles would have said something. He would have told us if he knew anything."

"Or he might be trying to protect himself or people he knows," she said, lowering the notes to look pointedly past Barrett at Kyran. "I think that will be—"

"He's not lying," Barrett seethed, stepping into her field of vision again.

Kat gave him a patient look that made him want to snatch the parchment from her hands and tear it to pieces. "Let's hope so." She moved to one side, and held the parchment and pen out to Kyran. "It just needs your signature, and I can go."

Pawing at his hip, Kyran reached into his purse and tugged his borrowed kerchief free, sending two pieces of paper fluttering to the floor.

"I've got it," Barrett said, bending to snatch the papers up, surprised he recognized one immediately by his own handwriting—the letter he had sent Kyran. Of all the things he thought Kyran would do with it, he'd never considered the mage might keep it on him. The thought sent a warm flutter through Barrett's middle as he handed it back, glancing at the second note with a curious frown. "Is that Lilyanna's handwriting?" he asked.

"Aye." Kyran sheepishly folded the note. "I need ta take it ta the chancery."

"Oh, is it an order for your false leg?" Kat asked, and the mage nodded. "I can take it with me and post it. I know the man. He's talented at his craft."

"Or I can take it when I go to write my report" Barrett countered, holding the note out to the mage.

Kyran paused a moment before he inclined his head. "Aye, as you like."

Barrett folded the note, and tucked it into his coat pocket, ignoring the amused snort from Kat.

"Regardless, I still need that signature," Kat said, holding out the parchment and pen again. "Just your cross at the bottom."

"Aye." Carefully, Kyran pinched the pen with his kerchief and bent to scratch an X next to the place Katherine pointed.

"Is that it?" Barrett asked as Kat examined the parchment.

"For now. I'm certain Hammond will be asking for more after this." She shook her head, drifting towards the door. "May your lanterns stay lit, and may we meet again, Kyran."

"And you as well," Barrett responded, following her to the door and shutting it behind her. "Insufferable," he scowled, stalking back to the table. Picking up one of the cups she'd left behind, he held it out for the mage, waiting as Kyran spread the kerchief over his palm. The cloth was filthy—stained black with blood.

"Wait." Barrett set the tea down again. "Let me see that."

Kyran ducked his head, shoulders hunching as he timidly set the bit of cloth in Barrett's palm. "I dinnae mean ta ruin it."

"Oh, it's not ruined. Just bein' put to good use." Barrett dropped the kerchief in the washbasin, fishing out a sliver of soap from beneath the stand. "I just thought you might not wanna wipe your cup down with it lookin' like this."

The mage made a soft noise of acknowledgement, the only other sound the tap of his nails against his walking stick and the soft splash of the washbasin as Barrett scrubbed the bit of cloth.

The water was quite grey by the time he deemed the kerchief clean enough. There were a few fraying threads around the edges from the mage's rough, frequent handling, but Barrett had also seen how Kyran had clutched it, worrying the embroidery when he was upset.

"I can make myself another one so I dinnae ruin that one," Kyran offered quietly. "I've spare cloth."

Barrett flicked a quick glance around the spare room. The only bit of cloth he could see that wasn't the quilt on the bed or clothes Kyran was wearing was the one extra shirt to the mage's name folded neatly atop the chest at the end of his bed. "It's all right. You can keep mine for now," he assured him, wringing the kerchief out and sending a bit of his magic into it to dry it off. "We'll get it washed up and find you a new one eventually."

He held the kerchief out to Kyran, who sighed in defeat but took it, if begrudgingly, and accepted the cup of tea with it.

Taking the seat across from Kyran, Barrett took up his own cup and tipped it back for a swallow. A vilely bitter taste filled his mouth in an instant, and he nearly choked trying not to spit the tea back out. "Graces, that's awful," he sputtered, holding the cup out as if it were poison. It was nothing like the honeyed drinks he'd gotten from the mess before. "I don't know if I can handle this. Need to get more of that Isleish whiskey. That stuff really knocks me out and tastes better than that tea."

"I dinnae take ta whiskey." The mage looked up from carefully wiping the rim of his cup. "Dinnae tell Murray."

"He won't hear a word of it," Barrett assured him, watching curiously as Kyran lifted the cup to his lips to take his first sip. The mage grimaced, a little shiver passing through him, but he didn't voice any complaints before taking a second sip, and Barrett forged ahead with choking the stuff down himself.

Despite the dreadful taste, it wasn't long before Barrett felt his scattered thoughts begin to grow quiet. He swirled the cup, peering down into the greenish brown liquid. If it didn't taste so ghastly, he might ask for more.

There was a soft noise from Kyran's direction, and Barrett looked up in time to see the mage swaying dangerously, his hand loosening around his cup.

"Whoa! Hey!" Barrett lurched out of his seat, just barely catching the cup as it fell from Kyran's limp fingers. "Kyran?"

The mage flinched, gripping the edge of the bed, his bleary eyes fixing on Barrett in what might almost pass for a glare.

"Sorry," Barrett said, easing back a step. "I'll, ah, just get goin' then. Let you sleep."

"Ye dinnae have ta," Kyran mumbled, head nodding.

Something warm fluttered in Barrett's chest at the mage's soft plea, but he brushed it aside. "You certain 'bout that?"

Murmuring something in Isleish, Kyran crawled up onto his bed and curled up on his side, tucking his leg underneath his kilt as he closed his eyes.

"Well, all right." Barrett chuckled to himself, easing back down in his chair. "I'll stay for a bit. Get some rest."

The mage said nothing, and in a few short moments, Barrett heard Kyran's breathing change to the long, slow breaths of sleep.

Letting out a long sigh, Barrett slumped back in his seat as the weight of the day finally landed on him. Graces, how had everything gone so wrong?

Chapter Thirty-Nine

Despite the abysmal weather and early hour, the guildhall's chancery was a flurry of activity as Barrett approached it. Secretaries, couriers, runners, and other guild members hurried in and out like a nest of ants hard at work. Inside was similarly laid out to the guild's post he had frequented in Oareford, only much larger and much busier.

Pushing past a harried looking scholar with crooked spectacles, Barrett found a stack of paper ready for use and a ratty quill resting in an inkpot, ink spattered across the desk. Pulling the note he'd taken from Kyran from his pocket, he bent over the desk and quickly scratched out a request for an appointment on Kyran's behalf. Sprinkling a pinch of sand over the note, he folded his arms, prepared to wait for the ink to dry when he spotted a familiar face amongst the strangers.

Not far from him, Ilham was leaning against another desk, apparently waiting for someone or something.

Barrett's mood darkened at the sight of her. The last time they spoke, she'd tried to get him to agree to make reports on Kyran without his awareness in exchange for information on his connection to the Old One. It had made little sense why the guild would ask such a thing, but after speaking with Kyran, he couldn't help a growing suspicion that something was going on and Ilham knew something about it.

He'd nearly made up his mind to confront her when another woman he recognized stepped up to the librarian, cupped Ilham's face and guided her down into a kiss.

Barrett immediately looked down, his ears warming, and he picked up the stack of papers to neaten it before stealing another glance, only to find both women looking his way.

"Barrett?" Alex laughed, and Barrett nearly immolated on the spot. "Didn't expect to see you here. What're you doing back in the capital?" she asked, approaching his desk. Ilham followed closely, her face nearly scarlet.

"I was part of the escort for Myles," Barrett explained, laying the papers back in the corner of the desk. "You?"

Alex reached for Ilham's hand and lifted it to her lips, grinning when the librarian's blush darkened with a shy smile. "Visiting."

Barrett felt his own face burn a little brighter. "I didn't know you were…with anyone. How long?"

"Before you and I even met. You never wondered why I never took you up on your offer for drinks?" Alex teased, sliding her eyes back to Ilham. "Don't tell me he's been after your attention, too?"

"No!" Ilham squeaked, her face darkening another shade.

"Oh, good." She flicked her eyes back to Barrett then down to the paper drying on his desk. "Another love note to your mage?"

His face felt like a scorching furnace and he scoffed to bury his own embarrassment. "It's for the artisan that makes false limbs. Lilyanna asked for it to be posted for Kyran."

"Meadows, right? He's good at his craft. I can have someone take it direct for you."

"Ah, thanks." He tested the corner of one of the letters, and, satisfied it was dry, shook off the sand and folded the letter around the note from Lilyanna. "Here."

"Why thank you. Take care of yourself. May your lanterns stay lit."

"And yours as well," Barrett said automatically, watching as they left together, his determination to confront Ilham faltering in the face of what was certainly a rare time with Alex. That was until he remembered the terrible sound of Kyran screaming. "Ilham, wait," he called, hurrying to catch up with them. "I…need to ask you something."

"Oh?" She turned to look up at him, her face still flushed and smiling. "What about?"

"The…" He glanced around them at the runners darting to and fro, and lowered his voice. "The research you were conducting about the Old One—who ordered you not to share it with me?"

The color drained from her face in an instant. "Barrett, I can't—"

"Can't what?" Alex asked, tugging at Ilham's hand to try to get the woman to look at her, but Ilham couldn't tear her eyes from Barrett. "Illy, what are you talking about?"

"The library," Ilham stammered, whirling for the door, towing Alex behind her.. "We… We can speak there."

"Ilham…" Alex said, following her out onto the lawn, Barrett just behind them. "What is this about?"

"Noth—" Barrett caught himself from dismissing her question. Secrets make for poor friends. "Before I went to the Isles, Ilham agreed to help me with some research. Now the guild has decided they'll only give it to me if I agree to provide information on Kyran. Without him knowing."

A deep line formed on Alex's forehead. "Is that true? Ilham?"

"Yes." The word was barely more than a squeak. "I don't like it, but I wasn't given a choice."

"Then make one. Graces, Illy…"

"Alex," Ilham reproached her, but Alex shook her head.

"No, you know how I feel about the guild's stupid secrecy. I understand not wanting to tell the world what they do, but the people making sacrifices for them have a right to know."

"It isn't that easy."

"Who—" Alex looked around, taking in the other people too, and started down the path, her hand around Ilham's. "I swear, if someone is threatening you…" she hissed once they were out of easy earshot.

"No. No, nothing like that," Ilham protested, but she sounded near to tears. It only deepened Barrett's suspicions.

"If you can't say who, then what is the guild planning with Kyran?" Barrett asked.

"I don't—I don't like being in the middle of this."

"You don't have to be," Barrett insisted. "If you can't tell me anything, then at least give me the file."

"And when they've found out you've read it?"

Alex let out a sigh. "They're asses, not mind readers. No one will have to know as long as none of us tells anyone."

"Please, Ilham," Barrett urged.

She shook her head. "The guild—"

"Hang the guild for a minute," Alex cut her off, pulling Ilham around until they were facing one another. "What's wrong with you? Why are you so scared to give Barrett a report you volunteered to make for him?" She leaned forward, rocking up onto her toes, and set her forehead to Ilham's as she whispered, "What did you find?"

Ilham squeezed her eyes shut, but she didn't pull away. "Too much. They know."

"Who?"

"Them. Head Scholar Marshal, Theona, Griswold, they know."

Barrett's shoulders stiffened. Of course, Griswold was involved. He was probably the one that had ordered Ilham.

Alex stilled, looking alarmed, and cupped Ilham's chin, raising her eyes. "Did they threaten you?"

"No," the librarian said, even as a tear slipped down her face.

A sneer curled Alex's lips. "Bastards," she snarled, gathering Ilham into her arms, and pressing her close. "Rotten bastards. I'll see every one of them to the Pit. Tell me where you put it. Is it in your desk?"

Ilham's frame shuddered, her fingers clutching Alex's shirt, but she nodded.

"I'll show him, then. You don't have to be anywhere nearby. I can meet you at the mess." Alex reached for Ilham's cheek, drawing her into another soft kiss. Barrett blushed at the sight and politely looked away. It was as if everyone had found someone while he had been away.

"Come on, hunter," Alex growled, stalking down the path ahead of him.

Ilham glanced his way as she stepped to one side, head lowered, and he felt a twist of guilt that he had upset her, even if he was angry. She was just as caught up in Griswold's schemes as Kyran was.

"Thank you," he told Alex earnestly when he caught up with her. "And I'm... sorry for upsetting Ilham."

She didn't respond, and Barrett sighed, folding his arms as they marched closer to the library. "So, how long have you two been friendly?"

"Few years. It's...hard, as you might imagine, since I'm away so often, but she's always here when I get back, and she always writes."

"Should've told me you had a lady when we first met," Barrett teased, pleased when Alex snorted at him. "I wouldn't have kept botherin' you."

"You were shyer back then. I had to let you down easy," Alex teased back, then fixed him with a serious look. "Don't think I've forgiven you for making Illy cry just because you made me laugh."

Barrett ducked his head with a light nod. "I've no idea how to make it up to either of you."

"Stick it to the guild, for one," Alex suggested as she raced ahead of Barrett and into the library. Once they were inside, Alex slowed and Barrett matched her pace as she led him straight to Ilham's desk. It was neat and organized, even the quills neatly lined at the top, their nibs cleaned. A mug half-full of what must have been coffee was set out of the way on a flat stone. And next to it was a familiar, neat stack of papers, tied with twine.

"This is the report," Barrett murmured and reached for it. "Alex, thank you—"

Her head lifted and looked past him, and Barrett turned to look, finding another scribe looking down into a book balanced in his hands, brows knit in thought. When he turned to look back at Alex, she was already five steps away from Ilham's desk, and Barrett followed after her quickly, tucking the report under his arm and rolling his boots as quietly as he could manage.

"I'll be heading to the mess," Alex said after they got back outside. "Make certain you keep that out of sight. I'll catch up with you later."

Barrett watched her veer off the path towards the mess and continued his own way back to the dormitories. He didn't stop until he was back in his room. He put the papers down on his desk, letting his head hang as it all hit him at once.

Griswold. Everywhere he turned, he kept hearing the guild captain's name. Kyran's arrest. The plan with the abomination. This file.

"Should have hit him harder," Barret sneered, smoke curling up from his fist.

He had to tell Kyran. The mage needed to know, and Barrett should be the one to tell him.

There was a flicker of magic from beyond his door, a familiar pull at his awareness, and Barrett felt his shoulders ease a fraction. Kyran was awake.

Chapter Forty

Kyran stared at the dim light streaming in through his window, his fingers wrapped around his prayer charm, but a prayer would not come. He should get up, should go and have breakfast, or a walk, or anything to get him out of his room, but all he really wanted was to lay there and fall back asleep. It was the first night in a long while he had been able to sleep without any nightmares, but they had been waiting for him when he woke, loud and demanding and overwhelming to the point of blotting out everything else.

Rattle. Rattle.

Kyran froze, fingers clenching around his charm as he strained to make out the sound as it came again, a soft, metallic rattling of the door latch, as if someone or something were trying to get in.

"It's just Barrett," he reassured himself, even as some frightened voice within him screamed that it was the demon, that it was its nails on the stone he was hearing, and he had to get up. Get up now.

"Kyran?" Barrett's voice called through the door. "I brought breakfast. My hands are full, and I can't—"

"Aye." The mage dragged himself out of bed, silently chastising himself for letting his thoughts spiral so wildly out of hand. "I'm here," he whispered as he used his borrowed kerchief to grasp the door latch, cool and solid against his palm. "This is real." He opened the door, swallowing his relieved sigh to find it was only Barrett, looking as disheveled as Kyran felt.

"Mornin'," the hunter said, holding up a basket for Kyran to see as he stepped inside. "Kept it as dry as I could. I didn't wake you, did I?"

"No," Kyran said, bumping the door shut behind them with his walking stick.

"That's good. Mead?" The hunter held up a bottle he'd produced from someplace and a pair of cups. "I can warm it."

"Aye, I could share a cup," Kyran said, taking a seat at the table while

Barrett began to unload his basket. There was fresh bread, oats with fruit, and even a tiny tureen of mushrooms.

They ate in relative quiet, something Kyran might have been grateful for any other day, but it was impossible not to note the anxious shiftings in the hunter. The way he kept glancing at the basket. Something was wrong.

"What is it?" Kyran finally demanded, setting his fork down, his hand straying to his amulet at his hip.

Barrett looked up, surprised. "What do you mean?"

"I'm na daft, Barrett. I can see something is off with ye. What is it?"

The hunter's eyes shifted evasively, and Kyran readied to duel the man if he tried to deny it, when Barrett let out a tight sigh. "There's… something we need to talk about."

Kyran felt his stomach drop to the floor. "You keep saying that," Kyran reminded him, his nails finding a ridge in his walking stick.

"I know," Barrett said, grabbing the bottle of mead and running his thumb over the wax sealing the bottle, which went up in a curl of smoke. "And there's a lot we should talk about. But this is about you."

Kyran watched the hunter pour two cups of mead, fighting the same brimming terror he'd felt when Barrett had walked into their room at the Drunken Wind with that warrant. Had the guild gone back on its word? Had Connal or Laird Dunbar found some other means to have him dragged back? Or, Graces forbid, had something happened to his family?

Setting the bottle down, Barrett reached into the basket and pulled out a stack of papers, letting them drop to the tabletop with a weighty thump. "I got this file from the library. It was supposed to have whatever Ilham compiled about the Old One from the guild's library. But when I went to get it from her, she said the guild demanded I trade for it."

Kyran's pulse hammered against his throat, his lines glowing dimly beneath his skin as Barrett lifted his cup.

"They wanted me to pass them information about you to get it."

The hole in Kyran's middle yawned wider, his face and hands tingling numbly. "What?"

"I didn't tell them anything," Barrett added quickly. "I wouldn't do that. Ever. I know I haven't been…completely honest about everything before now, and I want to fix that before I do anything else today, but you have to believe me. I would never spy on you like that, guild or not."

The hunter's eyes had gone wide, his face pale with real fear, and Kyran felt the edge of his panic ease. "Aye. I ken you're telling the truth."

"Ah, good," Barrett sighed with relief. He held out one of the cups to Kyran, waiting until Kyran took it before lifting his own to his lips, nearly downing it in a single draw. Kyran took a tentative sip, surprised by how warm and sweet the drink was. It was good, and he took a longer draw, letting the warmth settle in his belly.

Blowing out a sigh, Barrett set the cup down and ran his hands over his hair, pulling the tie free. "I'm...sorry again for not telling you anything. About the guild or hunters. Or me." He pinched the end of his glove and tugged it off, laying it on the table. "I never meant to keep things from you. I know you know—have probably known for a while—that I'm not a mage, like you."

"Aye. Ye're a witch."

Barrett winced at the word, eyes flashing with panic, but he didn't deny it. "...And?"

The hunter looked almost ill with anticipation, his starkly bare hand clenching the bottom of his sleeve, and despite Kyran's initial disgust and horror at the truth, he couldn't bring himself to see any of it in Barrett. Kyran knew what he had seen in the Inbetween—the way Barrett's eyes had changed just like Lilyanna's—but he'd also seen time and time again how Barrett had used that power to help people. To help Kyran.

"I ken it is...necessary," he said carefully, choosing his words. "The... demons. The lies."

"No." Barrett yanked his sleeve up, shoving it past his elbow. "Not the lies. Not anymore." He turned his arm, exposing his forearm and the blackened flesh marring his skin. "I have to hide these from regular folk, but I... I wanted you to know they're there."

"What are they?"

"They're called witch marks. When a hunter is gravely wounded, sometimes the demon expends energy to heal us. But it leaves us scarred like this."

Kyran tilted his head, studying the marks with knitted brows. He had never seen anything like them. "How did you get them?"

"This one was where I got bitten when you and I were in the Inbetween that first time. But the ones on my back are from... from my time in the demon realm. My body... it had to change. I had to... I had to surrender to survive there. Humans aren't meant to be there. It—" He lowered his sleeve, a soft tremor showing in his hands. "I have nightmares about it still. Feeling helpless. Out of control. You know about when it almost happened in the Isles, but..."

"It happened again?" Kyran ventured.

The hunter almost wheezed around a tight, bitter laugh. "That obvious?"

Kyran's attention switched to Barrett's face, moving along the cut that had nearly taken Barrett's eye. "What happened?"

Barrett flinched at the look, his fingers lifting to touch the tender scab across his face. "There was…another abomination. At Belldale. It attacked Myles, and I just…" His voice left him and he shut his eyes briefly, sucking down a deep breath and holding it for a long moment. "It happened so fast. One second I was attacking him, and my arm, my whole arm—it was black. I didn't lose control, though."

This time.

Kyran could hear the lingering remark between them. He looked down to his hands clasped in his lap so tightly the knuckles shone white. "What happens if you do?" he asked after a moment, voice quavering.

"The same as any other abomination."

The same as the broken body at the gates, or the man lying in his own blood upon a table. Another victim of the demon plague devouring Tennebrum, because what was a hunter but another casualty in the war against the beasts crawling out of the dark? As terrible and monstrous as it was, what other choice was there?

Kyran swallowed. There might have been one less life lost if he had been stronger, or able to control his magic better. But if he was able to gain more, to be stronger, then maybe there wouldn't have to be any more victims. He would be able to ensure Barrett never became one of them. But there was only one way for him to gain more magic. The needle-toothed demon had shown him.

He shuddered, and gulped down the rest of his drink to wash away the bitter taste of blood.

"Here." Barrett grabbed the bottle and started to pour them both another cup of mead, but hesitated when his eyes locked on something on the table.

The papers. An entire file. About the Old One. And maybe Kyran.

"We don't have to look at it today," Barrett quickly continued. "We can do it—"

"No. I want ta know." He needed to know.

Barrett nodded, setting the bottle down to reach for the file, drawing the papers out. "If you're certain."

"I'm tired of always being the last person ta ken anything. I want ta know."

"I know," Barrett assured him. He took a swift sip of his mead and set it aside in favor of the papers. "Let's get started, then."

Chapter Forty-One

COLD FURY ROSE like gorge at the back of Kyran's throat, his walking stick striking the cobbles in quick, hard clacks. The distant numbness of yesterday had faded, and all he could feel was wrath as his thoughts turned in circles.

He had listened as Barrett read aloud from page after page of vague references to the Old One made by countless hunters as far back as the guild had records. The oldest demon of the New Age. Then, they had come upon reports made by Barrett previously, and even Captain Griswold. Even the little bit Kyran had given the guild. But then the rest… The rest of the folder had been about Kyran, the Old One's only known living bairn, and it was obvious there were pages that had been omitted.

The file was proof in his eyes that he was less than a bondsman to the guild, he was an intriguing head of stock. A novel breed they wished to study.

It made him sick. Angry. Connal, the demon, the guild. Everywhere he went, he was just some thing to be used. Hurt. The guild had not outwardly been cruel to him, yet, but it couldn't be far off until they decided to lock him in a dungeon or cut him to see if he bled.

He reached for the sun he prayed with, holding it in his palm, but he still couldn't muster a devotion. Lumen didn't take demon kine amongst his worshippers. There was no other place for him than the Pit, if that was where demons went. He didn't know anymore. Maybe he would just disappear like the ones the hunters killed.

The thought sent a warm, hollow comfort spreading through him. No more nightmares. No more lies. No more pain. He could simply not be. No one else would get hurt because of him.

"Well, Graces carry my soul."

Kyran's fingers tightened around his walking stick at the low, creaking voice until he found the man he had overlooked seated on a bench nearby.

He was older, dressed in a priest's orange robe and yellow stole, and his face crinkled with a warm smile as he squinted up at the mage. "Kyran? Yes?"

"Aye?"

The man's smile widened. "I don't believe we've met properly. I am Myles." He shifted on the bench to face Kyran more fully, settling a cane across his lap. "This might be an odd sentiment coming from someone you've just met, but I am glad to see you are doing well, young man."

"Thank you?" Kyran replied uncertainly, trying to puzzle out who the man was until it finally clicked. "I ken it is you I owe—"

"You owe me nothing," Myles dismissed quickly with a wave of one gnarled hand. "I'm just a silly old man that happened to be in the right place. Though, if it isn't too much to ask, would you join me for a bit of this fresh air? I'd like to learn a little about this mysterious young man Kristopher beat the doors of the Pit down to deliver back into the Light."

Kyran felt a bit of color creep into his cheeks at the description, and he quickly dismissed his embarrassment for nonsense. "I ken he would have done the same for anyone."

"Perhaps," Myles agreed. "He is very kind and suffers the same affliction I do—what has been affectionately called a hard head." He chuckled to himself, and Kyran couldn't help a soft laugh.

"Aye, he has." But that wouldn't be enough to send a man into a realm of demons for someone he hardly knew, or across an entire sea, through the snow, to break into a castle's dungeon. That was...daft, to say the least. Friends. They still barely knew one another, but perhaps there was time yet. Before Barrett was sent away again, or before Kyran...

"You look troubled," the Lightbringer remarked, and Kyran's cheeks flushed darker.

"I dinnae mean ta wander," Kyran quickly apologized.

"Where did you go?"

"Just...thinking."

"About what? It looked awful important." Myles patted the seat next to him.

A hundred and one excuses to see himself off rose through Kyran, but where was he really in a hurry off to? His room? To sit at the ward? To wear the same patterns into the cobbles and mud he always did while there? To run away again?

"You don't have to tell me if you don't want to," the Lightbringer added, "But I feel rather like an old fool watching you stand while I yammer on."

Mustering himself, Kyran reluctantly lowered down next to Myles, tucking his walking stick into the crook of his arm.

"That's a bit easier on the neck." Myles chuckled, angling again to face Kyran. "You tall ones are like trying to see the top of an oak while standing at the base. Ah, but tell me. What is troubling you? I understand you have had a very difficult journey."

Kyran couldn't quite keep down a bitter sigh. "Aye."

"Barrett and I haven't had much time to catch up on current affairs since he left my House to bring you here. There is hardly any time to even tend the fires of the congregation as this plague worsens. I cannot thank the hunters enough for the sacrifices they make to keep us safe." He motioned a blessing with his fingers, and Kyran had to clench his walking stick to keep his hands from shaking with anger.

Here was a Lightbringer blessing hunters while Kyran and any other born a mage was cast from any House to be buried far from any Grace.

"Do you attend a House?" the Lightbringer asked, and Kyran stiffened in his seat.

"No, but my ma taught me the prayers," he said coldly, his nail tapping sharply against his walking stick.

"Was there not one where you lived?"

He gave the Lightbringer an arch look. "They dinnae build them atop the ben. There was one my kin went ta, but they dinnae suffer my kind."

Myles' shaggy brows arched so high they almost disappeared into one of his last remaining tufts of hair. "What's this, now? You weren't allowed to attend services because…you are a mage?"

Kyran nodded, the tapping growing louder.

"Well, I never," the Lightbringer scoffed. "What rubbish."

"I am na lying," Kyran said, pushing down a surge from his magic as his blood rose with his anger.

The Lightbringer held up his hands. "My apologies. You misunderstand. I am shocked to hear someone seeking Lumen would be turned away from his House."

"Oh, aye? Ye are? When there is a graveyard within these walls for the mages Lumen will na take ta his soil?"

Surprise and naked horror overtook Myles' placid demeanor. "Oh, Graces above, that's terrible. Why have they gone and done such a thing?"

Kyran lifted his hand, easing his grip about his power until his lines began to glow. "So we canna spoil the earth."

"Oh no. Kyran." The Lightbringer reached as if to take the mage's hand until Kyran pulled away from him. "I am so profoundly sorry that you have been made to feel like Lumen's light and Graces do not reach you. You are certainly welcome into his House, as is anyone that seeks to embody Grace. I will speak with the guildmaster about arranging rites for the departed as soon as I am deemed well enough."

Kyran didn't know quite what to say. He'd expected the Lightbringer to tell him what everyone else kept telling him—that as unfair and utterly mad as things were, he should learn to accept it. But Myles sounded so genuinely distraught, not just that Kyran was hurt, but at the idea that mages were being shunned from their place in Lumen's House.

It was as if a knot had come undone inside of Kyran. "Really?"

"Yes, of course. I am ashamed none of the Lightbringers that guard the Eternal Flame here in the capital ever sought to rectify this. For shame." Myles huffed, shaking his head before he looked up at Kyran again. "If you are in need of guidance for prayer, I would be more than happy to have you join me at the morning and evening bells. It would have to be here for now, unfortunately, if that puts you off."

Kyran's hand strayed towards his purse and the tiny sun charm he always carried. He'd only ever said his prayers with his family or alone atop Cairngorm, never with the guidance of a Lightbringer. "I ken I would like that."

Myles smiled warmly. "Good. Wonderful. I look forward to it."

"Aye, and, if it is all right with you, I'd like ta be there when you say Grace for the mages in the graveyard."

"Of course," the Lightbringer said with all sincerity. "I won't start a minute before you are standing there with me. And—ah." Something by the hospital door caught his eye, and Kyran followed his gaze to see an orderly patiently looking their way. "I see my time is up. If I were younger, I'd give them the slip, but I daresay my days of running anyplace are far and away," Myles puffed, managing to look quite sullen beneath his wrinkles.

Leaning heavily into his cane, the Lightbringer rose from the bench with a groan, his joints protesting loudly. "It was good to properly meet you, Kyran. I hope we will see more of each other while I am here. May your lanterns stay lit."

"And stars guide your way," Kyran offered with an inclination of his head.

He waited until the Lightbringer had passed through the hospital doors before the mage continued down the cobbled path towards the dorms, seized by a sudden determination. There were plenty more suns that needed to be made.

Chapter Forty-Two

By the Graces, Barrett regretted every last drop of drink he had swallowed. He stifled a wet burp, staring blearily at the folks filtering into the mess around him, before he let his head drop to the table again. Just a few more minutes, and he could head back and face Kyran after everything they read in that file, after everything Kyran told him. After seeing the face the mage made before and after reading those pages. Graces, maybe he did need another drink.

"Well, you look like something from the bottom of the Pit."

Barrett groaned, dragging himself upright again to look up at his sister. "Mornin', Kat."

"It's evening, you idiot. How long have you been in here?"

He struggled to drag an answer out of his sodden head. He'd come straight away after he and Kyran had finished the file, and Kyran had gone for a walk. When had that been? "Mmh, since this morning?"

"Morni—Kris—" She cut herself off, teeth clicking together with an evident force of will. She closed her eyes, taking a deep breath through her nose. "Is Kyran all right?"

Barrett's pulse leapt up into his throat. "Did something happen? Where is he?" he asked, struggling to scramble out of his seat.

Katherine set a hand to his shoulder and pushed him back down. "I don't know. Off doing whatever it is he does all day, I imagine. I just thought to ask since you're…" She nodded to the half empty bottle in front of him.

Barrett slumped back into his seat. "Oh. He… He's probably sleepin'."

"Like you should be."

He snorted, folding his arms on the table and setting his chin in his hand. "As if I could."

"You and him have a falling out, then?"

"No." He considered his empty drink for a moment. "Of sorts. I think I messed up."

"Mhmm." She didn't look surprised. In fact, she looked faintly amused. "Have you tried apologizing?"

"I did, but…"

"But?"

Barrett frowned, tipping his mug back for the last drop. "I don't know if it's enough. I wish I could…" He groped for the right word. "…comfort him?"

"Does he need comforting?" She pulled out the chair next to him and took a seat. "I never liked when Hammond or mum got it into their heads that I needed my hand held. I just needed to be let alone long enough to deal with it on my own, and then I just wanted them to let me rejoin them as if nothing had happened. Talk and drink and carry on as usual."

"He's not you, Kat."

She raised her brows. "Just to be clear, we are talking about Kyran?"

Barrett sighed, fiddling with his mug. "Yes," he finally said sullenly.

"Well, I suggest apologizing how every man that's courted me apologized, then."

"I am not courting Kyran," Barrett corrected her. "We're friends."

Katherine opened her mouth, then closed it before she continued. "And is that all you want to be?"

Barrett froze, his mind going a perfect blank at her question. "Do-Do I what?"

"I'll take that as a no," she said with a knowing smile.

"Wait. Wait, no. Kyran and I— We're just friends," he repeated, but she just chuckled, and Barrett felt the first fingers of panic tighten around his chest. "Kat. Kat, listen to me. Me and Kyran are just friends. You can't— Please don't tell Kyran whatever you think is going on. You'll scare him."

Katherine's expression sobered, her head tilting as she took in the sight of him. "I won't," she said at last. "But are you looking to pursue him?"

Barrett cut her a look. "Why do you think there's more?"

"I think everyone thinks there's more."

"Well, there isn't. Even if Kyran was… inclined, I couldn't… I don't know if I can, after…" He couldn't say his name. He couldn't say Raleigh without it tearing something out of him he couldn't face right now.

Katherine let him be and stayed uncharacteristically silent for a long moment. "Have you gone to see him yet?" she finally asked quietly. She meant Raleigh.

Barrett shook his head, not trusting his voice.

"You should go. Take a candle with you to burn when it's not raining."

He should. Barrett couldn't even say why he hadn't yet, but even just the thought of it was utterly terrifying. "I don't know," he whispered.

"It doesn't have to be now, but you should do it. For you and for him."

For Raleigh. Barrett nodded, silently agreeing. Raleigh deserved to be remembered. Honored. But Barrett was just so… scared of what he might feel, of how easily it had overwhelmed him before. He closed his eyes, pulling away from the deep, aching hole in his middle. "I will."

"Good. But if it's got you drinkin' like this, maybe it's too soon anyway. These things take time.

He tried to make a retort. Something silly. Something petty. But he found it difficult enough just to breathe. Barrett lifted his eyes to the ceiling, then shut them and forced himself to take a slow, deep breath. "I know," he replied after a long moment.

"As for your friend, buy him something tediously useless to present him with while you almost sincerely apologize for whatever it was that upset him."

Barrett groaned despite himself. "You're terrible at this advice-thing. Why did I even bother listening?"

"That—" she said, kicking her chair out as she smirked at Barrett. "— is the question you should be asking." She stood, offering him a hand. "Come on. Get up."

"What?"

"I'm taking you back to your room before you're sick all over the mess floor. I promise it isn't fun when they make you clean it yourself." Without waiting for his reply, she grabbed him under his arm, dragging him up out of his seat. "Come on."

"I am. I am," he groused, fumbling to get over the bench and nearly pitching over sideways as his legs refused to cooperate. Kat caught him though, her grip bruisingly tight as she hauled him up and slung his arm over her shoulders.

"Blessed Graces, you smell like a tavern floor," she swore, leaning away from him.

"Ha ha," he slurred, stumbling as she escorted him forcibly out into the blinding sunlight. His stomach gave an unsteady lurch.

"Do say something if you're going to be sick," Katherine warned him.

Barrett managed a sickly groan before he nearly dragged Katherine over with him as he heaved all over the grass.

She waited until he was only dry heaving before hauling him back upright and starting across the lawns again.

It felt an age before they reached the dorms, and Barrett was never so glad to see the inside of his room as when Katherine let him fall into bed. He started to close his eyes to go to sleep, when he heard his sister scuffing around. He entertained the thought of going to sleep anyway for a few tantalizing seconds before he rolled onto his side to see what she was doing.

She set the empty washbasin from the stand on the floor next to the bed, and a cup full of water on the nearest bedside table, along with a sealed note. "You received a reply to your letter," she told him, looking down on him in evident bemusement. "Get some rest."

Barrett managed a grunt, watching with just his eyes as Kat crossed the room and let herself out. He barely heard the latch click before he was asleep.

CHAPTER FORTY-THREE

THE SUN WAS hanging low on the horizon when Barrett finally stopped trying to fall back asleep. He felt dreadful—cotton mouthed and queasy, and more than a little ashamed.

His relatively unresolved conversation with Kyran and then Kat hung heavily over his aching head, and despite how ill he felt, he wished he had another drink to push the circling thoughts away. He didn't want to think about seeing Kyran cry, or what Kat's accusations had set stirring in Barrett's head. He didn't want to think about anything at all, and if it weren't for the letter Kat had left with him, he would have crawled back under the quilt and waited until tomorrow, but by then, it would be too late.

So, dragging himself off of his bed, and splashing some cold water on his face, he finally left his room.

It was only after a long moment of simply staring at the mage's door that Barrett was able to summon the nerve to knock on it. He waited, reciting in his head what he was going to say about the letter, but there was no answer, and, once he focused on the pull of his magic, no sense of the mage beyond the door.

He sighed. "Of course, he's not in."

Outside, the rain had finally let up, the grounds shining under a brilliant sunset that set guildhall aflame in golds and oranges. Among them, a flash of copper caught Barrett's attention and he felt his spine go rigid as he spotted Kyran disappearing around the corner of a far building. Despite having set out to look for the mage, Barrett lingered by the dormitory, a terrible sense of anxiety rising through him. What if he upset Kyran again? What if he made things worse, and the mage started avoiding him again? What if Kat hadn't kept her promise?

"Bein' ridiculous," he chastised himself, pulling away from the dormitory wall to follow Kyran, shoving his apprehensions down and out of his head.

But as he drew near, Barrett realized where the mage was headed. The graveyard.

Barrett's boots dragged to a stop, his heart thudding against his ribs faster and faster. He didn't want to go there. Could not go there and face what he knew was waiting for him. He waited for Kyran to stop, to turn away, to go another direction, but he moved forward with purpose towards the well-tended square of lawn at the far end of guildhall.

Barrett let out a tight, shaky breath and looked up at the sky and the lingering puffs of purple and orange. "Graces give me courage," he whispered and forced his feet forward.

With each step he felt as though his heart thudded harder and harder in his chest until all he could hear was a roaring in his ears.

And then he was there, his feet at the edge of the path, watching Kyran as he headed to the nearest gravestone. The mage stood there a moment, then carefully knelt, his head bowed. Barrett heard a whisper of Isleish, the syllables indistinguishable from that distance, but the intent was unmistakable. He was praying. Praying for the mages the Houses wouldn't take.

Barrett shouldn't be there, intruding on something so private. He rocked back on his heels, determined to leave, when Kyran's head lifted, and Barrett froze in his gaze.

"Sorry," Barrett stammered, easing back a step. "I can… We can talk later."

"What is it?" Kyran asked, cupping what looked like a lit taper in his hands.

Barrett tried to read if the mage was still upset, but Kyran's expression had returned to that cool implacability Barrett could never decipher. "It's kind of you to do this for them."

"Or madness," the mage said in a toneless, tired voice. "I dinnae ken if Lumen will even take our kind, even if that Lightbringer said he would, but I couldna leave them in the cold earth." He reached out, tracing his fingertips along the name carved into the headstone beside him. "I have ta believe there's some reason for us, though. That Lumen willna forget us for being made this way. He couldna, or what would be the point of any of it?"

"I… I don't know," Barrett stammered, utterly caught off guard by the change in sentiment from just the day before, where Kyran had decried his cursed bloodline. Maybe talking to him had helped. Maybe Barrett hadn't made everything worse after all. But what could he say now? Something significant. Uplifting.

He stared at the ground, wishing something inspiring would come to mind. The letter crinkled in his grip, reminding him of his intent when he came out here, but what had felt like a good idea to reconnect with the mage when he'd penned the initial letter now sounded like a hollow offering. He wasn't even certain Kyran would trust him enough to accept it.

Have you apologized?

Perhaps it was rotten timing, but if he didn't get it out in the air now, he wasn't certain when he would, or even could. "I wanted to apologize," he finally said. "Really apologize. For… everything. Everything I never said. I know I gave a hundred excuses before, but you deserved to hear the truth. I know we don't exactly know each other that well, but I meant what I said before. I care about our friendship a great deal and I… I was hoping you might forgive me."

He took a slow, quiet breath, nervously waiting for Kyran to say something, but the mage was quiet, his expression infuriatingly cool and hard to read. "Aye, I do," he said softly at last, carving a line in his walking stick with his thumbnail. "I'm still…angry, but I ken it isna with you. Ye are na the one that made things this way, and I'm…sorry ta have blamed ye after everything ye've done for me."

Something tight in Barrett's chest loosened at Kyran's words, and he ducked his head as his eyes began to burn in earnest. He had known to some degree how much it meant to him to make things right between them, but he had never considered that Kyran might feel the same way. It only went to prove how much he still had to learn. "I'd do it again," he said, fighting the coarse edge to his voice that threatened to turn into a sob. "I'm glad you're here."

Light flickered over Kyran's face, a flash of his runelines coloring his cheeks with faint blue light before the mage looked away over the headstones. Barrett followed his gaze, shame working into his belly over the fact that he did not know which one was Raleigh's.

Their quiet was disturbed as a lamplighter came by, quietly and quickly going about their work. Extinguishing his candle, Kyran slipped the taper into his purse, settling both hands about his walking stick. "I am done here if you would like ta get supper."

Barrett couldn't stop the grin from spreading over his face. He wasn't certain he could stomach food just then, but by the Graces, he was certainly going to try now. He—

The letter in his hand let out another plaintive crinkle, reminding him of the initial reason he had sought Kyran out.

"Ah, yes. Yes, I'd like to, but first, I, ah—I wanted to let you know that you got a reply to your letter." He held up the unsealed paper. "You have an appointment tomorrow to be fitted for your leg."

The mage blinked in naked surprise at Barrett's announcement, his whole demeanor shifting in an instant. "Aye?"

"And, if it's all right with you, I wanted to ask if I could come with you. Maybe not to the fitting, if that's too much, but I thought you might like someone to show you around. I know all the best places to get supper."

"Is that so?" Kyran said, a smirk at the corner of his mouth.

"Aye, it is," Barrett retorted, hiding his anxiety over the mage's answer behind a grin.

"I ken I could hardly keep you away if I tried," Kyran remarked,

"You know I would if you asked," Barrett assured him, his smile fading. Maybe he had pushed this too soon. Maybe he should have—

"Aye, I do," Kyran agreed, leaning into a walking stick. "When would we need ta leave for the appointment?"

"We? You mean…?" Barrett fumbled for words, because as much as he wanted Kyran to say yes, he hadn't really expected it at this point. "Ah, uhm, how about we talk about it over supper?" he managed to string together, his mind already racing ahead to tomorrow.

The mage agreed, and Barrett stepped to one side to let him from the graveyard, doing his best not to look at the headstones as he did, unwilling to trample the one shred of good news he'd heard in ages. Not today. He couldn't look today, but maybe when things were better. Maybe then.

Chapter Forty-Four

THE NIGHT PASSED slowly as Kyran lay awake in his bed, watching the shadows shift and move across his walls with the flickering lantern flame. It didn't matter which way he turned, or how long he lay there, sleep simply couldn't reach him through the squirming ball of knots that had tied itself in his belly, until he finally surrendered gracelessly to wakefulness.

Dragging himself from his bed, he went about getting ready for the day, washing up and tending to his leg before he let himself from his room to pay the ward a visit.

Effie greeted him first, running out the front door to take his hand with a delighted giggle. Sophie was not far behind, her mouth turned in wry amusement as she ushered them both in.

The weans were a welcome distraction from his difficult night. It was hard to linger on any disparaging thoughts with one lass chattering his ear off about writing classes and magic while the other patiently held out her doll for its hair to be braided, which he, of course, obliged.

It was over all too soon, though, the matron instructing the weans to head to their classes.

"I'll be back soon," he promised Effie, handing the lass her doll back, which she clutched to her chest like a talisman.

The good weather from the day before had miraculously held as the sunrise became a warm, dewy morning as Kyran crossed the ground to the northern gate. The gate itself was still in ruins after the abomination had destroyed it, but a towering wooden barrier had appeared in its place, the gatehouse's broken stones piled around the base for strength. Kyran must have been well and truly in his own world not to have noticed this scale of construction.

Kyran didn't recognize the guard on duty, who regarded him with thinly veiled boredom.

"Mornin'." It was Barrett's voice, but Kyran didn't recognize the stranger walking towards him until the man smiled.

The hunter had shaved. A few stray wisps on his neck had escaped the blade, and there was the barest knick of red on the corner of his jaw near his ear, but his face was otherwise clean and smooth, with the exception of the angry looking scab across his face. Not only that, but Barrett had taken a comb to his hair as well, which hung long and soft looking down his back. He looked almost like another person, one Kyran's own age.

"Ready to go?" Barrett asked, and Kyran shook his head clear.

"Aye."

Barrett stepped past him to address the guard, and Kyran couldn't help but notice the scent of fresh soap drifting from the hunter.

"Mornin'," Barrett greeted the guard. "Kristopher Barrett and Kyran Roche. We should have concession to—"

"Yes," the guard sighed, lurching up from her stool. "There hasn't been much commotion today, but I suggest you hurry and keep your heads ducked." She gestured for them to go through. "May your lanterns stay lit."

"And yours as well."

Squeezing through the gap, Kyran had to step over a mound of mud and rotting vegetable matter, the stink of it blending with the lingering scent of wet, burnt wood. Across the street, a Crown guardsman glowered at people as they hurried past, his cudgel beating out a rhythmic pace against his thigh. The buildings sported a few blackened scorch marks, but had fared better than elsewhere.

Looking over his shoulder, Kyran could see the front of the guild's wooden barrier splattered with more foul smelling debris.

"Things aren't always like this," Barrett assured him, but Kyran wasn't so certain.

It wasn't long before the cobbles began a gentle decline, and, as if they had crossed an invisible barrier, they were suddenly adrift amongst people. Tables and shops crowded the sides of the road, hawking every nameable ware, claims of goods from exotic lands ringing out over the constant hum of life and conversation. The smell of salt and fish gained in strength, but they could not cover the sharp tang of fire.

Kyran drifted closer to Barrett, nervously tugging his sleeves down over his wrists as he noticed the stares following him. He knew it wasn't necessarily because he was a mage. He was an Isleman. With his bright red hair and kilt, he looked every part the foreigner, but he still couldn't help examining his hands for any trace of his runelines as he quashed his magic down.

Barrett walked effortlessly through the crowd of people, weaving a path with Kyran right behind him. He couldn't judge properly just how long they had been walking, but finally they managed to break free of what had to be the thickest part of the crowd.

"Lot more folks out than I expected," Barrett commented as he paused at a crossroads. He looked up at the buildings, turning in place as if to get his bearings. "Ah, it's this way."

He turned left, the press of the crowd lessening. There weren't fewer people, but there were no stalls set up in front of the row of shops, whose doors were set open to catch the cool, salt laced breeze that tickled Kyran's nose. It was still strange, even after crossing the sea several times now, and he wasn't certain if he liked it or not.

"Here it is," Barrett finally declared, stopping in front of one of the shops.

Kyran squinted through the late morning sun up at the sign over the door. A small red bird was painted perched at the crux of an axe and another tool crossed at the center of the sign. There were letters arched above the image, likely the name of the place. He looked from the sign to the windows, but they were darkened, obscuring the wares within.

"You can see better from inside," Barrett teased from the doorway.

Kyran's mouth twitched before he ducked into the shop behind Barrett, hesitating just within at the change in light. The shop smelled pungently of wood shavings, and as his eyes adjusted to the lantern light, Kyran stood in awe at the wares surrounding him.

Among the tables and shelves crammed with knickknacks and dolls were a variety of walking sticks, canes, and, most fascinatingly, beautifully carved limbs of every intricacy. There were neat displays of legs, arms, hands, feet, and even fingers, all in different styles and colors.

Kyran stared at them all, burning with curiosity to know what it would feel like to wear one. He missed his leg—missed being able to run, to stand without having to hold onto something, to not have to live with the constant bone deep ache that never lessened and never fully went away without his magic to soothe it.

"And what may I do for you gentlemen today?"

Kyran looked away from the displays to the back of the shop, where an older gentleman sat in front of a warm fireplace, hands busily whittling at some project. His clothes were covered in flakes of wood, his build heavier with the same age that had sprinkled his dark hair with silver and drawn lines in his warm, brown skin.

"Good mornin', Meadows?" Barrett sounded uncertain.

"That's me," the man confirmed, setting his work aside and brushing his shirt off.

"I'm Kristopher Barrett. I sent a letter ahead."

"Ah, yes. My apologies for being so rude." The man got up from his stool and ambled over to them, trading grips with Barrett. "It is good to finally meet you in person." His gaze switched to Kyran as they shook, but anything he felt about the mage's appearance, Meadows kept tactfully hidden behind his smile. "And this young man must be Kyran."

"Aye," Kyran confirmed, shifting a glance at Barrett.

"Well, then. We don't get many Islemen in this country, and I think you are only the second in this shop." He offered his hand to Kyran. "My name is Anthony Meadows. A pleasure to meet you."

Kyran eyed the man's hand, imagining the rough texture of calluses across his palm and folding around his fingers, of skin damp against his. He folded both hands around his walking stick. "Aye, you as well."

Meadows frowned, his eyes flickering to Barrett for a moment before he resumed a professional smile. "I prepared a few things to show you after your friend here wrote me. I apologize if the selection is limited, but the Hunter was quite right—you are a very tall young man."

Kyran smiled thinly, glancing at Barrett again, but the hunter was looking down at his boots. "I dinnae realize there were choices," he said at last, his fingers beginning to tap against his stick.

"Well then, you have come to the right place to be educated on this very important purchase. I have brought a very many great things into the world that may help you. If you will follow me."

His arm swept past the fireplace to a thick, deep purple curtain, indicating for Kyran to go ahead of him. Clenching his fingers around his walking stick, he started for the curtain, when the man stopped with a soft tut.

"I'm afraid I'll have to ask you to stay out here." Kyran looked over his shoulder to see the man addressing Barrett. "It might be...uncomfortable for the young man if you were to come to the back while I take his measurements."

Kyran's fingers tightened around his stick. "My measurements?"

"Yes. It is very important these things fit with absolute precision if they are to be useful to you."

Barrett gave the man a worried look. "Could you let him take them, then you read the tape?" he suggested.

"I'm sorry?" Meadows blinked through his polite smile, obviously confused by the strange request.

Barrett fumbled for words. "I just thought it might be...awkward," he answered after a moment. He rocked back on his heels and instead addressed Kyran. "Will you be all right?"

"I promise I am accommodating," Meadows assured the hunter. "We will find what works for us."

Barrett nodded. "I'll be here if you need anything," he said to Kyran.

"Feel free to peruse the rest of my shop while I care for your friend," Meadows said, gesturing to the wares on display in the rest of the shop. "It may take some time even once he finds something to suit his needs." He turned to Kyran, his smile bright and crisp. "Shall we then?"

With a growing sense of anxiety, Kyran followed the man behind the curtain, perching on the very edge of the stool Meadows offered him while the man tugged the curtain shut.

"Now." Meadows turned to face him, clasping his hands almost earnestly. "I understand you may be nervous or concerned about what I may see, but I swear on my honor, that it is only so I may produce the best finished craft to accommodate your needs. To decide what type of limb you may need, I will need to take measurements of your good leg as well as the one I will be crafting, and measurements for the harness. I won't need you to dress down, as the harness can be adjusted, but I will need you to lift your fabric there so I may see your leg. Just when you're ready."

Kyran swallowed, the pit of his stomach threatening to lurch up into his throat. In any other circumstance, he would refuse. He would get up and leave, and never come back.

But just the idea that one of those carved limbs he'd seen on the shelves might be his, that he might just be able to stand and walk again, was enough to keep in his seat.

Looking anywhere but at the man or his leg, Kyran drew the edge of his kilt up to his hip, revealing the short stump, still covered in bandages, that was all that remained of his leg after the demon and then rot had claimed it. What was left was barely half the length of his right thigh.

Meadows then proceeded to ask him about the scars on his leg, which Kyran answered as best he could. "I see," the man said after Kyran had answered at least a dozen different inquiries. "Your scars are still healing, so you will likely experience some discomfort. That will lessen with time, though."

Next, the man bade him step from behind the curtain, and brought him a few different styles of prostheses to look at, and the different, confusing looking harnesses that accompanied each. Meadows was thorough, describing the aspects of each of the designs—both positive and negative—before insisting Kyran return to the curtain to try each on.

It took some doing. Kyran refused the man's help, wrestling with the heavy prostheses and a web of leather straps and buckles that went not only around what was left of his leg, but his hips and waist as well, each and every one adjustable to disperse the weight of the limb over his hips. Even then, all of the prostheses were too short, and he had to hobble around with his walking stick in an attempt to determine which he liked, which only served to make his stump and hips ache furiously.

In the end, he relied on the craftsman's opinion to select which he thought best. Of course, that was not the very end of things. After taking several measurements of both his good and bad leg behind the curtain, Meadows declared he would make something to Kyran's height.

"I will have it done by this evening," he promised. "Though I understand you may have other business you need attend. It will be here, safe with me, if you must delay your return. My only recommendation while you are out enjoying the city, is that you may wish to visit the clothier's quarter. It should be safe to wear the apparatus unencumbered in your own home, but it must be protected outside to remain in its best appearance." At the mage's perplexed face, he clarified. "You will require another boot."

A faint flush crept into Kyran's face. "Aye. Of course." He hadn't even considered that he only owned one boot at the moment.

"We'll get some boots after we find a bakery," Barrett suggested with mirth bright in his eyes. Kyran cut him a dry look.

"Wonderful," Meadows said with a delighted clap. "It sounds like you have it all planned out."

"We'll be back this evenin', like you said. May your lanterns stay lit."

"And yours as well."

CHAPTER FORTY-FIVE

KYRAN FOLLOWED BARRETT closely as they wound through a labyrinth of side streets and throughways until, almost miraculously, they emerged in the clothier's quarter.

The noisy crowd of the street was an unwelcome unpleasantness after the relative quiet and privacy of the shop, and a mild dread began to build in Kyran as he watched Barrett peek in windows and doors. Fortunately, it wasn't long before they found a cobbler's shop with a pair of boots that were remarkably similar to the ones Kyran had lost, which he immediately swapped out with the ill-fitted one he still wore that he had been given by Mrs. McCrory for the Great Hall in the Isles. The new left boot went into a sack Barrett slung over his shoulder, and the cobbler offered to take the old, unwanted boot. Kyran was all too happy to agree.

They ambled around the clothier's quarter a while longer, and Barrett used the opportunity to buy a new set of clothes for himself. None of it particularly appealed to Kyran, the styles and colors so vastly different than what he was accustomed to, and after a while, he found himself looking over clothing meant for weans. If he had any coin, he would have liked to get a new dress for Effie to wear. The lass had so little, but all of the money Barrett had given Kyran in Oareford had been lost when the demon had taken him.

"I think Effie might like that one," Barrett said, appearing abruptly off Kyran's left side and near starting him out of his skin.

He muttered an Isleish curse, turning on the hunter. "Finished, have ye?"

Barrett patted the sack he was carrying. It looked a little more stuffed than before. "Couple of shirts and a pair of pants since mine are going to rags." The hunter gestured to the dress Kyran had been looking at. "You were over here awhile. Why don't we grab it? I'm certain Sophie can help us tailor it for the lass."

"Aye," Kyran said slowly, digging at his walking stick with his nail as he tried to think of a way to explain why he couldn't, but there was no way of avoiding the truth, no matter how embarrassing. "I…dinnae have the coin you gave me anymore."

"I don't mind lendin' for it," Barrett offered, as if it were the simplest thing in the world.

"But I dinnae know when I can pay you back."

"You don't have to worry 'bout it," Barrett insisted sincerely. "I like helpin' where I can."

"Aye, but I dinnae like being a debtor."

Barrett's smile waned and he looked back at the little dress, his expression turning thoughtful. It was only a moment when he spoke again, the faintest of grins returning. "Then you can pay me back," he suggested. "Whenever it's convenient."

The mage gave him a wry look. "Whenever the guild decides ta pay me, ye mean."

"It'll be comin', don't you worry," Barrett assured him. "I got mine once a month while I was stationed in Oareford, though I've heard of hunters getting them more often if you stay at the guild, like we are now. Anyway—that dress? And don't worry about the cost. You'd be surprised how quickly you'll earn it back."

The hunter meant well, but it was still hard to agree to take his money. Kyran had never had a lot, but he'd never really needed it, not until he came to Tennebrum, and then he had been able to earn it. But for the past several months, he had been at the mercy of the guild, unable to do anything but rely on them. He intensely disliked being kept so utterly helpless and dependent. But this wasn't for him. It was for Effie, and that was enough to soften his composure.

Dinner they ate leaning against the wall of a baker's shop, which they found by simply following the smell—Barrett with his pork pie, and Kyran with onion. Barrett rambled as they ate, explaining how the pies would have been made, and the ingredients likely used.

Kyran smiled between bites, watching Barrett mime how to shape a pie crust. He hadn't known Barrett had once been apprenticed to become a baker under his ma. It was rare for the hunter to talk about anything personal. He had even stopped talking about Raleigh since the Isles. It had left many of their few days together strained for conversation. Kyran wished Barrett would tell him more. He felt like he hardly knew the man, but he understood all too well what it was like having things he wished to go unspoken. Maybe someday.

When they finished eating, Barrett disappeared into the shop again, reemerging with a custard tart for each of them balanced on his palm.

Kyran had never had one before, and was pleased to discover it was delightfully sticky sweet.

They wandered through the quarter a bit longer, but by then, Kyran was hardly paying attention to where they were going. His senses were rubbed raw and numb by the crowds and he could feel the edge of his exhaustion from his sleepless night creeping up on him.

It felt an age, but at last, they made their way back to Cardinal's Craftes where Meadows was waiting for them.

"You're back," Meadows greeted them from the back of the shop as they entered, standing to brush the sawdust from his clothes. "Perfect! Come, come, let me show you. You must try it on."

Kyran glanced back at Barrett, who offered him an excited smile and stepped clear so Kyran could pass by him and follow the man.

Meadows proudly stood by his creation as Kyran made his way to the back of the shop, and at the sight of it, he knew why the man was so pleased. It was beautiful, carved into a near perfect replica of a leg, down to the arching foot with delicate toes, the pale wood so smooth it could have been skin. Even the knee joint looked near enough to the real thing to pass idle scrutiny.

"Shall we try it on?" Meadows preempted when Kyran made no immediate remark. "You must try it on before you make your final decision, of course. One can never be too hasty with such matters. I must ensure a perfect fit before you leave, or it will not do."

Of course, it was this last fitting that proved the most trying. The leg was complete, but there was still the matter of the harness to fit. It was fortunate Meadows didn't have to make a new one, but was able to alter another he had to fit Kyran's slender waist and leg, but it took quite a while to adjust each individual strap to the proper length, especially since Kyran insisted on doing it himself.

At long last, though, it was finished. Meadows gave him a brief demonstration of how he should sit while wearing the leg, and tried to describe some of what it might feel like trying to walk with it, but Kyran hardly heard him. He was standing, his weight balanced precariously between his two limbs with no more assistance than his fingers clutched in the purple drape. He was standing.

"Come," Meadows encouraged. "Try it out. I am certain your friend will want to see."

"Aye," Kyran mumbled in reply, and started to reach for his walking stick, when he stopped. That wasn't what he wanted. He didn't want to keep walking with that hard bit of wood jammed under his arm. He already had enough bruises from it. He wanted to walk again like anybody else. So, he pulled the curtain back and, ducking his head, he walked.

It wasn't graceful. He was slow, his pace a bit uneven. His hips hitched just before he swung the wooden leg forward, breaking in a slight limp as he bore his weight down on his aching stump. But he was walking.

Barrett stood at the end of the aisle, his eyes alight with delight, and the smile on his face grew. "It looks really—you look really good."

Kyran pointedly fixed his gaze forward on the shelf he meant to reach, ignoring the flush that crept into his cheeks with a prickle of light.

It wasn't far, and it took an age to cross the space with his balance wobbling, but he never gave out. He stretched his hand out as he drew near and grasped the shelf, leaning on its sturdy strength as he rubbed at his aching stump.

It throbbed at the attention, and he let a slip of his magic free, the cold seeping into his muscle and bone to soothe the ache. The injury was still far from perfectly healed, and he suspected it would be a long while before he would be measurably free of the pain of it, but for now, it didn't matter. He'd done it. He'd walked.

"Wonderful!" Meadows applauded. "Simply wonderful! You are a natural."

"How does it feel?" Barrett asked, his gaze gravitating to the wooden leg with something like marvel.

"Good," Kyran replied, kneading his thigh. Even with the ache, he could not stop himself from smiling. He had walked. "It is good. I will just...need some time."

"You'll have all the time you need," Barrett assured him before he looked to Meadows. "The craftsmanship is remarkable."

"But of course!" the man all but bubbled, smiling broadly. "It is my pleasure. Though, I must ask if you managed to procure something to protect your new investment? It is the best way to ensure it retains its form."

"Oh, yes. Of course." Barrett's head whipped around to the nearest chair and he headed for it, slinging the pack off his shoulder and opening it up to remove Kyran's new left boot, along with the sock rolled inside.

"Please, let me fetch you a chair," Meadows said, bustling to bring one of the taller chairs he had evidently made. He lifted it with a grunt and carried it over, setting it down just next to Kyran. "Rest a moment before you are on your way."

"Thank you," Kyran grit through his teeth, settling a hand on the back of the chair as he carefully walked around it. Then, slowly, as Meadows had shown him, he stretched his replacement limb out in front of him and lowered himself using only his good leg.

It was hard, his tired muscles trembling with the effort, and he sat a bit harder than he meant to, sending a brief jolt through his injured leg and into his hip before his magic numbed the pain again.

Taking a deep breath through his nose, he raised his head as Barrett approached him, holding out the boot. "Do you need help gettin' it on?"

"No. I can manage," Kyran said firmly, accepting the boot.

He considered for a moment how he might accomplish putting it on before he saw the obvious solution.

Laying the boot in his lap, he took his new leg in both hands and folded it at the knee. The stocking went over it first, easy enough. Then, he loosened the laces of the boot as much as he could, even unlacing the top few holes, and began to work the leather over the carved foot.

It was not terribly easy, as the wood did not have the flex and give as an ordinary limb might, but after a few moments, he was lacing the boot up his new calf.

"So you can," Barrett said mildly and shook his head. He turned to the craftsman and extended his gloved hand. "Thank you again, Meadows. Your work is as good as every rumor I ever heard and better."

"Why, thank you," the man beamed, grasping Barrett's hand firmly. "An artist is always pleased to hear his work is admired. I am happy to have been of service to you both."

Meadows released Barrett's hand to face Kyran, beaming proudly down at his work. "You should find that it will become much easier to use your new purchase as you practice with it. Many of my customers need only a cane when they are in town, if that. And if there is ever anything you need—a repair, a question answered, anything at all— please feel free to call on me."

"Aye," Kyran said, tying off his laces. "Thank you."

"You ready to get goin', then?" Barrett asked and, eager as Kyran was to avoid the crowds outside, he couldn't ignore the pang he felt at the fact that they would soon be headed back to the guildhall.

"Aye, I ken so."

He shifted to the edge of his seat to get up when Barrett stepped in front of him, extending his gloved hand in a silent offer, as he had done so many times before. Kyran stared at his hand, hesitating. Then, lifting his own, he set it in Barrett's grip. The hunter's hand was warm—almost feverish—even through the leather of his glove, and his grip was strong but gentle.

A flicker of surprise passed Barrett's face before his smile deepened and the rims of his ears flushed red. He took a step back and offered the strength of his arm as Kyran stood from the chair and found his balance.

"There's an inn not far from here that I've stayed in before when I didn't feel like being around all the other hunters," Barrett remarked, as if nothing extraordinary had happened. Kyran felt a gentle squeeze against his fingers before Barrett's hand slid from his and the hunter stepped back. "The food's pretty good. Plenty I'm certain you'll like."

Kyran let out his breath, running his thumb along the inside of his palm where he could still feel the warm touch of Barrett's glove against his skin. "I dinnae think there will be time."

"What do you mean? There's plenty of time. We'll have all night."

Kyran's brows pinched. "All night?"

"I was going to get a room at the inn." Barrett shrugged, rubbing a hand along his bare chin. "Unless you would rather go back. I thought you might like some time away from the guild."

"Will they na come looking for us?"

"We'll tell them the fitting took more time. What are they goin' to do if you don't come back until tomorrow? Yell about it?"

Kyran gave him a thin smile. That was very much something he would expect Barrett to say. But the idea of a night away from the people set on using him like an intriguing tool was overwhelmingly tempting.

"Come on. I'll even buy you a drink," Barrett wheedled.

Kyran stifled a chuckle. That was something he expected to hear from Barrett. Why shouldn't he stay out and pretend he had nowhere else to be—that everything was simple once again. "Aye, but what kind of drink?"

Chapter Forty-Six

The inn was even finer than Barrett remembered. But then again, he had always arrived at night and left early in the morning, stumbling with drink and laughter.

It was something in the daylight, though, set apart from the buildings around it by a low, stone wall. Instead of the countryside stone of most of the buildings in Oareford had been constructed of, or the warped and slouching boards of the Drunken Wind, this one had been built of dark wood and plaster and stood a towering five stories tall. It really put the Drunken Wind in its place by comparison, especially when considering the clientele entering and exiting. Not a single person he could see wore anything less than fine. Captain Griswold would have been at home amongst them. Barrett looked like a pauper.

Shrugging their purchases higher on his shoulder, he held the door for Kyran, catching the glare of a man on his way out. Inside was thronging with people in richly colored fabrics, laughing and drinking. More than a few glanced their way, taking them in with a less than kind curl of their lip. He didn't recall ever facing such hostility before. But then again, there weren't people standing outside the guild when he was younger hurling insults and rotten food.

Nothing else had changed, though. Graces, had it really been more than a year ago now?

"And how may I help you this evening?"

Barrett brushed his nostalgia aside and did his best to smile at the man approaching them. He was heavier set, with a round face beneath his neatly kept beard, and though he was smiling as well, Barrett didn't miss the way his gaze shifted between himself and Kyran with a hint of suspicion. Barrett didn't recognize him.

"I'm Kristopher Barrett," he said, stepping sideways between Kyran and the man and centering his attention on himself. "I've been in correspondence about letting a room for this evening."

"You have?" The man's brow nearly disappeared beneath the black curls on his forehead.

"Yes," Barrett said, his patience running thin.

"The…hunter?" The man's gaze dipped to Barrett's chest.

Hooking his thumb beneath the neckline of his tunic, Barrett pulled the chain of his amulet until the pendant lay against his chest, glittering in the bright lantern light.

The effect was immediate.

All at once, the man's expression lit up with a friendlier smile, his ears darkening to a bright, ruby red. "My apologies, hunter," he said a little too loudly, waving over one of the serving girls. "You must be very tired. Sarah will take your things to your room for you. Will you be dining in the tavern or would you prefer a private meal in your rooms?"

"Private," Barrett growled, handing off the sack when the girl reached to take it.

"Very well, very well. Sarah, please show the hunter to his room. If there is anything at all you might desire, do not hesitate to tell Sarah." He stepped to one side, gesturing for Barrett to pass, a trickle of sweat making its way down his brow.

"This way, please," the girl—she couldn't have been older than fifteen—said, leading them towards the stairs at the far wall.

"You go ahead," Barrett said, nodding Kyran on. "I'll be just a minute. I want to talk to him about something."

Kyran hesitated, but a quick glance at the people watching them from their tables, and he was quick to follow the girl.

"You…wanted to speak with me?"

Barrett turned back to the other man, who was watching him nervously now. Good. "Yes. About my letter."

"Everything will be as you asked," the man assured him, dabbing at his forehead. "There's no need to fret."

"Good. I'll just get some drinks to—"

"I can have someone carry those," the man said, lifting a hand to signal someone to attend them.

"No need," Barrett dismissed. "I'd rather carry it myself."

The man looked utterly at a loss, signaling frantically. "Then let me just—ah, Jenny." He smiled in evident relief as another girl approached. "Get this man whatever drink he needs and show him to room seven."

Chapter Forty-Seven

THE ROOM WAS grander than anything Kyran had ever seen outside of the laird's castle in the Isles. It was spacious, nearly twice the size of his dorm at the guildhall, with a desk, a table, and two beds wide enough each could easily hold two people, and with proper pillows.

He was grateful the inn hadn't been far. Even using his walking stick to aid him, he was slow with his new leg, and he knew the pain he could not feel through the soothing cold of his magic would find him later that night. More than that, the edge of his exhaustion was creeping closer. He had only managed to snatch a bare few hours of sleep before he'd surrendered and risen to go to the ward, and it was telling on him.

Setting the sack the lass had taken from Barrett down at the foot of the bed, Kyran lowered himself onto the quilt, letting out a long sigh with relief at the gentle give of the mattress. Stars, but he had never lain on anything so soft.

Laying his walking stick carefully within reach, he flopped back on the quilt, reveling in the way he sank into the mattress.

"Glad my brothers are na here ta see. They wouldna ever cease calling me prince."

There was a faint thunk at the door, as if someone had kicked it rather than knock, and Kyran pushed up onto his elbow only to hear Barrett's muffled voice call through. "You decent?"

"Aye," Kyran called back, reaching to take up his walking stick again when the door swung inwards as Barrett let himself in. He had two heavy pewter tankards filled to the brim in one hand, and a jug in the other.

"I got us some drinks," he announced as he nudged the door shut behind him with his heel. "I think you'll like the cider," Barrett remarked, setting the jug on the table and holding out one of the tankards for Kyran. "Rivals even the Wind's for taste."

Tugging his kerchief from his purse, Kyran took the proffered drink, the heavy pewter bobbing in his grip. Drink sloshed over the rim and down his fingers soaking the fold of his kerchief.

"Sorry," Barrett said with a chuckle, settling on the bed opposite him

Kyran gave him an arch look, swapping tankard to his other hand, and shaking the drink from his fingers. They were going to be irritatingly sticky now.

"Room's nicer than I expected," Barrett remarked, bending to set his drink on the floor before he started working on removing his boots.

"Aye. *Princely*," Kyran agreed, earning a chuckle from the hunter.

Balancing the tankard on his knee, Kyran rubbed his kerchief between his fingers along the handle. He could not say anymore why he always used the kerchief to touch things before his bare skin. It was not even all things, mostly things people handed to him that he needed the extra barrier. He knew it was odd, but he didn't have a comprehensible answer as to why he did it, only that the very idea of *not* doing it sent a palpable coil of dread through him.

He passed the cloth to his other hand and wiped the rim before tucking the kerchief away again, and finally raised the drink to his lips. The sweetness of apple mulled with heavy spices struck his nose before the first drop touched his tongue. It was good, the flavor almost entirely masking the bitter sting of the alcohol. He took another long draught, already imagining he could feel the warmth of the drink pooling in his belly and running down his arms and legs.

"You're right. It's good," he told Barrett, idly watching as the hunter tugged off his second boot.

"Glad you like it." Setting his boots side by side, Barrett plucked the fingers of his right glove and pulled it free to drop next to them. He started to do the same with the left, then paused, his eyes flickering to Kyran, then away before he tugged at the glove again and slid it free.

The hand itself showed no deformation, but as Barrett folded his hands together and flexed them, the joints crackling noisily, Kyran caught a glimpse of the black mark along the skin of his forearm beneath the long sleeve, like a smudge of coal. His witchmark, as the hunter had called it.

Barrett glanced up at him again, offering a self-conscious smile before he reached up to tug at the leather tie in his hair. "Supper should be up soon. They have folks that bring it to your rooms here." He shook his head as the bit of leather came free, his pale, wheat gold hair flaring out to settle across his shoulders in tangled locks, a few thin wisps clinging to his beard.

Kyran consciously turned his attention elsewhere, his nail clicking against the pewter of his tankard. "I should wash up then."

"There's a basin behind the screen."

With a soft sound of acknowledgement, Kyran leaned over and set his tankard next to the bed. But as he reached for his walking stick, he realized something. "Barrett, I…ken I dinnae thank you properly for… for today." He touched his left thigh beneath his kilt, his fingers tracing over the hard, wooden thigh. He could still hardly believe it was there. That he had walked. "Thank you. For this."

Barrett's lips lifted in a pleased smile. "You're welcome, and I hope it helps. I really do."

"Aye," Kyran said softly. "I ken it will." He pulled himself upright with his walking stick, teetering for a moment before he got his balance, still unaccustomed to the weight of his new leg.

"How is it feeling?"

"My leg?"

"If you don't mind me asking."

Kyran touched his hip, the pain in his leg still numb beneath his magic. "Still healing."

"But it's getting better?" Barrett asked earnestly, and Kyran nodded.

"Aye, it is." Carefully picking his way around the bed, Kyran tried not to use the walking stick. It was much easier on the smooth wooden floor than it had been over the rough cobbles of the street, and his gait almost felt natural again.

There was a large basin and ewer of water behind the screen that had, to his delight, been supplied with a familiar soap. He pressed it to his nose, inhaling the sweet, earthy scent of heather. It smelled like home.

His eyes prickled, and Kyran quickly scrubbed his hands as he fought to choke down the pained sound caught in his teeth. He'd missed his home before, missed the comforts of his ma's tea and his da's hearth when he'd been up on the ben, all alone but for the snow. But never like this. Never without a certainty he would see them again. But now… Now, even if he died, his bones would be caged in Tennebrumian soil, his soul cast to the Pit. It wasn't fair, but he had never really known fairness.

Drying his hands on the cloth hanging from the basin's stand, Kyran wiped his face and mustered himself with thoughts of cider and a soft bed before he made his way back to his drink. Despite walking to the basin with little trouble, though, he found himself leaning into his walking stick, and he had to put his hand out to catch himself on the headboard as sat. He blinked, letting out a quiet chuff at the faint lightness in his head. "That was fast."

"Been awhile since you drank?" Barrett teased gently between sips of his drink.

"Only since I last saw you," Kyran said with a touch of amusement as he picked up his tankard, taking another long draught. "I havena the time, elsewise." Or the inclination.

"Oh, Graces, there's always time for a drink or two. Back when I was studying at the guild, my partner kept a barrel of ale under the table."

Kyran cocked his head at the hunter. He'd never heard anything of what Barrett's time at the guild had been like. "Is that so?" he prompted, curious to know more.

"It is," Barrett said with affected solemnity before he broke out in a grin. "Believe it or not, I didn't drink that much back then, but Graces, that boy could put away his drink and act perfectly normal. He had this man—maybe a friend—who would come by late at night with a small cart parked off to the side of the guild walls and— Graces, I can't remember his name. Dan…no. Dar... I can't remember. But, he would get me to help him carry this barrel out there with him to get it filled and bring it back. It wasn't against the rules to have spirits in your bunk, but I'm pretty certain if a captain had found that barrel, there would have been some petty punishment."

Kyran snorted. That sounded like something Barrett would do. He could almost imagine it—Barrett, his eyes younger, no beard on his face, grinning as he and another hunter carried a heavy barrel of drink between them under lantern and moonlight, trying not to attract attention from the other working members.

"I see you havena changed much," Kyran teased, taking another sip of his drink, the sweet taste going down as easily as water. Stars, but he was going to be in trouble by the bottom of this drink if it was already going to his head.

"Oh, I don't know about that." Barrett tipped his drink towards Kyran. "What about you? Did you ever do anything sneaky with your brothers?"

Oh, the stories his brothers would tell. "Murray always made certain my visits were eventful, and I always made certain his efforts never went unpaid."

The hunter's face lit up, his chest rumbling with another laugh. "All of your brothers are a bit wild. I can't imagine the things you all might have gotten up to."

"You heard some of it at the table that night. I canna remember if I heard it, but the goat is one of Tavish's favorite stories."

Barrett's smile widened and he looked down at his lap, both hands around his drink, his thumbs rubbing over the handle. "It was a good night."

"Aye," Kyran agreed, remembering fondly the long evening he had spent with his family, trading stories, drinking, and eating. By all the Graces in the Isles, he would give anything to see them again, well and happy.

"You know," the hunter murmured, tipping his tankard to peer into it, "I couldn't stand this stuff when I was a *wee bairn*, but Graces above, it's good."

Kyran flicked his eyes dryly at the hunter. "Oh, aye?"

"*Aye.*" Barrett winked at him and took a sip, sighing in satisfaction. "Strong enough to knock you down, but smooth enough to drink straight from the barrel. I see why Raleigh liked it."

Kyran sat a little straighter at the name. Barrett's former partner and another mage like Kyran. "That doesna sound like cider."

"Oh, it's not." He waggled the tankard. "Spiced rum. I can get you some if you like, but it'll take your breath away."

"Sounds like some of the whiskey Duncan brought me once," Kyran mused.

"It's a bit sweeter, but similar. Maybe you'd *take ta it* more than—"

There was a light rap at the door, and a young lass's voice that called through to say their supper was ready.

"I'll get it," Barrett volunteered, rising from the edge of his mattress. A lass stood in the hall, a large tray held before her. She curtsied carefully at Barrett's greeting, the red-brown of her hair sifting into her eyes.

"Your supper," she announced.

"Thank you," Barrett said sincerely, reaching to take the tray, but the lass leaned back just enough to make Barrett stop reaching for it.

"If I may?" she said instead, nodding into the room.

Barrett flicked a quick glance over his shoulder, his eyes meeting Kyran's, and the mage had the impression that he was asking him for permission, to which Kyran inclined his head.

"Ah, certainly," Barrett told the lass, stepping to one side to admit her. The hunter tucked a hand behind his back. Hiding the witchmark, no doubt.

She bowed her head, keeping her gaze trained downwards as she carried the laden tray to the table, though Kyran caught her eyes drifting his way. "Will you be needing anything else just now?"

"I don't think so, unless..." Barrett looked to Kyran again. "Do you need anything?"

Kyran tipped his tankard, peering into it. There wasn't much left in the bottom, and he was already near sotted with drink, but it was quite good. "Aye, I could use a wee bit more ta drink."

Barrett smirked. "We have drink."

"Then no."

"Nothing for me either," Barrett confirmed for the lass. Her eyes flickered between the two of them again before she dipped into another curtsey and excused herself, shutting the door behind her.

Turning the lock, Barrett went to the table and began to lay out the meal. Kyran watched him move from over the rim of his drink until Barrett looked up at him expectantly. "Are you hungry?"

"Aye, I'm coming," Kyran murmured. He started to lean over to set his drink down, and felt the room begin to sway. Oh, that drink had soaked in quite a bit more since he sat down.

There was a gentle tug at the tankard, and he lifted his head to find Barrett had taken hold of the heavy pewter.

"I've got it." The hunter gave it another little tug and Kyran slowly uncurled his fingers from the handle.

"Thank you."

Color crept up the hunter's neck, and he tipped his head. "Can't let you spill it," he teased, carrying the empty drink to the table.

Setting the end of his walking stick as close to the bed as he could, Kyran hauled himself upright. He leaned into the stick, waiting for the room to stop tipping around his ears before he attempted to cross the short distance to the table. It was not easy, even with his new leg. In fact, it made it more difficult, as he hadn't gotten used to the weight of it yet, and the odd hitch it put in his gait threatened to spill him over sideways, but he managed to make it to the table without incident, using his walking stick more than he would have liked.

He took his seat, nudging it out from the table with his walking stick before he carefully lowered himself just how Meadows had shown him. It was surprisingly difficult to lower himself with any amount of grace, and he sat quite a bit harder than he meant to when his good leg buckled, heavy from exhaustion and the good drink. He waved off Barrett's concerned glance, his face flushing with color at his own ineptitude. It was lucky he could not feel anything from his stump beneath the blissful numb of his magic.

He surveyed the table to avoid looking at Barrett just yet, and felt his brows raise. "Would you look at all that."

Instead of plating the meals separately for them all, the kitchen had sent up a dish of each food for them to split as they saw fit. There was a large bowl of roasted greens, turnips, and potatoes, scented heavily with herbs, a glazed tureen of what turned out to be stewed plums, a platter of roasted fish, a small pot of honey, and a what looked like almost an entire loaf of the palest bread Kyran had ever seen.

"Quite a feast, hm?" Barrett said , lifting the jug and refilling Kyran's tankard.

"Aye, a wee bit." Taking out his kerchief, Kyran wiped the handle of the tankard down again and took a sip of his drink, the sweet taste going down as easily as water. Stars, but he was going to be in trouble by the bottom of this drink if it was already making him go soft headed.

He watched a bit muzzily as Barrett took a plate from the tray and filled the plate up with a little bit of everything, except for the roasted fish. He hesitated, then tilted his head to catch Kyran's gaze. "I know you aren't fond of meat. Not even the smell. But I thought maybe you'd like to try a bit of fish? If you don't like it, I'll finish it for you. And if the smell is too much, I'll take it downstairs."

Kyran leaned over the table, peering at the fish. They were each at least as long as Kyran's forearm, their silver scales crusted with herbs and their bellies slit open and stuffed with lemons and salt, and was surprised to find the idea of eating one of them did not utterly repulse him, not the way beef and pork did.

"Just a wee bit," he told Barrett, curious to know if he might have found something more than oats and bread he might still be able to eat.

Cutting a piece from one of the fish, Barrett set it onto the plate and then slid the plate to Kyran along with a fork before he began to fix his own plate. "If you do like it, there's plenty," Barrett assured him.

"Aye," Kyran murmured, taking his time to wipe down each piece of cutlery before leaving the kerchief on his knee.

Barrett filled his plate quickly and topped off his own tankard before settling down across from Kyran. Rather than dig into the fish, Barrett speared one of the plums and popped it into his mouth, chewing through a sigh as he sank back into his chair. "Tastes just like I remember."

"Did ye come often?"

The hunter smiled down at his plate as he speared another plum. "I'm not certain I'd use the word 'often' but… anytime Raleigh had too much, he always wanted to come here. Not just for the rum—that was a bonus. He liked the food. Said it was *fancy*. Last time I was here was right before we left for Willowvale."

Kyran didn't recognize the name of the town from any of the ones they had passed through or that Barrett had mentioned before, but he was hesitant to ask. He was all too aware of the fate Raleigh met and the pain it had caused Barrett. It was a strange choice to pick this as the place to stay for the evening when it held so many bittersweet memories.

Tentatively, he prodded at the filet of fish, its flesh flaking easily under the sharpened tines. He was curious to know if he could stomach it, but his curiosity was tempered by the knowledge that if he couldn't, he would be unable to finish his meal without gagging on every bite. He left the filet for last, eating his fill of vegetables, fruit, and honeyed bread first along with generous swallows of cider until it was all that remained. Spearing a bit on the end of his fork, he took a cautious bite.

The taste was both familiar and strange. He had eaten quite a lot of fish as a lad catching them in the cold, clear streams and lakes of the Isles, especially during his time on Cairngorm. But those had been small, reedy little things compared to the fish on the serving platter. These tasted sweeter than he remembered, the flesh breaking into large, soft flakes. He took another bite, pleased when he only tasted sweet fish, and not the bitter memory of demon flesh.

"How is it?" Barrett asked.

"Well enough," he answered lightly, picking at the filet.

"I'm glad. It really is good. We didn't eat a lot of fish growing up. Kat isn't fond of it, but Raleigh…" Barrett's voice trailed off, his expression suddenly miserable. "Graces, I really didn't think when I picked this place. I'm sorry."

"For what?"

Barrett picked at his vegetables listlessly. "I wanted this to be something nice that you could enjoy, not an evening of listening to me *reminisce*."

"Barrett," Kyran said, waiting until the hunter's eyes met his. "I dinnae mind listening ta ye talk about your friend."

The tightness in Barrett's shoulders lessened, the misery in his face softening in what might have been gratitude. "He was more than just a friend," he said, reaching for his drink. "He and I, um…We were *together*, if you catch my meanin'."

Kyran's hand stopped halfway to his mouth, his tankard bobbling in the air. "Ye and Raleigh. "Ye were…" The mage's sentence trailed, his nail drumming against the pewter before he let out a frustrated huff. "Stars above, I canna think o' the word. He was your *leannan*?"

Even though Kyran was certain Barrett didn't know the word, the hunter's face blossomed bright as a snowberry from his cheeks to his ears. "We were, um… We fancied one another. Well, he fancied me first." He shook his head and let out a slow, wistful sounding sigh. "It was more than that before the end. But it feels so long ago now." The hunter's voice faded, and Kyran thought it might be the last Barrett spoke of it for the evening, but then he looked up again. "What about you? I know you spent most of your time away, but did you ever have a lass back home that caught your eye?"

"I'm a mage," Kyran reminded the man dryly. "They wouldna had anything ta do with me even if I was around, which was well enough for me. Twas never…" He hesitated, realizing what his sotted tongue had been about to say.

But then, did it matter?

Barrett had already admitted he was not drawn to the lasses; that his last lover had been a lad. Still, it felt strange, just saying it so forthright. It was never something he would have done in the Isles. Stars, he spent all his years trying to hide it. The hunter watched him attentively.

Kyran let his tongue finish its sentence, his face coloring modestly, "Twas never the lasses caught my eye."

Chapter Forty-Eight

BARRETT ONLY JUST kept his jaw from slacking in genuine surprise. Graces, but his heart had never jumped into his throat so quickly. After his conversation with Kat, he'd found an awkward shame in admiring Kyran the way he'd done upon meeting him, terrified the mage would find it offensive. Or worse, become nervous of Barrett's intentions. But to hear Kyran swayed in a similar direction as him filled the hunter with a strange, nervous excitement that overtook the heavy ache his memories had conjured.

"Is that so?" Barrett asked softly as he took in Kyran's reaction, the faint blush of his cheeks, the tapping of his fingers against his drink. "Did you have a lad that was your... What was the word? *Leannan?*"

It was impossible to miss the way the mage's cheeks flushed even more deeply, taking on the faint shimmer of his magic. "Aye. His name was Ben," Kyran admittedly quietly before hiding behind his tankard.

It felt like being let in on a secret. Barrett hesitated to pry, until he recalled Myles's advice. Graces, but the Lightbringer had been right. He really didn't know almost anything about Kyran even after everything he had heard and seen in the Isles.

"Ben," he repeated, watching how Kyran nodded somewhat meekly. "Did you just fancy him? Or were you two... together?"

"We were...together." The mage let out a heavy sounding sigh. "Though it took me this long ta ken he dinnae feel the same way about it as I did. I thought he was just scared."

"Scared?" Barrett waited for more, but Kyran said nothing right away. "Because you were a lad, too? Or, something else?"

"He dinnae like that we had ta hide it. I...never told him I was a mage, but he found out eventually. He wouldna see me again after that."

Barrett frowned, keenly recalling how Kyran had cried when he had told him he was human. Graces above, but if Barrett ever met the man that had made the mage cry like that... "It sounds like it ended badly, then?"

Kyran shifted in his seat, his nail tapping against his tankard. "I wouldna say we ended well, but I ken it wasna near as bad as what happened ta ye and Raleigh."

At the mention of Raleigh's fate, Barrett waited for the overwhelming, keen burst of pain. But all that came was that same dull, deep ache from before. He wasn't certain if it was the rum, or perhaps the conversation keeping him tethered. "Maybe, but that was different. It doesn't mean what happened with Ben wasn't awful, if that's what it was."

"Aye," Kyran sighed, taking another long pull from his drink.

"I'm sorry for that." Barrett finally picked his fork back up, forcing himself to eat a little before it got cold. He waited for Kyran to do the same, but the mage just drank from his cider. Before he could empty it, Barrett reached for the jug between them and offered to refill it once again. "For what it's worth, it's not… It's not like that here, in the guild. I mean you occasionally find folks who don't like it, and some folks think it's a little odd, but most don't care who you're with."

"And what of mages?" Kyran asked, his tankard bobbing dangerously again.

"No one ever…" Barrett hesitated, carefully trying to recollect those times he was with Raleigh, going into taverns, shops, inns, and everywhere else. "No one really cared one way or the other what Raleigh was."

"But did they know? Or did he hide it?"

Barrett was surprised by how quickly a chuckle rushed up his throat and shook his head. "No, he didn't hide it. He controlled water and the like. He was such a showoff. And he… He liked to play with his drinks when he got especially drunk."

Kyran snorted into his drink, lowering the tankard. "Bold as a fool."

"Maybe so, but no one minded him."

The mage made a soft noise, but he still didn't look up, and Barrett worried he had set the mage fretting again.

"We don't have to keep talkin' about any of this if you'd rather not."

"It's fine. I've just… I havena told anyone about Ben before."

"I appreciate you trustin' me with it," Barrett admitted, though he couldn't help smiling at the irony. "I, ah… I haven't really talked to anyone about Raleigh since… he passed."

"I ken that," Kyran murmured.

Barrett hummed absently, looking over the table again at all their untouched food. Kyran hadn't let go of his cider yet, but he didn't want to force the mage to eat. So, picking up his fork, he began to pick his way through the meal, surprised to find after a few bites that his appetite hadn't completely disappeared yet. "So, ah, what was Ben like, then? Before everything happened, I mean."

"Kind," Kyran answered with almost no hesitation, his gaze drifting across the room. "He was a verrah kind and gentle lad, but verrah nervous. He was always scared we'd be found out. Every time I saw him, he'd try ta say we shouldna see one another anymore, and I'd talk him around. I shouldna have bothered. I should have left, but I dinnae think I'd ever find anyone else."

Barrett swallowed roughly around a bite of fish, trying not to think too deeply about those last, soft words that he knew Kyran had not meant directly for him. But still, his stomach fluttered in earnest. "It sounds more than a little exhausting," Barrett sympathized. "It's… hard to look back, and wonder about what you should or shouldn't have done."

"Aye, and we canna undo the past, can we?"

Barrett felt that sentiment keenly. How many times had he wished he could have gone back and done any little thing differently to save Raleigh? "No. We can't. But we can move forward."

A quiet settled at the table, heavy and contemplative, but not so uncomfortable as Barrett might have thought it once. He reached for the honey, smearing it thickly over a slice of bread, then did the same for a second piece, leaning over the table to set it to one side on Kyran's plate.

"So how long were you with Ben?"

Kyran eyed the piece of bread, his mouth drawing into a slow, confused smile. "A few years, though I dinnae see him much in that time. Trying ta stay out of the laird's way."

"The laird can rot," Barrett scoffed and bit into his own honeyed bread. The loaf was still warm. "What did you do when you did get to see each other?"

Quicker than the bat of an eye, Kyran's entire face turned a shade of rose. "Climb trees. In the woods. And fish."

Barrett might have believed the mage if he hadn't blushed so fiercely. It was not the reaction he quite expected, and it was difficult not to grin in return. "Oh, aye? Were you fishin' with nets or hands?"

"We'd cast lines and tie them off."

Barrett couldn't hold the smile in much longer, and it broke with a low chuckle. "I was good at catchin' fish with my hands when I was a kid. Just little minnows. I always wanted to show Raleigh, but I always got distracted and forgot. He grew up in the city here, at the guild, and always liked getting out."

"I ken your water is a wee bit warmer as well," Kyran remarked, finally picking up the piece of bread Barrett had left him, and taking a bite.

"That it is," Barrett confirmed, watching as Kyran took a second, then a third bite, washing the bread down with some cider before finally investigating his food again, smiling to himself when Kyran speared one of the plums on his plate.

As they ate, Barrett tried to keep their conversation going, recalling a story of when he and Raleigh had gone out for drinks and food at a boisterous tavern close by the guildhall. Most of the patrons had been hunters, guards, and sailors, and Raleigh had, on a dare, been able to use his magic to pull the rum from his cup and float it in a small orb above his hand. Of course, that had been the moment another patron had brushed by, bumping Raleigh's shoulder, and sent the orb of rum flying, hitting one of the other hunters in the face.

Kyran snickered, remarking between bites how surprised he was that Barrett hadn't caught the drink, to which the hunter assured him he caught the next one after Raleigh heard his comment about his aim.

It was near the bottom of the jug of cider, with empty plates scattered in front of him, that Barrett realized he was still talking about Raleigh, still telling stories about him. He was smiling, even laughing. And it felt good. But even so, the pang of loss and aching loneliness remained. Except it wasn't so pressing or heavy as before. He could even ignore it when he had to laughingly ask Kyran to repeat himself—in Common— for the fourth time.

Instead of answering, the mage tapped his tankard. Rolling his eyes, Barrett moved the jug to pour out the very last of their drink. "I thought you couldn't hold your drink?"

Kyran smiled, showing his teeth, and said something in Isleish, lifting his fork to pick at the filet left on his plate.

Swallowing the last drop of cider, Barrett pushed away from the table, looking longingly at the bed. It looked especially soft and inviting now that he was comfortably full, and if he were alone, he'd strip down to his skin, spread out over that quilt and be out like a light. But he wasn't.

He picked at a hole in his sleeve, his thoughts churning until he finally came to a decision. "I should… get washed up and changed," he said slowly, fighting to get his tongue and lips to work properly.

Kyran's fork clicked against his plate, eyes darting up to Barrett, then past him at the window. "It's late, isna it."

"Gettin' there, certainly," Barrett agreed and pushed his chair away from the table. It groaned against the floor and creaked as Barrett tried to get up to his feet. The room spun briefly and he held onto the table as he righted himself. "I'll just be a moment."

Kyran murmured something more in Isleish while Barrett shuffled carefully to the side of the bed where the mage had left the sack of clothes.

"Aye, aye," Barrett replied automatically as he pawed through the sack, pulling out one of the new shirts he'd bought and a pair of trousers. He stumbled towards the ornate screen, taking small steps to keep from tripping over his feet.

Setting his clean clothes down on the edge of the basin's stand, he passed a final glance at the space of room he could see to make certain he wasn't visible to Kyran, then peeled out of his shirt. Even in his rum and cider-addled brain, he caught the unpleasant whiff of stale body odor.

He made quick work of washing up, enjoying the fragrant soap the innkeeper had provided. His pants were a little trickier to get out of, and he nearly fell over more than once trying to change into his clean pair. The shirt was far easier. The clothing was not perfectly tailored, but fit far better than the loose, threadbare set he had been wearing for the last few months.

There was a sudden clatter of what might've been Kyran's walking stick beyond the screen, followed by a crash. Barrett jumped at the noises and rushed out from behind the screen, only to find Kyran dragging himself upright on the edge of his bed. "Graces, you startled me," he said, resisting the automatic urge to help him upright, and instead fetched the fallen stick in case Kyran needed it. "You all right?"

"Aye," the mage slurred, crawling up onto the bed and collapsing onto the mattress with a long groan.

Barrett grinned at him and made his way over to his own bed. He slumped down onto it and stretched out, pleased at how his feet still had some clearance. Graces, it was nice for once. "I already miss these beds." The hunter chuckled.

Kyran said something in Isleish Barrett took to mean he would as well.

"Good night, Kyran."

There was no reply, and at a glance, Barrett could see the mage was already asleep, his face slack and soft. Barrett watched him for a moment, glad Kyran looked so relaxed and content in sleep. He deserved that much. To sleep through the night without the nightmares that had plagued him since Barrett had rescued him from the demon realm.

It wasn't long before Barrett felt his own eyelids fluttering lazily and he let them slide shut. The rum and cider had left his head feeling pleasantly foggy, and he found it easy to let his mind wander back to Kyran, remembering his smile and his laugh while Barrett spun his memories into amusing tales. He never would have imagined he could speak Raleigh's name, let alone speak stories of him, again. He wondered if he would feel the same way in the morning when he was sober, or if the effort of it would crush him.

Regardless, he resolved that when he woke up, he wouldn't let it ruin the rest of his time away from the guild. He wanted to enjoy this time with Kyran. He wanted the rest of this trip to be as perfect as he could manage.

Chapter Forty-Nine

"No... No. Ngh!"

Kyran's eyes sprang open with a jolt of alarm, his heart pounding in his chest. What—

The voice cried out again and Kyran scrambled upright, quickly looking around the room until his sleep fogged mind realized the voice belonged to Barrett, who was in the bed next to his. The hunter was lying on his back atop his quilt, his mouth moving in the light of their lantern as he muttered and twitched. He was dreaming.

"By all the Grace in the Isles," Kyran whispered, letting his head hang as he tried to slow his racing heart. He wondered if he should wake the hunter, or leave him be, when Barrett's mutterings broke in a sudden, harsh gasp that near startled Kyran from his bed. Barrett's fingers and lips twitched, and he mumbled something in a soft whimper. He said it again. And then again.

Kyran leaned forward, listening, and finally made out the word.

"Run." The man jerked in his sleep, but didn't wake. "Run," he whispered. "Raleigh."

The image Kyran had conjured of Raleigh, torn apart and eaten alive flashed through his mind, and he swallowed hard against the sickening lurch in his belly. Not a dream, then, but a nightmare.

"Barrett," Kyran called, trying to wake the man, but the hunter didn't respond, his breath beginning to hitch higher. "Barrett," he called louder, throwing his quilt back and swinging his bare feet down, pushing up— only there was something not quite right with his left leg, as if it didn't want to obey him.

He sat back heavily, catching his balance on the edge of the bed, and frowned down at his leg. He wasn't still sotted, was he? He pinched his thigh through the kilt, massaging it in case it had simply fallen asleep. Only it wasn't his leg.

He muttered blackly in Isleish, running a hand over his face to hide his utter embarrassment. "Thought it was real," he chuckled bitterly. He had forgotten, in just one evening, that he only had the one right leg. He had thought he was whole again.

"Raleigh…" Barrett called again, the tone sharper. "No…"

A wave of heat rolled over Kyran, and he felt his stomach drop as the lantern began to flicker dangerously.

"Barrett." Kyran used the side table to pull himself up, letting his blood slip to push the heat from his skin. "Barrett there's a…demon…"

In the light from his runelines, the air above Barrett shimmered like the summer heat off a stone at the peak of the day. And his skin. A whole swath of Barrett's skin, starting at his scarred hand, and covering near half his face was black as pitch. His demon. Barrett was losing control of *his* demon.

"Barrett, wake up you daft hunter!" Kyran shouted, his voice cracking and shrill, the air around him snapping with cold as his power overflowed his control.

The hunter let out a soft whimper, and the wick of the lantern flickered out.

"No. No!" Kyran panted, and lunged for the other bed. "Wake up!" he all but screamed, grabbing Barrett's shoulders and shaking him.

With a strangled gasp, the hunter's eyes flew open, and he grasped Kyran's wrists in a bruisingly tight, hot grip, peeling a startled shout from the mage.

"Let go." Kyran twisted in Barrett's grip, but the hunter's fingers didn't budge. "Let go!"

Barrett's eyes darted left and right, as if searching for something, before they settled on Kyran, and for an instant, he looked up at the mage through one eye of scarlet and black eye and one of summer blue. He blinked, and in that breath, the heat vanished from the room, the dark shadow invading Barrett's face and eye vanishing as if it had never been.

"Kyran?" Barrett whispered, his voice hoarse, brows furrowed in confusion before he snatched his hands away from Kyran's wrists like they were hot irons. "I'm sorry. Graces, I— What…"

"Ye were having a nightmare," Kyran said, balancing on his good leg as he pulled away from the hunter, rubbing his wrists. "And ye started ta turn inta an abomination."

Barrett's eyes went round as moons, the whites glaring in the light of Kyran's magic. "I did what?" He turned his hands over, then yanked his sleeves up, but there were only the black scars he already had. "Did I—I didn't hurt anyone, did I?"

He looked terrified.

Kyran shook his head, tightening his control of his magic as he heard the glass in the windows begin to pop and strain. "Na yet, but ye were losing control of your fire."

Barrett glanced past him at the dark lantern, then down to the table, a dawning horror stealing over him. "This… This has never happened before. I swear I'm telling the truth. You have to believe me," he pleaded, and of everything Kyran felt in that moment, he felt guilt the most keenly.

"I believe ye," he said, scratching at the skin where he could still feel Barrett's scalding grip. "But what by all the Graces happened?"

The hunter shook his head, burying his face in his hands. "I don't know. It's never… I've never had this happen before. In my sleep." He pulled his hands away and stared at nothing for a long moment before he got up from his bed. "We should go back to the guild." He plucked the glass from the lantern and pinched the wick, a warm glow filling the room again. "I'll talk to Griswold. Try to figure things out. It'll be safer there if…" He swallowed thickly. "If I need help."

Kyran nodded in numb agreement, leaning on the side table again as Barrett passed him to light the other lanterns. He didn't know what to say, or even what was rightly happening. He'd heard stories of demons taking over the witches they bargained with, the inevitable end to such arrangements. But that couldn't be the same for hunters, could it? A bad bargain to fight demons only to face an inescapable fate of becoming a monster that hunted the people they sought to protect.

That couldn't be all there was. No sane person would agree to such a thing. Unless…he hadn't known. As Kyran was discovering, the guild's very foundations were built out of lies and secrets. Why not one more? And if that weren't the case, it was certainly a possibility. A roll of the dice with each hunter that his demon would lose patience and take him for its own. It was madness, and yet, what other path was there? Unless…

Unless Kyran was strong enough to pull the demon out when the time came.

No, he decided, frost creeping over his skin as he bent to pick up his walking stick. He *would* be strong enough. He would not let the demons have anyone else. Not if he could help them. Guild and anyone else be cursed.

CHAPTER FIFTY

THE CLEAR SKY of the day had passed during Barrett's scant hours of sleep at the inn, and rain now fell in miserable sheets, soaking through his hair, seeping in around the collar of his coat and drenching the hems of his news trousers. He didn't dare call his fire to fend it off, not after what happened at the inn. Graces only knew what might happen.

Beside him, Kyran was silent, his tartan pulled up around his shoulders to shed some of the rain, but there was no glimmer of his runelines, his coppery hair clinging to his cheeks. He didn't look at Barrett.

So much for Barrett's grand plans. He wasn't even certain if the mage would want to be around him anymore after this, or if it was even safe. Then again, if Kyran hadn't been there, it could have been much worse.

Something was wrong. With his amulet or maybe even with him. Was it because of what happened in the Isles, or when he entered the demon realm? Or even before that, when he started speaking with his demon?

Whatever it was, he had to fix it. He couldn't keep losing control, or Griswold would retire him, or worse. He couldn't go back to just a powerless boy again, unable to fight, unable to protect anyone, not after he worked so hard to be a hunter. Not when people were relying on him.

No, he *wouldn't* give up his title as a hunter. He had taken his power from the demon in the Isles. He would *make* it stop.

There was no one but a solitary guard at the gate who waved them both in from beneath her shelter.

Barrett tried to think of what to tell Kyran, what reassurance he could offer or explanation, but all too soon, they were standing outside Kyran's door, and Barrett still hadn't thought of anything. "I'm…going to go see someone," he finally said when Kyran withdrew his kerchief. "I'm sorry I ruined everything. If it weren't for you—"

"Are ye going ta be all right?" the mage asked, catching Barrett off guard.

"I'll be fine," he tried reassuring him with a smile. "We'll…talk more in the morning?"

Something in Kyran's expression faded. "Aye, then," he said, fishing his key from his purse and turning to unlock his door. "Stars guide and keep ye."

"You as well," Barrett said, and Kyran's door shut behind him without another word.

Barrett stood there, listening to the sound of Kyran's walking stick and new leg moving away, wondering if he'd just made a mistake, but it was too late now. He had to fix whatever was going on with him first.

Locking his door behind him, he threw his wet coat off and yanked his amulet over his head, glaring at it. "You," he snarled at the gem, resisting the urge to throw it across the room. "You Graces cursed— What are you trying to do?" He waited a beat for that gravel toned voice in his head to answer, but it was, of course, silent. "Answer me!"

I was attempting to prevent a disaster, hunter.

Barrett's lips twitched in a furious snarl. "By trying to take control of me?"

Yes.

Barrett's fury turned cold at the bald admission. "Why?"

You were drawing my power in your sleep while you dreamed. If it had continued, you would have caused a fire, and the guild would have seen me hung in the archives. Or worse, you might have injured the Old One's offspring and summoned his retribution.

"You're lying."

What use do I have with lying to you?

"You... You just want me to lower my guard. You want to take control like you did in the demon realm."

If I had wanted that, I would not have relinquished my control in the first place, hunter. Why would I risk the guild hunting me when I can get everything I want right where I am now?

"You're lying," Barrett sneered, but he couldn't quite quash the flutter of panic rapidly growing in the pit of his belly.

You know as well as I, that if I desired to own your skin, I simply would.

Abruptly, the tips of his fingers went numb, and then his palms, his wrists, and he watched in terror as black, ashen flesh crawled above his gloves, spreading up his arms. "No!" He tried to throw the amulet, but his fingers were locked around it, unmoving, unfeeling as the numbness spread over his chest and wrapped around his throat. "Stop," he mouthed, his voice cracking. Not again. He couldn't— Not again.

"I suggest you learn better control instead of applying blame," his demon whispered through his lips.

And then, the numbness was gone, the black flesh vanished as quickly as it had appeared.

He staggered, catching himself on one knee as his body came back to him. He was free. For now, and only because his demon had let him go. Which meant the accident at the inn…

His breath hitched, and he raised his hand to throw the amulet away, but couldn't quite make himself. He needed it. If he wanted to remain a hunter, he needed his demon. But he still wasn't strong enough to control it or its power. He was a failure. Worse, he was dangerous, and if Griswold found out, it would mean an end to everything he had worked for.

"Graces protect me," he whispered, slipping the chain over his head again. The pendant hung heavy and warm against his chest, and his clothes began to gently steam as he drew his knees up and let the first sob claw its way out of him.

Chapter Fifty-One

BARRETT WATCHED THE flame flickering behind the glass of the lantern on his desk, struggling to figure out how to end the rambling letter he'd been working on to keep himself awake. Despite the heaps of crumpled drafts accumulating on the desk and floor around him, the letter was still a mess of scratched out lines, messily crammed in words, and blobs of smeared ink where he let his quill rest too long.

He'd always struggled with drafting reports, where everything was very cut and dry, but a personal letter he had no intention of sending to a person that couldn't even read it was apparently beyond him.

"Graces, help me, I am an idiot," he sighed, rubbing aching temples as he reread the disjointed and long-winded rambling that had somehow become even more incoherent despite his efforts. It was supposed to help gather his thoughts, but instead, he'd apparently let them range with the depth of the drink he'd gotten from the mess last night.

He caught a glimpse of the sodden sentiments scrawled crookedly near the middle of the letter, and he crumpled it to toss with the rest. He'd have to burn the lot. Lumen forbid anyone actually read them.

He'd just drawn a fresh sheet when he heard the familiar clack of wood on stone passing in the hall. He glanced at the window and the weak light filtering in through the rain pelting the glass, and tossed his tatty quill onto his desk. Maybe breakfast and a strong coffee would dig the words out of him that he needed.

Throwing on his coat, he shivered as he stepped out into the hall, his breath clouding in the air. He caught a glimpse of faint blue light illuminating the grey stonework before it vanished in an instant, and he smiled sheepishly at the mage standing just a few feet from him.

"Mornin'," he said, watching the light trickle back into Kyran's runelines as the mage relaxed. "Heard you passin' by and thought I might see about breakfast."

"I'm on my way ta the hospital," Kyran said slowly, flicking a look up and down Barrett, his brows rising. "Did you lose a fight with a quill?"

Barrett frowned before the mage's meaning occurred to him. "In a way." He chuckled dryly, scrubbing his cheek with the heel of his hand, wincing at the grating stubble that'd already grown back. "How bad is it?"

"I ken it must have been fierce."

Barrett snorted. "*Aye*, it was."

Rolling his eyes, Kyran started down the hall again. "I dinnae ken how long I'll be at the hospital."

"You're not ill are you?" Barrett asked, suddenly worried the mage had caught his death drenched in winter rain last night.

"No, but Lilyana may want ta see me."

Barrett started to ask why that might be when his tired mind finally noticed how Kyran was holding his walking stick. Instead of tucking it beneath his arm and stooping to bring his weight to bear on it, he held it more like a staff out before him, moving it in tandem with his new false leg.

A swell of emotion tangled up in all that had happened yesterday threatened to overtake Barrett, and he swallowed hard, stepping forward to get the door. "That's all right," he said, the edge of his voice catching. "I might ask about some of that tea we had the other day while I'm there. Could use a quiet night."

Kyran hummed in reply, ducking beneath the lintel and out into the rain, a white mist wrapping around him like a cloak as little flecks of ice bounced off his hair and shoulders to scatter across the frozen cobbles in his wake. Barrett watched, taken in by the fae spectacle.

"Graces above," he whispered, turning up his collar as he followed after.

They said little as they crossed the grounds. Barrett tried to summon some of the words from his letters he'd tried to write, but couldn't bring himself to speak the fragments he was able to recall when he began to shiver even in his coat. Graces, he hadn't been that cold since the Isles. He had his demon to blame for that, too.

By the time they reached the hospital, his hair and face were drenched in frigid rain and bits of ice, and he shivered pathetically in his coat.

"Are you all right?" Kyran asked, brushing ice and frost from his clothes and hair as they stepped inside.

"A-Aye," Barrett chattered, fishing around in his coat pockets once he was under the hospital's sheltering roof, but couldn't find the leather tie he used to keep his hair tamed. "You go ahead. I'll be waiting."

The mage looked concerned, but he didn't say anything more,

disappearing down a hall at the back of the lobby.

Barrett stamped his feet, folding his arms over his chest as he tried to warm up, but the cold seeped deeper than his skin. Blessed Graces, but he didn't remember being this cold when he was young. How in the world did anyone stand to be outside without magic to keep them dry and warm?

He caught a glimpse of an orange stole, and a gnarled hand lifted in greeting from across the waiting room. "Myles?" The last he'd known, the Lightbringer had been bedridden after being caught in the attack at the college. The trap Griswold had set. Barrett still hadn't forgiven the captain for that.

"Good morning, Kristopher," the Lightbringer said, shuffling over to him. "I hope you don't mind me saying this, but you look miserable. What happened?"

Alot. "Bad weather."

"It has been trying as of late," the Lightbringer said, nodding sagely.

"You look…better," Barrett offered awkwardly.

"That is thanks to you." Myles chuckled, his face going ruddy. "I'm embarrassed to say it seems my latest bit of excitement was nothing more than a fit of nerves."

"I'm glad. Not that you… But that you're all right."

"Why thank you. I'm not holding you up from something, am I?"

"No. I'm just…waiting for someone."

The Lightbringer nodded, his brows lowering, and Barrett swore he was being scrutinized. "Well, if you're not busy, maybe you'd like to come and take a seat for a little bit? You seem like you have a lot on your mind."

Barrett nearly resisted, nearly made up some excuse to walk away, but then he was being ushered along behind the Lightbringer into his private sick room and directed to a chair.

"Sorry I don't have anything more comfortable to offer," Myles said, lowering himself stiffly onto his cot. "But what little adventures have you been up to since we last spoke? You look like quite the different person with your beard gone. And don't think I didn't notice the new clothes."

Barrett flushed, picking at his new trousers. "I got them while I was out in the city. With Kyran."

"That sounds exciting. How did Kyran find the capital?"

"I think he enjoyed it, for the most part. He doesn't like crowds," Barrett added, trying not to think of last night.

"That's wonderful to hear. I'm not certain I'd find it as titillating as I once did. Too many memories in these old streets."

The riots. Barrett looked the Lightbringer up and down, but he simply couldn't see the same sharp fury as the protestors outside the gates or the malignant cunning Kat believed the man possessed. He still couldn't believe her wild accusations. Myles would never.

"I can see you have a question," Myles said, settling back against his pillows. "Ask away."

"No, it's… It's nothing. Just…"

"Go on," the Lightbringer encouraged, nodding congenially.

Barrett let out a tight breath. There was nothing to ask that he didn't know the answer to already, Kat's doubts be cursed. Except… "How did you come to Belldale?"

The man blinked in surprise, the first time Barrett had seen the man so. "I had thought your guildmate would have told you. He was the one that asked me if I would attend that House while he was visiting Oareford to collect you and Kyran."

"Griswold?" Barrett asked, scarcely breathing when the Lightbringer nodded.

"That's the one."

The captain again. Graces, everywhere Barrett turned, there Griswold was again. It couldn't be a coincidence. Kyran, Myles, the abominations. Even Raleigh. Why hadn't he noticed it before?

"I left Oareford not long after you did to travel to that poor village," Myles continued. "I'm truly sorry not to be there any longer. If there was a place that needed Lumen's guiding light, truly it is a House besieged by demons."

"I'm sorry, Myles. I… I need to speak with someone," Barrett said, rising from his seat.

"That's quite all right, but what about the person you are waiting on?"

"I'll be back," Barrett dismissed, starting to leave, when there was a tug at his coat. He looked down to find Myles gripping the hem, giving him a reproachful look. "It's important."

"So is your friend," the Lightbringer chastised. "Would you like me to tell him where you've gone?"

"Ah, yes. Yes, please. Tell him I've gone to talk to someone and I'll meet him at the mess." If Griswold didn't try to kill him. Barrett wouldn't go down quietly, though. He'd make certain everyone knew.

Chapter Fifty-Two

KYRAN SHUDDERED AS he left the examination room. Lilyana had been waiting for him, as he'd expected. It had only been what was fast becoming a routine exam, but it always left him unsettled. The chirurgeon hadn't touched him, merely examined his leg and asked him a few simple questions about his pain and sensitivity and if he wanted more tea sent to his room before sending him away, but simply exposing himself—his *leg*—like that felt too terribly intimate. He didn't like how incredibly vulnerable or uncomfortably aware of his body it left him, and he found himself tugging his shirtsleeves down while he clenched his control around his power as tightly as he could, though it bucked against him.

"Ah, Kyran."

The mage turned as the Lightbringer he had met at the hospital before approached him, smiling brightly. "Lightbringer."

"Myles," the man corrected gently. "It's good to see you again. I was asked to give you a message on behalf of Kristopher."

Kyran cocked his head at the name before he distantly recalled it as Barrett's given name. "Aye?"

"He wanted me to let you know that he has gone to speak with someone and will meet you at the mess when he has finished."

Kyran's lips thinned. "I see."

"It must have been important. He was in quite a state about it."

"I ken he was." Kyran looked down, thinking for a moment, before he made up his mind. "Thank you for the message, Lightbringer."

"I wish it was better news," the man sighed, reaching up to ruffle the last bits of white frizz clinging to his bald pate, drawing Kyran's eye to a green bruise. "You and I will have to catch up soon. Maybe the three of us should have dinner some time once they finally let me out of here. I am looking forward to being able to continue my duties as a Lightbringer once more." He waved his hand dismissively, folding it atop the other on his cane. "But don't let my rambling hold you up. You two enjoy your breakfast. May Lumen's Light guide you and keep you safe."

Kyran's fingers tightened around his walking stick. "Aye, you as well."

He didn't go to the mess hall. Making a short trip back to his room, he went instead to visit the ward.

The weans were playing outside, tossing a leather ball back and forth, chasing hoops, or simply each other. The rain had finally tapered off, but the clouds still hung heavy and grey above.

He spied Effie in an instant, staring back at him, a point of stillness amongst the other weans. She clutched a doll to her chest, her face lighting up with excitement before she broke into a run as fast as her feet could carry her, and all but threw herself around his knee.

He planted his stick more firmly, catching his balance before he reached down to tousle her hair. "Morning lass."

"You're here!"

Kyran looked up as Moira broke from the crowd to join them, spattered in mud from head to toe.

"Good morning," she beamed, then let out a dramatic gasp. "You have a new leg!

"Aye, I do."

"Can I touch it?"

Kyran eyed the lass's muddy hands. "I'd rather you dinnae."

"Can you show us your magic again?" Moira asked, clasping her hands and sticking her lip out as far as she could manage. "Please?"

Kyran blinked, caught off guard by the request.

"Effie drew me a picture of it," Moira declared, looking quite proud. "She draws lots of pictures. Most of them are really scary, but this one was of you, and you had stuff coming out of your hands, and you were fighting a monster!"

Kyran looked at the younger lass, who looked inquiringly up at him. He wasn't certain if he was more surprised the lass had drawn him, or concerned that she had been drawing monsters.

Disentangling Effie from his leg, he lowered himself to his knee, and then his hip, then laid his walking stick across his lap and pulled his new limb into a more comfortable position. He looked about him until he found a decently sized puddle within reach. Extending his hand over it, he focused his power down into the water. With a rolling crackle, the puddle flashed to ice in nearly the blink of an eye.

"You glowed again!" Moira gasped. The other weans in the yard were watching now, some wandering closer.

"Aye."

"Does that happen every time you use your magic?"

"Aye."

"Wow." She walked over to the frozen puddle, tapping it with the tip of her shoe before she crouched, working her fingers under the edge of the ice.

He was as amused as much as he was baffled by the lass's fascination. It was a sight better than seeing her run terrified across the lawn, though.

Effie made a soft sound to get his attention, unwinding an arm from her doll to fish in her dress pocket. She pulled out a neatly folded piece of paper and held out to Kyran.

"Oh, thank you." He accepted the paper, unfolding it against his knee. Inside was a drawing in charcoal, slightly smudged after being folded, but still easy enough to make out. At the center was a small girl holding the hand of someone very tall dressed in what had to be a kilt with little hatched lines drawn in it for the pattern. It was him, or Effie's depiction of him, standing next to her, both with smiles drawn on. In the background was unmistakably a house and other people, also wearing kilts, except for one drawn at Kyran's right side, holding his other hand. That one had trews, long hair, and a long coat. Barrett.

It was a drawing of him, holding hands with Effie and Barrett, surrounded by his family in the Isles at his da's house.

The pain was sudden and intense, as if someone had closed their fist around his heart and squeezed. The corners of his eyes prickled threateningly, and he gulped for air around the swelling knot in his throat. "Thank you, lass," he managed, looking over the picture again as he remembered the night she had drawn, standing out in the snow, his hand extended to the man he owed his life.

He might have been nothing but an oddity to the guild, a demon blooded tool for them to study and wield, but Barrett...

A raindrop landed on the corner of the page with a loud plop, and he quickly tucked it close.

If he had been born a human, he would have been a farmer. He would have bred and broken horses for the laird. He would have grown up surrounded by his family, his brothers, his sister, ma, and da. What happened in the stable would never have come to be. He wouldn't have come to Tennebrum, wouldn't have been dragged into the demon realm and tortured. Wouldn't have had to stand in the Great Hall while someone bought his freedom. He would have lived a normal, peaceful life.

But that wasn't what he had been given, and he would never have it.

Reaching out into the rain, he let his control slip just enough his blood glowed faintly through his translucent skin. Where the rain struck his palm, it bounced, hitting the ground by his boot with a little clink. Others did the same, raining down in little ice chips.

There was no way to take away the curse he had been born under, but he could turn it back on the beasts that had set it on him. He could be the monster in the shadow that kept the rest at bay, so there were no more *weans* like him or Effie.

All he had to do was accept it, stop fighting the truth, and do what he knew he had to.

"That's a neat trick."

Kyran whirled at the unexpected, familiar voice, looking up at Finley, who peered down at him over her scarf. She was dressed much as she had been every time Kyran had seen her, bundled against the cold, only her eyes visible. "*Madainn mhath.*"

She chuckled, pulling her scarf down from her nose and mouth. There were shadows under her eyes he hadn't noticed in the front room and she looked as haggard as Kyran felt. "I don't think I know a word of Isleish."

"Good morning," Kyran repeated in Common.

"Morning. Anyway," she retorted, casting a wary eye up at the sky, "I'm certain you can guess why I'm here, but I wanted to let you know we'll be meeting in the arena again tonight just after sundown."

Kyran felt his spine bend under the weight of his exhaustion at the thought of pulling himself into the Inbetween again tonight. "Aye, I'll be there."

"Good. Make certain you get some rest before then. I—" She looked down the path suddenly, and Kyran followed her gaze to Barrett coming their way down the path. "I suppose I should let you get back to your friend." She was smiling, but there was a note of irritation in her tone that rankled Kyran. "May your lanterns stay lit."

"And yours as well." He watched her leave in the opposite direction of the hunter, frowning at the brief interaction. He didn't know the other mage very well, but something seemed off.

"You're going to get muddy down there," Barrett called when he got near, his eyes tracking the other mage. "Was that Finley?"

"Aye," Kyran said, gathering his walking stick.

"Not more orders from Griswold, I hope," the hunter growled, folding his arms.

"No, she was only letting me know ta meet in the arena tonight."

"What's she want with you at the arena at night for?"

Kyran picked at a splinter on his walking stick. "Practice."

Barrett's brows rose dubiously. "At night?"

"Going inta the Inbetween."

The hunter's eyes went wide. "By all the Graces, why would you—"

"So I can get out when I am taken again," Kyran cut him off, pulling his hand from his walking stick and reaching to stroke the top of Effie's head. "Nowell will be there as well."

Barrett's shoulders slumped, and his eyes slipped closed before he finally bowed his head. "Right. All right. Do you still want to get breakfast?"

"Aye. I wasna certain if you did. The Lightbringer said you left."

Barrett shook his head, wincing apologetically. "I went to talk to someone, but he was at some meeting. I couldn't get in." He twitched as a raindrop landed squarely on his cheek, and shrugged deeper into his coat. "If you'd rather not…"

"I ken I should." Kyran turned to Effie again, holding the folded drawing out to her. But the lass wouldn't take it, clinging to her doll. "I'll be back soon," he assured her, pressing the paper against her knuckles, but she shook her head, looking up at him plaintively. Unwilling to argue with the lass, he carefully tucked the drawing away in his purse. "Thank you, lass," he said, meaning every word.

She smiled brightly in return, shuffling back as he cumbersomely got up from the ground.

"If it'd be more comfortable, I can bring breakfast back to the dormitories for us like the other day," Barrett offered, twitching as another raindrop pelted the tip of his nose.

Kyran smirked at the hunter's expense as a bit of ice bounced off his shoulder. "Aye, if you like."

Chapter Fifty-Three

BARRETT WOKE TO the sound of splashing and the unsettled feeling of not knowing where or when he was. And it was cold. He shifted uncomfortably, tucking his nose unto the crook of his arm to warm it, and cracked an eye open just enough to make out a room that wasn't his.

"Are you awake, then?"

The hunter rolled his head onto the pillow of his arm to see Kyran washing his hands in the basin. "I think," Barrett croaked, slowly peeling himself up off the table he was folded over. "Graces," he mumbled, stretching as he took in the room, including the window, which was dark behind a sheen of frost. "Is... is it that late?"

"Aye. I was just about ta wake you before I left."

Barrett sat back in his chair, absolutely dumbfounded. He racked his brain, trying to remember some part of the day, but the last thing he could recall was eating breakfast and deciding to rest his eyes. "I... I'm sorry. I didn't mean to—"

"It's fine," Kyran said, picking up the rag from the side of the basin to daub at his hands. "You were about out of your head trying ta stay awake. Gave the wall a good hard look for a while."

Barrett felt his face warm. He had a vague notion of trying to hold his eyes open between bites of food. He looked around the table, noting the neatly stacked remains of their breakfast and odd collection of tiny whittled suns, one of which was stained with freshly dried blood. One of Kyran's amulets. He supposed that was why the room was so cold. He was surprised the pull of the mage's magic hadn't woken him. He must have been very deep asleep.

There was, however, something missing that concerned him. "Have you eaten since this morning?" He looked up at the mage, who didn't quite return his gaze as his stomach let out a plaintive growl.

"I'll take that as a no," Barrett said, chuckling weakly. "You should have woken me. I'd have gone and gotten it."

Kyran set the rag back on the edge of the basin and came around the table. "I was busy myself preparing for tonight," the mage said simply, picking something up off the table and holding it out to Barrett.

"I saw," Barrett said, leaning forward to take whatever Kyran had. His brows shot up at the sight of a small, carved sun resting on Kyran's palm. It looked nearly identical to the one he had seen the mage praying over every morning, the center of the sun covered in swirling lines that curled and twisted around one another.

"Ta keep you through the night."

Barrett's cheeks warmed in vague embarrassment, but he couldn't stop the smile that stretched his face as he picked up the charm, careful not to touch Kyran's palm beneath. "Thank you," he said, turning the charm over in his palm, the wood cold against his skin. "You know, I used that whistle you made me while I was in Belldale."

"Oh?"

"Worked like a charm."

"Of course, it did," Kyran scoffed, and Barrett smiled until his cheeks hurt.

"Are you headed to your practice now?"

"Aye," Kyran said, tucking his bloodied amulet away and taking up his walking stick.

"Do you mind if I walk with you?"

"As you like."

Barrett tried to read the mage's cool expression, but he couldn't make out if Kyran was pulling away or truly felt no particular way about it. Everything seemed fine between them, but he never had managed to talk to Kyran about what had happened at the inn. Instead, he had unsuccessfully chased after Griswold and then slept the whole day. "Kyran, are you... Are we all right?"

The mage looked back at him, his hand resting on the door's latch, his kerchief spread over his fingers. "What do you mean?"

"After..." Barrett's throat tightened around the words, and he had to force the question past. "Well, with what happened the other night..."

Kyran tilted his head, considering him, and Barrett felt his mouth go dry. "You are a hunter, are you na?" He waited, and Barrett nodded meekly. "And hunters work with demons, aye?" Barrett nodded again. "If I am going ta blame anyone, it is going ta be *that* selfish beast," he said, his eyes lowering to the outline of the amulet under Barrett's shirt. "And if it tries it again, I will make certain it never does again."

A threat? Barrett felt his demon stir within him, his skin warming, and he knew a thrill of panic.

"*Don't,*" he cautioned it silently.

Don't what? the beast simpered. *If the mageling thinks the wounds my brothers have given him smart, he should try to make good on his threat.*

"The Old One—"

Is the only reason I wouldn't pull him apart and swallow his bones. I would only hurt him enough to ensure he never dared to cross me again.

"If you hurt him—"

It would only be in self-defense, hunter. You had better warn him.

Barrett swallowed, prying his tongue loose from the roof of his mouth where it had glued itself. "You can't."

Kyran's eyes narrowed, his runelines brightening a hair in anger, and Barrett rushed to clarify.

"It's strong. Maybe stronger than the needle-toothed demon, and I… I don't want you to get hurt trying to save me if I become…an abomination."

"I am going ta get hurt, Barrett," Kyran said, his voice even. "I'm a mage. That's why I am going ta get stronger."

Barrett stared, taking in the determined set of Kyran's mouth as the mage's words rang in his ears, his chest suddenly full of something terrifying, a maelstrom of emotions that left him drowning. "You…"

Outside, the distant peal of the House's evening bell rang out over the city, marking the last of the day.

Kyran glanced past him, his magic flickering out as he mastered himself. "I have ta go."

A cold fear flashed through the hunter before he remembered the mage's obligation that evening. "Al…alright. I'll come find you for breakfast, then?" he said, managing a shaky smile.

"Aye. We'll give Effie her present."

"Of course." There was an awkward pause before Barrett finally said, "May your lanterns stay lit."

"And yours as well."

The mage left then, leaving Barrett standing alone in the middle of Kyran's room, grappling with the tangle of emotions warring beneath his ribs. Taking a trembling breath, he pushed his fingers through his mess of hair, squeezing his eyes shut as reason began to creep in.

"Oh Graces, curse me to the Pit."

Chapter Fifty-Four

THUNDER RUMBLED OVERHEAD as Kyran crossed the guildhall, keeping his head bent against the wind and rain. It was as miserable a night as he had experienced since coming to the guildhall, but even now, he could see runners scurrying to and fro carrying messages across the grounds, lamplighters tending the lanterns, and other guild members hurrying between buildings.

Stars, he hoped Barrett would be all right for just a little while. Kyran could still see the hunter's face, wide-eyed and grey with terror, and he couldn't help a trace of frustration that Barrett didn't think him capable of keeping the threat he'd made. Perhaps not yet, not if the hunter's demon was as powerful as Barrett made it out to be or as Kyran had witnessed himself. But soon. He just needed more practice to hone his control and a strategy to strengthen his magic. As of yet, he only knew of one method, revolting though it was.

Nowell and Finley were both waiting when Kyran stepped beneath the sheltering awning of the arena.

"Thank you for coming promptly," Nowell said as the mage approached. His brows were raised, watching the pellets of ice gather around Kyran. "That is an… *interesting* application of magic." His gaze shifted to Kyran's legs and he let out a soft *huh*. "How's that suiting you?"

"Well enough," Kyran said, leaning into his walking stick to take the pressure from his leg.

"That's good to hear," Finley cut in. She was bundled up in her coat again, a knitted cap pulled so far down her head, it nearly hid her eyes. "And, now that we're all here, Nowell, I wanted to make a proposal for this evening's practice."

The guard captain looked nonplussed at being interrupted, but he gestured for her to continue.

"Since we've all had adequate time to rest between…happenings here at the guild, I think tonight would be the best opportunity to make our first real push to reach our goal."

Nowell folded his arms as he considered the suggestion. "I think that would be a good use of our time." He looked to Kyran. "I trust you're rested after your *holiday*?"

"Aye," Kyran assured him, chafing at the way the man implied Kyran had done something wrong.

The guard captain sighed, looking up at the ceiling. "All right. I'll need to send a runner to let the captains know about the possibility of a longer excursion. Time is… strange, the deeper we go, as I'm certain you're aware, Kyran."

He was, of course. It was always disorienting to experience the divergence of rational time after slipping out of the human realm. The first time the demon had dragged him into the Inbetween, he and Barrett had been there for what couldn't have been more than a few minutes, but when they escaped, an entire night had passed. They had all three experienced a similar phenomenon here in the arena, where a few seconds entering and then leaving the Inbetween stretched into hours of waiting for the others.

"Get the lights while I chase down one of these boys. And do not start until I am back and give the word." He didn't budge until both Kyran and Finley had given their assent, then exited the arena, leaving the two mages alone.

Finley snorted, her eyes crinkled with amusement above her scarf. "You think he'll try to have us added to the ward next?"

"Aye, I ken he would," Kyran agreed drily.

She shook her head. "The lanterns, then?"

They took opposite directions around the inside of the arena, then waited at the center next to the very last upon the post for Nowell to return. Thankfully it wasn't long before he returned.

"It's done," the guard captain announced. His hand settled against the pommel of the sword at his hip. "Ready?"

While uneasy about the proposal, Kyran found himself starting to warm to the idea of making the demon realm tonight. This had been what all of this practice was for—to find a way to reach it so he could get himself out again. And today might be the day he finally accomplished that.

He touched his purse, reassuring himself his amulet he had been working on was still there. "Aye. I am."

"Good," Finley answered, stepping uncomfortably close. "I think this will work best if all three of us go in and take turns pulling us deeper, that way no one tires over much. I read in Hunter Barrett and Captain

Griswold's reports that they did it by holding onto one another, so we'll need to take hands."

Kyran balked at the idea. It was true, Griswold and Barrett had always had to take hold of him to pull him through the Inbetween and, he assumed out of the demon realm, but he still wasn't taken with the idea of clinging to Nowell and Finley for the next several hours.

Nowell let out a grisly sigh that indicated he felt much the same way. Finley was the first to lift both her arms, palms up. Nowell followed suit, slapping his gloved hand down into hers and then offering his opposite to Kyran.

Fighting the revulsion crawling under his skin, Kyran took Finley's hand first, finding it papery, dry and hot. Nowell's hand was no easier to bring himself to grasp, but at least the glove had the familiarity of Barrett.

"I'll start," Nowell offered, taking a long, measured breath. A moment later, Kyran could feel the world sloughing away as the darkness pressed over them. It was a slow pull at first, the ambient sounds and smells of the guildhall fading into nothing, giving way to suffocating silence. A few minutes passed like this, Nowell breathing around each pull, until he finally paused.

"Finley," the guard captain signaled.

Kyran heard her chuff and felt her hot hand twitch in his. Then her runelines lit up with a pulse of power, releasing a wave of heat with it. For a moment, she scarcely looked like herself. Between the shadows of the Inbetween and the molten glow of her magic, she bore far too close a resemblance to the needle-toothed demon.

Then, she pulled, the sensation of the Inbetween rushing past them with such a ferocity that even Nowell let out a sharp noise.

"Pace yourself," Nowell snipped at her. When her magic faded, apparently signaling the end of her turn, Nowell called, "Kyran."

Taking a settling breath, Kyran reached out into the pitch dark with his magic, and pulled.

It hurt, the inky dark resisting his every inch forwards, but it wasn't nearly so difficult as it had been to tear his way into the realm. Minute by fraught minute, he dragged them forward, Nowell and Finley barely noticeable weights behind him.

"That's enough," Nowell said after an interminable amount of time. "I'll go again."

They went on like this for some time, trading off at Nowell's command. But after each round, gradually, the guard captain's tone became different. Harsh and ragged, as though he were straining.

"Can you manage?" Finley asked after Kyran had finished pulling them deeper again. The press of the Inbetween was nearly suffocating now. They all felt it. But Nowell was the most affected of the three of them.

The hunter glowered at her. "I'll be fine. I've just never been this far down. I am… adjusting."

"Perhaps you should *pace yourself*," she suggested. Nowell didn't respond, instead drawing them in deeper. It was becoming hotter, the pressure so much that Kyran's ears and head were aching even when he wasn't the one pulling.

"We're almost there," Nowell said haltingly as the space around them drew taut, pressing down on them with all the weight of a *ben*.

Then, in an instant, the skein of darkness tore, and they all but tumbled out onto a ledge of terribly familiar ashen stone.

Kyran sucked down a grateful breath, letting his magic burn in his veins to give them light as he took in their surroundings. His stomach dropped between his boots.

Surrounding them on every side were the leering grins of demons.

Chapter Fifty-Five

BARRETT HOVERED AT the edge of the arena, glancing up at the lighting sky, but there was no sign of Kyran or the others. He had felt the pull of their magic last night, of them slipping into the Inbetween. He'd nearly gone racing out into the night, except the bell had remained silent. Not a demon, then.

He waited another hour, and then another, willing himself to feel something—anything—that might indicate the mage was returning. But there was nothing. Something must have gone wrong. The mage should be back by now. What if they'd met trouble? What if they'd been captured? Or hurt? Or worse?

"I should have gone with them," Barrett muttered, his worry blossoming into panic before he realized he knew someone that was almost definitely involved.

Barrett stormed across the grounds to the college, taking the stairs two at a time to the captains' offices, glancing at the placards until he found the one he wanted. Grabbing the handle he shoved the door open, glowering at the man behind the desk.

"You—" he growled before he noticed the other people in the room.

"Do you make a habit of barging into rooms unannounced?" Kat snapped, folding her arms over her chest. Beside her, the guildmaster looked on in stony bemusement.

"I…" Barrett stammered, taken aback by the unexpected audience until he remembered why he was there. "I need to talk to the captain."

"We are in the middle of something, Kris. What's so important?"

"Kyran is missing," Barrett snapped, his eyes switching to the guild captain who hadn't even looked up from his notes. "And I *know* Griswold knows something about it."

Kat's scowl dropped, her expression softening. "What?"

Barrett took a step forward when the air pressure in the room shifted, and Barrett's stomach curdled with dread as the door slammed shut behind him.

"He is not missing," Griswold finally said. "I presume Kyran has told you about the experiments he was asked to conduct?"

Experiments? Barrett felt the knots in his stomach try to rise into his throat as he thought of the file Ilham had presented after asking him to report on Kyran to them. "No. He told me he was practicing with Nowell. And, that they were trying to reach the demon realm."

The guildmaster's brows rose, and he wondered if Kyran was not supposed to tell him anything. Graces, he hoped he hadn't just condemned the mage under guild law.

"You are correct," Griswold confirmed. "So, you have your answer."

"But it's been a day."

The captain let out a long suffering sigh and lowered his notes, folding his hands on his desk. "And you were gone almost a week when you disappeared. We anticipated this kind of delay."

Barrett bit back a frustrated groan. "But what if something happens? How will we know? How long is too long?"

"Kyran is with a senior mage and the captain of the guard," Kat cut in. "I'd wager they're fine."

"You don't know that!"

"If they haven't returned after a week—" Griswold said.

"A week?" Barrett gaped.

"—Nowell recommended not sending a rescue party," the captain continued. "He also advised that we were unlikely to successfully prevent you from going, and so to have you consult on a best possible route." The captain's mouth turned faintly wry. "As you have the most experience in this area."

Barrett could hardly believe what he was hearing. Either about Kyran or Griswold's admission. "If that's the case, then I think we should go now, not in a week."

"Kyran is with two very capable guild members, as well as being competent himself," Griswold pointed out, massaging his temple. "I am certain they are well equipped to deal with any obstacles they encounter."

"But why send him at all? Why Kyran, of all the people in the guild? What does the guild want with him?"

"He is a guild member, and one of the few not engaged in the matters at Belldale. " Griswold said, letting his hand fall from his temple.

Barrett felt his last thread of patience snap. "That's bullshit!" he snarled, fire crackling across his hands and up his arms. "Stop lying to me! What does the guild really want?"

"Barrett," Kat warned, reaching for him. "What are you—"

"Don't!" Barrett snapped at her, twitching his shoulder away. "If you know—" He looked at Griswold again. "If you don't tell me, I will do everything in my power to—"

"And what is it I am supposed to tell you?" Griswold asked, his hair and clothes beginning to stir. "You already have the facts."

"What are you planning? I know about the guild's file on Kyran."

"Barrett, there are files on all of us," Kat sighed. "That is the scribes and librarians' whole purpose."

"Not like this." Barrett cut his eyes to Selah, who watched passively, apparently content simply observing all of this. "There are notes from before he was at the guild. Letters from the laird from over a decade ago about a mage born in the Isles after an out of season snowstorm. You knew about him, and you left him up there until…" Barrett choked on the memory of what Kyran had told him had happened to him, what had sent him fleeing across the Isles and into Tennebrum, and still it hadn't been far enough to escape.

"You knew, and you still waited. And then you tricked him into signing that contract. And no sooner did he get back here before you started using him in these…*experiments*, when he's barely started recovering. Then you used all of us as bait to…to what? *Lure* abominations to make Kyran fight? That was awfully convenient, wasn't it?"

The papers began to rustle restlessly on Griswold's desk. "What are you implying?"

"I know about Myles. I know you're the reason he's here. Why he was in Belldale." Barrett leaned forward, the smell of woodsmoke filling his nostrils. "Everywhere I've looked, I've found your name, Griswold. And then this talk about traitors? How do we know it isn't you?"

"That's enough." The pressure in the room flexed with Griswold's voice, and Barrett clapped his hands over his ears at the sharp pain that lanced through his head.

"Bastard," he hissed.

"Hammond," Kat said, touching his shoulder, and the pressure eased. "You should tell him."

"He is not in control," Griswold said, his tone cutting. "He is untrained and brash and—"

"And you should tell him," the guildmaster spoke up at last, her voice calm and even, but firm enough that Griswold immediately paused. "Keeping him in the dark has not prevented his interference yet. It would be easier to simply have him remain involved."

The captain inclined his head ever so slightly. "As you wish, guildmaster." He settled back in his seat, folding his hands on the desk once more. "We are losing this war, Barrett."

Barrett looked from one face to the other, not quite comprehending what Griswold meant. "What?"

"Our war with demons. Every year, there are more and more of them crossing over, killing people and destroying our cities, and every year we have fewer hunters to face them. We are losing, and if something does not change, there will not be enough of us left to protect anyone."

Barrett felt the color drain from his face, the fire on his arms flickering out. He looked at Kat, her face more haggard than he had ever seen. Then he looked at Griswold, the captain's neutral expression replaced with something anxious. Graces, was it really as bad as that? "But what does that have to do with Kyran?"

"We cannot continue to simply repel the demons that crossover. Trying to spread our numbers so there might be a hunter within reach for every demon that comes through makes us vulnerable and leaves far too many unprotected. So, I have proposed a new strategy—we move the warfront to the demon's territory and eliminate them at their source."

Certainly Barrett hadn't heard that right. "In the demon realm?"

"From a series of fortified outposts in strategic places where we could engage demons before they can cross over, and hunt the rest down before they can become threats."

It sounded mad. Outposts and hunting demons to extinction. Yet, there was some sense to it. Putting out a fire at the source instead of only where it spread to. "But why Kyran?"

"Because he has been there before."

"So have I," Barrett reminded the captain sharply.

"With your demon's interference," Griswold reminded him in turn. "But I am more interested in maintaining Kyran's involvement to see if his sire might be lured into helping us."

"The Old One?" Barrett looked from Griswold to Selah. "You're mad."

"I am not planning to ask it if it would like to join our ranks, but if Kyran is among those that will be under attack, I am hoping it will be motivated to protect him, or at the very least, not attack us."

"That's..." Barrett groped to find any way to describe how utterly mad of a plan that was. "You were there in the Inbetween and at the guildhall when it appeared. You saw what happened just from it crossing into our world. What it felt like just to stand near it."

"Yes, and I've also seen it appear twice now to protect the mage without attacking anyone directly."

"You don't know if it will do that again."

"That is a risk worth taking if there is a chance we might not have to confront it directly." The guild captain reached up to push his hair from his face, letting out a long breath before he straightened in his seat again. "Have I explained myself sufficiently, then?"

Not even close, but Barrett doubted there was anything else Griswold could say that would make any of what he just said make more sense. "What about Kyran now, though? Why a week? Why not now?"

"It is dawn," Selah pointed out.

"And it hasn't even been a full day," Kat said, squeezing Griswold's shoulder before she let her hand slip from it. "If they don't come back in a day or two, then we can decide what to do."

Barrett looked between them, at their utter unconcern. "And why shouldn't I just go in after them myself right *now*?"

"Because it is dawn," Selah repeated, folding her hands. "And as one of the few seniors currently at the guildhall, you are needed here in case of another attack."

"Fine." They weren't going to listen to him, no matter how much he argued. They thought he was simply frightened and paranoid. They hadn't faced that needle-toothed demon's determination over and over and over the way he and Kyran had.

Without another word, he left, slamming the door shut behind him. But he hadn't made it more than a few steps down the hall before the door opened behind him.

"Kris," Kat called sharply. "Kris!" He kept walking. "Kristopher!"

The sharpness of her voice made him flinch, but he stopped and whirled to face her. "What?"

"Seriously?" she scoffed as she briskly caught up to him. "I need to know you're not going to do something stupid."

"Like what?"

"I don't know, lock yourself in a cellar so you can disappear again?"

Barrett's scowl deepened. "At least it worked."

Kat pressed her lips together, but inclined her head in acknowledgement. "I know, but this is different. I get it. He means a lot to you, and you're worried, but you can't act rashly."

"But what if he is in trouble? What if he needs help?" Barrett nearly shouted. "I'm sick of the guild trying to *use* and *study* him. It's cruel to make him go there. He's been through enough."

"I may not be in the know on this, but I don't think Kyran would have gone unwillingly. He knew what he was getting into. You can't let yourself feel responsible for everyone. You—"

"Don't." Barrett took a deep breath. "Just don't. I don't want to talk about it. I know—I… Why do *you* even care?"

"Excuse me?" Kat folded her arms. "You want to ask me that again?"

"I just don't get it," his voice rose. "Why do you—you were never—"

"Don't you *dare* say I was never there. I don't think you remember a single time I came to check on you when you were drinking yourself to death in that seedy little inn in Oareford. It was bad, Kris. I've seen your low point. I don't think you can make it back if you go there again, and if you spend every minute fretting over Kyran, it's going to happen again."

His jaw squeezed so tightly his teeth ached. There was so much he wanted to shout at her for. They had never got on, not really, and ever since he had come back things had felt…different. "Why do you care?" he asked, his voice weak. "I know you and Pa never wanted me to be a hunter. Neither of you were ever around. And when you were around, you were always such an arse, and I—"

"I kept you out of the house," Kat interrupted hoarsely. "So you wouldn't have to see how Pa talked to Ma. You think *we* bicker a lot? They *always* fought. Maybe I went about distracting you the wrong way, but I didn't want you to be like him. Being a hunter isn't for the faint of heart, Kris. People die doing this. People die in front of us. Sooner or later it's going to be you or someone you know. I'm not— I'm not saying it isn't worth it, but I've seen how you react, and I don't think you can take it again."

Her words stung. Everything about them. He wished he hadn't heard any of them and could just ignore how much they made him feel. It was too much all at once. Barrett took in a sharp breath and turned away without meeting Kat's eyes.

"Where are you going?"

"To get a bloody drink," he muttered bitterly.

He heard her boots against the floor approaching him, but didn't expect her to grab his wrist. Barrett yanked his arm, but she held fast. He opened his mouth to shout at her, but a sudden cry threatened to overtake him in that moment and he just clamped his teeth shut, snarling in frustration while fighting back the stinging of his eyes.

"Kris," she said, her voice so soft it sounded like a stranger. Barrett pulled at his arm again and she let go. "Please. Don't. Please, just think about what I told you last time."

"What else am I supposed to do?" Barrett muttered bitterly. "Sit on my hands and wait? Hope he comes back?"

"You could always come train with me," Kat offered. "It doesn't have to be a sword. I know you're all right with a bow, and I've seen you throw hands. You've got the instinct, but—"

"But I'm not a *prodigy* like you, right?"

She gave him a dry look. "That's hardly fair. I was dragged into this young by pa. You like to think he and I got on, but we…I've always been in his shadow. It was Hammond that finally helped me get past that."

The admission took Barrett by surprise. For all he was blood with Kat, it never really struck him like it did just then how little he really knew about her. Not to say he forgave her for the years of misery she put him through as a boy, but it was a light he had never even considered her in.

She cleared her throat, shifting feet awkwardly before she continued. "The offer stands. We could go right now, if you wanted. Or later, if you want to get some rest. I know you haven't gotten much rest."

There was a bitter part of him that wanted desperately to push her away, to go get the drink he had set his mind on. But there was truth to her words. He remembered those days after his pa had retired and his mother had left. The drinking. The snide comments. The disappointment. Graces, it was no wonder Kat had stayed at the guild instead of coming back to Willowvale when their mother had left.

He tried to digest everything and felt an ache starting in his temples. Blowing out a sigh, he reached up to massage the ache away. "I don't… I don't think I'd be able to sleep, anyway," he acquiesced stiffly.

She clapped his shoulder. "Come on, then," she said softly, stepping past him to lead the way.

Barrett followed. If nothing else, perhaps a bit of fighting would wear him out enough to sleep a little and not spend every waking moment worrying about what Kyran might be facing. And what Griswold wanted him to face next.

CHAPTER FIFTY-SIX

KYRAN FLUNG HIS hand up, focusing his magic as it came surging out of his blood when something collided with the back of his knee. His leg folded like wet snow, his false leg pulling him off balance, and his head hit the ground with a solid crack. A wave of nausea rolled through the mage and he nearly retched as he rolled to his belly, his pulse hammering at the inside of his head.

"Finley!" Nowell barked, cutting through the vicious ringing in Kyran's ears. "What are—" The guard captain's voice warped into something throaty and dry before Kyran heard the man fall.

Despite every urge not to, Kyran peeled one eye open and cautiously turned his head to see the man down on one knee, his eyes glowing bright red through the black spreading through the whites of his eyes, bleeding out into his skin. He was losing control of his demon,

"You?" Nowell ground out through his teeth, and Kyran followed his gaze, of Finley standing before them. "You planned this?"

"For a very long time," she said plainly, unwinding her scarf.

"Traitor!" Nowell snarled and lunged forward, drawing his sword, only for his legs to buckle beneath him, sending him careening to the ground.

Sniffing, Finley stepped around him, as her scarf dropped to the ground along with her hat to reveal her face. One eye had bled black, her iris burning bright red with power. Even as he looked, Kyran could see fine lines of inky black growing down her cheek.

"Stars, no," Kyran whispered, dragging himself to his knees.

"It's distasteful, I know, but how else is a mage going to stand up to an entire nest of witches?" Finley said, approaching Kyran. " It *is* a pity I didn't have you at my disposal before now. You would have made a fine skin for me. But maybe once this is over…"

"*Falbh dairich fhein,*" Kyran snarled up at her, at the demon speaking from inside her, because that wasn't Finley. It couldn't be.

Her smile turned simpering, and she turned away, facing the circle of demons. "I've already softened him for whomever wants to claim him."

A cacophony of perverted purring rolled through Kyran's senses, filling him with dread as he felt them probing at his mind like little splinters under his skull.

"I was beginning to wonder if you would even make it through," a voice simpered from the crowd.

"You are impatient," Finley tutted.

"Am I?" the other voice hissed, and the splinters probing at Kyran vanished as the beasts jostled and shoved one another to move out of the way as the speaker came forward. It wasn't another demon, but an abomination. Its frame was small, barely half Kyran's height, moving in a long rolling motion of its many, many legs. "You are stalling," it said, addressing Finley. It didn't even quite have a face, only the suggestion of one masked by the jagged ends of what looked like more limbs reaching out from beneath the ashen skin of its bare head, only its bare torso betraying the human beneath its twisted form. "We have waited long enough. You promised us a feast, yet have remained insufferably idle."

"We could have acted sooner if not for your interference," Finley chastised it.

"They were…unsuspecting, and it would have been enough, if not for your…" It's mockery of a face slid towards Kyran, and he felt its will peer at him in an ingentle press against his mind. "*Pet.*"

Kyran's lips drew back in a snarl, frost creeping across his face as shoved the demon from his head contemptibly. "I am na a *pet*," he hissed.

It purred again, the sound bleeding into something like a hearty chuckle. "That is what they all say. Still, you are just *one…little…mageling.* And we…" It tilted its head, as if casting its gaze to the group of demons hawking hungrily. "We are *many*. And we are *hungry*."

Bending, Finley clamped her hand on Kyran's shoulder in a bruisingly strong grip, dragging him upwards. In a flash, Kyran grabbed her wrist with a burst of magic that made the soft flesh under his nails turn white and hard.

The woman shrieked, yanking her hand back, leaving bits of her skin stuck to his fingertips. "You—" She raised her hand as if to strike him, and Kyran let his power pour out of him, driving her and several of the demons back as the stones beneath him gave a thunderous crack and split.

"I am na a *pet*," he repeated, dragging his good leg beneath him and, with both hands on his thigh, managed to push himself up to his feet again, gritting his teeth against the pounding lingering behind his eyes.

"And neither is she. Let her go."

A wave of unease rolled through the demons, their excited chitters fading and they eased backwards.

"*This-s-s one,*" came a raspy voice from the crowd. "We cannot take *this one*. The Old One will know. The Old One will find us."

"That's right," came Nowell's strained voice from behind Kyran. He was struggling to his feet, his body twitching and convulsing at random, but clutched in his hand was Kyran's walking stick. "It will. Did it…while he was at the guild."

The unease ratcheted higher as the demons began to hiss and snarl with indecision. Kyran flexed his magic again, letting the frost spiral from his feet like a web. Their apprehension at the display was palpable.

"Wretched cowards," the abomination behind Finley hissed at the rest of them.

"Kyran." Nowell's voice was ragged with pain as he stumbled to the mage's side. "You have…to warn the guild. I'll…" He let out a strangled shout through his teeth, nearly losing his footing as he shook his head. "Ah, go. You have to…go!"

No. You will not.

The words seared into Kyran's skull like a brand, not just the soft, rasping tones of a demon's voice but Finley's, echoing inside and out of his head as if he were a bell rung.

He didn't know what to do about Finley or Nowell, how to help them, but *this* he knew well by now. "I said, *falbh dairich fhein!*" he snarled, pitching every drop of his magic against them both.

Something thumped against his belly, and the pressure against his magic vanished as a wall of fire sprang up mere inches in front of him.

"Go!" Nowell shouted over the deafening roar of the flames pouring from his upraised hand, his other holding Kyran's walking stick against him. "Run! Now!"

"What about you?"

Nowell shoved the walking stick into Kyran's hands. "I'll keep them busy long as I can. Whatever it takes. You can move faster, and you've got to go, *now.*"

"But—"

"The guild needs to know! Go back the way we came! I'll be right behind you."

Kyran wanted to argue, wanted to face the demons and fight. But another look at the sheer numbers crowding around them and Nowell's face contorted in pain as bony ridges began to push their way out of his cheeks, and he knew it would be a wasted effort. He had to warn the guild of what was coming.

Closing his eyes, he reached for the space Inbetween the realms, the ache in his head instantly turning to a hammering throb.

It was harder this way, trying to find a tether to pull himself back in, to escape the boiling heat and cacophony of the demons. The pain in his head sharpened and for a horrible moment, he feared he might not be able to slip back.

Then he felt it—the way they had come, still open enough that he could pull himself through.

A violent snarl made him turn to look back, to see Nowell collapsing back down, his body convulsing beneath his skin, nearly pitch black now.

"No!" the guard captain shouted abruptly. "I will *not* let you join them!" Lifting his sword, Nowell plunged it deep into himself with a hoarse cry.

"Nowell!" Kyran screamed, but the scene vanished before the words even left his mouth, disappearing into the oppressive dark of the Inbetween.

For an awful moment, Kyran couldn't move, couldn't think. Nowell was dead. He'd killed himself right in front of him. He was dead.

The guild.

Grasping that single purpose, Kyran clung to it like a lifeline as he dragged himself through the Inbetween. He had to get back. No matter what, he had to get back. He had to tell them what was coming.

He trudged through as fast as his power would carry him, but each pull ripped through him, leaving him winded and weak, growing more and more lightheaded.

There was a pulse of power behind him, so far away he barely noticed it. The pressure around Kyran's head slowly loosened and he knew he was close. But whatever had come into the Inbetween with him, it was gaining fast. He struggled to move faster, to make his escape before he had to turn and fight whatever was coming for him, but it was all he could do to keep up his sluggish momentum.

There was another pulse, and then a long dreadful nothing as Kyran focused every dreg of power on getting free of the Inbetween. He was close. He could feel the stretch of the world against him as the fabric between places resisted his passing. He fumbled at his hip, feeling for his amulet when something slammed into his back, knocking him forward onto his belly. He twisted, swinging his walking stick with a tightly controlled flash of power.

The demon caught his arm mid-swing, hissing loudly as Kyran pressed his power into it. Rather than let go, it tightened its grip and slammed his arm down, almost knocking his stick from his grip. The familiar hot, knife-like pain of another mind invading his began to rise, and he had to yield his magic to focus enough to keep it at bay.

A dribble of hot, burning saliva dripped onto him as the thing let out a thick, gurgling noise. "Such a treat, such a treat," it hissed. "You thought you could sneak away? Never."

"Let go," Kyran grunted through his teeth fighting to get his hand out of his purse, but his arm was pinned beneath him, and it was everything he could do to concentrate enough to keep the demon out of his head.

He felt it slither and prowl through his thoughts like a worming tongue, not to torment him, but to taste him. He tried to push it away, to lock it out, and in that moment, the demon curled a limb around his waist and suddenly began to skitter back, away from the edge of the Inbetween.

Panic, bright and silvery, shot through Kyran like lightning, and every thought of keeping the demon out of his head vanished with a visceral *need to get away*. He erupted into a frenzy of nails and teeth and kicking, his magic boiling out of his blood as he fought to escape the arm holding his hips.

The demon yowled, the vice grip of its mind releasing and clarity slammed back into the mage. Head whirling, Kyran sank his nails firmly into the strange, foreign flesh of the demon's arms, and his magic surged into it. The limbs steamed and crackled and the demon shrieked at him, but did not let go, taking him further and further from the light.

Then, Kyran's fingers finally closed on his amulet. Power surged into his blood, his lines burning under his skin, tearing another pained howl from the demon. But instead of turning the full force of his magic on the beast, Kyran reached out with his power and dragged himself back towards escape. Towards other hunters and daylight.

The demon shrieked louder and louder, trying to scrabble out of Kyran's grasp. It nearly made it, but rather than let it run, Kyran snatched at it, catching its arm and yanking it down before grappling it. He was not about to let it escape and come to find him another night. No, it was coming with him.

Struggling, he got his arm around its neck and locked his elbow under its chin. It gurgled and hissed, teeth snapping at the air uselessly as he dragged it. It was harder, towing the beast along, but Kyran held fast as he found the seam between realms and shoved his magic against it as hard as he could.

"No!" the demon wheezed as the seam began to give. "No, not there!"

With a jarring sensation like missing a step, the pressure in Kyran's head released, and he stumbled out into the murky light of a single lantern.

"No!" the demon screamed, dragging Kyran to his knees as it thrashed and kicked. "No, no! Go back! Must go back!"

"No ye will na!" Kyran ground through his teeth, pouring magic into the beast, holding tight as it began to convulse and writhe, its body steaming and smoking as its skin cracked and shriveled under a layer of black frost

Then, as quickly as it had started, it ended. The demon went limp in his arms, the magic fading so quickly from his senses he wondered if it might be a trick, and clung to its corpse as it continued to simply dissolve until it simply fell apart into ash.

With an exhausted sigh, Kyran let himself slump on the ground, his eyes almost slipping closed when the sound of boots pounding down a set of stairs drew him back with a frown.

He moved to sit up, but just lifting his head sent a wave of dizziness through him and his vision blurred darkly. Stars, it had taken everything he had to escape. "Barrett?" he called weakly, trying to crane his head to see the hunter. It had to be Barrett.

"Oh Graces, is that the mage?"

A lad barely older than Tavish came into view, followed closely by a second lad that looked to be even younger.

"Careful," the second lad cautioned. "He might be another one of those abominations."

"Where am I?" Kyran croaked, dragging himself back to his knees.

"Belldale, beneath the House of Light. What're you doing down here?"

There was another surge of magic, not a stray pulse, but a storm that simply kept building and building, pressing against Kyran like a wall.

"Demons," one of the lads said, stepping off the stair to come to his side. "Elijah, tell the captain."

"All right."

Kyran shrank from the lad's offered hand, snatching his walking stick up and dragging himself to his feet as he felt the air behind him suddenly tear itself apart with a vicious howl.

"Come on!" the lad barked, grabbing Kyran's arm and dragging him up the stairs. "Go, Elijah, go!"

Before Kyran could even protest, he was all but shoved unceremoniously through a doorway into a narrow hall. He stumbled, catching himself on the wall as the door slammed shut behind him.

"Get Captain Fairclough!" the lad bellowed, the other lad pelting down the hall. "Tell her they found a way in!"

Chapter Fifty-Seven

BARRETT WATCHED AS the last dreg of grey light faded from the sky outside his window, his thoughts turning in restless circles.

Three days. It had been three whole days since Kyran had gone to the arena, and Barrett knew something must have gone wrong.

He'd tried to be patient, to pass the time, to try to do anything to keep himself from throwing his quilt over his window and blowing out the lantern to try and squeeze between the realms. He'd even let Kat beat him nearly senseless with a wooden sword in the name of practice until she'd told him not to come back until he'd gotten some sleep. But he couldn't. Not when he didn't know what could happen.

A cold tendril of dread slithered across his scalp and he wondered, briefly, if it was his silent demon stirring. He pulled up his sleeve, rubbing his thumb over the witch marks, the same way he had nearly every hour all night, terrified he'd find they'd spread. He'd had nightmares before, but bad as they had ever been, they had never caused him to lose control. And worst of all, Kyran had seen it. Had seen what was happening to him.

They looked normal for now, but if he went to the demon realm, that would assuredly change. Graces, he never wanted to feel that sensation again, that helpless, numb sensation of watching his body operate without his control. But if he had to do it to save Kyran, he would.

There was a rap at his door, and he yanked his sleeve down, nearly tripping over his pack as he raced to answer it. Graces, let it be news of Kyran or orders to go and find him. Yanking open his door, he found Alf waiting for him. The runner looked a mess, shirt untucked and hair sticking in every direction, as if he'd just woken. "Yes?" he prompted.

"You're wanted in Captain Griswold's office," the boy said between haggard yawns.

Barrett's pulse leapt. "Did he say what it was about?"

The boy shrugged. "Not in particular. Just wanted me to get you."

Barrett let out an irritated sigh. That sounded like him. "All right. I know the way. Thanks."

Abandoning his room, Barrett pulled his collar close against the slow, frigid drizzle that had been falling nonstop since the disastrous night at the inn, and started across the grounds for the college at a quick clip. The grounds were quiet, the cobbles slick with mud and the first thin veneer of ice, glittering yellow in the lamplight. It only made him even more heartsick, and he prayed in earnest he hadn't waited too long.

Trudging up the stairs to the third floor, he rapped at the door, waiting until he heard Griswold ask him in.

The guild captain was seated at his desk again, papers spread out before him with a scattering of rocks pinning them to the surface. Standing beside him, hands clasped, was Selah.

"Barrett," Griswold said, gesturing to the empty chair angled before him. "Come in and close the door, please."

Barrett did as he asked, looking between the two of them suspiciously. Something was wrong. "What's happened?"

"We've reassessed our plan, and want to make entry into the demon realm to offer assistance or recovery."

Barrett nearly lurched out of his seat. "When?"

"Possibly tonight if you—"

"Yes. I'm ready. I can go now."

"Good, but it will be a few hours at least. We've drawn up a list of supplies to bring should this—"

Outside, a bell began to toll. The tone was low, deep and long, sending a heavy chill down Barrett's back as he felt a surge of power rolling over the guild. And not just one. It felt like Belldale all over again. Only they hadn't nearly the number of hunters at the guild.

"Curses. It's happening already," Griswold said, rising from his seat. "Barrett, with me. We will defend the hospital. Selah, if you—"

"I will begin the evacuation of the college," she said, moving briskly for the door. "Send all noncombatants to the mess hall."

"What do you mean *already happening?* What about Kyran?" Barrett protested, nearly knocking his chair over as he hurried after them.

"We will still search for him, but protecting the guildhall comes first."

"I…" Barrett wanted to protest, wanted to run to the arena and go to look for Kyran himself like he should have days ago, but he could already feel the pull of demon after demon tearing its way into the guildhall.

And there were a lot more innocents.

"Curse the Graces," Barrett breathed. "And may our lanterns stay lit."

Chapter Fifty-Eight

KYRAN'S HEAD SPUN as he tried to piece together what was happening. Finley had turned into an abomination and Nowell…

"Where is this?" he asked the hunter guarding the door.

The lad looked askance at him, brows raised in concern. "Belldale," he repeated.

Kyran's stomach lurched. This is where Barrett and Griswold had come right after their return from the Isles. "How far is that from the guildhall?"

The lad's brows rose another degree. "Nearly a week of travel. Are you all right?"

A week? Kyran could hardly believe what he was hearing. Stars above, how in all the blessed Graces in the Isles had he wound up days away in another town? He was sure he had gone right back the way he had come. Had he done something wrong? What about Finley and the other demons? What about the guild?

What about Barrett?

"Listen…" the lad said, speaking slow and cautious, the way one might to a spooked horse. "If you go up those stairs there—"

"Marcus?" a woman called sharply, appearing at the top of the stairs the other lad had gone up. She was much older than the two lads, and she moved with a purpose as she approached them, trailed by the lad that had run to get her and another man. She stopped next to Kyran, giving him a quick look up and down. "Who are you and how did you get here?" Kyran didn't miss the way her hand moved to rest on the hilt of her dagger at her hip.

"Kyran," he answered. "I—"

"The mage?" Her eyes widened, looking him up and down again.

"Aye. I—"

"Captain, what do we do?" the lad at the door interrupted. "There's demons coming through under the House."

The captain's eyes switched to the lad, and then the door, her lips pulling back from her teeth before she spat a curse. "Back upstairs. All of you. Now."

"But—"

The door rattled in its frame as something heavy collided with it from the other side.

"Now!" She looked pointedly at Kyran, waiting for him to follow the others before she came behind them, casting a quick look over her shoulder as the door rattled again.

Kyran paused at the top of the stairs to catch his breath, taking in the room beyond with an unsettled feeling of displacement. It was obviously a House of Light, the benches clustered to create wards of injured and barriers to entry at the doors. He really was no longer at the guildhall he had entered the demon realm from.

The captain slammed the door shut behind him, barring it before she spun to face the hall. "Hunters!" she bellowed over the noise of the people milling in frightened clusters. "There has been a breach in the basement! Bar the doors. I want teams to move benches to barricade civilians and injured at the back of the House away from any doors or windows. Stand the benches on end and lash them as we have time to block as much fire as possible."

The hunters jumped to follow orders, fearful cries going up from the crowd, and the captain turned to Kyran. "Now you. Are you with the guild?"

"Aye."

"Can you fight?"

Kyran drew himself upright, crushing his exhaustion down. "Aye."

"Good. I want you with the injured and civilians as part of our last line of defense. Join with whichever team is coordinating there. We'll sort out the mystery of your unannounced arrival once the sun rises."

A scream cut through the noise of the hall, and a bench went clattering to the floor as one of the injured that had been lying upon it lurched upwards, their skin quickly dying an inky black.

Stars above…

"Abomination!" the captain bellowed. "All hunters—"

There was another scream, and another, as more of the grievously wounded spasmed and contorted, their skins changing color. It had been a trap. A perfectly laid nest of beasts waiting for the command. Just like in the demon realm. Just like Finley.

"—evacuate now!"

The inside of the House erupted into pandemonium.

Hunters and ordinary townsfolk scrambled for the front doors, tripping, grabbing, clawing their way over one another to get away from the abominations as the once injured sprang to unnatural health and began to turn on the nearest people with teeth and claws.

"Let's go!" the captain shouted at Kyran, grabbing his arm, and dragging him away from the scene.

Kyran twisted in her grip, stumbling as he fought to keep his balance. "Let go! Why are we running? Those people—"

"Are going to die anyway if we don't get outside and regroup," she snapped.

"We canna just leave them!" Planting his false leg and walking stick, he yanked his arm free and ran before she could grab him again, angling for the nearest abomination pursuing a townsman. Raising his hand, he let his control over his power slip, but the glow that traced the lines of his blood up his arms was a pale imitation of the bright starlight it normally shone. He was nearly at his limit. Just a bit more, and he would be as good as dead, as would the rest of the innocent people that the guild captain was abandoning.

Tamping down his control, he shifted his stance, wrapped both hands around his walking stick, and swung.

The abomination, consumed with hunting the helpless man, did not even notice the stick as it struck with a loud crack and sent it staggering sideways. The man that had been pursued by the abomination scrambled out from under it and quickly got to his feet. "Thank— behind you!"

Kyran didn't have enough time to even turn before something slammed into his back, pinning him to the floor, its hot breath rolling over his back and neck. He kicked against the floor, trying to find purchase so he could shove the thing off of him. Black, curved talons bit into the floor by his shoulders and locked him in place. Something hot and wet dripping on the back of his neck.

His magic burst into brilliance. "Get off!"

A scalding blast of heat erupted behind him and black flames licked past him. *Barrett?* The abomination above him shrieked. Someone shouted, and a second later the weight left Kyran's back.

"Watch out!" someone yelled.

"I've got it!"

Kyran twisted upright just as the abomination was collapsing to the ground, the hunter from the stairs facing him. He tugged, tearing the long blade of his dagger free of the beast, and the abomination collapsed. "Elijah, keep your eyes up," the young hunter said and rushed towards Kyran. It wasn't Barrett. Just another hunter, wielding the same fire. He extended a hand towards Kyran. "You all right?"

"I ken I will be," Kyran said, staggering upright and swiping a hand over his neck. It came away sticky with what looked like drool, and he suppressed a shudder of revulsion as he turned to the next charging beast. "You take—"

A loud boom echoed through the House, and Kyran tore his eyes from the man twisted by demonic power to the front doors. They were shut. They'd all been shut in.

"Marcus," the shorter hunter whimpered. "Marcus, they—"

The young hunter that had helped Kyran, Marcus, took a quick look around the room and pointed towards the back. "Back there. It'll be easier to defend. Elijah," the man gestured towards a small group of villagers that had skittered away from the doors, "get everyone rounded up." Then he looked at Kyran, blowing out an exhausted sigh and shaking his head. "I don't know how you got here, but I'd be glad for any help keeping those things off Elijah and the rest."

Kyran looked out over the survivors, at the remaining abominations, faces caught in mocking, rictus grins, their bodies still swathed in weeping, bloodied bandages. "Aye," he said through gritted teeth, his fingers aching where they clenched his walking stick.

"Good." Marcus didn't wait a second longer and rushed to engage an abomination headed straight for Elijah and the group of people with him.

A second beast prowled along the wall, its eyes locked on Kyran. "A mage," it hissed through its wide grin, a bit of drool dribbling past its lips.

Kyran slipped his knife from his boot. "If ye ken what's good for ye, ye'll take ta that window."

With an ear-splitting shriek, the abomination leapt with unnatural grace, long arms outstretched. Kyran twisted out of the way. Something snagged in his hair, yanking his head back. He stabbed blindly over his shoulder, his knife biting into flesh. Its scream pitched high, like a wounded dog.

The grip vanished from his hair and he nearly tumbled back onto the floor, fighting to keep his balance as something slammed into the basement doors, the wood groaning behind the weight.

"They're already in!" someone screamed, but Kyran didn't dare look, his eyes locked on the abomination retreating from him.

"Kyran! Come on! We have to go!" Marcus shouted, and Kyran backed towards the sound of his voice until the abomination reached the wall and disappeared out the window.

Whirling, he found most of the group gone, disappeared through another door into the back of the House, and the hunter gestured frantically for him to hurry.

Falling in at the back, Kyran kept his eyes cast out into the House for any other abominations when a terrible roar bellowed from behind the basement door, and every lamp and candle in the House flickered out. His heart leapt into his throat, and his lines burst to watery brilliance beneath his skin, lighting the darkness.

"Go," he urged the townsfolk, raising his voice above their panicked screams as the strained door shook, and creaked, and finally shattered. "Go now!"

CHAPTER FIFTY-NINE

BARRETT RACED BEHIND Griswold for the door, but the captain was moving at an absolutely unearthly speed, his wind tearing a wake down the hall behind him that nearly knocked Barrett off his feet.

"Bastard," Barrett growled, shielding his watering eyes as he took the stairs two at a time.

The front doors were open when he reached them, rain blowing inside. He vaulted down the front stairs, racing after the captain's retreating back, when a deep, rasping howl sounded over the guildhall, drowning out the sound of the bell and the rain. Another howl shivered through the air, joined by a second throat, and then a third as fire went up in a flare of bright yellow-orange in the dark.

Gritting his teeth, Barrett stretched his legs, flying over the wet grass, his boots sliding in the mud as he cut a path across the lawn for the hospital, when a shape came barreling out of the twilight between lamps. Throwing his hand up, the rain flashed to steam as he reflexively called his fire, the crimson flames throwing the beast into stark relief.

It looked like the hideous progeny of some unholy coupling—a fusion of the human form and demonic features. The limbs had been extended, the pale human flesh morphing into blackened, animal-like claws it could use to run on all fours, and its human face had been forced into a hideous, rictus grin by a pair of ebony tusks that protruded from its lips by several feet. Its eyes, blue as the waters of a lake, fixed on him with a hateful zeal before it twisted away and fled with an all too human sound of fury as his fire lashed across its hide.

Barrett's stomach threatened to turn as he threw another ball of flame after its heels. That was the fate he faced if he could not learn to control his power better. He started to pursue it when he heard screaming from across the lawn and another bright orange light lit up the other side of the guildhall. The hospital. It was burning.

The lawn stretched on and on, but at last, he could make out a steady stream of people fleeing out the front of the building. "Barrett," the captain's voice said at Barrett's ear, though there was no sign of the man. "You take the top floor. I'll take the bottom. We have to clear the hospital."

"I'm on it!" Barrett shouted back, even though he had no idea if the captain could hear him.

It was utter chaos within. People must have retreated into the building when the demons began coming through. They had started to rally together in knots here and there, frightened and panicking in the whirlwind of bodies and power—not only from the abominations, but the hunters. They pulled at Barrett's senses from all sides, tearing at his attention, fighting to pull him in every direction.

His boot caught on something, nearly toppling his tentative balance, and he nearly lashed blindly out at it until he made out the form of a man clinging to his ankle by one hand, obscured by the stark shadows thrown by hunters' and demons' fire. But he was not so hidden Barrett couldn't make out the man's mouth moving in silent pleas for help, the words caught in thick, red bubbles of blood that dribbled past his lips. His tunic was torn nearly to sodden shreds, and Barrett felt his gall rise when he noticed the grey-pink loops peering between the quilted fabric and the man's other hand desperately holding his own insides against his belly.

"Oh, Graces…" The demons. More must have come up here in the hospital, not just the arena. They were already in here with the sick and the injured, the people that weren't even hunters from in the city. These people had been helpless.

He started to reach for the man, though he had no idea what he would do to help—he had to do something—when a hoarse scream of pain from up the stairs stood every hair on Barrett's arm upright. He knew that scream. He had heard it in Belldale, right before he had— "Myles!"

He staggered to his feet, turning to go up the stairs, then stopped, looking down at the man again. He couldn't just leave him. He needed…

As Barrett bent close again, he finally noticed how still the man had gone, how his eyes no longer focused on anything. He was gone.

Swallowing thickly, Barrett tore his eyes from the fallen man, and ran, taking the stairs two at a time, letting his fury boil over. Enough was enough. This—all of *this*—was too much. He was going to kill every demon he could get his hands on, and more.

The air turned to thick, black smoke as he reached the landing, and it took all his will to keep his watering eyes open. He tucked his mouth and nose into the crook of his elbow as he carried forward blindly, but he could barely manage more than a few quick gasps as every breath set his lungs and throat on fire, his nose streaming.

"Stupid old man," a voice hissed from somewhere ahead, followed by a terrified whimper of pain.

"Graces, no!" Barrett tried to move faster, but he was near blind. Shapes loomed out of the oppressive smoke, bodies and chunks of stone that had fallen. He couldn't even make out the walls now, feeling his way forward until he stumbled through a doorway where the smoke thinned, lit up by the bright, fiery runelines burning beneath an abomination's skin. He bolted forward, but the fire was already leaving its hand, licking across the Lightbringer, who screamed in agony.

"NO!" Barrett plunged right into the fire, bracing against the force and heat of it with a pained groan before he could summon his own fire to protect him and Myles. "Leave him alone!"

"Get out of my way," it sneered, eyes bright against its familiar face.

"Finley?" He pushed back against her fire, drawing deeply from his demon's power until the tips of his fingers began to blacken again. He couldn't worry about that, not if he wanted to save everyone.

"She can't hear you, hunter," the abomination sneered.

Oh Graces, it was her. But hadn't she gone with— "Where's Ky—"

A sleek, ashen arm struck through his fire, catching him right in the gut, nearly doubling him over, then grabbed him and threw him aside.

"Stop!" Barrett wheezed, snatching at Finley's ankles, who kicked him away, stepping past him. "Don't hurt him! He doesn't deserve this!"

"It doesn't matter to me," Finley hissed, voice warping, becoming less human as she looked down at the Lightbringer. "He is a gift to my little mage."

The word nearly stopped Barrett's heart. "Kyran? Is that— Where is he?"

"Look around," the abomination purred, spreading several of its limbs in mocking placation. "I'm certain someone is using his skin after I took such pains to—"

"Shut up!" Barrett snarled, hate carrying him to his feet. "You're lying. Where is he?"

Its face drew in a sharp toothed grin. "Dead. Long live the Auld One's wrath."

With a wordless, furious roar, Barrett lunged for the abomination, flames licking along his arms. It caught his wrist with one of its limbs, and Barrett swung his other fist without hesitation. The hit landed with a sound of sizzling skin, but the abomination didn't even stagger, cackling as fire burst from every inch of the beast. He screamed, his skin boiling, but he refused to stop, swinging again and again, pushing more fire and strength into each hit until one of the abomination's limbs connected solidly with his mouth. The taste of blood blossomed in his mouth and he nearly lost his grip on it. Barrett spat out a swear. "Where is he?" he shouted.

"Gone along with its wretched sire!" the abomination howled, raking its claws over his cheek, nearly catching his eye as it opened three lines of fire down his face. It twisted as if to flee, and Barrett snatched the front of its rags, wresting his dagger-arm free. With a snarl, he thrust his dagger forward again, and caught another solid hit to his jaw as the abomination twisted out of his grasp. He lunged after it, the blade nicking flesh before the abomination scurried out of reach, its eyes locked on Myles as the Lightbringer crawled into a seated position.

"Why are you doing this?" he screamed, planting himself between the horror and the Lightbringer.

"What do you care, hunter?" it mocked, throwing another burst of fire at him that he easily deflected with a quick burst of his own. "What is it you think I am doing?"

"You're destroying the guild!" Barrett said, letting loose a stream of fire at the beast, but the abomination merely sprang backwards, clinging to the wall like a great spider.

"And have you ever stopped to consider that this entire farce is the guild's fault? A pact for power for them both? The demons gain power and a pool of half-breed children they can use. The guild needs people to be afraid. To need them, and pay them." Its smile turned simpering as the building shuddered around them as if it were on the brink of coming down on top of them.

"You're wrong! If demons didn't come here and kill people, there would be no need for the guild. For any of this!"

Using the long, hooked claws at the ends of its many, many fingers, the abomination crawled onto the ceiling, scuttling over it as easily as the floor. "Are you certain you haven't swallowed all those guild lies a bit too deeply? Maybe let your own demon whisper in your ear about power?"

The hair on the back of his neck rose and he glanced down at his hands, horrified to find they had turned a coal black, the nails transformed into long, hooked claws. "It's not like that. Hunter's demons are different."

"Are they? Or is that what you tell yourself?"

"I—" The building groaned around them and Barrett nervously looked at where the flames were beginning to show, licking across the wood. He needed to get out of there, needed to get Myles someplace safe. He—

A flicker of movement drew his eye back to the abomination just as the beast launched itself from the ceiling straight at him, limbs outstretched, claws bared for his throat. He raised his dagger, ready to spear the beast through its shriveled heart, when something collided with it with a thunderous *boom*, sending it cartwheeling across the room.

Standing in its place was Griswold.

"Hold your fire," the captain ordered, raising his hand at the abomination. "That's Finley. She's one of our mages."

"I know it is. But she's an abomination," Barrett snapped, turning his dagger in his hand when a tempest howled through the room. He froze, terrified that the guild captain meant to put him down like he had in Belldale, until the abomination dropped to the floor, thrashing violently. Barrett almost couldn't look as the too human face gaped for air, one hand clawing at its throat while another reached for Griswold.

"Barrett, the Lightbring—"

With a horrible squelch, the demon tore off one of its own limbs and struck the captain hard enough to knock him off his feet, the churning air vanishing in an instant.

"I'll be back for you, old man. Make no mistake," it hissed, vanishing through the smoke.

Cursing viciously, Barrett gave chase and nearly tumbled out the broken window the beast had disappeared through, just barely catching himself on the frame. "Curse the bottomless Pit."

"I'll follow her," Griswold said, and Barrett pulled himself back inside to see the captain getting to his feet, favoring one side. "Get the Lightbringer to safety, then come and find me."

"But wh—" Before Barrett could get his question out, the captain rushed the window in an explosion of wind and leapt. Barrett swore, clinging to the frame again as the captain's wake nearly pulled him out after. "Bastard."

Pushing away, he hurried to Myles' side, kneeling by the Lightbringer. Myles' skin was shiny and red, with ugly yellow blisters beginning to show. The wisps of his hair had vanished; he looked at Barrett from where he clung to the remains of his through wide, terrified eyes.

The shame hit him like a slap, and Barrett instinctively folded his arms, hiding the claws and blackened flesh as if he were five again. "Myles, I…"

"Thank Lumen you made it," the Lightbringer wheezed, knuckles creaking as he slowly let go of the cot's leg. "I thought I would finally join the Eternal Flame."

"Not if I can help it," Barrett said, his eyes stinging with smoke. "Can you walk?"

"Yes, I just need a little help." He held out his hand to Barrett, a faint smile crooking his mouth even as the building shuddered around them again. "We all need a little help sometimes."

"I know." The stinging turned to a steady burn, and Barrett's breath hitched when he offered his gnarled, demon marked hand, and the Lightbringer took it without hesitation.

He pulled Myles to his feet and looped an arm over the Lightbringer's shoulders to keep him steady as they made for the door. The man felt like nothing under his arm, light and frail as a bird.

A loud boom rocked the corridor as they reached the stairs, raining dust down from the ceiling on their heads. The smoke had thickened into an impenetrable blackness and Barrett's lungs were on fire.

Grasping the railing with one hand, Barrett felt his way down the stairs, eyes and nose streaming, boots sliding in whatever unseen horrors slicked the stair as the building groaned fatalistically. He tried to move faster, shifting his hold on the Lightbringer around his back and under his shoulder, mouthing a steady stream of curses as the heat built and built, pressing against his skin.

There was a crash somewhere out in the murk, and Barrett's grip on the Lightbringer tightened, urging him forward faster and guiding him around unseen obstacles.

They were nearly to the bottom when there came a terrible shrieking roar from all around them, growing louder and louder and louder until Barrett could hardly think around the deafening scream. He cursed as his boots caught on fallen stone and bodies, nearly sending him to his knees as he stumbled towards the square of night he could see, half-dragging, half-carrying Myles with him over the threshold. Oppressive heat and smoke gave way to the hard pelt of rain, and Barrett knew a moment of exhilaration as he sucked down a clean breath of air.

"We made it." He laughed. "We made it."

"So we did," Myles said weakly, stumbling in Barrett's grasp.

The hunter slowed, steadying the Lightbringer, when the hospital let out a low, thrumming boom Barrett could feel as much as hear. He turned, mouth gaping as he watched, transfixed, as the building crumbled and sank itself, fire filling the sky with a hungry roar.

"Oh, Graces."

There was a touch at his elbow, and he started, spinning as he raised his hand, fire dancing along his fingers, only to find Tacita, her face and coat running with water.

"I'll take him," she said, nodding to the Lightbringer when Barrett stared in blank incomprehension.

"Myles, he's—"

"A little worse for wear, I'm afraid," the Lightbringer said, patting Barrett's hand before accepting Tacita's. "Luckily, Kristopher was there in the nick of time."

"Well, I—"

"Are you injured?" Tacita interrupted brusquely, her gaze moving past him.

Barrett glanced over his shoulder, eyes raking over the dark and the fallen littered over the stones at the front of the hospital, rendered indistinct by the harsh light of the burning hospital. None of them moved. "I… No. I'm fine. Did you see Captain Griswold?"

"Towards the college. If you find any other injured, send them to the western gate."

"Selah said to get everyone to the mess—"

"We'd never make it across the grounds," Tacita said. "We're safer in the gatehouse while you and the others clear the guildhall. If there's nothing else, may your lanterns stay lit."

"And yours as well," Barrett said automatically.

"And may Lumen light and guide your way," Myles murmured, offering Barrett an encouraging smile through the tracks of rain running down his cheeks before Tacita turned away, leading the Lightbringer off into the dark.

He watched them until they were out of sight, caught between wanting to follow them to make certain the Lightbringer reached someplace safe, and going to find Griswold until he heard another loud boom from across the guildhall, a gout of fire shooting up into the air from the direction of the college. Of Griswold.

"Curse the Graces." Turning his dagger in his grip, Barrett took off across the lawn, his legs and lungs burning. But he had to keep going. For Myles. For the guild. For Kyran, if he was still alive. The thought of the mage being lost, or worse, an abomination himself like Finley nearly undid him right there. He was going to find that abomination and tear off its limbs until it told him where Kyran was, captain's orders or not.

CHAPTER SIXTY

THE DOOR SLAMMED shut behind Kyran, and he hadn't even a chance to take in the hall they had fled into before Marcus let out a curse. "There's no bar."

Kyran's belly dropped. "Ye canna—"

"I'll hold it." Marcus set his body against the door as it rattled violently in its frame. "It won't hold long. Find a place we can take them."

"No, Marcus—" Elijah rushed to press his uninjured arm against the door.

"I'll be fine," Marcus assured him and pressed his hands against the walls to brace himself against the door. "Go on, get back to the front. You can clear the way faster than I can."

Elijah sucked down a breath. "I can't—"

"You can. Remember your training. Go!"

Shoulders straightening, Elijah stepped away and easily pushed through the crowd of people. The door banged behind Marcus again. He looked at Kyran and started to say something when someone shrieked at the front of the group.

"Back! Get back!" Elijah's voice bled over the crowd, now backing into Kyran and Marcus.

Setting his teeth against his discomfort, Kyran shoved his way into their midst, his skin crawling as people pushed and shoved against him, almost carrying him back before the crowd parted as fire lit up the other end of the hall.

Demons.

"Cursed stars," Kyran swore. Every way they turned there were more of the beasts. He spotted Elijah, his good arm thrusting forward with a powerful burst of wind that caught Kyran by surprise. The wind rivaled what he had seen from Griswold, forceful enough that it sent the nearest demon tumbling back through the doorway they were coming through. But more poured out. They pushed against one another and knocked each other over in a vicious stampede, fire licking along each of them.

"They're everywhere!" Elijah shouted and forced another burst of wind out that pressed some of the demons back up against the wall. But some withstood it and crept forward. "We're trapped!"

Kyran's blood flashed beneath his skin, and he stepped in front of Elijah as he unleashed a short burst of frigid cold, carried violently by the hunter's wind. He smiled mirthlessly when the closest demons froze in place and those against the wall fell.

"I'll take them," he said, letting loose another tightly controlled flash of power, desperately aware how dim his blood was growing.

The young hunter's breath fogged in the chilled air as he looked up at Kyran with something like awe. "Everyone," he called, turning down a hall leading away from the demons. "This way, this way! Stay behind me!"

Kyran moved closer to the demons, watching the light fade from his skin as he menaced another demon. The beasts cowed. Perhaps they remembered the threat of his sire from their realm. But soon, one of them would grow bold again. They were too ravenous, too greedy to do anything else.

And then what? His magic had nearly run dry. But he'd faced the very same circumstance before, deep in the belly of the Inbetween, caught between its crushing heat and the needle-toothed demon's claws. And he'd done what any other demon-blooded kin would do, though he didn't understand at the time. His amulets weren't the only source of power.

It happened quickly. One of the demons leapt at him, molten hands gathering fire that resisted the chill of his magic. Kyran caught it before it could tackle him, but reeled when their magic collided together and he felt the demon try to pierce into his thoughts, but it was like a worm wriggling against stone, searching for a crack amongst the mortar.

He steeled himself, trying not to think about what he was doing, to only think of what it would give him, *why* he was doing it, and not why his mouth watered as he stretched it open and sank his teeth into the beast's wrist. Blood, hot and bitter, burst over his tongue, and he fought not to retch as it poured down his throat.

The demon thrashed against him, but the shrill screams faded until they were utterly distant as power pooled in Kyran, starting in his cramping stomach and quickly spreading through each limb and digit, and with a sudden clarity, he dug into the demon's mind, wrenching every ounce he could manage. When the demon fell limp in his grasp, he let it fall motionless to the ground. The action drew the attention of the other demons, which bolted down the hall without warning towards Kyran.

He felt them like stones against his thoughts, cutting and sharp, but nowhere near the dangerously precise attacks he had withstood before. He loosened his control just for a flash, freezing the nearest beasts where they clung—the walls, the floor, the ceiling, wherever they stood. Using his knife, he carved a line down the back of the nearest beast, running the blade across his tongue as he turned to let out another pulse of magic down the hall.

Spirals of frost and ice laced over every surface, every demon until they were as still as stone. They were weak, pathetic things, and it scarcely took any effort to reach into each one of them, carving out their power for himself.

The wood and stone groaned around him as he let his magic run wild, until he could only sense a few more demons. He turned towards one, but instead of a demon, there was a young man, pressed back against a door with a small aura of heat around him.

Marcus. The hunter stared at him, eyes wide open, looking like a frightened, cornered animal.

Kyran crushed his power down, reaching for his sleeves, his stomach lurching up into his throat. "Are ye…" He looked past the hunter at the door, at how still it was. "Are the demons gone?"

"I-I think so," the hunter answered quickly, but didn't move away from the door. "What… What did you do?"

The mage looked down at his hands, at the blood frozen to them, glittering darkly, and shoved away the disgust that threatened to make his stomach turn inside out. "I…took their power."

"You—you—" Marcus stuttered, then lowered his voice. "You should—" He gestured vaguely at his own face. "There's… blood. It'll scare them."

Kyran's throat closed around what would have been sob. He started to reach for his kerchief before he stopped himself. It was Barrett's after all. He shouldn't soil it.

Tugging on his sleeve again, he wiped his face, smearing black along his shirt.

Marcus slowly moved away from the door and flicked his eyes over Kyran. "I didn't know mages could do that," he said quietly. Kyran didn't miss the tremble in the hunter's voice. "We should rejoin the others. Make certain no one is hurt. Maybe hold out until everyone outside settles."

"Aye," Kyran mumbled, following the hunter the direction the others had gone. It was impossible not to notice the way Marcus wouldn't quite put his back to him.

Half-breed.

An anxious murmur went through the small gathering of villagers when they opened the door. Marcus waved an arm to quiet them as he pushed the door shut behind Kyran.

"They're dead and gone," the hunter said firmly. "We're safe for now. There's still fighting outside the House, so we'll stay here until things calm down. Everyone, get comfortable."

"I found some candles," Elijah said, pushing his way to the front of the group. "I need you to…"

Marcus pinched the wick of the nearest candle, and a small golden flame came to life, illuminating the cramped room. It looked like someplace the Lightbringers of the House would have slept.

Seeing the hunter effortlessly light the candles reminded him of Barrett. What he would give to trade this room full of silent people for Barrett's mindless prattle.

"He shouldna be here," a woman spoke up, her voice colored by a thick Isleish accent that took Kyran by surprise. "He'll draw the demons here."

"Not any more than us," Elijah retorted, offering Kyran a tired, earnest smile.

"Ye dinnae understand," she snapped. "He's a half-breed. They'll come ta him if he doesna turn on us first." She fixed Kyran with a glare, but there was disgust and fear behind those eyes that he hadn't seen since leaving the Isles, and he felt himself shrink towards the door. "Ye need ta leave."

"You need to shut up and be grateful he's on our side!" Elijah barked back at the woman.

"And what would ye know about gratitude pretendin' ta be a lad?"

"Georgie," Marcus said loudly. "He's not going anywhere. He's stronger than either me or Elijah. If you're not comfortable with him here, you can kindly go outside."

The woman pursed her lips, her eyes narrowing icily, and, folding her arms over her chest, she settled into a furious silence.

But the damage was done. With the exception of Elijah, everyone cast a wary glance towards Kyran. Even Marcus kept his distance, busying himself by lighting whatever candles they could find and spreading them throughout the room.

Elijah came up to him after not too long, holding out a small flask. "Don't let them bother you. They don't know any better," he said softly. "Thought you could use a sip or two."

"Ah, thank ye." He fumbled his kerchief from his purse and took the flask, wiping the lip and starting to tip it back when he caught a whiff of the contents. His nose wrinkled. Whiskey. He'd know the smell anywhere. But stars above, could he use something to soften his head, even if it was just for a mite.

He poured a measure into his mouth and forced himself to swallow, his jaw clenching almost on its own at the harsh taste.

Elijah giggled as Kyran handed the flask back. "Thought all you Islemen liked this stuff."

"That one's a mite rough," Kyran defended.

"Marcus likes it," the hunter remarked with a little smile and slid the flask back into a pocket on his belt. "I hate it, but it helps with my arm."

Kyran took in the sling, wincing in sympathy. "Aye, I ken what that's like."

He saw the hunter look down where Kyran's leg should have been, but his gaze didn't linger there. "You're one of the guild mages?" Elijah asked quietly.

"Aye. Kyran," he replied.

"What are—how did you get here?"

We are many. And we are hungry.

"It was an accident," Kyran said, his nail worrying at his walking stick. Stars, he needed to find someone to send a letter. The guild needed to know what was coming. And Barrett… Graces, he would think Kyran had been taken again. He might try to go back into the demon realm where the rest of those beasts were waiting.

"Well, I'm glad you arrived when you did," Elijah continued almost cheerily. "I thought we were all—"

"Elijah," Marcus called, beckoning the hunter over. Elijah offered Kyran an apologetic smile before heading over to Marcus, who wrapped an arm around Elijah's shoulders and led him to one of the few chairs. Then he cast a wary look at Kyran.

He deserved it. Kyran knew that, had accepted that every cruel thing Connal and the needle-toothed demon had said had turned to truth. He had embraced that he was meant to be nothing more than a tool of the guild to fight and kill demons. But in that moment, he felt only shame and a deep, deep guilt that he could still taste the bitter blood staining his mouth even after the burn of the whiskey had faded. He'd known what he was doing when he decided to accept his blood. But he hadn't considered what it truly meant to become the monster he'd always been told he was. He could only pray no one else found out.

That Barrett never found out.

Chapter Sixty-One

Thunder clashed above the guildhall, the noise blending with the clamoring bell and the sounds of battle. All of it was muddled by the steadily strengthening downpour. It was as if the sky had opened up and was emptying itself over Barrett's head. He squinted through the sheeting rain, his dagger ready for any beast that tried to take him, but the entire world had fallen away beyond the veil of the storm.

"Come on. Where are you?" he hissed and swiped the rain from his eyes. His boots slid on the slick cobbles, but he didn't dare leave the path with no landmark to guide him. "Curse you, Griswold."

"In the arena! Go! GO!"

Barrett's head snapped up, the grey wall of rain suddenly resolving into the arena where his sister held a pair of demons at bay with nothing more than her sword. She should have been at the mess hall with everyone else. She—

There was no sound, or even a flash of fire to warn him before something slammed into his back so hard his feet left the ground. He had just enough time to see Finley, her face twisted into a terrifying mask of jutting bones and teeth as she galloped by before he hit the ground. He bounced, the speed of his flight carrying him into a roll, and he tumbled over the grass, his elbows and knees taking the brunt, until he finally slid to a stop in the mud.

He lurched to his hands and knees, dizzy and struggling to take a clean breath. He picked his head up and watched as the abomination veered towards the arena.

"No! Kat—"

"Katherine!" Griswold's voice shouted across the lawn.

She saw Finley and turned, her sword caught in the middle of a parry against one of the demons harrying her. Barrett felt a scream at the back of his throat as it collided with her claws first.

A column of wind howled across the lawn, tearing up chunks of earth and ripping the planks from the arena. The wind plucked the demons and Finley from the ground and flung them screaming out into the storm with a bestial shriek of rending air.

"Kat!" Barrett shouted, his voice ripped away by the raging wind. "Kat!" Rain as sharp as needles pelted as he staggered to his feet. He shielded his face as the column dissipated, flinging bits of wood, frozen water, and clumps of muck as big as his head. Kat had been at the center of that.

Letting loose a string of curses, he ran for the entrance, leaping the deep rut the column had cut into the earth and the debris it had scattered. He caught a glimpse of Katherine on the floor, the ground beneath her undisturbed, and Griswold standing over her, before he was drawn to the figure at the bottom of the arena, leering up at him.

"Enough!" Barrett snarled and raised his arm as he strode past Griswold. Finley or not, he couldn't let it hurt Katherine. Or Griswold. Or anyone else. His lips curled back as he let the power rush out from his palm. He clenched his fingers, shaping the fire into a tight, rushing torrent of flames.

The abomination lifted its hand to try and block his fire, but it staggered at the force of it. Barrett advanced, forcing it back farther and farther away.

"Oh, did I touch a nerve, hunter?" the abomination cackled and steadily backed away.

"Shut up!"

There was another ominous rumble in the distance, and the abomination grinned, showing every one of its teeth. "I think our mission was a success."

"What are you—" A terrifying groan began to fill the air and Barrett gasped at the sight of the college nearby. It was beginning to lean, one of the supports collapsing and part of the building crumpled, sending a wave of fire, dust, and debris flying out.

There was a massive surge of power, and Barrett flung his arms up, ready to take whatever attack the abomination had for him next, when the beast simply vanished into the shadows.

"No. No!" He searched the arena, throwing short bursts of flame to light up the furthest corners, but it was empty. The abomination had fled back into the Inbetween. "You won't get away there," he sneered, focusing his power to pursue it into the Inbetween.

"Barrett."

Barrett ground his teeth at Griswold's voice and whirled to face the man. "What?"

"Stay on Finley. I need you to capture her by any means." the captain said, kneeling by Katherine and gathering her into his arms. It was only then Barrett could see the blood. The front of her blouse was in shreds, and what looked like pieces of skin before the well of blood obscured everything.

Barrett's breath left him and he let out a harsh, "*No.*" He sprinted across the ground towards the captain and his sister.

"I'm— I'm fine," Katherine insisted in a thready voice and tried to push Griswold's hand away from her belly. Her face was pale and ashen. "I'm— I'm—"

"No, no, no—" Barrett's breath caught tightly in his throat. Not Katherine. He couldn't lose Katherine. Not now. He breathed harder, sucking in breath after breath, but it wasn't enough.

"Barrett!" Griswold snapped. "Stay on Finley. *Go.*"

"How am I supposed to—?" Barrett cut himself off, trying to get ahold of his rapid breaths. He had to focus. "I'll—I'll try."

"Good. Don't lose her." Griswold looked down again, gentling Katherine when her head eased back against his chest and she let out a low groan. "I have you. Don't worry."

Barrett nodded, but he couldn't get to his feet. Couldn't tear his eyes away from his sister. Would this be the last time he'd ever see her? "Is she…"

"I'm taking her to the chirurgeons now," Griswold said sharply and lifted Katherine in his arms as though she weighed nothing. "They will see to her."

"Tacita and the other healers are in the eastern gatehouse."

Griswold nodded. "I've got her. Now go. You can't let Finley get away."

Barrett took one last look at Katherine before Griswold took off towards the gatehouse. Then he turned towards the arena and ran, taking the stairs two at a time. He planted his feet in the center of the arena and concentrated on feeling for the Inbetween.

It came easily, his magic pulling him down between the realms almost before he could even think it. Even the resistance was less as he followed in Finley's wake, tracing the pull of her power as she fled.

He thought she would dive through the Inbetween to the demon realm, to where she and Nowell and Kyran had gone—where Kyran might still be. But all too soon, he realized they were not going deeper. He was simply following her through the Inbetween. And he was closing in.

The Inbetween was thinner here. The darkness was not as oppressive and he could breathe easier. After what only felt like seconds of running, he spotted the glow of Finley's runelines. He shot a gout of fire towards her and grinned wickedly when it struck her back, nearly knocking her off her feet.

Catching herself, she spun and laughed as she slung a line of fire without breaking pace. Barrett barely ducked the fire's path. The heat of it alone made his eyes water.

"Look at you," it said, Finley's voice colored by a second, rasping tone. "Chasing me like a mad dog while your guild burns. I'd think if anyone would understand what I was trying to do, it would be you."

"You don't know what you're talking about," Barrett growled. "I would never side with demons."

She flung another searing arc of fire and Barrett had to bring his own fire to shield them, crimson flames licking outwards in a dome around them.

"I wasn't talking to you, hunter," it simpered. "Born and lived and died a beautiful martyr. A hero to all but the poor wretches you let your beasts savage, and their spawn you indenture." Then it jerked its chin up, leering down at Barrett imperiously. "How many mages has your line made, Barrett? I'd wager at least as many as one old, fallen Lightbringer."

"What are you talking about?"

It let out a giddy laugh and quickly pulled away into the darkness as more limbs began to sprout from her body, carrying Finley's distorted body forward like a great spider.

"Get back here!" Barrett roared, pumping his arms as he raced after her when an unearthly wail rolled up from the depths of the Inbetween, stirring the heavy dark with an unnatural chill wind.

He knew that sound well.

"You hear that, demon?" Barrett shouted. "Finley knows what the Old One did when he came to the guildhall to protect Kyran! You don't stand a chance if he catches you!"

Her voice came calling from the dark ahead of him, "I told you, the mageling is gone. Run away somewhere with my hounds at his heels. My use for him had run out."

"He would never help you. And he's not gone!" Barrett insisted. He had seen Kyran survive stronger things than this abomination. He had to still be alive. He—

The air just in front of him ignited, and Barrett barely had time to shield his face. His eyes watered from the searing heat and he juked to one side as another ball of fire came hurtling his way. "Cursed demon," he growled, digging his boots into the solid nothing of the Inbetween as he sprinted after her. His lungs began to burn as he chased her on and on until, with a jarring suddenness, he felt the Inbetween begin to thin. She was leaving, headed back to their realm.

And then the ground simply vanished beneath him. Barrett gasped sharply as the visage of stone walls and wooden floorboards suddenly ruptured from the darkness. He didn't even have time to cry out in surprise before he hit the floor, boots first, with a tooth jarring thud, stumbling to stay upright when he collided with someone and they went down in a tangle.

"Sorr—" The word wasn't even half out of his mouth before he recognized the bright emerald eyes looking back at him. "Kyran!"

There was a deafening crack of splintering wood, and Barrett whirled to see Finley disappearing through the shattered remains of a door, fire licking up the walls in her wake. People were screaming, cowering at the furthest corners.

"Damn the Graces," he cursed. He wasn't about to let her get away after he had chased her this far. He lurched to his feet when bitter cold flashed across his skin.

"You," Kyran hissed, his lips drawn back from his teeth in a terrifying sneer and his skin limned in blue-white fey light. "You—"

Barrett raised his hands, alarmed to find them blackened with hooked claws at the end of each finger. Kyran's magic slammed into him and he nearly doubled over. "It's me!" he wheezed, his lungs burning with cold. "Kyran, it's me!"

"Barrett?"

Barrett looked over his shoulder at his name, surprised to find another familiar face. "Marcus?" But Marcus was in Belldale. How—

The other hunter had his hand raised, fire already kindled in his palm.

"I'm not—"

"It's him."

Barrett turned to Kyran again and the mage's lines dimmed as he picked himself up off the floor.

"This isn't what it looks like," Barrett said and sucked down a breath as the frigid air tempered. "I'm still me. I just— I have to go after that abomination. The guild—"

"How do we know it's really you?" Marcus threatened..

"The other ones dinnae talk like him," Kyran answered. "They talk like demon kine." The mage gave Barrett a level look. "He said my name."

A knot caught in Barrett's throat and he let his hands fall, the frost encrusted across his shirt and face flashing to steam. "I have to stop Finley. Griswold wants her alive."

Kyran's eyes went wide, flicking to the door behind Barrett. "That was her?"

"*Aye.* Marcus." Barrett turned to the younger hunter. "You stay with these people. I—"

"We," Kyran cut in, stepping up to Barrett's side, and the hunter finally took in the blood and dirt covering the mage. "I ken what the captain wants."

Barrett's brows knit in confusion before he remembered what had happened the last time Griswold had involved Kyran with abominations.

I was trying ta take the demon out of that lad, but I wasna strong enough ta do that and protect myself.

That was what Kyran was going to do. He was going to rip the demon out of Finley.

"All right. *We'll* stop her. Marcus, Elijah, you all stay with these people. Keep them safe."

"May your lanterns stay lit," Elijah called as Barrett stepped into the hall.

"Yours as—"

Before he could finish the invocation, there was an all-consuming roar that tore through the House of Light, rattling it down to its foundations, the walls and floorboards convulsing. Barrett stumbled sideways into the wall, clinging to the stone.

"Kyran!" He caught the mage as his knee buckled, pulling him to the wall.

"What's happening?" Kyran shouted over the noise, his grip tight on Barrett's arm.

"I don't know!"

There was another awful roar and a deep, thrumming *crack* of rock splitting before they were falling again. A scream ripped from Barrett's throat as the room tore apart around him.

Chapter Sixty-Two

KYRAN'S STOMACH LURCHED up into his throat as the ground split beneath his boots. There was no time to cry out before he and Barrett plunged into an awful, weightless, nothing, as if the hand of Lumen had reached down to tear the stones beneath them apart and cast them into the Pit.

And then there were arms around him, clutching tightly as they careened off a pile of rubble, peeling a scream out of Kyran as his bad leg struck stone, his vision blotting white as they rolled down a shifting pile of debris, and slid to a stop across rough stone. He laid there, unable to think, to move, to do anything until the grip of pain began to ease under the numbing touch of his power.

He slumped against the floor, his breaths loud and rasping in his ears as he came back to himself.

"Are you hurt?"

Kyran cracked an eye open to find Barrett looming protectively over top of him, hands on either side of his shoulders as stones and bits of wood still raining down around them, bouncing off the hunter's back as he shielded him.

"Leg," Kyran managed, drawing himself up from beneath the hunter. "I'm fine."

Settling back on his knees, Barrett grabbed Kyran's walking stick and pressed it into his hands. "Are you sure? Can you walk?"

Another tremor shivered through the stone beneath the mage, sending a shower of rocks and dust down over them.

"Aye." Gritting his teeth, Kyran rolled onto his hip, clumsily getting to his knees where he could plant his walking stick and pull himself to his feet. His muscles trembled at the effort. He'd known he was still ill after his time in the demon realm, but he hadn't confronted it so directly before now. Stars, he was tired, and even now he could feel the deep, throbbing ache in his leg pulsing up through his hips and back even through his magic. "Cursed beasts," he swore quietly and leaned into his walking stick to take some of the weight.

Barrett didn't rise right away, one of his hands wandering up to the side of his head, coming away with some bright, fresh blood. Panic lanced through Kyran's middle. "Are ye all right?"

"Mmh," Barrett grunted affirmatively and flashed a smile at the mage before leveraging to his feet. "I think I see a way out," he said, fire kindling along his arms, sending a faint scarlet light out into their surroundings. It looked like they had fallen into a room below the House, not the Pit, though it was impossible to make out more than a few feet in any direction through the dust hanging in the air.

Kyran followed close behind, carefully maneuvering around broken rock and beams. He tried not to look too closely at the hunter's blackened arms or how his long nails curled around his dagger. He looked ragged, covered in sweat and mud with his clothes scorched in places, his face bleeding.

"Cursed Graces." Barrett came to a stop ahead of him, his head craned back where part of a wall had slumped down to reveal a rectangle of night air. "Hold on." Backing up several paces, Barrett sprinted at the wall and leapt, catching the tip of the ledge. Legs kicking, he managed to scrabble up, straddling the stone. "It leads outside," he confirmed and looked back down at Kyran. The hunter started to lower one of his blackened hands but paused, staring down at his own limb. His jaw flexed before he offered the hand out to the mage.

It would only be for a moment, Kyran assured himself, and handed Barrett his walking stick.

The hunter took it and tucked it under his other arm before reaching to take Kyran's hand. Even though he braced himself for the contact, he didn't expect the feverishly hot, papery-dry skin. It took every ounce of willpower not to yank his arm back and instead tightened his grip as Barrett pulled him up on the ledge where he could swing his legs over.

"Go ahead," Barrett said and held his grip steady as Kyran angled himself down. The moment his feet touched the ground and he straightened, Barrett let his hand go and followed him out before passing his walking stick back over.

A thick pall of fog and smoke cut off Kyran and Barrett from the rest of the world. Kyran could hear fighting, people shouting and screaming, demons wailing, but it had a strangely distant quality.

"Can't see a Graces' cursed thing," Barrett swore at his side, slowly turning in place.

Kyran shut his eyes, sweeping his magic out through the fog, feeling for Finley, when he felt a sudden draw. "On your left!"

Barrett gasped and reached for Kyran's arm, shoving him back. The mage's back hit the wall of the House as an abomination galloped by on its centipede-like legs, its body consumed by fire. The heat was so great he had to close his eyes, the air suddenly thick with the choking scent of burnt hair and meat.

Beside him, Barrett coughed violently before letting go of Kyran's arm to put himself between the mage and the abomination. The flaming beast scraped its body down the side of the House as if trying to peel the flames from its flesh, leaving globs of burning skin behind before it disappeared into the fog.

"I canna sense Finley," Kyran said, rubbing his arm where Barrett had grabbed him.

"I have an idea of where she's headed," Barrett said. "Come on." The hunter led the way down the side of the house at a quick pace, keeping close to the wall. Bits of burning flesh lit the fog all around them with haunting crimson and orange flickers of light.

"It's coming back!"

Kyran started to turn at Barrett's warning, then dove to one side in time to see the abomination's outstretched claws scythe through the air just inches from his chest. It slammed into the side of the House, its head rolling on its shoulders to follow him with its ruined face of fingers.

"You again?" it hissed through its wide grin. A bit of liquid flesh dribbled between its digits as it launched from the wall, darting away as Barrett charged it.

"Stay with the House—I'll handle it!" the hunter shouted, dagger in hand, a burst of fire roaring from his palm. The abomination skittered to one side, evading Barrett's fire as it circled him relentlessly, trying to get behind him.

Scooping up a handful of mud, Kyran pulled his arm back and quickly judged the beast's path before throwing the frozen muck. The beast flinched where the frozen ball struck its hindquarters, ice spiraling across its skin. Barrett lunged, burying his dagger in its flank. It twisted with a roar, trying to swipe at Barrett. The hunter barely ducked before pulling his dagger out and plunging it back in. When it finally collapsed, Barrett pushed himself upright and flashed a grin at the mage.

"Nice throw," he said as he caught his breath.

"Thank ye," Kyran chuckled, getting cumbersomely to his feet again.

Kyran balked at the wave of heat that rolled over him as they rounded the back corner of the House and shrank behind Barrett. Before them was Finley, her body sprouting a multitude of grotesque insectile limbs that she used to tear at the bricks of a tower that filled Kyran with an inexplicable dread.

They were the same ashen grey as the brick of his prison in the demon realm.

"Graces, she's getting through," Barrett swore. Fire wreathed his arms before he grappled the abomination.

Finley let out an infuriated shriek, two of her limbs twisting back to try and grab Barrett, but all she could do was uselessly claw at his hair and tunic, bereft of fingers to grasp him.

"I've got—"

Without warning, Finley whipped around and slammed her back into the tower with a sickening crunch.

"Barrett!" Kyran gasped.

The hunter's eyes rolled back into his head and he went slack, sliding limply from her back. "Troublesome hunter!" she snarled and pinned beneath her boot.

"No!" Kyran raised his hand, shaping his magic, but he wasn't quick enough. The back of Finley's fiery fist cracked across the hunter's face. His body jolted from the strike.

The air around Kyran flashed to frozen white fog, and he heard Finley scream as he carved into her just before he felt something rake at his mind, a claw scratching along the inside of his skull.

"You stay out of her head or I will eat you alive from the inside, mage," Finley sneered. "Hollow you into the perfect skin. I will leave nothing left for your precious sire!"

"No!" Barrett's rough voice ground out. Kyran cracked his eyes open to see the hunter shakily pushing to his feet. He lunged for Finley while she was distracted and caught several of her arms under her shoulders, pulling her tight against his chest. "You leave him alone!"

Finley screamed and writhed against him, fire lashing out all along her misshapen body. Everywhere it struck Barrett it left behind ashen, black skin. With a strenuous shout, the hunter pushed her down to her knees.

"Kyran!" he bellowed from behind Finley. "Do it! Do it now!"

Closing his eyes, Kyran focused on what he wanted of his magic, what he had to do, and felt his lips twitch back from his teeth before he sank his magic into Finley again. There were no memories, though, no flash of images or scents he didn't understand. Instead, his teeth closed around a perfect void. He pressed harder and dug blindly, searching for some piece of Finley or the demon, some stray memory or thought, but there was nothing. It was as if he had fallen into an abyss.

Something shifted, like a door closing, followed by the faintest prickle of pain. It was not until he tried to pull away that the nothingness began to fade. The empty black took shape and form until he recognized the grey, ashen landscape of the demon realm.

Sweet, young thing.

Kyran's vision spun, and suddenly, he was looking up at the multi-limbed demon. Its voice came from within a face of flexing, straining fingers.

Do not be frightened, little halfling, it whispered in Finley's warm, scratchy voice as a hand reached to touch him.

He flinched away, starting again when he caught a glimpse of himself. He was no longer himself. He was a *wean*, barely taller than Effie, his clothes tattered and charred. He must have slipped into a memory. This had to be Finley.

I will protect you, the demon curmured. *Teach you to use your power as you grow stronger.* It bent, arms reaching to gather him closer, the fingers of its face folding back to show a mouth full of sewing needle teeth and a second eyeless face grinning within it.

Mageling, the eyeless face taunted in that soft, hissing voice he would never forget. *I will take good care of you until you ripen.*

Kyran sneered into its face, trying to lift his hand to send his magic lashing into it. There was another faint, prickling sensation behind his eyes before the demon simply dissolved. the whole world blurring and running together like smoke that smelled hauntingly of hay.

"No..." He pressed his hands over his ears and staggered backwards until his back hit the rough stone of a foundation. He could feel the dry scratch of hay under his cheek. He tried to open his eyes, but they only squeezed shut more tightly, tears streaking down his cheeks. "No no no..."

"No!" a woman was screaming on the other side of the wall. "Please!"

There was warm, ale-scented breath against his ear, and Kyran curled more tightly into himself.

"It's all right," Finley murmured. "He will be done soon. I won't let him hurt you."

The woman's voice behind the wall pitched higher, turning to an animal shriek of pain before she broke into ragged sobs. "Stop. Don't. Stopstopstop."

A warm, gentle touch pressed against the back of Kyran's hand. "Don't listen."

"Barrett?" Kyran tried once more to open his eyes. To lift his head. Anything.

"I'll protect you. I want you to be okay. As okay as you can be, y'know?"

Kyran's voice broke in a soft, aching whimper at the words. Words he keenly remembered. But he couldn't be sure it wasn't something miming the hunter's earnest voice. "You're not… You're not here."

"I will always be here."

"No! Ye're a demon!" Kyran shouted, fighting to close his fist, to reach for his amulet, to open his eyes, *anything* to ground him. He couldn't move or feel in this memory—illusion— whatever it was he was trapped in. It was as if he had ceased to exist.

"Aye, da was right. You're nothing more than a demon blooded mongrel."

He felt another hand at the back of his neck, pressing him down, and then another ghosting along his thigh, another at his waist, grabbing his belt, wrapping in the fabric of his kilt, covering his mouth, touching and grabbing and squeezing and pressing every inch of him. He could do nothing more than scream.

"Ye are na real!" he screamed, trying desperately to call his power, but he felt nothing. No wild bucking of his magic against him, no flood of power. "This… this isna real!"

With a furious wrench, Kyran finally tore his eyes open, only to find everything around him had changed again. It wasn't the stable or the burning hospital, but the ashen stone of the demon realm he laid on. And above him, its eyeless sockets boring down into his, was the frail, ghostly figure of the Old One with one of its hands wrapped around his leg.

Mine.

With a sound like creaking ice, pain flashed bright and hot through Kyran's thigh. His back snapped into a taut bow of agony as another scream tore out of him. Fire flashed past, and his leg snapped off in the demon's grip like brittle ice as a pair of arms wrapped around him, dragging him away as the Old One reared and howled in pain.

"I've got you," a voice whispered and the arms laid him down on something soft and warm. "I've got you now. You're safe." Someone was stroking his hair, and he shuddered feverishly. "I'll protect you. Just relax…rest…"

"Barrett? I—" Kyran tried to speak, to protest, to make any sound at all, but his tongue was too heavy. Everything was too heavy. He sank into the fever warmth cradling him.

"Rest…"

Chapter Sixty-Three

BARRETT NEVER THOUGHT silence could be so terrifying. There was so much terror happening elsewhere, but Kyran stood silent and immobile, like a statue of fey light and frost. A steadily growing dread continued to build that something had gone wrong. Something worse than what had happened in the guildhall last time. Even Finley had gone slack in his arms. He only hoped that meant whatever Kyran was doing was working.

"Come on…" he urged quietly, afraid that at any moment, a demon or abomination would ambush them from the fog. "Come on, Kyr—"

Finley jerked abruptly in his grasp and the back of her head connecting solidly with his mouth. He spat out a swear, nearly lost his grip on her.

"Hold still!" he shouted. Fire flickered up along her arm and rolled over her ashen cheek,. Barrett drew upon his own fire and flexed his fingers. "You don't have to do this, Finley."

"Oh, but I have been planning for far too long not to."

"What? Planning what?" Barrett asked, trying to keep her talking and distracted from whatever Kyran was doing.

"You haven't put it together yet, hunter? I am going to wipe every one of you off of this miserable rock, and I am going to make certain there will never be another one of you again!" With a furious snarl, she reared back again, catching his nose this time and his vision flashed white, tears springing into his eyes as she shoved him away.

I can finish this, his demon's voice whispered at his ear and his steps steadied for just a moment as numbness crept up his legs.

"No. *I* can do this," Barrett growled and stamped his boots as he focused on the feeling of his feet against the coarse ground. He turned to keep Finley in sight as the abomination circled them. "He just needs more time."

"Oh, does he?" Finley simpered. Kyran let out a sharp, pained whimper, his body seizing.

"No!" Barrett lunged, scrambling to catch the mage as he collapsed. "Kyran?" He gave the mage's shoulder a hard shake, but he was limp and unresponsive. The glow had completely faded from his skin, and Barrett couldn't sense a single ounce of magic coming from him. "Kyran? Come on. Come back. Wake up, please."

Hunter.

The mage's eyes fluttered and his lips twitched, almost as if he could hear Barrett. Tears began to streak down the sides of the mages' face as another pained whimper slipped out.

HUNTER.

A pair of claws clamped onto Barrett's shoulders, slamming him to the ground. Suddenly, there were hands all over him. His hips, his shoulders, his hands, his knees, even his hair as Finley crawled over him and pressed him down into the ground.

"Fin— stop," he wheezed, his lungs aching. "You have to stop! You have to—"

She is gone, hunter. Put my dagger through her, take your mage, and flee.

"No!" He fought to suck down a breath. "Kyran said—"

Your mage is—

"The mages are *mine*," Finley laughed. Her nails bit into Barrett's wrists where she grappled with him. "You should join us in our liberation."

Barrett tried to break free of her strength. His fire blazed all around him, but she didn't recoil. "*You*—" The hunter gasped as the word rolled its way past his lips. He hadn't said that. Magic and strength swelled violently in his arms as he twisted one free of Finley's grasp and snatched at her hair. "*Your hubris against the hunters will be your downfall.*" His demon. Barrett's demon was controlling him, talking to Finley and her demon.

His demon snatched the dagger from his hip and thrusted it up at Finley. Barrett fought for control with every bit of strength he had and his dagger hand flinched. The abomination caught his wrist and slammed it against the stone so hard he cried out and dropped the dagger.

"*Hunter!*" his demon sneered threateningly as his fingers curled into a fist.

Don't hurt her! Kyran—

A scream ripped out of him as something pierced his skull. All at once, he felt as if he were choking and drowning, as if his heart had been broken, and an endless amount of grief swept over him.

GET. OUT.

Instantly, the pain vanished and Barrett's eyes flashed open. A low, stone grinding growl rumbled deep in his chest, but it wasn't from him. He could only watch as his demon wrenched his arm from Finley's grasp and backhanded her hard enough to send her sprawling. His body got up, catching one of Finley's arms as she raised it, fire licking up her arm and across her cheek. He saw what was coming a moment before his demon twisted the limb with a sharp yank. Finley shrieked.

What are you doing? Barrett screamed silently, wishing more than anything at that moment that he couldn't hear the way she screamed in pain. *Don't—*

"*You didn't want me to kill her,*" his demon said with his own mouth, tossing the limb aside. It lifted his boot and stomped down on her knee and then her ankle, landing a bone shattering kick to her middle before it stepped away. "*That will keep it occupied.*"

Sensation flooded back into Barrett, and his knees buckled at the sheer overwhelming *feeling* of being able to perceive anything but his own thoughts again. "You son of a—" he wheezed.

Do not waste the time I have bought you, hunter. Tend to your mage.

Barrett tore his eyes from where Finley lay curled on her side, sobbing softly as her demonic limbs tried to drag her.

Barrett lowered to his knees next to the mage as his stomach dropped to his boots at the sight of him. Kyran's eyes had fallen open, staring at nothing. Just like— "No. No, not again. Kyran. Kyran!" He grabbed the mage's shoulder again, shaking him, but Kyran's head lolled limply. Biting out a curse, Barrett reached for the mage's face, hesitating for just a moment before he gingerly cupped his cheek, turning his face to look up at Barrett. "Please."

"He can't hear you."

Barrett cut his eyes up at the abomination. It was closer, its insectile limbs dragging Finley's body towards him. Finley still lay on her side, tears streaming down her face, her expression one of mute agony. The voice came from a new protrusion, a second mouth splitting the side of her face with a lipless gash filled with shards of teeth. It grinned at Barrett.

"Mages are so easy. So soft. I only had to touch those old scars to tear them open again."

Fire kindled along Barrett's fist and he flexed his fingers. The captain wanted Kyran to save Finley from the demon that had taken hold of her, but if it came to it, he wouldn't let it hurt Kyran anymore than it already had. "Stay back."

"He's hollow, hunter. Empty." It stretched one of its limbs towards them, the end a serrated, hooked barb. "Bloody skin."

"Shut up!" Without thinking, Barrett snatched Kyran up and stepped farther away from the beast. Its claw gouging the earth where Kyran's arm had lain. "I said stay back!"

There came a howl from the fog behind him, and Barrett whirled as another abomination came galloping from the dark. Its face was a mess of twisted limbs and half-melted skin. Clutching Kyran to his chest, he threw himself backwards. His back hit the wall of the House as the beast's limbs scythed through the place he had been, tearing up chunks of earth.

"Damn the Graces," he growled and hunched over the mage to protect him from flying dirt and stones. He could hear the thing coming around again even as Finley's abomination crawled closer. "Kyran," he called urgently and moved along the wall, away from Finely. "I don't know what her demon did to you, but you're stronger than this. You've got to wake up. Please. I need you—"

With an ugly gasp, Kyran's lines flashed a blinding blue-white, searing Barrett's skin, eyes, and lungs in an instant, but he held on tight, his heart all but stopping as the mage's brilliant eyes focused up at him.

"Barrett?"

Chapter Sixty-Four

DOWN, DOWN, DOWN, Kyran sank into the warm, comforting embrace of nothingness. His thoughts drifted apart and spun away like snowflakes. It was so, so mercifully quiet. So peaceful. As if he were falling into a long, long sleep.

"Come back. Wake up, please."

The peace and nothing felt good, exactly as he had imagined in his room looking at his knife. Everything would simply fade away to nothing. Stars, he had dreamed about it, looking up at the walls of his prison in the demon realm, of simply laying down and never opening his eyes again. To just *not be*.

"Kyran…You're stronger than this."

The voice cut through the quiet like a knife. Kyran squeezed his eyes more tightly, trying to shut out the voice, to simply fall away from everything.

"You've got to wake up."

There was a sensation, sudden and hot as a slap against his skin. He twitched away from it, willing himself down into emptiness, but the heat persisted, a brand against his cheek solid and real, burning away grey fog wreathing his thoughts. And he remembered. He wasn't simply floating in nothing. He was fighting Finley.

"Please."

He had tried to attack the demon within her, to destroy it. But it had gone wrong. This wasn't a pit or even nothing. He was trapped inside his own head. And that other voice. That was…

"I need—"

That was Barrett.

"—*you*—"

With a start, Kyran's eyes flashed open, his breath catching at the sharp, needling pain behind his eyes that radiated down along his throat into his lungs, his arms, and pelvis. Dragging his eyes upwards, he found not the twisted parody of Barrett he half-expected, but the hunter's bruised and battered face smiling through fresh tears.

"Barrett?" he slurred, struggling to even form syllables beyond the splinters burying themselves in his head.

"Thank the Graces." The hunter exhaled sharply. Kyran wobbled, disorientated, and grasped at the hunter's clothes. Barrett kept him upright with an arm around his shoulders and a hand at his elbow. "Are you all right?"

"Head," Kyran said thickly and lifted a hand to press his palm firmly against his temple. His vision swam as something squirmed beneath his skull. "Still..."

"So there *is* still enough of you left to talk."

Gooseflesh erupted down Kyran's arms. He turned, his stomach lurching nauseously to find Finley's broken, twisted form crawling towards him. The mage was sobbing, her human limbs dragging as demonic legs pulled their shared body forward like some sort of hideous growth.

Shh... you need your rest, he heard like a whisper behind his eyes. *You don't need to get up yet.*

A heaviness, like a thick, woolen blanket laid over him, pressed down on him, easing the sharpness in his head. It was trying to draw him in again.

"No..." he slurred, loosing his magic, pushing blindly at the whispers.

Enjoy the warmth. Enjoy the quiet. It's been so long since you've had a peaceful rest. Just sleep.

"Kyran? What's wrong? What's happening?"

More. He needed more power. Another demon. A—

His fingers closed around hot metal.

"What are you—?"

He felt it. Not Barrett, but his demon. Raw, hidden power and strength that slammed into his senses like a wall. But it wasn't just the demon. There were whispers and growls and chittering noises. Dozens—no, *hundreds* of demons calling out in a disorganized cacophony. And over all of it, coiled back like a viper, was the hunter's demon.

Let go of the amulet, mage.

Barrett's hand left his elbow, clasping tightly over Kyran's. "Do it. Take it."

Hunter, you cannot allow him—

"Take it! Now!"

With a cry, Kyran shoved his power into the vast, swirling maelstrom of the hunter's amulet. A vice grip seized him, holding him back. The demon's snarl bled into the sound of Barrett screaming. They both collapsed to their knees. Barrett squeezed his hand tighter. "Let him have—" Barrett spoke hoarsely. "He needs—" Briefly, the grip holding Kyran back eased as if being pulled away.

Kyran reached as deeply as he could into the chaotic well of power and the voices rose, a cacophony of shrieks that wrapped around him as he began to drink. Power flooded into him, a scouring heat pouring into his blood that burned beneath his skin, in his muscles, deep within his belly, and in his skull like a wild, thrashing beast He tried to focus, to shape the power, when a scalding pain shot through his leg.

He screamed, clutching his leg, expecting to find the all too familiar image of the needle-toothed demon sinking its teeth in to strike bone. But it was Finley—the demon growing from her, its claws wrapped around Kyran's leg just above his boot as it lurched upwards on its other limbs, maw opened wide.

Now, mage.

A voice Kyran didn't recognize thrummed through his blood, murmuring at his ear low and gravely. Almost without his having thought it, his hand raised, grabbing the blackened growth on the side of Finley's face.

It was as if a dam had burst inside of him. Raw power roared through him, carving into and through the abomination like a butcher's knife, fileting its memories, its thoughts, its very being out of Finley. They screamed through Kyran's mind, too much, too fast, and yet perfectly, terribly clear. Decades of existence branded into the inside of his skull in an instant.

But the demon would not go quietly. Even as his power tore it apart, it fought.

Through the blinding torrent of memory, he felt its claws at his hip, another set sinking into his side.

He tried to move, to turn away, to push it away, but his body was locked, rigid and immoveable as the essence of the hunter's demon poured through him. But then, the feeling of claws faded. The overwhelming heat. The ache of his leg. His skin. His throat. He couldn't gasp. Couldn't close his eyes. Couldn't scream.

So this is what my brothers covet.

Kyran's mouth twitched into a smile without his consent and his eyes lowered on their own to the blinding blue-white light of his blood shining beneath his skin.

I understand the allure.

A demon—Barrett's demon—was inside him, controlling him the

same way the demon inside Finley was controlling her.

Panic clawed up from Kyran's belly, silvery and bright, and he tried to shape his magic, to push the thing out of him. But nothing happened.

The demon laughed through Kyran's mouth and let Finley drop to the ground. *Do not worry. I've no intention of making my home here. You may tell your sire I saved your life when next you meet him, so long as you do not try to steal from me again.* There was a measured threat in its voice.

Then, all at once, Kyran's breath hitched in a loud, shocked gasp. His knee buckled as sensation rushed back into his body. A woman was crying, the sound piercing through him. Finley was there, lying on her side. Not a speck of black on her skin. Her veins were not even glowing. Her arm was twisted the wrong way and curled tightly against her chest.

"It's—" Kyran whipped his head around to see Barrett. The hunter's face was pale as the snow as he looked at Finley. "It's gone," he whispered.

Except it wasn't.

Kyran brushed the back of his hand over his face, wincing as rough crystals of ice scraped across his skin, and looked down at Finley again. The demon was no longer in her, but it wasn't gone. Not entirely. Its memories crowded Kyran's thoughts, its power joining his own in his blood, and soon it would be given a name in report after report as its successes were recorded into guild history.

They had killed it, but not before it had left its scars on the guild and all of Tennebrum. They were too late.

There came a distant howl, echoed by others in the dark, and Barrett snapped out of his awe. "We should find the others," he said, moving past Kyran to carefully gather Finley in his arms. She didn't resist, her eyes fixed on nothing. "She needs a healer."

"Aye," Kyran said, his voice hardly more than a harsh whisper as he gathered his walking stick. It took every ounce of strength to draw himself to his feet, the wool of his kilt creaking with frost as it pulled away from the stones. All around him, the earth was blasted with ice and under it, the surface was churned and scorched by fire.

"Are you all right?"

Kyran looked up at the hunter, and the exhausted concern writ into his features.

"I mean, I know— I saw what was happening," Barrett continued. "What it was doing to you, and—"

"It isna something linen can fix," Kyran repeated back to him, leaning into a walking stick.

The hunter's face greyed. "Are you... Are you going to be all right?"

Kyran's gaze lowered to the broken woman in Barrett's arms, the knowledge of how her entire life had been warped and ruined by the thing inside her now etched into his skull. He hadn't saved her. But he might have given her a chance. "I ken I will be."

Chapter Sixty-Five

BARRETT COULDN'T QUITE believe the state of things around him. The whole way around the outside of the House, his eyes wove over the shadows, expecting something to leap out at him and Kyran. His ears burned with the anticipation of hearing an inhuman howl. But there was no howl. No scream. No demons or fighting. Only a grey silence as smoke and fog closed in around him.

There was already a small cluster of hunters gathered at the front steps, with others slowly coming in through the dense fog, some carrying injured with them, others carrying the dead.

"Here," Barrett led Kyran to a clear spot on the steps. "We can rest here while everyone regathers."

"I am fine on my feet," the mage insisted, settling his weight on his good leg, but Barrett could see the slight tremble in the man's fingers before he could hide them.

"As you say," Barrett said softly and adjusted his hold on Finley.

"Hunters!" Captain Fairclough called from the midst of the group before she rounded the stairs and came into view. She looked rougher than most, blood spattered across her, but hale. "I need volunteers to sweep the House and make certain it is clear of abominations and demons. Once it is declared clear, we will focus on removing bodies and making room for the healers to work with the injured."

"Fairclough," Barrett called out to her and offered a tired smile when she spotted him with a baffled look of surprise. "The House is clear. We—"

"That remains to be seen. Wounded go by the wall. You and I will have a chat later about how you got here. Again." Her eyes fixed briefly on Kyran before she turned away. She pointed out three people and sent them through the broken front doors.

At the center of the knot of hunters, hemmed against the solid wall of the house, were the unlucky. Some huddled together in frightened knots, others lay where they had been put, swathed in bloody makeshift bandages. And around them, in greater numbers, were bodies, shapes beneath linens, blankets, even shredded dresses that had been laid over them to shield them from the living. So many.

Barrett set Finley down as gently as he could on the cold, filthy stone. She said nothing, still staring straight upwards, breaths coming in shallow gasps. Graces, but it looked so painfully familiar, and there was still nothing he could do but leave her.

The night stretched into a grey eternity of waiting. The air was still and quiet. Even the hunters were silent, staring into the grey murk. The only sounds were the quiet moans and whimpers of the wounded. The chaos had simply evaporated. It reminded Barrett of the Inbetween, a vast nothing beyond time and place.

He kept checking to make certain Kyran was still nearby, half-expecting to turn around and find him vanished. But the mage was always there when he looked. He looked haggard, eyes distant and posture withdrawn. Barrett did his best to keep himself between the mage and the rest of the crowd, to give him what space he could. It was a meager comfort, but Barrett didn't know what else he could offer until he could find somewhere private to speak to Kyran.

It was an age before the hunters came back from inside the House, declaring it secure. Fairclough immediately began barking orders. Barrett and the other able bodied hunters worked quickly to move the injured inside, while everyone else was tasked with gathering things that Georgie could use to tend the injured. Soon, the House was full of frightened, injured hunters and villagers alike, laid in rows near the front of the House where the damage had been the least severe on scavenged canvas and cloth.

Barrett had only just finished laying the last wounded man on a makeshift cot when Fairclough found him again and tasked him with helping to put out any remaining fires in the village. With an exhausted sigh, Barrett went to find Kyran. The mage had taken up next to Finley, watching over her while she waited to be seen by Georgie.

"Hey," Barrett hailed, smiling when Kyran raised his head. "Captain's sending me out with the others to help in the village, but I wanted to make certain you were all right first."

"Aye, I'm fine."

He looked anything but fine, but there was little Barrett could do. "Okay. I'll come find you as soon as I'm back here, but if there's anything I can—"

"Barrett?" Elijah's friendly voice called out from the end of the makeshift cots. The young hunter walked briskly towards them. "Captain sent me to get you. She wants us to see to the village right away."

Barrett sighed and pressed the heels of his hands into his eyes, willing the exhaustion away. When he lowered his arms he spotted the mage giving him a wry, if exhausted, grin. "All right," Barrett groaned. "I suppose we should go, then, before she strings me up." He gave Kyran a final look, flashing what he hoped was a convincing smile. "I'll be back as soon as I can," he promised, hating that he had to walk away. Every time he got to see Kyran, it was as though something was pulling him away.

Marcus was waiting on the steps outside, a bandage covering the hand he raised in greeting.

"You both with me?" Barrett asked.

"Seems so," Marcus answered. His expression softened when Elijah passed Barrett. "I tried to get them to let Elijah rest, but—"

"I'm fine," Elijah argued. "We should get started, though. Sooner we're done, sooner we rest."

Descending the stairs, Barrett ventured out into the village to see what could be done. But as he followed Elijah and Marcus into the ruins, it became increasingly clear there was nearly nothing left of Belldale. What hadn't been ruined before the assault was burned and broken. So many of the buildings were beyond saving. All they could do was smother the flames to keep it from spreading. The smoke veiled the sky as the sun rose, casting the village in an eerie glow.

Occasionally, they passed another group of hunters, tasked with clearing debris out of the streets, or, for those with stronger stomachs, clearing the mutilated bodies, or what was left of them. Barrett couldn't remember what he'd last eaten, but he lost it when two hunters passed with a cart full of limbs, bloody lumps of flesh, and offal. Faces rendered beyond recognition.

At last, the sun rose behind the smoke-veiled sky, casting the ruined village in an eerie glow.

"I think we've done about all we can do," Barrett said, his heart sick from seeing the rampant destruction the demons and abominations had wrought despite the guild's every effort to protect these people.

When he, Elijah, and Marcus finally returned to the House, much of the debris had been cleared and swept away. The windows were boarded up. Lanterns had been relit. There was a gentle murmur of conversation and the smell of cooking food permeating the building. Blessed Lumen, it was hardly the House Barrett had left.

"There you are."

Barrett looked around to see Fairclough headed his way and held back an exhausted groan. She was as bad as Griswold.

"You two may go," she said, nodding to Marcus and Elijah. "Get some food and find somewhere to bed down. I want everyone inside the House."

"Yes, Captain," the two hunters said in tandem. Elijah spared a glance towards Barrett before Marcus tugged him along, leaving him with Fairclough.

"As for you…" She folded her arms, looking Barrett up and down. "While I'm happy to have the extra help, I wasn't expecting any more hands before the next supply wagon, which clearly hasn't arrived."

"I didn't come with a wagon," Barrett hedged, uncertain how much he should tell her, or if she would even believe him.

Her brows rose archly. "Then give me a reason I shouldn't stick you and that mage before you can turn into another pair of abominations, hm?"

Her hand came to rest on her hunter's dagger, and Barrett all but leapt backwards, throwing his hands up defensively. "What—" He looked around, at every pair of eyes watching their confrontation. "What're you doin'? I was fightin' them same as you and everyone else here."

"So you're telling me that you *didn't* come through with one of those monsters?"

"I… did," Barrett admitted, grinding his teeth. Curse Griswold's secrets. He wasn't going to let Fairclough hurt Kyran or him for his blasted secrets. "The guild was under attack last night too, and Captain Griswold ordered me to chase the abomination he was pursuing here."

"Through the Inbetween?" She sounded understandably skeptical.

"Yes."

She looked him up and down again, brows knitting. "Barrett, right?"

"That's right."

"There was a report—"

"Of how I went into the demon realm and came back?" Barrett filled in, letting his hands drift down to his sides after Fairclough nodded. "Yeah, that was me."

"And the mage? How did *he* get here?"

"The same way. You'll have to ask Griswold for more details."

Fairclough scoffed, rolling her eyes. "That bastard? I'd have better luck squeezing water from a stone." That gave Barrett a chuckle. Fairclough stepped back, her hand falling from her dagger. "I'll have word sent with the next report that the two of you are here. Get yourself fed and rested. As long as you're able, you'll be part of tonight's patrol with the others."

The knots in Barrett's shoulders eased, and he let out a breath. "Aye."

Shaking her head, Fairclough marched off to bark more orders at idle hunters.

Dismissed, Barrett headed straight to where he had left Kyran and Finley. She was unconscious, but Kyran was not by her side. He looked down the rows of resting patients, but there wasn't a lick of copper hair.

He felt a stab of panic, and quickly squashed it down. The mage must have been sent somewhere else. There were plenty of places in the House to be out of sight.

He stopped the first person he came to and asked them about Kyran, but they simply shook their heads and shrugged, explaining they'd been busy and hadn't noticed. He tried someone else, much to the same effect, and again.

Frustrated, he searched the room until he saw the Isleish healer, Georgie, and several assistants tending to the wounded. She was the last person he wanted to talk to, but she was the most likely to know where he had gone. "Have you seen the other mage, Kyran? He was with Finley last I saw him."

She wrinkled her nose, glowering down at her work bandaging a villager's hand. "That one? He took a whole roll of my linen and went off that way." She jerked her thumb towards the back of the House. "Good riddance."

"Good rid—" Barrett just barely kept himself from shouting the woman down. "You—"

"*I* am verrah busy, as ye can see, so kindly bugger off."

Clenching his fists, Barrett bit his tongue. With a muttered oath, Barrett left her to her work and followed the vague direction she had sent him.

The back hall was not as well-lit as the front of the House, battered lanterns flickering here and there, their wicks left low since everyone had been confined to just the front of the House after the partial collapse near the tower. Everyone but for the magic Barrett could sense further in. He followed it, certain it was Kyran. But there was a margin of doubt that another abomination had secreted itself away in the House, unnoticed in the panic and chaos, and walked right into the room where Kyran had tucked himself away.

The door was open, so he peered inside, relieved to see the mage seated on the broken remains of a bed with his back mostly to Barrett. His kilt was hiked up his left thigh, the buckles and straps of his harness lying loose as he pulled his false leg free.

Barrett froze, his eyes locked on the bandaged stump and the red seeping through, fear lighting in his belly. "Kyran—" He said the mages' name sharper than he intended, making the mage jump in surprise. "Your leg, are you— Are you all right?"

"Aye," Kyran said and yanked his kilt down, his eyes flashing up at Barrett.

Barrett quickly looked down at his feet and tried not to pay attention to how hot his face felt as he turned around. "I'm sorry, but I— It— That was blood, wasn't it?"

The mage sighed, the old frame creaking. "A few of the scars opened up. I ken I will live."

Barrett winced. That sounded painful. "Is there anything I can do?"

There was a muted rustle of cloth, and another creak of the bed frame. "I've what I need."

"All right." Barrett sighed, feeling a bit useless. "I'll just step out. Give you a moment—"

"It's fine. I'll be done soon enough, and I ken well enough that ye'll mind yerself."

Barrett paused, already reaching for the door behind him, and let his arm drop. "Well, all right." Folding his arms, the hunter leaned against the doorframe, wincing at the ache in his skull that was beginning to settle in. "I talked to Fairclough. She said she's gonna send word to the guild that we're here."

"When are we going back?"

"I… I don't know. When the guild or Fairclough says, I guess. I hope the guildhall isn't as bad as this."

"The guild? Is the ward—the *weans*—" There was panic in the mage's voice, and Barrett felt a flush of cold roll over his back.

"I don't know," Barrett answered and allowed himself to sink down to the floor. "It was… absolute chaos. Griswold tried to rally everyone, but we were all spread out and there were so many." He should have been optimistic. Reassuring. But everything felt so…

He dropped his head into one of his hands, trying desperately to remember if he had seen any of the children. All he could remember was smoke. Carrying Myles to Tacita. Katherine screaming. The blood.

"Stars above," Kyran whispered, the words bleeding into a string of Isleish.

"I'll write a letter to Sophie," Barrett offered. "And I can ask Fairclough for any updates from the guild while we're here. She'll know before anyone else."

Kyran made a noise in acknowledgement, and they lapsed into quiet, broken only by the soft rustle of fabric as Kyran tended his leg.

Barrett fiddled with the pommel of his dagger, itching to do something more useful, but had to settle for being content with being nearby. At least he could do that, after everything from demons to lairds to the guild itself had conspired, purposefully or not, to keep them on opposite sides of the continent and even in different realms since the first night they met outside of Oareford. But they had always found their way back. Barrett made certain of it.

Chapter Sixty-Six

KYRAN TURNED THE bit of wood in his hands, shaping the pointed tip of the sun's ray, but the charm was more or less finished, and he was out of things to keep his idle hands busy while he waited. It was all he had done since the demons had retreated. Day after day of waiting and watching, but the demons hadn't returned, and Fairclough had no orders for him other than to guard the injured within the House.

He felt useless. Barrett was gone most of the time, through no fault of his own. Fairclough had him and the rest of the hunters without too severe of injuries salvaging materials from what remained of the village to repair the House of Light and construct shelter for what few people remained. But the hunter still found time to eat with Kyran and appeared from time to time during the day to spend a few minutes talking about anything while he gulped down water. It was a welcome break from the monotony, and Kyran found himself looking forward to the hunter's brief visits where he would chatter about the droll weather, bland food, whatever Fairclough had him doing.

But the waiting was preying on him more and more, with nothing but time to think, for the memories that weren't his to bubble to the surface, filling his thoughts. He wished he could write, could pour them out someplace to give him some sort of peace.

There was a soft moan from the cot he was seated beside, and he watched as Finley tossed in her sleep, expression pinched with discomfort. She'd woken once or twice since Kyran had taken to sitting by her, but she'd never said a word, only stared up at nothing. He'd murmured to her anyway, relaying to her what had happened since she last woke, or mumbling his way through a bit of Isleish song.

With a harsh clang, the bell overhead began to ring, and Kyran lurched to his feet, shoving his carved sun into his purse as he hurried to the door. A small party of hunters were rushing up the stairs, Barrett among them. The hunter came to a stop in front of Kyran, setting his hands to his knees and panting to catch his breath.

"No demons?" he asked quizzically, peering past Kyran into the House.

"I wouldna be standing here if there were," Kyran said, craning his neck to see down the road. It looked like—

"Horses?" Barrett straightened, squinting towards the entrance of the village. "Is that—" His back stiffened, and whispers broke out throughout the group. "That's Selah."

"The guildmaster?"

The riders came to a stop in the square, five singly mounted, another three hitched to carts of supplies. And riding at the head of the column was none other than the guild's leader Selah, her hair pulled up into a severe bun, dressed in heavy skirts. Next to her was another familiar face.

"And Alex," Barrett added, wiping his brow. "They got here fast."

Alex scanned the crowd of hunters, her eyes locking on Kyran, and she smiled, lifting a hand in greeting before she handed her reins off to someone, and started towards them.

"Bless the Graces, you two are a sight!" Alex said as she approached them.

"What's happened at the guild?" Barrett asked, pushing through the crowd to meet the courier. "Is Kat all right?"

"She's all right—"

"What about the ward? The children? And the Lightbringer?"

"Slow down!" Alex gave the hunter a grim smile that sent an anxious shock through Kyran before she continued. "The children are all right. The ward burned, though, along with the hospital and part of the college. I don't know about Lightbringer Horne. I was kept busy."

"Why is the guildmaster here?" Kyran asked and moved to stand by Barrett

Alex pursed her lips, glancing back at the guildmaster. "She hasn't said. I imagine it's her business anyway. I'm here for you two."

"Us?" Barrett asked. "How did you even know we were here? "

"I didn't," Alex answered. "Griswold said there was a good chance of it, though."

"Did my letter make it through?"

Alex shook her head lightly. "I don't think so. A lot of couriers were recalled. I barely did any deliverin'. Anyway, pack your things—we're headed back to the guildhall right away."

"We... don't exactly have any *things*," Barrett said with a light chuckle and scratched at his chin. "Are we leaving now?"

"Unless you've got unfinished business?"

"Aye," Kyran spoke up quickly. "I need a moment."

"Well, when you're ready, I'll be waiting at the stables. May your lanterns stay lit." She bounded back down the stairs, producing a stack of letters from the satchel on her back as she approached Fairclough.

"You goin' to see Finley?" Barrett asked, and Kyran nodded, picking at a splinter on his walking stick. "You need anything for the road? Bandages or anything?"

"Aye. I can—"

"I'll get 'em. Georgie was in a mood this mornin'. You take your time and say what you wanna say."

"Thank ye," Kyran managed a grimacing smile, and carefully picked his way up the stairs, grateful to put the crowd behind him.

Finley was where he had left her, her eyes tracking him as he approached.

"I'm leaving," he told her, looking down so he wouldn't have to hold her gaze. "I dinnae ken when you will be coming, but I'll come ta see you when you do. I'm sorry. For everything. Stars guide and keep you ta the path."

The other mage lay silent, her gaze fixed on him. He wasn't certain she had even heard him. He knew that struggle too well.

Barrett found him at the door. He walked with the hunter down the steps of the House, but they only got a few feet before someone called out, "Barrett!"

Marcus and Elijah were coming towards them. Barrett went to greet them and Marcus paused, looking aside at Kyran before reaching to shake Barrett's hand. "We heard you were leaving. Wanted to thank you for all your help—again."

Elijah broke away, approaching Kyran with a soft smile on his face. "I wanted to thank you, too. If you hadn't arrived, I don't think we would have made it out of that House. And, um—" The young hunter held out a small, wrapped bundle to the mage. "Just some provisions. I know you'll have food for the road, but I thought you both would like some bread that *isn't* stale."

Kyran blinked, then fumbled out his kerchief to accept the gift. "Thank ye."

"You're welcome. May your lanterns stay lit."

"Aye, yours as well." He watched the hunter rejoin Marcus, tucking against the taller hunter's side. Without even looking, Marcus settled an arm around Elijah, pulling him close, and Elijah sank into the embrace. A sharp, bitter hurt needled at Kyran, and he quickly looked away, pointedly ignoring the sting in his eyes.

"Maybe we'll see you when they decide to send us back to the guild," he heard Marcus still speaking with Barrett. "Just… be careful on your way back."

"We will be. May your lanterns stay lit."

"And yours as well."

"Kyran?"

Descending the last of the stairs, Kyran joined Barrett, keeping his eyes trained out on the lightning streets so he wouldn't see how Marcus drew Elijah away. At least not directly. He followed Barrett, keeping just off the hunter's shoulder as they crossed the square to the stables.

Kyran moved to one side to wait, when Barrett stopped next to him.

"Hey," the hunter said softly, shifting closer until Kyran leaned away. "What's wrong?"

"It isna…" Kyran clenched his teeth around his sharp tongue, his nails drumming against his walking stick. "I need a moment."

"Of course." He could hear the worry in Barrett's voice and watched the hunter's boot take a small step towards him. "What can I do?"

Kyran shook his head, squeezing his eyes shut as he pushed down the circling thoughts and raw, stinging memories until his head felt quiet again. It wasn't a peaceful quiet, like standing out in the falling snow, but more like cotton or water in his ears. It would do.

But Barrett persisted. "Whatever it is, you can talk to me about it. Kyr—"

"Hey, boys!" Alex's voice interrupted them, leading Sweetheart over by the bridle. "The sooner we get going, the sooner we can stop for some decent food."

"Sweetheart. I've missed you," Barrett cooed. stroking the mare's neck, who kept a weather eye on Kyran.

"We're taking one of the wagons back with us. They've just about finished unloading it."

Kyran sighed, mostly in aggrievance at still being unable to ride, but also in anticipation of the long, bumpy road ahead in the back of a wagon. Again. At least it was away from here, he reassured himself as he followed Alex and Barrett along the square.

Chapter Sixty-Seven

THE JOURNEY BACK to the guildhall was far more pleasant than the last time Barrett had made the trek, despite the rain. There was Alex to talk to, who insisted they stay at inns instead of camping every night, which meant hot food and dry, soft beds. And while they were eager to get back to the guildhall, there was no dire urgency this time. And yet, Barrett couldn't help but anxiously fret as day after day passed with hardly a word spoken by Kyran.

Forced to ride in the back of the wagon, the mage spent his time gazing out at the countryside, speaking only when spoken to directly. In the evenings, he picked at his meals and retired early to their shared room, but every time Barrett rolled over to look at him, he found the mage awake, eyes heavy, and runelines glowing dimly.

At first, Barrett worried Kyran was slipping away again, back into the nightmares he had been trapped within before. But as the days slowly passed, and the mage continued to rise and at least go through the motions of breakfast and conversation. Instead, Barrett began to worry if Kyran was *drawing away* instead, like he had at the guildhall, only there was nowhere to go in the back of a cart.

The hunter tried to reassure himself that he was overanalyzing the mage, that they'd both just survived another nightmare and had a lot on their minds. But as they drew near the guildhall with nothing improved, Barrett finally decided he couldn't avoid the conversation any longer.

He waited until after supper and ordered a large, stiff drink to take back to the room with him. He knocked, waiting until he heard Kyran's answer to let himself in. The mage was seated on his bed, his false leg removed, and a pile of dirty bandages next to the washbasin. Barrett could just make out the spots of blood still dotting them, although they were nowhere near as bloodied as when they had left Belldale.

"Everythin' all right?" Barrett asked, stiffly lowering himself onto the opposite bed. The bruises and aches from the long night at the guildhall and Belldale had finally begun to fade, but they weren't completely gone yet.

"Aye," Kyran said, running his fingers over the empty place in his kilt where his leg had once been. "It's just…slow ta heal. I blame the rain."

"If you need something to help keep dry, I can—"

"It's well enough under my kilt," Kyran said, drawing himself up onto the bed and curling on his side.

Barrett gulped down the mouthful of drink he'd taken, sputtering as the mage shut his eyes. "Wait. Wait, before you go to sleep, I wanna talk to you about somethin'. Just a moment."

Kyran peered up at him, his eyes dark in the low lantern light. "Aye?"

Barrett scratched at his beard, wincing when his nail caught the tapering end of one of the scratches Finley had given him. "It's just… We haven't talked much since… Graces, since we stayed at the inn in the capital. And I know you saw what happened to me in Belldale, and I just wanted to explain—"

"I ken well enough what happened." He said it so calmly, so evenly, and Barrett's pulse hammered against his throat.

"No, you see, it was helping me—"

"No it wasna. Demons only help themselves."

Barrett's stomach dropped somewhere between his boots. "I— I just needed more control to use more of its power so I didn't hurt any—"

"It's lying."

"But why would it… Why would it need to do that?"

"It's a demon. It canna help itself." Kyran pushed up on his elbow, holding the hunter's eye. "I meant what I said before, at the guild. If it tries ta take you, I willna let it."

There was a stirring then, within Barrett, and for one terrifying moment, he thought his demon would make good on its threat from last time. But with a passing sense of amusement, the beast faded out of his awareness again.

He let out his breath, raising his drink to his lips and swallowing until he had to come up for air. "Graces."

"Are *you* all right?"

Barrett chuckled drily. "*Aye*. I just… You've been so quiet, I was worried you… Well, that you didn't want to be around me anymore after…everything." It felt silly to say it out loud, but it was no less true.

"If I dinnae want ta see your face, I wouldna have agreed ta share a room," Kyran pointed out, and Barrett snorted again.

"Of course." He'd been worried for nothing then. "Well, aside from your leg, how are you holdin' up?"

Kyran sighed, his gaze drifting to the lantern on the bedside table. "I canna sleep."

"Nightmares?" Barrett hazarded, and Kyran nodded.

"They're worse. And I worry for the lass. If she's all right."

Barrett's chest ached for the mage. Graces, but he deserved more than strife after strife. "We'll be at the guildhall soon," Barrett tried to reassure him "You should ask Lilyanna for more of that tea when we get there."

The mage grimaced. "Aye. Foul stuff."

"That it was, but it was the best sleep I ever had," Barrett chuckled. "I could use some myself." And at least one night not spent fretting over his own nightmares recurring. He still wasn't certain what he would do once they were back at the guild again, and he was consigned to his room again. "Maybe with some honey," he suggested, breaking from his thoughts. He would just have to figure something out.

Kyran hummed in agreement, sinking down on his bed again, head pillowed on his arm.

"I could get you a drink," Barrett offered, tilting his cup towards Kyran. "Something to help you slip off."

"I could stand a drink, so long as it isna whiskey."

"I think I can manage that," Barrett chuckled, getting to his feet. "Something sweet, right?" He caught the mage's groan as he let himself from the room, and smiled to himself, feeling all the more foolish for having waited so long to talk to Kyran.

Chapter Sixty-Eight

THERE WAS A crowd outside the guild's gates when they arrived at the capital. Alex had warned them, but Barrett still started when he saw them. Men, women, and even children crowded the guild's walls, many of them injured or filthy, their voices an incomprehensible roar of anger. There were guards, both guild and Crown, at the gate to keep the masses from rushing into the guildhall. They parted as Alex guided the cart into the gatehouse and reformed directly behind them as the crowd surged forward.

A guardsman Barrett didn't recognize stepped forward to see the sigil Alex held up and they were waved hurriedly inside. Barrett let out a tense sigh as the noise of the crowd grew muted behind them with the thickness of the walls. He braced as they entered the guildhall proper, not quite ready to see the devastation the demons had wrought to the venerable old hall, but he wasn't prepared for what greeted them.

There wasn't a place untouched by the demons' destruction. What buildings were left standing were scorched, bits of canvas draped over caved roofs and collapsed walls to fend off the rain. The lawn, once green and vibrant, had been churned to mud. And the cobble walking paths were charred and broken in places.

"Graces," Barrett whispered.

"It's something, isn't it?" Alex said as she dismounted from the driver's seat and leaned into a stretch. "Now, orders were for you two to head over to the library to—Hey!"

Barrett tore his eyes from the tower to find Kyran already out of the wagon and crossing the muddy lawn away from them. He looked past the mage and spotted the ward.

"It's all right," he said to Alex, already following Kyran. "I'll make certain we get to the library."

"Barrett, wait," Alex groaned but was soon out of earshot.

"Wait up," Barrett called as he jogged to catch up to Kyran. "I'm comin' with you."

It was evident as they drew near that the ward hadn't escaped unscathed. The grey stones had been stained black, and the front door as well as much of the roof had been recently replaced.

Kyran reached the door first, tapping it with his walking stick. They didn't have to wait long.

Moira opened the door, her eyes going wide and round as dinner plates before a grin broke across her face. "Effie!" she squealed, disappearing back into the ward with the patter of bare feet. "Effie! Effie! It's him! He's back!"

"Moira! The door," came Sophie's voice from someplace within as Kyran pushed the door open with his walking stick and ducked beneath the lintel.

He'd hardly made it two steps within when, with a loud wail, Effie threw herself at the mage.

Barrett saw the walking stick go one direction, Kyran the other, and lunged to catch the mage's elbow only to slide in the mud he'd tracked in on his boots. They went down in a heap. Moira guffawed at them.

"Graces, sorry. I'm so sorry," Barrett sputtered as Sophie rushed into view. Barrett scrambled back up to his knees, his face ablaze with embarrassment.

Kyran blinked upward, his expression dazed before he cut a look at Barrett, but the hunter didn't miss the flush of pale, watery light in the mage's cheeks.

"Effie, you get on your two feet right now and apologize," Sophie scolded, stamping over to them.

Throwing her arms around Kyran's neck, Effie sniffled loudly then began to cry, big heaving sobs that shook her entire body.

"Well," said a worn, familiar voice. "This certainly is quite a lot of excitement this evening."

Barrett's eyes snapped up to the robed man seated at the hearth. "Myles!"

"Welcome back, Kristopher," the old Lightbringer said and lifted a bandaged hand as Barrett got to his feet. He looked in good spirits despite the bandages covering much of him.

"You're all right?" Barrett asked, coming around the table.

"A bit banged up and bruised, but still kicking.," Myles chuckled, watching the scene unfold behind Barrett as Sophie fussed over Effie and Kyran. "My acolytes have already threatened to come and fetch me."

"I can't say I blame them. You've had bad luck since you left." Barrett pulled the old man into a hug.

"Not luck at all, Kris," the Lightbringer sighed, squeezing him back. "Just old mistakes coming back to roost."

Barrett pulled back, searching Myles' face for a trace of meaning at the mention of *old mistakes*, but the Lightbringer only looked regretful with no trace of his usual lighthearted smile. "What do you mean by that?"

The Lightbringer was quiet for a long moment, peering past Barrett at Kyran and the others before answering softly, "I told your Captain Griswold already, but you deserve to hear it from me."

He gestured to the chair across from him, and Barrett sank into it as his pulse gradually began to thud in his ribs as he thought of Kat's words about the Lightbringer. It couldn't be true. Not Myles. Not him. "You don't have to tell me right now."

"No, I had better before I lose my nerve. I've already been sitting with it near two weeks while you were gone. You already know about my past with the Cult of the Guiding Light," the Lightbringer began, folding his hands in his lap. "That they…that we sought to expose the guild and its hunters for what they were. We told ourselves it was justice, that we were bringing the truth to light." He let out a little bark of a laugh. "Hypocrites and frightened fools, all of us."

Barrett shifted uncomfortably in his seat. Myles had been an anchoring stone for Barrett over the last half a year, a source of wisdom and patience. It was unnerving to see the man as he was now—a former member of the people that Barrett had just had to face down, who had left so many wounded and dead on the steps and under the rubble in Belldale.

"What you may not know," the Lightbringer continued, "was that there was a sect of the movement that went farther than the others. They became convinced that if they removed hunters, then demons would have no reason to come to this world. They would stay in their realm, while humans remained in theirs."

Barrett's skin went cold. Graces, it sounded all too familiar.

"But while they could shout their ideas and rattle their fists in the street, they had no way to enact their beliefs." He cracked a smile at Barrett. "Hunters aren't what you might call a pushover in a fight."

The Lightbringer looked into the fire, his hands twisting and worrying in his lap. "I think things wouldn't have gotten so bad if Lumen had made demons less cunning. The sect told us they found one of the things hiding beneath their meeting place, but instead of attacking them, it struck a bargain. It told them it had heard of their plan, and it had come to offer its help to end the hunting of its kind, but it needed their help in turn. If they would offer themselves, the demon would gift them its power."

Myles shook his head. "The fools were blinded by their beliefs, just as we all were. It started with just members of their sect offering themselves, and those they could convince to join them. But by the end, they would take anyone they could catch alone and drag before the beast. Those of us that knew had taken to traveling in groups, or at the very least pairs, but I…" He squeezed his eyes shut, pressing one gnarled hand to his face. "I had forgotten something at home. I was only going to be just a minute. Just a quick nip back."

He lowered his hand, his eyes heavy beneath his scraggly brows. "I don't remember much. They threw a sackcloth over my head and took me somewhere. I could hear voices. Demons as well as men. And then it was as if someone had set the inside of my head on fire and…"

The Lightbringer shook his head again, drawing a deep breath through his nose before he pressed on, the words trembling. "And then I was standing at the door of my house. Everything was on fire, and there were demons everywhere. My house was empty. My wife… I didn't remember how I got there, but I knew. I knew I had… I still have no recollection of what happened after they took me, but I know what the others did. What I must have done. I've heard all the stories of what happened during the riots."

"You…?" Barrett leaned forward, reaching to touch the Lightbringer's hand, the bandages rough and cold under his fingers, but there was no pull of magic. He was as he had always been. A man. But that couldn't be. Not if Myles had been… "You became an abomination?"

The Lightbringer shrugged helplessly. "It wasn't my will."

"I know," Barrett said quickly. "I'm sorry. Graces, I'm sorry that happened to you."

Myles gave him a watery smile, patting the hunter's hand. "The Graces work through us in many different ways. Sometimes they have to work a bit harder to reach us stubborn old men."

"I'll say," Sophie cut in, stepping into the firelight. "You are supposed to be resting, not frightening the children."

"My apologies," the Lightbringer said, bowing his head humbly.

"Sorry," Barrett added sheepishly, shrinking back in his seat. "Maybe I should—"

"You stay right there and warm up by the fire while I get the kettle on."

Barrett could have melted at the offer of something hot to drink after the long, cold, rainy trek back from Belldale. If he never set foot outside the guildhall again, it would be too soon. "That sounds good."

"Aye," Kyran agreed from where he still sat on the floor, stroking Effie's hair between murmurs of Isleish. The sight of mage on the floor, arms wrapped tightly around Effie, and face buried in her mop of hair pulled hard on Barrett's heart.

"Thank you, Sophie," Myles said, sinking down into his chair, when he tilted his head down past Barrett. "Why hello there."

Barrett found Moira staring up at him with wide eyes.

"You made the demons go away, right?" she asked, clutching her hands to her chest.

"Well, it wasn't just me," Barrett corrected her. "All of us together made them go away."

"Can you tell us how you did it?"

"Ah, uhm." Barrett glanced around, not quite certain what to say. "I'm no good at storytellin'," he hedged and guided Moira to sit by Kyran. "But I think the Lightbringer might have a funny story or two." He looked back at Myles, catching the Lightbringer's gaze. "He's good at saying things people need to hear."

"Yes, please," Moira cooed, dropping down next to Kyran and leaning against his side. The mage didn't even flinch. In fact, he had acted calmer than he had the entire time they'd been away.

Barrett's chest ached as he selected a chair to settle into, but he quickly pushed the feeling away. "I think we could use a good story or two," he said to Myles, giving the man a tired smile. "It's been a rough month."

There was no mistaking the glimmer of tears in the Lightbringer's eyes, but, drawing himself up, he angled himself to face the children and smiled.

"So it has. Why don't I tell you all the story about when the stars first appeared."

CHAPTER SIXTY-NINE

THE WARD WAS quiet except for the crackling of the hearth. Kyran had fallen asleep against the corner wall some time ago during one of Myles' stories about rabbits, field mice, and acolytes. Moira had listened with rapt attention up until her head began to nod, and she curled up on a drape of Kyran's kilt, her head pillowed on his knee. After several minutes of mumbled assurances that she wanted Myles to continue the story, she had started snoring softly. Effie had fallen asleep last, sniffling into Kyran's chest, little fingers clutching his shirt.

Even Barrett was fighting to keep his eyes open, despite his whirling thoughts over Myles' revelation. He and Kyran hadn't gotten much rest the entire way back from Belldale. Graces, they hadn't had much while they were still at Belldale, and he still hadn't figured out what to do now that he was back *at* the guildhall.

"Kristopher?" Myles said, his voice gentle, and Barrett smiled at him. "Yes?"

"I am certain you have questions—"

A light knock made Barrett jump, tea sloshing out over his gloved hands. He set the mug aside, cursing quietly to himself, when Sophie answered the door.

"Well, good evening Alf," she said, stepping to one side to admit the runner. He looked no worse for wear, despite the state of the guild. Tired, of course, but unhurt. Barrett allowed himself a sigh of relief.

"Evening, mum," Alf greeted Sophie, looking past her until he spied Barrett and then Kyran. "Hunter," he said, keeping his voice to a whisper. "You and Associate Kyran have been requested by Captain Griswold. I'm to guide you when you're ready to go."

"Of course, we have." The guild captain was going to want reports and information. Supper and a real bed were going to get even further away.

"Let me put down the little ones," Sophie said, stooping next to Kyran to gently lift Moira into her arms. The girl stirred, mumbling a few words before curling into the matron's arms. "I'll be back for the other."

Barrett forced himself out of his chair, stretching and hiding a yawn before he dropped to a knee in front of the mage. "Kyran," he called softly.

The mage twitched, eyes flicking open and searching until they found Barrett. He relaxed and sank against the wall again. *"Madainn mhath."*

Barrett grinned and tried to repeat the Isleish back. Kyran gave a light snort, no doubt at Barrett's awful pronunciation, but he saw the corner of the mage's lips twitch.

"Sorry to wake you," he apologized and moved when Sophie came back to scoop Effie out of Kyran's arms. The girl didn't even stir. "Griswold's askin' for us."

Kyran groaned, mumbling something in Isleish that was doubtlessly similar to Barrett's own thoughts on the situation.

"I know, I know," Barrett commiserated with a chuckle and stepped back to allow the mage to get up. "I suppose we'll be seeing you," Barrett said to Myles with a sigh. "Are you sleeping here or just visiting the children?"

"Sophie has very kindly set up a place for me to stay," the Lightbringer said, smiling wistfully towards the hall where the matron had disappeared. "Too drafty in those tents they set up out there."

Barrett wracked his brain, but he didn't remember seeing tents. Then again, their arrival had gone by in a sort of haze. The Old One could have been standing out there, and he wasn't certain he would have noticed.

"May your lanterns stay lit, and Lumen's light guide and keep you," the Lightbringer said.

"And yours as well." Stepping away from the hearth, Barrett turned Alf, gesturing for him to lead the way. "So, where is Griswold?"

"At the hospital. Or what's left of it," the runner said as they stepped out into the freezing drizzle.

Right. Alex had mentioned the hospital. He'd forgotten in his excitement to see Myles well. "What do you mean 'what's left of it?'" Barrett asked, shrugging deeper into his leather coat and shooting Kyran a playful glare when the mage's runelines lit up, the rain turning to frozen fog around him. "Is it still standing?"

"Sort of. You'll see."

Alf's words made much more sense once the hospital finally came into view through the haze of fog and rain hanging over the guildhall. The building was little more than a pile of still smoldering ash and rubble nearly as large as a house. A cluster of tents had been set up nearby, a stream of runners, hunters, and other guild members coming and going.

He led them to a tent near the outermost edge, holding the door flap open for them. Inside, Captain Griswold sat at a small table giving directions to several other runners who all nodded and ran past Barrett and Kyran out of the tent. Beside him, Katherine lay in a cot, propped up by several pillows and a blanket over her lap. The whole of her chest and belly were covered in bandages beneath her parted blouse, dark mottled bruising showing against pale skin where the linen didn't cover.

"Kat!" Barrett blurted out and wove his way past the runners before he knelt by her cot.

Katherine lifted her hand at his approach and smiled thinly. "Kris. You're all right."

"More or less."

"Better than I fared. Cursed beasts." She laughed, the sound hardly more than a rough cough.

Barrett winced at the sound. "I'm… glad you're all right. I was worried."

"Oh, that so? Could've fooled me with how quick you ran off."

"What? No, I had to—"

"It was a joke, Kris."

Griswold looked up from his papers he had been scribbling a note on and leaned back until the chair creaked to give Kat a soft glare. "You need to be resting."

"I'm bored, Hammond," his sister snipped back, but lowered her head back against the pillows and folded her arms carefully over her belly. "Gotta get my licks in somewhere."

Unphased, Griswold sat back up and looked past Barrett to the boy still standing at his shoulder. "You may go, Alf."

"Right." The runner dropped the tent flap behind them, closing them in.

The captain took a moment to collect himself with a tight breath before he looked to Katherine, then Barrett and Kyran. "I am glad to see my suppositions were correct."

"Right. It's good to see you both too," Barrett said and got back up to his feet..

The captain flashed him a rare, wan smile, and picked up a stack of paper, tidying it. "It seems from what I have read of Fairclough's reports so far that you two were successful in aiding Finley?"

Barrett winced. "You could say that."

The captain's brow lowered, his attention switching to Kyran. "Were you able to learn anything?"

Kyran shifted beside Barrett, his nails tapping against his walking stick. "Aye." The captain was silent, obviously waiting for more, and Kyran ventured a question. "What is the guild planning ta do with Finley?"

"Once she is well enough to travel, she will be brought back to the guild where Tacita and Lilyanna will determine when she is well enough to be interrogated by the scholars. They will determine where we proceed from there, if she will stand trial before the Crown or be pardoned on the basis of her having been possessed against her will."

"She was an abomination. Of course, it was against her will," Barrett argued.

"Yes, and we do not know what that might have done to her. She may be dangerous."

"Or she might be frightened. Hurt. She might not even wake up again." Like Kyran nearly hadn't. There was no Old One coming to rescue Finley.

"All of that is being considered."

"Course it is," Barrett sneered. He wanted to believe the captain, but after everything he had found the guild hiding about Kyran, he wasn't certain anymore.

Kyran was quiet, eyes steady and hard, before he finally inclined his head. "All right." He cast a quick glance at Barrett that the hunter couldn't quite read before he continued. "The Lightbringer said he told you what happened the last time in the capital, aye?"

Griswold tipped his head, flicking a quick glance at Katherine before he picked up his quill and dipped it in his inkpot. "Yes. He was able to confirm details from back then that we had only guessed. It has provided some much needed context for what has been happening recently, though its complete veracity is difficult to ascertain."

"He didn't lie," Barrett snapped. "Myles wouldn't make something like that up."

"I am not suggesting he would, but there are details that are unusual," Griswold countered. "First and foremost, how and why he is here today in the state that he is in."

"The demon left him for a better skin," Kyran said.

Gooseflesh rippled down Barrett's neck and arms at Kyran's choice of words. It sounded far too much like what the demon had said when taunting him about the mage. "What do you mean by that?"

"When it realized it was losing the battle in the capital, the demon found a different skin it could hide beneath, one it could slowly feed from ta get stronger."

"Finley," Griswold said, and Kyran nodded. "And her being a mage would have masked its presence. That explains a lot."

Barrett looked between the two of them, suddenly grasping what Kyran was saying. "You could tell all of that when you were…looking?"

A little shiver ran down Kyran's spine, his gaze becoming unfocused. "Aye."

Barrett knew that look too well, remembered keenly what Kyran had described when trying to put words to what happened when he and demons fought without frost or fire. Graces, to have been inside the mind of something like that demon.

"What of Guard Captain Nowell?" the captain asked, changing the subject. "I haven't received any reports on his whereabouts."

"I didn't see him in Belldale," Barrett answered and turned to Kyran, who was staring down at his boots.

"Nowell is dead," the mage said, his voice flat, the tapping of his nail growing louder, more insistent. "We were ambushed in the other realm. The demons and abominations were waiting for us, and Nowell's demon started ta take over him when we entered. He told me ta run while he held them back and fell on his sword before his demon could take him."

They were all quiet. Neither Katherine nor Griswold said anything, and Barrett couldn't muster anything to say. The longer he stared at Kyran, the more his quiet, odd behavior suddenly made a terrible sort of sense. There were so many hunters that had perished, but to hear about Nowell…

"Thank you for informing me," Griswold said quietly. "That is all for now. See that you get to a scribe immediately, both of you. Then, send the reports directly to me."

Without so much as an acknowledgement, Kyran left the tent. Barrett wavered, looking from Griswold to Katherine, until he finally got out a quick, "May your lanterns stay lit," before he hurried after the mage.

He didn't know what to say. He couldn't quite wrap his head around the idea of the guard captain never being at the gates again. Barrett may not have gotten along with him, but he'd been a strong hunter, and another veteran lost while the demonic activity in Tennebrum continued to escalate. And for Kyran to witness it. Barrett knew what it was like to see someone die—not just a stranger but someone that he knew.

"Kyran," he whispered the mage's name when they were several paces away from the tents. To his surprise, the mage paused, but didn't pick his head up. "I—I didn't know. I'm sorry you went through that. And that I kept prying."

Thunder rumbled threateningly from the horizon, and Kyran's shoulders rose. "You dinnae know," he repeated back to Barrett.

"I still should have—" He sighed and stepped around the mage. "If there's anything I can do, even if it's to give you some space, or if you want to talk about it, please let me know."

"I dinnae ken if there is anything ta be done. I've never..." Kyran's mouth tightened in discomfort, his eyes shifting someplace else—anywhere but at Barrett. "I saw him fall on his sword after he told me ta run, and I canna help but think I should have stayed and fought. That maybe—"

"You did the right thing." Barrett bent, catching Kyran's eye. "If you stayed, you might not have made it back."

"Or I might have taken some of the beasts out before they could—"

"Or you could be dead with Nowell." Barrett wished he could take the mage's hand, but he smiled instead. "And I'd rather have you here. And I know Effie feels the same way."

A soft flush of blue-white light crept in Kyran's cheeks, his lips parting when a loud, low growl interrupted whatever Kyran had been about to say. The mage's flush darkened, and Barrett realized it was the mage's stomach and not a roll of thunder.

He let out a helpless laugh. It was so ridiculous and so normal and he couldn't believe how much it surprised him. "Maybe we should grab a bite to eat?" Barrett suggested between chortles. "We can take it with us to do the reports."

"Aye," the mage agreed, coloring bright pink beneath the glow of his blood all the way to his ears, his mouth turning in a scowl.

"Don't give me that look, please." Barrett tried to stifle his laughter and looked towards the mess, glad to see it still standing. "Come on. I'm starving."

CHAPTER SEVENTY

Kyran dragged his gaze back to Ilham and forced himself to focus, fingertips smarting as he picked at a ridge in his walking stick. His head felt swollen and tender, throbbing with every lub of his pulse, and he could feel the last shred of control fraying, threatening to leave him utterly untethered. He didn't want that. He wanted to leave. To breathe air that wasn't close and thick with dust. He didn't want to talk about any of this anymore.

"Aye."

Ilham leaned back in her seat, brows creasing in evident concern. "I... think this is enough for now. We can meet another time to fill in more details, and—"

Kyran got up, twitching his sleeves down as he all but ran out of the stacks. He'd hardly made it to the end of the aisle before he found Barrett seated backwards in one of the library's chairs, his head tucked in his arms, fast asleep. It was the first time Kyran could really study the hunter since they'd reunited at Belldale, but for all his new cuts, bruises, and scars, he was still very much the man he'd met in Oareford, tangled hair and all.

At a particularly hard clunk of Kyran's walking stick, Barrett started in his seat, squinting blearily around until he saw Kyran. "Hey," he said, his expression softening into a smile. "You finish up?"

"Said it could wait another day."

"That ought to be a bit of a relief, eh?"

Kyran shrugged, leaning into his walking stick. "Aye, if I dinnae have ta come back."

Barrett gave him a sleepy grin, pushing his hair out of his face. "I could cause a ruckus later, give you a chance to sneak out of the library."

"I ken I'd wake one evening ta Griswold at my door," Kyran sighed.

Barrett snickered before he had to smother a yawn with the back of his hand. "I'm certain we could give him the run-around for a while."

"Oh, aye? Before or after ye fall asleep on your feet?"

"Hopefully before, else I might end up with a face full of mud." The hunter chuckled, dragging himself up out of his seat. "I think you should rest, though. You nearly dropped your head into your soup twice earlier."

"Says the man sleeping in a chair." Kyran scoffed, picking his way through the stacks to the front of the library.

"It was a comfortable chair," Barrett excused and pushed the library door open to reveal the thunder from before had become a downpour. The hunter sighed and leaned against the door. "Graces cursed weather."

Kyran loosened his grip on his magic, the pounding in his head easing ever so slightly as lines of light traced beneath his skin. The air around him flashed to white, and he stepped out from beneath the protective shelter of the library, the rain bouncing off of him in little hard pellets.

"It'll be nice to sleep in a bed, though, with no time to get up and nowhere to go," the hunter began to prattle, unbothered by the ice drops bouncing off of him. "One more day of riding, and I think I might have gone mad myself."

Kyran hummed in reply, but sleep was possibly the last thing he was looking forward to at the moment just behind speaking with any of the librarians or scholars or guild captains just then. There were always plenty of nightmares waiting for him in his dark, empty room.

"You all right?"

Kyran looked up at Barrett, reading the concern writ into his features. "Aye. Bright and bonny as the sunrise. I just…I think I'll walk for a bit before I lay down," he excused himself. It wasn't quite a lie.

Barrett was quiet for a beat, then nodded, pulling his coat collar up around his neck. "You mind if I walk with you? It's just…I feel like I haven't even seen you since Avonmouth."

Kyran shrugged, but he couldn't help a faint smile at the hunter's admission. "As ye like."

They fell into a comfortable silence, keeping a steady pace in no particular direction. The quiet, at least, helped Kyran's frayed nerves, and Barrett's presence at his side was an unexpected comfort. They had scarcely spent any time around one another since the Isles, and when Kyran had found himself thrown into Belldale with swarms of demons bearing down, somehow, the hunter had found him. Again.

Around them, the guildhall was in shambles. There was hardly a building untouched by the fires and demons, part of the plan enacted by the demon that had taken hold of Finley. Even a good portion of the college had collapsed into a heap of charred stone and wood. Kyran carried on past it, burning with a terrible curiosity and dread.

The mage's graveyard hadn't changed since he last saw it, the neat rows of headstones still surrounded by carefully tended grass, unmarred by the battle that had clashed all around them. But it felt different. The seething, righteous rage he had felt at seeing them here, abandoned by Lumen and all the world had withered. Now all he could feel was shame and a guilty sort of pity. What he had done in Belldale was exactly why he would be buried here and his soul left to fester in the Pit.

"These were what you were making on our way back from Belldale," Barrett said as he drifted forward into the graveyard.

Kyran traced his eyes amongst the headstones, picking out the suns pressed in wax he had placed with prayer and reverence and sincere faith. "Aye." It felt silly to admit now.

"Why the wax?" Barrett asked softly, tracing his fingers over the rays of one of the charms Kyran had left. "Why the sun?"

"It is an Isleish tradition ta bring Lumen's Grace ta those that need it."

Something changed in the hunter's face. He inhaled softly as his gaze passed over the headstones then walked to the next, and the next, and then he stopped, and exhaled shakily. "Thank you," he said to Kyran, voice wavering. "Thank you for doing this for them." Barrett knelt, his fingers brushing the wooden sun there. "For him."

Raleigh. It couldn't be anyone else.

"Aye. I…had only hoped someone would do the same for me," Kyran said, grasping the hollow loss he felt for the first time. Grief for what he never had, and never would have.

"I would." Barrett said the words so softly, Kyran almost missed them. A tremble had started in the hunter's fists, carrying up to his shoulders and even his jaw as he struggled to speak. "If something happened— Lumen forbid—I would." He swallowed thickly and looked at the mage, his eyes glossy and red with tears.

An ache twisted in Kyran, one even his magic couldn't quell. It wasn't quite grief for the end he knew would come one day, nor was it joy at the hunter's promise, but something of the two of them. *"Tapadh leat,"* he murmured, voice cracking on the words.

Barrett smiled, watery and wan, before he looked at the headstone he knelt at again. "You know… I've been meanin' to come here. But I—" His voice cracked and he swallowed again.

"Aye." The word was past Kyran's lips before he even thought it, his feet already carrying him to the hunter's side as he reached for the kerchief in his purse to offer the man. "Here."

He meant it as a comfort, but Barrett's composure crumbled at the sight of it, a hard sob tearing from his chest. "Graces," he swore between wrenching sounds and collapsed his face into his hands. "I was too scared to come. I haven't been here since he—since Raleigh died. I should have come before. He's been… He's been all alone."

"He wasna alone," Kyran said, looking out over the graveyard, at the other mages that had been killed before their time. They didn't deserve it. None of them had chosen this life. The curse of their blood

"But I should have. I couldn't— And he's— I couldn't come here."

"It's all right," Kyran soothed, kneeling next to the hunter, and gingerly touching Barrett's elbow.

Barrett tried to say something more, but the words were drowned by the broken noises coming from him.

Gently, almost timidly, Kyran set his other hand to Barrett's shoulder, squeezing to let the hunter know he was there, when the hunter leaned forward and dropped his head on Kyran's shoulder. Kyran froze, utterly bewildered, his body twitching with the urge to pull away out of the touch. Instead, he forced a deep breath through his nose and carefully moved his arms around the hunter's shoulders, murmuring a soft string of Isleish as he gentled the man.

Barrett sucked down a shuddering breath that dissolved into another rough sob, sinking onto Kyran's embrace. "I should've…I should've…" the hunter croaked, only pausing when Kyran murmured more Iselish to him.

The mage carried on until the sobs began to finally subside into choking little sniffles. They sat that way for some time, the rain soaking into Kyran's hair and rolling down his back, the only sounds Barrett's sharp breaths and the rolling cadence of Kyran's half-nonsensical Isleish he murmured over and over at the hunter's ear.

Eventually, Barrett's soft gasps and sniffles stilled into shaky breaths, and even that abated after not much longer. Kyran could feel when the tremors finally ceased, before Barrett slowly picked his head up, hands falling away from his face.

He blinked at Kyran, his pale eyes rimmed red, swollen and tired. Then his eyes dropped low on Kyran's face before he suddenly leaned back out of the mage's arms.

"I-I'm sorry," he said quickly. "I didn't even realize—"

"It's fine. Dinnae worry yer head over it," Kyran assured him, crossing his arms over his suddenly cold chest, letting his magic slip free again to ward off the rain.

Barrett's lips twitched into something like a smile. Despite the state of his face, he was miles better than when he had first stepped into the graveyard. "Thank you."

Kyran felt his pulse quicken, cheeks prickling with embarrassment, and he suddenly found the bouncing bits of ice far more interesting to stare at. "I couldna let ye just keel over. could I?"

Barrett gave a choked laugh and finally accepted the kerchief when Kyran held it out again, pressing it to his eyes. Kyran looked away, back out into the graveyard again, unable to keep from thinking of who else might be grieving the people buried beneath the guildhall, unable or simply unaware there was a grave to mourn. Because for all their monstrous blood, they had families too. People that loved them, that grieved them when they were gone. Even Kyran.

He spotted the sun pressed into Raleigh's headstone, and his fingers found the rough, pointed rays of the carved charm in his purse. He would finish what he started. Not for Lumen, but for Barrett. For Finley.

For Raleigh.

When Barrett picked his head up, he appeared a little more composed.

"I ken my ma would offer ye a spot of tea," Kyran said, withdrawing his hand from his purse and picking up his walking stick he'd laid aside.

The hunter smiled. "Some hot tea sounds good right about now."

"I can fetch a cup from the mess for ye."

"That's kind of you, but I…I don't think I could take being alone right now." Barrett lifted his hand to sweep his rain-soaked hair out of his face. "Would you mind? If I…if I stayed with you? Between the nightmares and the…" His eyes flickered towards Raleigh's grave and he visibly shuddered. "I—I don't think I can—"

"Aye," Kyran cut him off. "Long as ye if ye dinnae mind my scratching at bits of wood."

"I don't mind it at all," Barrett confessed, getting to his feet and offering Kyran his hand.

The mage hesitated for only a moment before he took Barrett's hand, letting him help him up. "Ye say that now," Kyran chuckled as they started down the path together. "Murray threatened ta cut my fingers off when we were last there."

"You know I wouldn't."

"Aye, ye ken I could throw my knife first."

"A trick you've still to teach me."

Kyran chuckled, wiping a clump of ice from the corner of his eye. "Aye. That I do."

Authors' Note

Thank you so much for reading Witchfire, the second installment of our first series, The Dark Inbetween. If you've been with us since the release of the first book, Frostfire, we thank you graciously for your patience. Neither of us anticipated a four-year gap between books. We both had many life changes that proved difficult to work around, but we've been working on the rest of the series and are excited to show you what else is in store for Kyran and Barrett.

If you enjoyed their story, and would like to see more, we would be forever grateful if you left a review wherever you purchased the book to let us know.

If you would like an exclusive look into our current writing projects, we do have a newsletter that gives you a look into what's going on behind the scenes. You can also find us on most social media sites.

www.thorneandivey.com

www.ingramcontent.com/pod-product-compliance
Lightning Source LLC
Chambersburg PA
CBHW061630190726
48289CB00006B/1543